THE SILVER VORTEX

FICTION

The Egyptian Sequence:
Hatshepsut: Daughter of Amun
Akhenaten: Son of the Sun
Tutankhamun and the Daughter of Ra
The Ghost of Akhenaten

Guardians of the Tall Stones:
The Tall Stones
The Temple of the Sun
Shadow on the Stones
The Silver Vortex

Weapons of the Wolfhound
The Eye of Callanish
The Lily and the Bull
The Tower and the Emerald
Etheldreda
The Waters of Sul
The Winged Man
Child of the Dark Star
The Green Lady and the King of Shadows

MYTHS AND LEGENDS
Crystal Legends
Three Celtic Tales
Women in Celtic Myth
Myths of the Sacred Tree
Mythical Journeys: Legendary Quests

More information is available from
www.moyracaldecott.co.uk

THE SILVER VORTEX

by

Moyra Caldecott

Published by
Bladud Books

Copyright © 1987, 2000 Moyra Caldecott

Moyra Caldecott has asserted her right under the Copyright, Designs and Patents Act, 1988, to be identified as the Author of this work

First published in Great Britain by Arrow Books in 1987

Electronic editions published by Mushroom eBooks 2000

This edition published in 2004 by Bladud Books,
an imprint of
Mushroom Publishing, Bath, UK
mail@mushroompublishing.com
www.mushroompublishing.com

All rights reserved. No part of this publication may be reproduced, stored in a retrieval system, or transmitted, in any form or by any means without the prior written permission of the publisher, nor be otherwise circulated in any form of binding or cover other than that in which it is published and without a similar condition being imposed on the subsequent purchaser.

ISBN: 1-84319-318-3

Contents

Introduction		3
1	Wardyke's shadow	4
2	Isar and Deva	18
3	Urak locates her heir	29
4	The ghost-owl	47
5	The search for Guiron	58
6	The scarlet dress	69
7	Farla	75
8	Gya and Isar	83
9	The seeking spell	90
10	Urak's treasure	101
11	The island	106
12	Deva	120
13	Lark challenges Wardyke	128
14	The Hall of Records	136
15	The fire-mare	150
16	The silver vortex	154
17	Deva's return	166
18	Wardyke's 'friend'	174
19	Sekhmet and Ra	188
20	The seven doors	197
21	The Festival of the Moving Stars	206
22	The last raid	223

For my family and friends
visible and invisible
with my love

Introduction

In this book we have to presuppose the reality of reincarnation, i.e. the continuance of life before and after death, and the reintroduction of the same 'spiritual entity' into the physical realm in different times and places, often for the purpose of working out some unresolved matter from a previous life. In the present day, a large proportion of the world's population, mainly in the East but growing rapidly in the West, holds this belief. In ancient times the Celtic Druids certainly had faith in reincarnation; indeed, debts were often carried over from one life to the next, payment legally enforced. The Bronze Age people of this book, *c.* 1500-1450BC, lived long before the Iron Age Celtic Druids came to the British Isles... but the belief in reincarnation was probably already here, hinted at in ancient legends and expressed in the circle, the spiral and the vortex – their most frequent and insistent symbolic images.

In this book we also have to presuppose that the realm we see with our eyes and kick with our feet is only one of the many realms we inhabit. Invisible presences are everywhere – either emanating from ourselves, or belonging to other realms altogether – and as 'real' as anyone we might invite to dinner.

The Temple of the Sun at Haylken is called Avebury in modern times, and is still to be seen in Wiltshire, England. "The Haunted Mound" is now called Silbury Hill. Both monuments are thought to be nearly 5000 years old.

Chapter 1

Wardyke's shadow

Urak caused the drum to be sounded deep into the night, her bony hands moving too fast for human sight as she beat the taut hide hour after hour in the oppressive and listening darkness.

The voice of the drum and the voice of its echo mingled and blurred, rumbling and growling until the sky answered. Only then did Urak lift her hands and give the high, thin call that would give the drum rest. When the lightning came it picked out her figure on the top of the mountain, arms wide and high, head tilted to the sky, counting with her heartbeats the pacing of the thunderclaps. Nearer the storm came, and nearer – until the thunder struck at the same time as the lightning.

'Bring me a worthy acolyte...' was the message the rising wind scattered among the mountains, hissed through the branches of the trees, hurled through the narrow ravines.

'Give me a name... a face... someone to call... someone to teach... someone to carry on my work...'

The long cloak she wore flapped around her and cast giant shadows across the valley. For a moment it looked as though she would lift off and beat her wings into the storm.

'I have been tormented by fools...' she howled. 'Send me someone who will learn quickly... who will understand...'

She was an old woman, her skin a mass of folds. The hair that swirled around her was as white as smoke, never cut since the moment of her birth. She had sent away a score of apprentices in her long life, never satisfied, never ready to share her deepest secrets with anyone she did not consider her equal. But who could ever equal her, mighty witch-woman of the mountains, seasoned sorceress of nearly a hundred summers? Lately she had felt time slipping away from her: she could hear death whispering behind her, and she knew she had trained no one fully to follow her.

She tried to hold the rain back for she knew that once the rain burst from the black cloud that pressed so heavily down on the brow of her mountain, the storm-power she needed to use would be defused. With her own will she forced the cloud to hold its burden.

Once again her voice rang out.

Once again the wind carried her message.

In the livid light before the next whip-crack of thunder, she thought she glimpsed another figure on the rock platform beside her.

Her thin body was shaking with the strain of calling the storm and holding it poised. There was almost unbearable pain in every limb – but she knew she must hold on.

The next flash confirmed that she was no longer alone.

A man was before her – his eyes, the eyes of the dead.

She closed her own eyes and saw him still, held as an afterimage, accurate in every detail.

'Your name?' she asked in the language of the dead.

'Wardyke,' he said, his voice crackling like dry kindling in fire. Wardyke! She knew the name from a time when he had been her apprentice... one who had pleased her more than most.

'Wardyke,' she hissed, and felt the first hard hammer-blow of the rain. 'Give me a name! Give me someone worthy to train as my heir, someone who will succeed in destroying the Temple of the Sun where I have failed, someone who will make Guiron wish he had never been conceived in the womb of Time – let alone born to cross my path in this life...'

Wardyke smiled darkly. He too had been the victim of Guiron's power as High Priest of the Temple of the Sun. It was Guiron who had refused him the final prestigious mark of initiation into the priesthood after his long and arduous training at the Temple. It was Guiron who had masterminded the forces that had defeated him on the field of battle. And before that – in another lifetime – there had been another wrong not yet paid for... Wardyke had a great deal of bitterness to share with this wild and fearsome woman of the mountains.

He smiled because he knew a way to avenge both Urak and himself that was so neat, so economical, so marvellously simple and cruel, that she could not help but be delighted with it. He would give her a name that rang in the heart of both Guiron and Kyra, his two most hated enemies. He would give her an heir that no one would suspect until it was too late: an heir that would destroy the Temple from within. Urak would not regret calling his shadow up from those dark regions in which it had lain festering for so long. She would be proud of her one-time pupil. She and he would achieve together what neither of them had been able to achieve alone.

'Deva,' he said, his eyes darker than a cavern that had never seen the light. 'Deva, daughter of Kyra.'

Urak did not know the name Deva. She did not know the name Kyra. Her quarrel had been with Guiron and, before him, with other High Priests of the Temple of the Sun who had tried to prevent the spread of her power.

'Who is this Deva?' she called. 'Who is this Kyra?' But the pressure of the cloud above her was now too strong for her to hold back and she could feel her will giving way, her body crumpling. The image of Wardyke was fading, the echo of his words diminishing until finally it was drowned out by the thunderous beat of the raindrops on the rock as the cloud burst. On her knees in the deluge she still tried to reach him, tried to learn more about the name he had given her... but all she could hear now was the clamour of a million tiny chattering rain voices warning her that she might pay dearly for the name she had been given, that she should not accept it lightly...

The slave who served Urak, Boggoron, found her in the morning, soaked through and shivering, gibbering a name he did not know. He carried her to her cave and saw that the hearth fire was banked up. The storm had passed and the mountains rang with the sound of water on rock, birds greeting the sunshine, a shepherd calling his sheep.

The same dawn saw Deva, daughter of Kyra, many days' journey to the east of Urak's mountain fastness, stirring and waking beside her husband Gya. A thin beam of sunlight driving through a small gap in the curtain pricked her eyelids like a needle. She tossed her head impatiently and turned over, her back to the window. But the damage had been done. She was awake and the birds, uttering every variety of trill and pipe and warble, insisted that the day was already under way and she was missing it.

She turned back again to the young man still asleep beside her and pulled the rug aside so that she could see the firm and muscular landscape of his back. She kissed the nape of his neck and then worked her way down his arm, pausing to give his elbow a sharp bite. He woke with a jerk and slapped at the place she had bitten. She laughed and bit him on the hip. He heaved over on his back and took her roughly in his arms, shaking her and then kissing her. But now that he was awake and she had him roused, she suddenly lost interest and pulled away, slipping from the bed and taunting him by standing naked just out of his reach. She felt restless, as though she wanted something, but she didn't know what. A short while ago it would have been Gya. Then she could not have enough of his loving. But now... She reached for her wrap and covered herself.

He stared at her intently for a few moments, and then turned his shoulder to her, his fists clenched. He knew her well enough not to insist on anything when she had that expression on her face. He was fully awake now, and angry. He was angry with her and angry with himself. He wished he was not bound so close to her: wished that he could live without her. He told himself a thousand times that he had not chosen her – she had chosen him. He had walked into this community, its wood and reed houses clustered in the valley of Haylken near the Temple of the Sun, a free bowman, the hero who had helped to overthrow the armies of Groth, honoured, admired, in a position to take any woman he wanted. He could see them now, the young girls, clustering around him, their eyes begging for the slightest crumb of his attention. But Deva had swept them all aside. With a flash of her jet-dark eyes and a swing of her long raven's-wing hair she had led him firmly from the others and set him beside herself at the victory feast. He had been astonished at her beauty and her boldness, and awed by the splendour of her dress, the great clasp of amber and gold that held her light cloak to her creamy-white shoulder, the gold bracelets that gleamed on her slender arms. He remembered, as a drowning man remembers the last glimpse of dry land as he sinks beneath the surface of the water, the comfortable and rounded contours of Farla, a less frightening beauty, on the other side of the long table, before he succumbed completely to the spell of Deva, daughter of the High Priest Khu-ren and his wife Kyra, mighty Lords of the Sun, the most powerful and respected people in the land.

Deva was getting dressed. He could hear her moving about the room. What would she do so early in the morning? Today was probably market day. She would be out before anyone else, making sure she had first choice of all the goods the merchants brought in, all the food the farmers stacked in such neat piles. She needn't have bothered – for everyone knew her and everyone loved her and she would be given the first chance to acquire anything worth having that came into the Haylken community this day. Sometimes he called her a magpie. She seemed to need to accumulate things. He had seen her so often, flushed and bright-eyed, bargaining for some length of cloth or basket of willow wands that he knew she didn't need. Crowds would gather round her, enjoying the heated exchange between the young woman and the salty old merchant, egging her on as she lowered the value of the goods for barter. And then, when she had him cornered, she would suddenly lose interest and move on to the next one. He would have thought the merchants would hate her for the way she teased them, but they did not – and nor did he. They, like him, probably remembered the times when she gave in suddenly, capriciously, beautifully.

She leant down and kissed the top of his head just before she left the room and he heard her humming as she stepped lightly out into the early morning sunlight. 'Next time,' he thought, 'next time I won't let her get away with it.' He drifted back to sleep, pleasantly imagining how he would make love to her the next time she woke him as she had this morning.

Isar awoke troubled. For the first time in many years he had dreamed about his father – not Karne, who had brought him up with loving care, but his natural father, Wardyke, who had raped his mother Fern, and who had been killed in the war between the Spear-lords.

As soon as he opened his eyes the dream began to slip away, as an intruder would when the master of the house begins to stir. Isar lay on his back staring at the wooden beams above him and the thatch that kept the weather out. The grey light of early dawn had entered through the window he kept unshuttered in all but the worst weather. Lark, who lay beside him still wrapped in sleep, hated the dark and was comforted to see the stars from their bed. She was usually awake with the dawn like her namesake, but this day she lay curled up with her hand over her eyes as though she didn't want to face the day.

Isar tried to remember what he had dreamed. The impression of Wardyke's presence was strong, but he could recall none of the details. He wished Lark was awake. He felt the need to talk about Wardyke. Strange after all these years! He thought he had put him out of his life forever. He kissed the shoulders of his wife and held her close. She stirred and turned to him with a sleepy smile. Lark, the girl who had saved his life more than once during that dreadful conflict with Groth and his followers, her tongue cut out on Na-Groth's orders, a stranger to the Haylken community, was yet as close to him now as his own heartbeat.

Drifting between sleep and waking, Lark caught the shadow in Isar's eyes and touched his lips with her fingers. She couldn't speak but she could communicate with her hands, her eyes and her thoughts, and she had taught Isar that tongue-talk is only a very small part of the human dialogue. But Isar needed to use word-sound this morning, he needed to push out into the open what he was feeling. He needed to rid himself of the strange, haunting mix of emotions he had always had regarding Wardyke... As he talked Lark listened quietly, fascinated – her intent grey-blue eyes never leaving her husband's face, seeing how he wavered between the love and loyalty of the distant past and the revulsion Wardyke had generated more recently. She saw an image of the man, tall and lean, with dark and penetrating eyes, aquiline nose, sharp and determined chin. The image was so clear in her mind's eye she wondered for a moment if he were really there, in the chamber, watching them. She shuddered and buried her face against Isar's shoulder. She prayed that the old chain was well and truly broken and that Wardyke would never again return to interfere in Isar's life. With Guiron far away, Wardyke dead and Deva apparently happily married to Gya, it had seemed as though Isar was free at last to live a new life – but now, she wondered...

Kyra was already in the Temple when the first light came. She too had sensed the stirring of an old danger and was preparing to combat it in the most effective way she knew – by calling on the help of the spirit-realms, by gathering strength from her peers across the world and across time. Khu-ren, her husband and High Priest of the Temple, was not with her. He had celebrated the turn into spring with them – the moment when the sap begins to rise and the travelling birds return – and was now on a progress through the land, visiting other communities, encouraging and strengthening bonds with the mother Temple, and making a particular point of calling on those priests who were failing to keep up regular contact through the thought-channels.

Like a silver shadow she slipped over the wooden bridge that spanned the deep protective ditch round the huge circle of standing stones. She greeted the night watchman and he stood aside for her, smiling as all people smiled when the Lady Kyra passed by. Khu-ren, her Egyptian husband, was admired; but she was loved. Although she had a married daughter, her step was still as light and firm as a young girl's, and her hair, standing out around her this early dawn, was still like a fiery cloak of spun gold.

'Stay in peace,' she said softly as she passed.

'Go in peace,' he replied. It was too early for the dawn ceremonies – but the Lady could go where she pleased.

The grass under her bare feet was cold, a touch of late spring frost sparkling like powdered crystal on the leaves and stalks. She hardly felt it, pleased to be treading directly on the earth.

She did not use the three tall stones at the centre of the inner northern ring, the most sacred and powerful place in the whole system of circles, but went directly to her favourite stone – one she always turned to when she had a personal problem. It was an outer stone of the northern ring, the one against which Khu-ren had stood in that long-gone time when she had first called the Lords of the Sun to her aid, when she had not yet seen him in the flesh but already knew from his spirit-form that she loved him.

She leaned her back against it, looking outwards to the mighty stones of the main circle and the ridge beyond them. She would have seen nothing of the landscape surrounding the Temple even if it had been light, for the ridge would have prevented that, but she could always see the sky. She tipped her head back so that her golden hair flowed over the stone. She watched the subtle and gradual adjustment of colour tones as the earth prepared to receive the Light-giver, the King of Kings. She knew the sun was only the visible cipher for the invisible God, the Nameless One, but the miracle of the rising never ceased to fill her with awe. The sky was lightening to the purple of iris and gentian. One by one the stars were disappearing until, in a pale green dome, one enormous diamond hung, the morning star, the herald of the day, with its entourage of birds.

Her husband, Khu-ren, in a distant forest, waking on his bed of moss and dry fern, looked up through the high canopy of branches and saw, blazing through an intricate net of twigs and new leaves, the morning star. He looked into its eye and smiled, knowing that Kyra had found a way to be with him; and then he frowned, for the star was already gone, and a shadow had touched his heart. Was it a warning from Kyra about dangers he would have to face, or was it a call for help against dangers that *she* had to face? He started to compose himself for spirit-travel, preparing to join her in the Temple – where she must surely be in order to send out such a powerful beam of thought. Before he could leave his body, however, he was distracted by a sound from above and to the left. He turned his head to find that he was being closely watched by the huge and unblinking eyes of an owl.

Khu-ren felt strange – as though he were under some kind of spell, as though someone were deliberately suspending time, deliberately holding him back. He became totally absorbed in his observation of the owl. Every detail of feather and beak, of folded wing, of claw on twig, fascinated him. All the time the light was growing stronger and the creature clearer. Its eyes seemed to stare dispassionately into his innermost thoughts, and by doing so, seemed to blot them out one by one, until his mind was left a blank. He no longer remembered the message of the star, no longer remembered that he had been about to try to make contact with Kyra.

At last the owl moved, and was gone instantly, disappearing into the shadows as though it had never been. Khu-ren ran to the foot of the tree on which it had perched, but there was no sign of it – nor had he heard any sound of beating wings. If it had been an apparition, its 'sending' was not from the Temple. He had not missed the malevolence of its penetrating gaze. Hastily he gathered up his possessions, anxious to leave the place.

In the great house of the Spear-lord, overlooking the sprawling community of the Temple of the Sun at Haylken, Kyra's brother Karne half woke to find that his wife Fern was not beside him, and turned over to sleep his dreamless sleep. She often left when first light came. He knew if he looked for her he would find her in her garden. There were three children apart from Isar, and the only time she really had for herself was before they woke in the morning. Sometimes even that was taken away by their youngest, who woke with the birds, but this day, mercifully, he was lying with his thumb in his mouth, breathing steadily, when she crept past him. Karne was the Spear-lord of his village, the first of his people to have that privilege, and the Spear-lord's lady had not only her own family to attend to, but a constant stream of supplicants and guests.

Fern loved the early morning. It was true the night gave one respite from the noise and bustle of the day, and the difficulties that seemed insoluble at sunset were often sorted out when the mind was still; but the darkness carried its own burdens, and nightmares could creep in below one's guard. In the morning everything was fresh and new... all good things seemed possible.

She drew her woollen cloak closer over her night shift. It was still very cold, but she knew the sun was returning, and she could stand anything as long as the sun was on its way. Winter was not a good time for her. She hated the long dark when her companions, the plants and the trees, shut themselves down. For months she could have no communication with them. The wind howled through their bare branches with its own voice, not theirs, and she felt alone when she walked over the crackling brown bracken of the forest.

Now everything was stirring again. She could feel the movement inside her rowan tree when she rested her cheek against its bark. Every cell was vibrant with activity – the sap rising through the twigs, pushing out the leaf shoots and the tiny curled blossom buds. Everywhere the earth was cracking open as the green shouldered its way out of the dark towards the returning sun.

Every morning and evening at the same time three geese flew diagonally over her garden, uttering their strange raucous cries. She smiled as she heard them approaching now. Their regularity was comforting though she could never understand why they flew from one apparently identical pool of water to another a few miles away each day and returned to the first each night. Sometimes they dropped feathers for her as they passed. She had a collection of bird feathers in a little wooden box Isar had made for her, the lid beautifully carved with images of birds. She sometimes allowed her daughter Inde to look through them and choose some to play with. The best and largest ones she herself had woven into the slender golden ring she wore around her head sometimes on ceremonial occasions. Her long red-gold hair had a few strands of grey in it now, and she was not as slender as she had been as a young girl, but when her hair was piled on top of her head under the feather crown, and her best green cloak was caught at her shoulder with an amber and gold clasp, she did not look like the mother of four children, one of whom was already grown to manhood.

The geese passed but dropped no feathers this day. Fern went from plant to plant in her garden, tenderly freeing a shoot from the weight of a stone here, placing a stick for a tendril to grasp there. For some reason she began to think about Wardyke. Puzzled, she told herself it must be because she was paying such attention to the new growth coming through. It reminded her of the time her forest began to grow again after Wardyke had cruelly burned it down. She had hated Wardyke and he had raped her, but she no longer carried bitterness for this. Had not this evil brought about her handsome and much-loved son Isar? But she found it difficult to forgive the burning of her forest. She still woke sometimes in the night with tears streaming down her cheeks, unable to tell Karne what was troubling her. It seemed to her she could hear her green children screaming as the flames devoured their branches and tumbled the trunks that had taken so many centuries to grow. It was true a new forest had sprung up again from the charred remains of the old one – buckthorn and dogwood, hazel and alder and ash – but her mighty oaks and the yew trees that seemed to have been growing from before time began were gone, and in this life she would not see them grow to that size again.

'Why do I remember this now?' she thought angrily. 'It's a long time since I've had that dream.' She shook her head, trying to shake away the memory. The light had been steadily strengthening since she left her bed, and the long rays of the sun were beginning to pick out the frost crystals on certain tall grass leaves so that they momentarily blazed with light and then dissolved. 'I will not think of Wardyke,' she told herself. 'He has no place in our lives now.' But her tryst with the dawn had been spoiled and for once she was not sorry when she heard the call of her second son, Jan.

Jan was a boy of eleven summers, restless and energetic, usually his father's companion when he rode or strode about the valley, but not averse to working with his mother in the garden when there was nothing else to do. He came running down the path, ready for the day, impatient that no one else was up and about, chewing on a piece of yesterday's loaf, a large apple from the last of the winter store in his hand.

Fern straightened up and smiled. Jan was good company – perhaps he would help her dig a trench for the new plantings. She sent him off in search of an antler pick she had put somewhere at the end of the summer and he left with a good grace, glad to have something to do. 'How tall he is growing,' she thought, 'hardly a child any more.' Inde, her daughter, was a year older, but shorter than he and very different in temperament – passive, steady, reliable but somewhat unimaginative. Jan was quicksilver – never still, never dull, alternately surprising them with his maturity and shocking them with his childishness. If anyone could drive the shadows out of her thoughts it would be Jan. She was glad he was up and about.

Unaware of the shadow that was beginning to stalk the quiet community of the Temple of the Sun in the valley of Haylken, Guiron, now a very old man who, after years of wandering, had finally come to live beside the great Nile river in Egypt, went about his daily business. His friend Userhet, also a man long retired from active life, was teaching him to read the writing of his people.

When Guiron first exiled himself from his homeland, Britain, where he had been High Priest of the mighty Temple of the Sun for more years than he cared to count, he made sure that an ocean lay between him and those he loved and whom he felt he had betrayed. But the narrow ocean was not enough. On a clear day he could see a faint smudge of white on the horizon, the white cliffs of his birthland, and he found himself gazing at them, remembering the past with nostalgia, when he should have been seeking the future.

Sadly he gathered his new possessions together and set his face towards the north-east. There he found the climate harsher and the people less friendly. He told himself as he battled against wind and storm and driving sleet, as he was turned away from hearth after hearth, as he heard the wolves singing in the forests and the prey of the bald eagle screaming, that he deserved no more. He journeyed perpetually, seeking some sign, some sage who would teach him something he did not yet know, something that would help him overcome his own nature and free him from the guilt he still felt for what he had done.

In the long dark winter of the far north, where the sun hardly rose for half a year, he thought for a while he had at last found such a sage, such a teacher. The Mogüd, a wise-man, a shaman, holed up against the winter with his apprentice, his grandson, took him and gave him shelter in his rough hut of reed and hide, smoke blackened and stinking of dried fish. He had found Guiron on the verge of death, lost in a thick fog, shivering and frightened, his long years as High Priest forgotten. It was as though he was the first man, crawling on his hands and knees, faced by the primeval void. The Mogüd had lifted him up in his huge arms and carried him until they were on a slope above the fog and Guiron could see a blaze of stars. He wept like a child, knowing that he had forgotten the splendour of existence and had succumbed to unforgivable despair. It was the Mogüd who gradually gave him back himself.

Outside the tight little world of the shaman's hut the wind howled and the snows piled up. The three of them lived on a sparse diet of dried meat and dried fish. Edible mosses and lichens gathered in the good weather were a welcome supplement. The two old men managed reasonably well, but the growing boy's eyes grew wild and feverish as he became hungrier and hungrier.

Guiron watched the boy's training with interest, the very frenzy of his hunger being used by the old man to prod him into states of trance. The shaman's way was different in many instances from the way of the Temple of the Sun. When he told the Mogüd how differently they worked, the Mogüd said it was because they had a different end in mind. He said that the Lords of the Sun mastered the skills of earthly spirit-travel and could roam the world in search of their peers, but he aimed at leaving the earth altogether and flying to the celestial world of the gods above. Yet even among the shamans of his line there were different methods of working. There was the 'ladder' method, where one trained slowly and laboriously to climb step by step to the celestial regions; and there was the method of the eagle, where one flew instantly and directly to one's goal. He was trying to train the boy to fly – for this was the way with which he was most familiar.

As the winter grew deeper and deeper, and there was no end to the howling of the wind and the darkness that pressed close around them, Guiron and the boy became more and more disorientated, more and more prone to shaking fits and morbid dreams. The Mogüd watched them carefully, eking out the food and water.

One day Guiron woke to find the Mogüd muttering incantations and preparing something in a small wooden bowl. He was taking a pinch of powder from one leather pouch, and a handful of herbs from another. Gradually he mixed together a great many different substances. Guiron watched closely. He could feel that this day was going to be different from the others and he wondered if it would bring him the wisdom and relief he sought. The firelight flickered on the shaman's face – the contrast of light and deep shadow making an impassive mask of it. Guiron glanced across at the sleeping boy, his tousled hair catching the light but his face still in darkness, unaware that from today there would be no turning back for him.

The Mogüd completed his preparations and called his two students to his side. The old man and the young boy crawled out of their sleeping rugs and stretched, looking hungrily at the rough shelves that housed what food was still left so late in the winter. The shaman shook his head. Today they would not eat. Today he had something much more important for them to do. He produced two ragged cloaks of eagle feathers from a pile of dusty objects behind the food store and bade them put them on. With some distaste, Guiron pulled the half-rotted garment around himself. It scarcely covered his shoulders. But the boy's face lit up when he saw what his grandfather held in his hands, and he eagerly reached out to take it. His was the longer cloak and he wore it proudly, smoothing out the feathers that were ruffled and out of place, adjusting it until it lay around him like folded wings.

Then the Mogüd took out two pipes and filled their bowls with the mixture he had been making. Solemnly he lit them and handed one to Guiron first and then one to the boy, indicating that they should smoke them. Guiron hesitated a moment, wondering what the shaman was up to, but the boy trustingly put the pipe stem in his mouth at once. Guiron met the Mogüd's eyes and hesitated no longer. In accepting the Mogüd's teaching Guiron had agreed to suspend his own judgement... a thing no teacher at the Temple of the Sun would ever have advised – or indeed allowed.

He drew heavily on the pipe and felt the warm smoke filling his lungs.

Satisfied that his students were in the mood to obey him, the Mogüd took out a drum and began to beat it. For a while Guiron squatted on the floor dreamily smoking his pipe, listening with detachment to the music the Mogüd was making. Then, gradually, it began to seem as though the beating of the drum was coming from inside him and he felt the urge to move with it, to express it, to dance...

Guiron and the boy danced round and round, faster and faster.

Then it seemed to them that the giant form of the Mogüd stood over them and commanded them to fly, commanded them to overcome the pull of the earth and to fly... to fly above... beyond... to fly like the eagle.

The urge to fly, the belief that he could fly, was all that was left of Guiron's consciousness. He spread his wings, his feathers ruffled in the dark wind and, straining muscle and sinew, he lifted at last to the air – and flew.

The agony of muscles that had never been used before was almost more than he could bear, but the Mogüd's voice drove him on, and the passionate desire to fly like the eagle held him to his course. He banked, he turned... his eye as red as a dying sun saw the earth a thousand leagues below him – a blue pearl, luminous in the darkness that surrounded it.

'Ai,' his bird-voice called. 'Ai... ai... ai-i-i...'

The stars, like a handful of diamonds flung into a shaft of sunlight, glittered for a moment and then disappeared. He was among the 'gods'. He could see their forms: some huge and menacing, others slender and wraithlike, some bedecked in jewels and rich fabrics, some in simple robes of white, some with the shape of men, some alien and weird... All with masks.

Guiron was filled with terror. 'If only I could see their faces,' he thought. 'If only I knew who they were. If only I could look into their eyes.'

His human frame could take no more. His wings failed him and he spiralled down and down through darkness and cold to fall with a sickening thud at the feet of the Mogüd.

After a long time he opened his eyes.

He was in the smoky hut of the shaman. Beside him lay the body of the boy, with the wizened form of his instructor crouched over him, rocking on his heels, keening.

The boy was dead.

Shaking and confused, Guiron rose and stood beside them, gazing down at the body of the boy, the shell, the pathetic little pile of flesh and bone still in the cloak of dead and lustreless feathers.

Guiron felt sick and sad. He turned away and crept into his sleeping rugs in the corner. He lay down with his face to the wall and pulled them over his head. He was weary, weary. He was no longer sure what was right and what was wrong. He had had great faith in the Mogüd – but now he wondered. He felt dissatisfied, as though he had been cheated in some way, as though his flight had been an illusion induced by smoking the pipe and not as he had always understood such flights should be – a reaching of the actual soul, the eternal Self, towards the higher realms. He had always believed that these higher realms were not literally above the stars, but out of Time and out of Space altogether – a question of quality rather than of position. No wonder the 'gods' he had seen had been masked – they were no more than figments of his own imagination performing the role he demanded of them, like actors in a play. He had not really wanted to see behind their masks, because, if he had, he would have known them for what they were. How he longed for some One he did not know, some One he could not know... the Nameless One beyond all self-deception and illusion.

The Mogüd had suggested that the Lords of the Sun were earth-bound, and Guiron admitted it was this earth-realm that concerned them most – but only because without an understanding of what they were here and now they could not adequately prepare for what they were to become. When they reached for the celestial realms they wanted to be sure they could distinguish what was real and what was not.

In the spring Guiron left the Mogüd, seeking the sun and a teaching that he could better trust. It was thus that he had come, at last, to Egypt.

Guiron's admiration for Userhet knew no bounds. He was an adept of the highest order and a master of his country's enormous and complex store of knowledge. Coming from a culture that wrote nothing down, but learned everything by direct transmission from teacher to pupil, Guiron was fascinated by this, to him, new way of learning. He begged Userhet to teach him how to decipher and to inscribe, hoping perhaps to find among these elaborate glyphs something that would lift him far beyond himself. Userhet, in turn, was interested to learn what he could from the traveller – for what had been certainty when he was young now seemed, in old age, not so simple, not so certain.

While Wardyke and Urak hatched their plans for vengeance against him in Britain, Guiron lived a pleasant life in Egypt, full of hope that he had finally put to rest the old and troublesome web in which he had once been caught.

Chapter 2

Isar and Deva

Urak dismissed Boggoron and prepared to make the search for Deva, daughter of Kyra. There was a flat, smooth slab of black stone just outside the entrance to her cave, very different from the grey limestone on the rest of the mountain, and this she swept carefully – using a small brush of eagle feathers tied with a wolf-skin thong. Then she polished the stone with a soft cloth of doeskin. When she was satisfied that it was spotless she arranged a circle of red jasper pebbles on it, smooth and river-worn. In the centre of this she marked a pentacle, using a piece of white chalkstone.

There was one more thing to do. From a thong around her neck she untied a flattened disc of flint with a hole in the middle. She laid it in the pentacle so that it formed a small circular holding plinth. Then she went to a niche in the darkest part of her cave and drew out a snakeskin pouch. From this she removed a sphere of dark, almost black, smoky quartz. She had shaped and polished it from a huge single crystal until it was a smooth black ball, a scrying stone with a mirror surface.

The sun was rising fast, shining through the branches of the tall trees that grew in the valley well below the witch-woman's cave, their crowns on a level with her floor.

She arranged the black sphere with great care, edging it from side to side until she was satisfied that it was perfectly centred. Then she waited, squatting cross-legged beside it with her back to the cave, facing the forest and the sun. She was ready the instant the sun rose above the tree tops and blazed down on to her table of symbols and artefacts. As the sunlight reached the black sphere, it illuminated not only the surface but the depths as well. As Urak leant closer and peered into it, she seemed to catch a glimpse of a huge circular temple of standing stones surrounded by a deep ditch and a high ridge; by burial mounds; by encampments and settled villages. She knew at once that this was the Temple of the Sun at Haylken, the centre from which all the thousands of stone circles throughout the land drew their strength and to which all who wanted to be of the priesthood gravitated for training.

The vision was gone almost as soon as it came. The sun had climbed higher and the angle of its rays no longer focused the light in that particular way. But Urak had seen enough. She knew the place. She had been there as a child, taken by her parents to be offered for training – partly because her family were convinced that she was a natural candidate for the priesthood with her strong psychic abilities, and partly because she was such a headstrong and difficult child they did not know what else to do with her. They hoped the famous Temple discipline would tame her and give them and the rest of the family and their neighbours some respite from her increasingly sadistic tricks. But she had refused to stay. There was something about the Temple that made her uncomfortable.

She had passed all the tests the priests put her through and everything seemed settled, when suddenly she started to weep and stamp her feet, and demand that she be taken home. She could see the eyes of the High Priest now as though it were yesterday – looking into her own with that disconcerting, steady, penetrating gaze. He knew then why she could not stay and quietly told her disappointed and protesting parents to take her home. Before they left he drew her aside and made various secret signs and passes over her head. When she demanded to know what he was doing in her small piping child's voice, he looked at her very gravely and murmured, more to himself than to her: 'I have done what I can... but I fear you will one day prove to be too strong for us.'

At the time she had not taken much notice of the enigmatic words and, indeed, was so delighted to have won her battle to be going home that she had apparently forgotten them until this moment. Now, as they came back to her from some deep storage region in her mind, she took them as a sign that she would be successful in taking whatever or whomever she wanted from the Temple.

'So, Deva, daughter of Kyra, you are at the Temple of the Sun. But your destiny does not lie there and there you will not stay.'

Urak replaced the precious black sphere in its pouch and returned it to the depths of her cave. The red jasper pebbles were placed in their own pouch of wolfskin beside it. The pentacle she rubbed out with spit and her index finger. The flint with the hole she returned to the thong around her neck.

She had located her heir. Now all that remained was for her to claim her and train her.

The sun was much higher now, shining down into the valley that lay at her feet. The sides of the gorge were steep, birch and hazel and mountain ash clinging to the silvery grey walls of rock, ferns and moss flowing from crevices where soil had gathered and retained some moisture on the surface. Most of the rainwater in these mountains disappeared down sinkholes and drained away in an elaborate series of underground rivers and waterfalls. Urak knew that her mountains were hollow. What looked like gigantic slabs and mounds of solid rock were mostly thin shells of limestone over vast underground passages and halls. Guiron, in banishing her to these mountains, was unwittingly giving her access to a labyrinth which served her both as a luxurious dwelling and a hideaway where no one would ever be able to find her.

Isar was preparing for a journey. Kyra had expressed a wish for a very special wooden bowl in which to keep her precious collection of double-ended crystals, and Khu-ren had asked Isar, the Temple wood-carver, to make it for her as a surprise. Isar had looked through the seasoned wood he had in store and found that none of it was suitable. He remembered a huge old oak he had once seen in a forest some distance away, so old that half of it had been brought down in a storm, while the rest remained standing black and gnarled with age, but still putting out fresh green shoots in the spring. He was by no means sure that it would still be there for him, but it was so far off the beaten path he had hope that it would not have been spotted by any of the woodsmen. On the fallen part there was a huge oak burr that would do very well for Kyra's bowl.

He set off along the ridgeway that led towards the north, soon striding past a place the locals called the 'field of the grey gods' – that strange and haunted field where his palace had once stood in a past life, long-gone, ancient days. He remembered a time in this present life when, as a child, he had been taken there by Wardyke and glimpsed for a moment something of the splendours of that distant past life of his. He remembered also how Kyra had come seeking him and angrily pulled him back to the present.

But the field was soon past and he forgot the shadows it contained as a skylark trilled above his head. The huge circular Temple of the Sun was no longer visible, nor the plumes of smoke from the long wooden buildings that surrounded it. Even the mysterious flat-topped hill beyond the Temple that some people thought was a haunted burial mound, but which he believed to be a holy mountain raised in the ancient days to be close to the moon, the sun and the stars – even that had finally disappeared from sight. Everywhere the soft flush of hawthorn blossom drifted like white mist over the green, while underfoot all manner of small flowers peered out – the tiny crocus and the violet, the tall speckled snake-head fritillary so sacred to the Temple, the primrose, the lover's periwinkle. What had been bare fields a few weeks before were now emerald green as the barley and the wheat began to grow. The high ridge took him into the forests at last, but he still had a long way to go. Oak did not grow comfortably on the chalk and was not commonly found among these gentle white hills.

About midday he rested in the sunshine with his back against a tree. He was tired and soon dozed off. The sun had moved a long way and he was in the shade when he woke, startled, at the sound of someone approaching.

'Deva!' he called out in surprise. Kyra's beautiful daughter was indeed standing in front of him, out of breath but smiling broadly. She was dressed in travelling clothes, close-fitting buckskin trousers under her thigh-length tunic, boots laced up to her knees and a short cape flung jauntily over her shoulder. Her long black hair was plaited and tied back so that her face was completely clear of it. Her jet-black eyes were sparkling.

'Yes, Deva,' she said cheerfully. 'Not an apparition or a dream or a ghoul. Deva in flesh and blood!' And she laughed as she held out her hands to him.

Delighted, he took them in his own and allowed himself to be pulled to his feet by her.

'What are you doing here?'

She stood on her toes and kissed him lightly on his lips: a butterfly wing could not have administered a lighter touch. He squeezed her hands warmly and kissed her where her hair joined her forehead. For the moment, in the joy of seeing her so unexpectedly, he had forgotten that recently, on more than one occasion, he had intercepted a look from her that made him uneasy.

'I'm going to Farla's wedding at Hael,' she said, naming a village not far from the very place where he hoped to find the oak burr. 'I heard you were probably on this road and I hoped I'd catch up with you. I've been running most of the way!'

He grinned. 'It would be good to have your company,' he said lightly. 'But we'd better get on if we want to reach Hael before nightfall.'

But Deva was hungry and thirsty and they stayed a while longer for her to eat some of Lark's freshly baked bread and drink from his water-skin. She had left in such haste she had not brought any provisions for herself.

Isar cast an anxious look at the sky. It was later than he wished and a billowing mass of clouds was piling up on the horizon.

'If we don't start soon we'll be caught in that storm,' he said. But she insisted that she was still tired and needed more rest.

'Those clouds will take a long time to reach us,' she protested.

But a wind had sprung up and they were moving with alarming speed across the sky.

'Come,' he insisted, and held out his hand to help her to her feet. It had been pleasant for a time to sit at the roadside talking of this and that, but he was beginning to feel impatient to be on the way again.

As he pulled her up, she stumbled slightly and fell against him. There it was again – the look in her eyes that should not have been in any woman's eyes for a man not her husband. He moved away quickly and started to stride forward. She followed, two steps to his one, complaining that he was walking too fast. He did not slacken his pace.

It was not long before the clouds completely covered the sun, and they were nowhere near Hael when the rainstorm broke.

The distant landscape disappeared under a heavy veil of grey and the wind roared and rattled in the forests, rubbing and beating the branches of the trees together. Isar looked back at Deva and saw that she was almost being knocked off her feet by the fierceness of the gusts. He raced back to her and took her arm. Everything loose seemed to be whirling around them and everything rooted was being tugged and shaken. Then the first drops of rain fell, heavy and fast.

'We'd better take shelter,' Isar shouted against the wind and she nodded. The road here was wide and exposed, a ridge above the forest to the left and the open country to the right. They were already almost soaked through. He looked desperately around, but there was nowhere to go except down into the forested valley and hope that they could get below the wind and under trees clustered thickly enough to keep off most of the rain.

They slipped and slithered over the deep matting of wet dead leaves and down a steep slope, hand in hand. The spring growth was not as thick as they would have liked and most of the trees afforded very little shelter. The noise of the gale in the branches and the increasing orchestra of sounds in the valley as the stream swelled, rushing and gurgling over the rocks, put them into something of a panic. What if a tree blew down? They had both seen trees uprooted by gales, huge branches snapped like thin twigs.

'There!' shouted Deva suddenly, and pointed to a place where there was an overhang – a cliff that leaned over a turbulent stream and a ledge halfway up and out of reach of its fury. They edged their way over a crumbling scree to reach it, clinging to saplings, not letting one go before they had another in their grasp. At one time Deva lost her grip and her footing and slid some way before the huge old stump of a tree halted her. The black leaves on the forest floor were dangerously slippery now and it was some time before, bedraggled and scratched and out of breath, she reached Isar's side again, and they were both comparatively safe and dry on the ledge.

She was shivering and he put his arm around her as they sat close together, watching the rain pouring into the forest, listening to the wind howling and shrieking in the high canopy above them.

They looked into each other's eyes and laughed, exhilarated and happy that they had outwitted the onslaught of the elements. Isar kissed her wet cheek with a grin, and hugged her. The innocence of their childhood love had returned and for the moment Isar was no more than the cousin the much younger Deva adored. The far-memory of the more complicated adult love, and the life they had shared centuries before which had ended so disastrously, was dormant, sleeping below the surface, biding its time.

They had thought they would only have to shelter under the overhang for a short while, but the rain showed no sign of abating. After a while the wind eased off, but there was no break in the steady drum of the raindrops.

Isar unrolled his woollen cloak and wrapped it around both of them. Deva nestled into his shoulder.

He half expected her to say, as she had so often done as a child, 'Tell me a story, Ia... the one about the revenge of the wolf-princess.' This was one of her favourites – largely, he thought, because he had to accompany it with suitable howling and snarling.

She must have remembered those days too, for she looked sideways up at him now and there was a mischievous twinkle in her eye.

'Tell me a story, Ia,' she said.

'The wolf-princess?' he asked: but she shook her head and laughed.

'No – that's a child's tale. Tell me the one about the storm that opened up a hole in the earth and those who fell through were not heard of again for a thousand years.'

He smiled, telling the old tale... the sadness of those who had lost their families and lovers... the passing of time on the surface of the earth so that generations lived and died, while for those who had fallen into the hole and now lived in a magical land more beautiful than any words could tell, hardly any time passed, at all.

Deva listened with delight to the descriptions of the splendours in the other world – the crystal towers, the shimmering forests, the lakes so clear that the diamond sands beneath them shone night and day and boats sailing on the surface of the water cast no shadows, for the light was coming as much from below as from above. But when he reached the part where the earth opened up again and the lost people emerged excitedly to look for their loved ones and found that the world had changed beyond belief and no one was there who could recognise them, tears gathered in her eyes and she gave a sob.

Isar held her close, suddenly realising why Deva had always loved this tale. Had she not waited as ghost-lady of the lake beside the Haunted Mound for centuries for his return... and when he had at last returned, nothing was as she had hoped.

Forgetting everything but the passion of that ancient life, he gathered her even closer and kissed her deeply. Had they been wrong to try to break the thread, change the pattern? Were they not destined? He felt her response to his kiss. She was winding herself around him like a vine. His heart was hammering painfully, and from being so cold he was burning hot. How he desired her at that moment! But consummation was not possible on that tiny, crumbling ledge, and discomfort broke them apart. Trembling, he drew himself up and away from her, and found that the rain had ceased and the night was coming on rapidly.

'Deva,' he said sharply. 'We must go.'

She looked at him, dazed, puzzled – and then with extraordinary bitterness. She picked up a loose stone and hurled it with all her strength away from her. It hit the trunk of a tree and ricocheted against two more before it fell with a thud to the valley floor. To her it seemed he was calmly folding his cloak and preparing to leave. Because his back was to her she could not see that his hands were shaking so much he could scarcely make the folds.

Isar's wife, Lark, had something to tell his mother, Fern. For some time she had suspected that she was pregnant and now she was sure. Her body was gradually changing. She could feel the subtle adjustments it was making. A new soul was nesting in her and she had to prepare for the physical nurturing of it until it was ready to take its own place in the world. She had held off telling Isar because twice before she had conceived and had had a miscarriage, and this time she did not want to raise his hopes until she was sure the soul would stay. She had been on the verge of telling him before he left to fetch the oak burr, but his long and anxious talk about Wardyke had put a thought into her head that she wanted to examine before she told him anything. Fern was the one to tell. Fern, the mother of Isar. Fern, who had known Wardyke.

Lark had long since accepted the inconvenience of not being able to use word-sound. The people she loved had all grown accustomed to interpreting her hand language. But today for the first time in a long time she wished desperately that she could speak. She wanted to talk, to pour out, to relieve the pressure on her mind with floods of sound as other people did. With her kind of talking one had to say exactly what one wanted to say and no more.

Fern was at home and greeted Lark warmly. She loved her eldest son's wife and was always delighted to see her. They walked out into the garden together, the older woman's arm around the girl's waist. Knowing that Lark could not talk, Fern did what most people did, talked a lot herself. She chattered on about this child and that, about this plant and that, about her husband, Karne, who had gone off with his two eldest children, Inde and Jan, to look for the plants Fern needed for the water garden she was preparing. They were standing beside the wall of heavy boulders he had built to dam the stream at the bottom of their garden, when Fern finally realised that Lark had not just come to pass the time of day but had something important she wanted to say.

'What is it?' she asked, looking at the girl's hands and not her mouth.

Lark hesitated. How to begin? How to express the complicated and probably unfounded fears she had? How to ask the question she feared to ask?

But first she had good news for Fern. That would be easy to tell. She placed her hands on her womb and smiled. Instantly Fern hugged her.

'You're sure?'

Lark nodded vigorously. Fern knew the history of Lark's miscarriages and put them down to the horrors of the time when Lark had been Na-Groth's prisoner, the slave of his formidable queen. 'There must be shadows in Lark's heart that will take years to dispel,' Fern had told Isar after the second disappointment. 'Give her time.' By the look on the girl's face now, the shadows were lifting at last. Or were they? Fern caught something under the surface of Lark's smile that told her there was something more Lark wanted to communicate and that it was not as good as the first piece of news.

She suggested they sat down, and Lark gladly complied. They sat facing each other on two of the larger boulders, and Fern composed herself into the mood of relaxed quiet that would make it easier to understand what could not be said in words. She watched Lark attentively. She saw that she was worried, that she was worried about her child. Was it because of the previous miscarriages? No. Did she feel ill? No. Did she not want the child? Lark's response left Fern in no doubt that Lark wanted to bear her child, but – and here Fern came up against that hint of shadow again. Could it be that it might not be Isar's child? She remembered the agony of the time when she herself discovered that she was carrying Wardyke's seed. The quick and reproachful look she received through Lark's tears told her that this was not the problem.

What then? Perhaps she had been given some sign about the child's former lives. She asked if this was the case and knew from Lark's reply that she was now very close to an understanding.

Because the question of Wardyke had scarcely come up since Lark had joined their community, no hand-sign had been devised for his name. Now, in desperation, Lark mimed again and again the two words 'war' and 'dyke' until Fern suddenly grasped what she was saying.

She went cold. Wardyke! Fern remembered how he had been in her own mind recently and how she had felt the stirring of the old malevolence.

'What about Wardyke?' she cried.

Laboriously Lark communicated in her own way that Isar had been suddenly troubled by memories of Wardyke one morning – and that she herself, since the time he had mentioned it to her, had been having a series of recurring dreams in which Wardyke featured. She would be walking down a path, and in each dream the path was different, but on each path her way was finally blocked by a tall dark figure in a long black cloak. She never saw his face – but she knew it was Wardyke. He never spoke to her. As soon as she saw him her terror was so great she turned round and ran back down the path. Every morning she had the dream she woke up out of breath, as though she had indeed been running.

Fern frowned. This was not good.

'Perhaps,' she said tentatively, though she had very little hope that what she was about to say was true, 'it is not a message dream at all – but just one of those one has when one is worried about something. You say you have only had it since Isar spoke to you about Wardyke?'

Lark shook her head. 'I had it the night Isar began to think about Wardyke... before he spoke to me about it!'

Lark remembered that she had encountered the dark cloaked figure in her dream that very night. She had not known then that it was Wardyke, and, in that first dream, she hadn't turned to run, but stood her ground on the path gazing at the figure, ill at ease, but not yet in real fear. Isar had woken her before either of them made their next move. She had forgotten the dream entirely until it began to recur and she associated the figure with Wardyke. That she had first seen the figure in her dream before Isar spoke about Wardyke worried Fern.

'Perhaps...' she said, wishing wise Kyra was with her to give advice, or even Karne with his down-to-earth common sense. 'Perhaps,' she said, 'if it occurs again... I mean, if – if you meet the figure again, you shouldn't run but challenge him to show himself and say what he has to say. Perhaps you could even tell him to go and leave you alone.'

'I fear,' Lark indicated, her grey eyes swimming in tears. 'I fear – this child...' She put her hands on her womb and her face was so wracked with suffering Fern put her arms around her and held her close. So Lark feared that Wardyke might be returning through the gate of her body, his dark soul insinuating himself into their lives, his shadow lying between them.

Fern held her even closer. She wished she could say no, this was not happening; no, this was not possible; but she had felt his cold shadow on her heart and, it seemed, she had felt it the very morning Lark first dreamed her dream and Isar poured out his memories.

The two women clung together and neither could give the other comfort.

Fern's garden grew silently and imperceptibly around them. A bud started to open. A leaf unfurled.

At last Fern pulled herself together.

'Come, dry your eyes,' she said, pushing the girl gently away from her. 'We must be sensible. We must be practical.'

Lark's eyes asked a great many questions. Fern was thinking rapidly.

'We must ask Kyra. She'll be able to probe into the other realms and find out for us.'

Lark's face cleared. Of course, Kyra – the great priestess, capable of travelling through time and space and through all the realms available to humankind outside time and space. She would know. But then Lark's heart sank again. If she knew for sure that it was so – what would she do? She shivered. Would she terminate the life in her womb? The life she had longed for – her child? She dreaded and feared to make such a decision. But if she let it live – what evil would it wreak? And if she did not – who was she to decide who should live and who should die? Who was she to deny Wardyke a chance for life and, with life, a chance to change?

Fern witnessed her turmoil.

'I'll speak to Kyra,' she said reassuringly.

Lark shook her head.

'No?'

'No.'

She made Fern promise to say nothing to anyone. She wanted to think about this by herself. She wanted to be sure that she was ready for whatever Kyra might find out when the moment came, and she even decided not to tell Isar anything until she was surer in her own mind what she wanted to do.

Chapter 3

Urak locates her heir

The village of Hael was preparing a wedding feast. One of their most popular young farmers, Geb, was marrying the young woman he had been in love with all his life – Farla, daughter of By-ek, the chief Elder of the village. Geb had waited a long time for her consent. He had asked her first when they were young children and regularly every year at the spring festival since then. But, although she was fond of him, she had made it clear she was not in love with him and would prefer their friendship to remain as it was.

When she was fourteen she had chosen to leave Hael for the Temple of the Sun, to train as priest. At first her enthusiasm and dedication had been unshakeable. She had no doubt that she was destined to be one of the Lords of the Sun, the highest of the ranks possible for the priesthood. At that time the High Priest Khu-ren and his wife Kyra were the only initiates of this level at the Temple, but so quickly did Farla learn what her mentors set before her, and so single-minded was she in the pursuit of the difficult and arcane knowledge of the Temple, that Kyra herself recommended her for the special training. She was a good way through this when she began to lose self-confidence, and one year when Geb asked her to leave the Temple and marry him she actually considered it.

In the end she refused him as usual, but she watched him leave this time with something like regret – appreciating for the first time the steadiness of his stride, the comforting strength of his thick-set shoulders. The very earthiness that had irritated her before, now began to be appealing.

What she was trying to do was so difficult, so complex, so subtle. If she had tried to explain to him that when she was sitting silently, rock still, apparently doing nothing, she was in fact travelling the universe, exploring invisible and intangible realms unknown to him, learning from guides and teachers he did not even believe existed, he would not have understood. She was always surprised that he was so persistent; they had nothing in common. They were, literally, worlds apart. She could only surmise that he saw her always as the attractive, good-humoured village girl she had once been and never grasped at all that there was a whole other side to her nature – a side which was rapidly being developed at the expense of the one he knew.

When she was very tired and failed for the fourth or fifth time to achieve the state of consciousness that her teacher was expecting of her, she thought of Geb and longed to be the girl he thought she was. 'How easy,' she sighed, 'to fall back into the village ways and have nothing to worry about but the earth-realm.' But then, almost immediately, she remembered how unsatisfactory that realm could be – how limiting it could seem once one had experienced life enhanced by an awareness of the rich and various invisible and transcendent realms. She put Geb aside and concentrated once again on her training.

One day a young girl came to the Temple. She was lonely and anxious and Farla took her under her wing, remembering how she had felt those first few months away from home. Iren, the new student, was quick to learn and progressed admirably – but on the way she developed a passionate admiration for Farla which Farla at first enjoyed, but later began to find disconcerting. She could do no wrong in Iren's eyes. Farla was to Iren a great spiritual being whose every word and every move ought to be emulated. It was the disparity between who Iren thought she was and her own feelings of inadequacy that finally drove Farla into the arms of Geb.

Walking the muddy track now, driving geese before her for the wedding feast, Farla thought back to the day she had made the decision to settle for what Geb had to offer and reject the vast potential of her life at the Temple. It had not been a sudden change of heart – though to her friends it appeared so. She had been finding the strain of living up to Iren's vision of her, and Kyra's expectations of her, more and more irksome.

She had found her mind wandering far too much when she should have been concentrating. In her work this could often be dangerous. Time and again Kyra impressed on her that the difficult skill of travelling in other realms was not sought to satisfy idle curiosity – and to forget one's original purpose while undertaking it was to ask for trouble.

'We seek to become familiar with the invisible realms only so that we can use the knowledge gained there to help us in this realm,' Kyra said. An analogy she gave was of a small child who sees around her a certain horizon and bases all her decisions on what she can see within that horizon. The adult, taller than the child, can see further. But the priest, who can travel above the earth-plane, can see further still, so his or her decisions are based on a much wider understanding of what actually is the reality.

'And yet,' Kyra warned her more than once, 'don't think you know everything just because you know more than those who are outside the Temple. You are still only capable of seeing part of what there is to see – and for this reason it is imperative that you have integrity of motive. If your motive is true and good, there will be little danger that you will go far astray. But' – and she never ceased to stress this – 'if you lose quality of intention, you will lose quality of result.'

One day this lesson was driven home to Farla in a way that plunged her into despair and finally decided her to leave the Temple.

A young child who seemed to be dying had been brought to her. Iren had persuaded his parents to come to Farla because she believed implicitly that Farla was capable of producing great healing energy. Farla certainly had on occasions proved herself a very sensitive and effective healer. But this day she could not reach the right state of consciousness to channel the necessary healing energies. Gya, Deva's handsome, flirtatious husband, had crossed her path the evening before and left her in no doubt that he would like to take her to bed. She had rejected his advances immediately and sharply, but she had lain awake all night thinking about him and dreaming of how it would be if she had accepted. Now, she knew, she should send the boy and his parents to another healer – but she accepted him, flattered by Iren's total faith in her, and the parents' trusting and beseeching eyes. She started the process of going into the Silence, her hands resting lightly on the child laid out on the couch before her. Iren stood opposite her, her eyes filled with admiration. How she longed to be as advanced and as skilled as Farla! The parents sat to one side, holding hands, waiting confidently for the miracle they were sure Farla would perform.

It was then Farla began to have doubts about herself. The Silence did not come as easily as she had known it in the past. When Kyra first trained her for this she had said that there were no words to express the feeling you had when you entered the Silence. There were no guidelines, no maps, no explanations. You would just know when you were there. And, after many puzzled and abortive attempts, Farla had known when she was there. Gradually it had become easier for her to reach that state, so that now there should have been no problem. But there was a problem. Like a lamp-flame that flickers in the wind, some moments she felt herself filled with energy from the spirit realms and ready to work on the child, but the next moment it was as though she was alone in a dark and empty place. She began to be afraid. What if she did not succeed? What if Iren saw that she was not as wonderful as she had thought? In bitter shame she knew she would not succeed – because she was thinking more of herself than of the child.

The child died.

Farla looked at the faces of his parents and at the face of Iren, and walked away. She could not think of words to say to comfort them. She had let them down.

The next day she left the Temple and returned to Hael.

Isar and Deva did not reach the village of Hael until late evening. It was already dark when they turned off the road and took the track down to the village. The dogs were out to warn them off at once and, for the first time since they had left the shelter of the ledge, Isar and Deva came close together. They huddled back to back as the dogs ringed them, barking. Isar called out soothing words but both had their carrying pouches off their shoulders ready to use as weapons of defence if necessary. To their relief a man's voice called out a sharp command and the dogs retired a short way, growling, still watching the intruders suspiciously. Then they were surrounded by men with torches demanding who they were and what their business was. Deva took Isar's hand and Isar was glad of it. The flickering of the torchlight and the hostile, wary figures looming so suddenly out of the dark had startled them – though they were relieved that the dogs had been called off. It was Deva who rallied first.

'Deva, daughter of the High Priest of the Temple of the Sun,' she said haughtily, stepping forward. 'And Isar, son of Spear-lord Karne. Is this the way Hael greets guests invited to the wedding of Farla and Geb?'

'Guests are not expected to arrive so late at night,' was the surly reply, though the man who gave it – the one who had originally challenged them – modified his tone.

Another stepped forward from behind him and held out his hands in welcome.

'Greetings, Deva, daughter of the Lord Khu-ren and the Lady Kyra. Greetings, Isar, son of Karne. You are welcome. You must forgive us for our caution, but there are sometimes human wolves who roam the forests at night and prey on sleeping villages. I am By-ek, Elder of Hael, father of the bride.'

'Greetings, By-ek,' Deva said coldly. She had been frightened by the dogs and resented that she had shown it. But the warmth of the welcome that overwhelmed them as soon as it was known who they were soon made her smile. They were escorted to the village centre excitedly: those who were asleep were woken and a huge fire was lit. Isar stood back and watched, amused, as the whole village began to revolve around Deva. It was as though no one else existed. Kyra's beautiful daughter had stolen all hearts. He had seen this happen many times before. Since she was a very small child she had had this power to attract and hold – to centre everything on herself. Isar was sure that there was not a person present who was aware of anyone else. Only he – because he knew her so well – could stand aside to watch. But even he – when she suddenly turned and sought out his eyes and laughed and waved at him – could not restrain the leap his heart gave. Did he still love her? 'No,' his mind answered. 'She is selfish, fickle, sometimes even cruel.' He knew he was better off with Lark, who created a peaceful environment for him where he could think his own thoughts and be his own self. But...

Annoyed with himself, he turned away and moved further from the fire, deeper into the shadows. There he encountered a young woman standing as quietly as he.

'Farla?' he enquired. He had seen her at the Temple during the time she was a novice, but had never taken much notice of her. She was a well-rounded young woman, though not plump. There was a scattering of freckles across her nose and cheeks and her hazel eyes were quick to sparkle. Her hair was brown, tinged with ginger and golden lights. She was not beautiful in the way that Deva was, but she was very pleasant to look upon and when she smiled she became beautiful. Her expression was now troubled. It was for her wedding Deva had come and she should have been beside her at the centre of the celebration.

'What is it?' he asked her gently.

Farla looked at him. She remembered him: the wood-carver. A slender young man with red-gold hair like his mother, eyes always dreamy as though he was not seeing what actually was there before him, but always what he as an artist could make of it. She remembered his wife, the dumb girl with the large, expressive eyes. Isar and she had always looked so close – so absolutely as though they belonged together. She had envied them their certainty. If only she could be as sure about her life! She had left the Temple which she loved, and a life that had meant a great deal to her, to live as a bird with its wings clipped, with Geb, but she was still unsure if she had made the right decision.

Kyra's words when she told her she was leaving still haunted her. 'Everyone approaching the final steps of initiation feels inadequate and wants to run away.' Had she been too precipitate? Kyra made her feel that even the child's death might not necessarily have been her fault. She pointed at the complexity and mystery of the healing process, the crucial timing of it, the readiness of the patient to be healed, the subtle karmic roots of the illness, many of which might be beyond the skill of the healer to uncover. Perhaps the illness had gone too far. Perhaps the child himself was blocking the flow of energy by his doubts. Or his parents' anxiety might have set up such a field of negative vibration around the child it was impossible for the healing energies to get through.

Farla listened, but she knew in her heart that even if the child's death had been inevitable whatever she might have done, she had still failed to go into the Silence properly and she had still failed by allowing her own little earthly self to intrude in a matter that should have been dealt with by her higher self.

She had worked hard to fit back into the ordinary world since she returned to the village, and hoped she had finally done so – but Isar brought back vividly the flavour of the Temple, of a place that had no bounds, of a place that was in touch with the whole world and the furthest reaches of the universe... and she had become unsettled all over again. Her questing heart and upreaching soul would not be still. She was lost between two worlds and feared that she belonged nowhere. Besides, on another level altogether, the sight of Isar and Deva together brought back the longing she undoubtedly felt for Gya. She saw the way Deva looked at Isar, and she resented that she had rejected a night with Gya which she would very much have enjoyed, because she was trying to honour their marriage; a marriage which now seemed not to matter that much to Deva.

She sighed and Isar asked her once again what the matter was.

'Nothing,' she replied.

'Ah – but sometimes "nothing" hurts more than "something",' he said wryly.

Instantly her eyes filled with tears. She wondered if she could talk to Isar. She felt he would understand. He was of the Temple and yet not of it. He respected it and abided by its teaching, but had taken no vows. But she was prevented from saying anything further by the arrival of Geb, who, momentarily recovering from Deva's spell, had noticed that his bride was not with the circle in the firelight.

Farla turned away at once so that he would not see her tears and Isar distracted his attention by asking him if he had any idea when the village intended settling down for the night.

Geb laughed. 'We're usually asleep long before this,' he said. 'But we don't often have a visit from the High Priest's daughter.'

'The High Priest's daughter has been travelling all day,' Isar pointed out. 'And I'm sure she would be very grateful for a chance to rest.'

Farla had recovered and slipped her hand through Geb's arm.

'Come,' she said. 'We'll go and see what we can do.'

Isar watched them go, and wondered what the problem he had seen in Farla's eyes, was.

At last the village settled down and Deva and Isar were shown places to sleep in Farla's family home. Deva and Farla lay side by side in one bed, with Isar beside them on the floor. The parents had wanted to give up their bed for Deva, but she refused the offer and they had settled for this arrangement.

Isar lay awake for a long time, wrapped in his cloak, staring into the darkness, hearing the whispering and the creaking of the wooden bed as the two young women tried to get comfortable before finally dropping off to sleep. Deva had insisted that she would travel on with him in the morning to find the oak burr. It was a day or two before the wedding and she said they would be back in good time for the celebrations. From the way she put it, Isar could tell she was counting on his staying for the wedding. He began to feel that their meeting on the road had not been a chance encounter at all but had been very carefully contrived. Well, if it was, she would not get her way. He was going on alone and he was returning to the Temple by a different route – alone.

He must have dropped off to sleep at last, because he woke with a start and for a moment was completely disorientated. He reached out for Lark beside him and felt a cold, hard, alien floor. He turned his head to where he would normally see the stars and met a darkness so black it seemed solid. His heart pounded with alarm. There were sounds of snoring and breathing in the room that should not have been there. And then, in relief, he remembered where he was.

He shut his eyes again and set about adjusting his mind more gradually to his situation. When he opened them he was feeling quite calm and collected. He knew exactly where and what everything was in the room although he could not see it. The sagging bed of wood and hide strips that contained the bulky figures of Farla's parents was off to the left and Farla's siblings were lying in a huddled and untidy heap on the other side of the central hearth, the two eldest after Farla having been banished there for the night to make way for Deva. Beside him was the other bed, the one with Deva and Farla. He turned his head towards it, wondering if Deva was asleep, and saw something that made him gasp. At the foot of the bed were two figures. It took a moment for him to realise that they were unlike any he had seen in the village and indeed unlike any he had ever seen.

They were contained in an eerie glow that illuminated them completely without throwing any light on to the rest of the room. One was a very old woman, so old that Isar would have expected her to be bent double, but instead she was standing tall and straight, thin, wizened, but as strong as a warrior. Her white hair flowed round her like a cloak almost to the ground. On her head she wore a close-fitting cap of feathers, and when he looked more carefully he saw the eyes of an owl staring at him from her forehead. The cap was in fact made of the skin of an owl – feathers, eyes, beak, ears still intact. Her own eyes below the owl's were directed at the figure of Deva on the bed.

As Isar watched, the old woman raised her right hand and silently pointed a long, thin finger at Deva. Every finger on her hand was adorned with a different ring, the huge stones glinting in the uncanny light. Beside her, her companion leaned forward to get a better view of Deva, whose arm was flung out across Farla, her long lashes dark against her fair cheek. Only afterwards Isar questioned how he could see so much detail in pitch darkness. The old woman's companion was a small man as hunched and twisted as she was straight – of middle years, Isar thought, and clad in outlandish clothes, the skins of wild cat strung together to make some kind of haphazard cover for his ungainly naked body.

Isar found he was watching the scene – after the initial shock – as though there was nothing unusual about it. And then suddenly the two figures disappeared and the room was totally black again.

He sat up hastily and peered at the place where he knew the door to be. It was impossible for the visitors to have moved so swiftly across the room that they could have opened and shut it again without his hearing or seeing it. It was a crude kind of shutter and had to be lifted into place each night. He had to accept that this had been a supernatural visitation. He began to shake and he pulled his cloak closely around himself. Who? Why? Their attention had specifically been directed at Deva. Should he tell her? It might frighten her. She was being singled out – pointed out. Who by? To whom? For what purpose? His heart was hammering. He could still see the figures in his mind's eye so vividly he could almost believe they were still there. Perhaps he had not seen them at all? Perhaps he had still been asleep and they were only part of his dream? He lay down again and tried to compose himself and think clearly and sensibly. Was it a dream?

He knew it was not.

As the night slowly wheeled away and the grey light of dawn came through the cracks around the window and door shutters, he knew that after seeing what he had seen he could not leave Deva alone. He would keep her by his side until their return to the Temple. He would not tell her what he had witnessed – but he would tell her parents as soon as they arrived back. Kyra and Khu-ren would know what to do.

The branches hung low as Isar and Deva penetrated deeper and deeper into the forest away from the well-travelled paths. Even hunters and woods-men seldom came this way. Everywhere the fern was beginning to push out tightly coiled stems, holding the young fronds close and clenched until ready to release them. The trees shimmered with a pale and silky green light.

Deva had been astonished how quickly Isar agreed to take her with him. The evening before, she had been sure that he would refuse. But this morning at her first suggestion he had instantly accepted, and since they left the road he had been extraordinarily solicitous and protective. He held branches for her. He lifted her over marshy ground, though he knew perfectly well she was as capable as he of leaping over it. She wondered if finally he was beginning to desire her as much as she desired him – and she was almost frightened by the thought. She had never been quite sure why she had decided so firmly that they should not share this life as they had shared others, but decide she had – and many times she had regretted it.

The attention he was paying her now should have made her happy. But somehow it was making her uneasy instead. The expression in his eyes was anxious and brotherly. Why was he treating her like this? She pulled her arm impatiently away from him when he next tried to help her over a stream. This was not what she wanted of him. She felt constricted by his solicitousness – even angry. Suddenly she started to run.

As quick and light as a young doe, she sprang over mossy boulders beside the stream and away over the deep layers of leaves that covered the forest floor. Before he realised what was happening she had disappeared into the thicket. For a time he chased after her, calling her name, but soon even the sounds she had been making ceased. He found himself far off the track and there was no sign of her. It was not the first time in his life he had been angry with Deva.

What should he do now?

He called and called but there was no answer. In growing alarm he realised that they were both lost to each other – and lost in the forest. He remembered the vision in the night and wondered if the two figures he had seen had anything to do with their present predicament. He blamed himself for bringing her into the forest. She might well have been safer among the villagers. He remembered that Farla was highly trained in Temple lore even if she had not reached the final grades. Perhaps his best plan was to return to Hael now and seek her help.

Miserably he started to retrace his steps as best he could, following the trail of twigs he had crushed. But before long he lost the trail, and found himself going round and round in circles over the same ground, with no familiar landmarks to give him a clue whether he was near or far from his destination. He became more and more agitated and less and less capable of making decisions. At last he sat down again and tried to calm himself. Kyra's insistence that one should always find one's way in one's heart before attempting to find it in the external world, came back to him.

She had told him that, when he was looking for something he had lost, he should stop worrying about it – he should even busy himself with something totally unrelated to the object he sought. 'The agitation of your mind,' she said, 'hides it from you. It is as though you have been stirring up the mud in a pool in a desperate attempt to find something on the bed of it. If you let the mud settle and the pool become clear again, you'll be able to see to the bottom of it quite easily and find what lies there.'

It was some time before he could calm his mind sufficiently for the 'mud' to settle. He tried to think of Lark, but she seemed very shadowy and insubstantial. Deva's vivid and quicksilver beauty was with him at every turn. He decided to concentrate on Kyra, calling to her over and over again for help. He had absolute faith in her – faith in her strength as a woman, as a friend and as a mother, and in her capacity as Lord of the Sun, as soul of a million years.

He knew she loved Deva without reservation, though Deva had caused her many griefs. If anyone could find her lost daughter, Kyra could.

Gradually the quiet began to take over. He did not know how long he sat thus, cross-legged on the forest floor, letting the names and the images of Kyra and Deva flow through his mind like water. But when he became conscious again of where he was and what had happened the sun was well past the zenith. Quietly he stood up and stretched, feeling his limbs cramped and stiff as though he had been in that one position a very long time. He no longer felt anxious. What would be would be. He set off walking – not knowing whether he was heading towards Hael or away from it – but within a very short time he saw the smoke and thatch of the village ahead of him.

He sought out Farla immediately and told her what had happened.

At first she said there was nothing she could do, afraid to open those channels to the other realms she had so carefully closed when she made her decision to return to ordinary village life. But when he told her about the owl-woman and her horrible-looking companion that he had seen hovering over Deva in the night, she agreed at once to try.

She withdrew from the village to a little glade she knew nearby. She sat cross-legged on the grass in the centre of a circle of silver birch trees. A light breeze shivered the slender twigs, still only lightly touched with green. She tried to concentrate as Khu-ren had taught her – choosing one leaf of the thousands around her, trying to enter it with her imaginal mind to seek out the hidden pathway of the sap that flowed in its veins and follow it down through the twig, the branch, the trunk to the root, there to feel the earth around her – the same earth on which Kyra stood, the same earth that linked all earth's living creatures... She had always found this method, of all the ways she had been taught, the best for her. 'In meditation never strain... never force yourself to do something that doesn't come naturally to you.' Khu-ren's words rang in her head. 'What works for you is the method you must stay with.'

Khu-ren was on the road, travelling, when he thought he saw a silver birch tree growing beside the path suddenly take on the aspect of a woman. He stopped and blinked and looked again – but now it was no more than a tree with silver-white bark and tiny shimmering leaves. He walked on – but once again, out of the corner of his eyes, he had the decided impression that it was a woman. He stood still and allowed the image to manifest more clearly. Now it seemed that it was a young woman he recognised:

Farla, Kyra's favourite student. Farla, who had left the Temple to marry a farmer. The image faded.

Why? he asked himself. Why? He frowned. He had just left a village where there was a very formidable evil force. An entire family was being systematically killed by a curse-spell. He had saved the life of the last one only with tremendous effort. In his questioning of the villagers he had learned that this family had had a child called to be the apprentice of a sorceress. They had refused to let it go – and one by one they had died. No accidents, no illnesses – just death.

Could Farla be connected with the events in the village? He didn't like to think so, but he had been puzzled as to why she had left the Temple training so suddenly. The kind of thing he had encountered in the village was often the work of a man or a woman who was disaffected, resentful, the possessor of undisciplined psychic powers without the necessary spiritual stature to contain them. This was the reason why the Temple was so anxious to call all youngsters who showed unusual psychic abilities to training at the Temple, and this was why a great deal of the training was on control and discipline – and even more on trying to instil a lively sense of responsibility and an understanding of the nature of good and evil. He hoped he was wrong about Farla... but why had she appeared just at this moment when his mind was occupied with the question as to who was playing so powerfully on the fears of the villagers?

Farla started, her heart pounding. As clearly as though he were standing only a short distance from her she had seen the image of Khu-ren. As suddenly as it had been there, it was gone.

She had been trying to reach Kyra – but it was Khu-ren's words about the method that had been uppermost in her mind, so it was Khu-ren she had found. She was excited that she had not forgotten everything, though the fact that she was so off-target made her nervous. She felt she had blundered into his presence and blundered out again, and was not at all sure if she could repeat what she had done. She suffered more than a twinge of regret for all she had given up.

Taking a deep breath she tried again... and again. But no further glimpses of either Khu-ren or Kyra were forthcoming.

Back in the village, Farla found Isar waiting for her, anxious to know if she had made any progress in contacting Kyra or finding Deva. He ran eagerly to meet her.

'No,' she sighed. 'I can't do it. I've lost the power. In the morning, if she has not found her way back here, we'll have to send out an ordinary search party.'

She turned away from him to hide her tears of frustration.

Kyra felt restless and depressed – but she was not sure at first if it was due to missing Khu-ren, anxiety about some of the work at the Temple that was not going well, or something more sinister: the sense of a shadow beginning to reach out for the bright heart of her world.

She retired to her favourite room in the house and prepared to go into the Silence. Before her, on a low table of yew wood, was a fine cotton cloth Khu-ren had brought from Egypt, his native country. She sat cross-legged on the floor beside it and began to compose herself for the task ahead, withdrawing her mind gradually from the teeming thoughts of the busy day. She did not try to fight them off, for that would have made them more persistent than ever. It was as though she made an appointment to deal with each one at a specific later time – and, content that they would indeed be given her attention later, they retired peacefully, leaving her free to concentrate on the matter in hand.

As one after the other left her, she narrowed her attention to the white cloth on the table. She fingered its edges, thinking about the plants growing in that hot and distant land from which it was woven; thinking of the weavers themselves living their lives in such a very different environment, part of such a very different culture, and yet making the same motions with their hands that the weavers of her own country made, thinking the same sort of thoughts, dreaming the same kind of dreams. She thought of the day her husband gave it to her, and of her decision to use it in this way. It was so fine and soft compared to the rough wool and flax weaving of her own country. It would do well to cover something special, something that was sacred to her that she did not want seen or touched by others.

When she was sure she was close enough to the Silence, she lifted the cloth and laid it aside. Before her on the tabletop lay her collection of crystals. One by one she picked them up and held them in her hand. It was as though they were light caught and held in solid form, so beautiful, so harmonious, so deeply suggestive of the mysterious spirit realms that are invisibly with us all the time – and yet at the same time reminding her of the solid earth, its generous and marvellous gifts and secret splendours.

Each had a story to its finding, and each was of particular significance for Kyra, but one in particular seemed to her more magical than all the others. She reached for it now and held it up to the shaft of sunlight that shone through the window. It was a quartz crystal, as transparent as clear water, faceted to perfection – and within it was another, smaller, quartz crystal, equally perfect. Her heart always beat faster when she saw it. It seemed to her to suggest the individual soul within the greater matrix of eternal spirit.

As she gazed into the depths of this double crystal, the light flashing and echoing from facet to facet, within and without, she felt herself leaving the confines of her everyday self and expanding her awareness to that of her greater, eternal Self. In that state she felt Urak's threat to their lives, though as yet she had no idea of what the threat consisted.

She glimpsed an old woman, almost skeletal, with sunken cheeks and ash-white hair, sitting cross-legged at the mouth of a huge gaping hole in the side of a mountain, her knees like sticks poking out on either side of her from beneath a skirt of coarse black wool. At first Kyra could not make out what she was doing, but then she saw that between her bony hands she held a dark crystal orb. Her thin lips were muttering some incantation that Kyra could not hear. From time to time she passed her hands over the orb as though she was having difficulty seeing into it and was trying to clear it of some misty impediment. Around her, in the air, Kyra could see strange geometric and arcane signs flickering strong and flame-like one moment, weak and vapour-like the next.

She was startled by the apparition but knew that if she did not act quickly, before the witch-woman consolidated her spell, she would lose the opportunity. She could sense the web of evil the woman was trying to weave with those signs – though she still had no idea of its specific nature or against whom it was directed. She believed that it had relevance to the shadow she had recently felt closing in on their lives.

Kyra's hand trembled very slightly as she raised her precious crystal closer to her eyes. She called on all the inner strength she had, the clear steady light that was the core of her being, and directed it through the crystal in her hand to the old woman in front of the cave.

Hastily Urak covered her black scrying sphere. The flash of light that had just leapt from its surface had almost blinded her. Angrily she paced about her cave. Someone was interfering. For the first time in her long life someone was reaching out for her. She was accustomed to being the one who spied on the lives of others, who controlled, manipulated, interfered... Could there be a sorcerer more powerful than she?

She was annoyed that she had been so precipitate. She uncovered her sphere. She must find out the source of that light and take measures to prevent anything like that happening again.

But gaze as she might she could not see what had caused it; neither did it come again.

Kyra had spent all the energy she possessed and was lying on a couch in her chamber exhausted, the crystal still clutched in her hand.

Boggoron, Urak's 'familiar', left the mountain fastness at dawn. He had his instructions and he expected to enjoy carrying them out. He had lived most of his life among the high crags and secret limestone caves where he had been abandoned by his parents as an infant, and would probably never have lived long enough to know that the rest of the world existed had Urak not found him and cared for him. He worshipped her and never questioned anything about her. He accepted humbly the withering scorn she poured on him sometimes, frustrated as she was by the slowness of his wits and the clumsiness of his body compared to hers. There was no physical deformity that made him bend and twist the way he did; no misshapen leg that made him hop and stumble. He shaped himself to his own vision of himself. He believed he had no right to live except as tool for Urak. He believed he was not fully human. And it served Urak's purposes never to disabuse him of these misconceptions.

When he reached the open hills and the long rolling landscape, he began to feel a little uneasy. He hated being looked at and liked nothing better than to spy on others – but here there was very little cover. The first man to greet him was astonished when he jumped and slid away. 'Up to no good, I'll be bound,' the farmer muttered, wondering if he should count his sheep. But there was no need. Boggoron was not seeking meat this journey. He was after something much more important.

He had covered a great deal of ground and was beginning to feel the exhilaration of being his own master for a change, when he suddenly found himself unaccountably sleepy.

'Oh no!' he thought irritably. 'She's going to call me back.' Just when he was enjoying the journey, the new sights and sounds, the marvellous variety of people. He tried to fight the feeling of drowsiness – but could not. He lay down beside the road he was travelling and was instantly asleep. In his dream Urak appeared to him, as he knew she would. She was in the form of an owl with a mouse in its beak. He found himself running over the fields, following the shadow she cast on the ground, running faster than he thought it was possible for any man to run – until suddenly the running became flying and he was in the sky winging after her. She dropped the mouse deliberately and precisely on one of the roads leading off from a crossroads. He noticed that of the four stones that marked the directions, the one indicating the road to the north where she had dropped the mouse was pockmarked with little holes, while the others were smooth and grey.

He woke and found that he'd been asleep no more than a moment. No shadow had moved.

'Well, at least I don't have to go back,' he muttered, and started walking again.

He found the crossroads, as he knew he would, and took the

northern path beside the strange pockmarked stone. The feeling of freedom was gone. There was nowhere he could be that would take him out of range of her surveillance.

As the night grew darker the forest began to change character. The silence brought about by the cessation of birdsong at sunset was soon filled with all kinds of rustlings and cracklings and squeakings as the creatures who thrived when the earth had turned its face from the sun came into their own: creatures that could see Deva – but which she could not see.

She was exhausted and frightened. She could not understand how she could have become so utterly lost so quickly. Surely Isar was not far away, nor Hael itself more than an hour or two distant. She had no idea how large the forest was, nor how rarely it was penetrated this far.

She sank down upon a bank of ferns and knew she could go no further. Her voice was hoarse from calling; her legs scratched and aching. She lay back and shut her eyes. How long would the kaleidoscope of shadows turn round and round in her mind? Tree after tree moved past her, black as a moonless midnight, branches reaching out for her and lashing her face, brambles fastening their tiny claws into her.

Deva must have dropped off to sleep at last, but she woke in a cold sweat to hear the sounds of some large animal moving near her. She sat up instantly, crushed bracken leaves sticking to her hair, her cheek and her clothes. She peered into the darkness, now no longer so dark. Dazed, she blinked and stared. Moonlight was shafting through the branches and making patches of the forest floor less dark. She crossed her arms and hugged herself, partly with fear and partly with cold, trying to stop the shivering that threatened to give her presence away to whatever nocturnal predator was snuffling close by.

She thought of running, but she knew she couldn't run in that darkness; and even if she ran she might well encourage whatever it was to pursue her. She waited, desperately afraid. She felt a jagged stone against her foot and tried to loosen it from its bed of earth and leaves without making a sound. Working on the stone took her mind off her fear, and when she had prised it loose she gripped it between both feet and drew it towards her. The sounds the heavy animal was making were getting louder and closer. She made a dive for the stone and held it ready in her right hand, staring with close attention at the break in the bushes towards which the sounds were heading.

At last a snout with two bright eyes appeared, closely followed by the large but not ungraceful white and black body of a badger. It seemed not to notice her at all but stepped out into the patch of moonlight, closely followed by its mate and a string of young. Deva relaxed her grip on the stone in her hand. It felt strange to be so totally ignored by the animals – almost as though she were not there at all or had been accepted as part of the forest itself.

She watched until they were out of sight, deep in the undergrowth again, and then stood up and stretched. She wondered if now she was rested it would be sensible to try to walk on. The purposefulness with which the badgers had been moving made her feel that the forest was not such a labyrinth after all.

She took a step, and turned her ankle in the hole she herself had created by prising out the weapon-stone. She winced and rubbed it anxiously... worried that she might not be able to walk on it. Gingerly she tested it and found that it hurt a great deal.

'Stupid!' she muttered to herself. How many stupid things had she done in this one day? She bit her lip, but she was determined not to cry. 'Why not?' she muttered bitterly. 'No one would see if I did.' But even as she thought this she felt that she was being watched. She spun round and stared into the shadows. She told herself that the place must be alive with small nocturnal animals, many of which would be hiding under the twigs and the leaves observing her. But she still felt uneasy and looked up.

On a branch in the moonlight a huge owl was sitting, its eyes fixed on her as though she were its prey.

In the morning Deva bound her ankle with a strip torn off her tunic. It was swollen and painful, but she was determined it would not hold her back. She sought and found a sturdy stick and began to hobble through the forest. In daylight her predicament did not seem so bad. She had no doubt that she would soon break through to clear country where there were villages, or she would find a path. She set her direction by the sun, and blamed the blind circles of the evening before on the fact that she had not done so.

She was bitterly cold and remembered with something more than nostalgia the warmth of Isar's body against hers as they sheltered from the storm. The longing she had to be with him again was overwhelming. Gya, her husband, and all they had shared together, meant nothing to her any more. They had been strangers when they married, and they were strangers still. But Isar and she – now that was different! Their roots went very deep. She had been a fool to let him go. Savagely she hit out at a fern stem about to unfurl and knocked its head off with her stick.

'I'll have Isar again – come what may!' she said aloud. 'We should never have been parted.'

A few moments later she found a path and confidently set off along it.

Already her ankle was feeling better. The mist that had been clinging to the damp ground was lifting and the sun was beginning to warm the air nicely. She shrugged aside the terrors of the night and began resolutely planning how she would set about parting Isar from Lark. She knew it would not be easy. Everyone loved Lark, and she knew Isar himself had a very close and deep relationship with her because of the dangers they had faced under Na-Groth, and the fact that Lark had on more than one occasion saved his life. But when Deva wanted something, it was very unusual for her not to get it. She had no doubt that Isar, in spite of appearances to the contrary, was already hers.

The village she eventually came upon in the valley was still under mist, but the dogs and geese alerted the villagers to her arrival and she was soon surrounded by surprised but solicitous and friendly people. It seemed she was not the only visitor this chilly spring morning. A man had arrived a short while before her from the southwest and was already warming by one of the hearth fires.

When she heard this her heart leapt, thinking that it must surely be Isar. But she was disappointed. The man sitting cross-legged on the floor beside the smouldering wood of the central hearth was small and weedy, his shoulders hunched as though he were deformed, his grey hair matted over a low forehead. She took no more notice of him as she wolfed down the bread and milk the villagers pressed on her. It was only when she was replete that she glanced up at him again. As she met his eyes she was startled to see that he was staring at her intently, and that in his stare was something of recognition and something of triumph.

Chapter 4

The ghost-owl

Old as she was, Urak was still as agile as a mountain goat. She knew Boggoron had found Deva and she was excited. She left her cave as soon as the sun was high enough to melt the gleaming frost crystals, a stole of lynx fur over her bony shoulders and a long woollen cloak keeping her warm against the breeze that came off the snow still lingering on the high peaks. She felt like celebrating and she wanted a crowd. She had long since lost all contact with the villagers who lived in the valleys. It was decades since she had emerged from the mountains in physical form, and no villager would dare venture into the gorge itself and brave the terrors of meeting the fearsome owl-woman against whom generations of parents had warned their children. Sometimes she had been lonely – but lately very rarely. She found the local villagers, when she spied on them, stupid and boring. No, when she was lonely it was other company she sought.

She made her way along the steep sides of the mountain until she came to a flat slab of rock, clear of pebbles and boulders. It was edged on the north side with spindly trees, nearly all of them twisted and deformed by the long struggle to find root-space in the meagre topsoil. There was one tree with which Urak felt a particular affinity. It was a dwarf oak, stocky and muscular, hardly taller than herself, growing from a crack above the platform, with a huge root that could be seen exposed along its whole length at eye level – growing sideways, not downwards, along a fissure. Sinuous as a huge serpent, its weathered surface was flaky and scaly – more like bark or the skin of a dragon than root fibre. It always excited her. She could feel the power with which it forced its way through the rock, the brute strength, the eager and restless energy. Trembling, she touched it and trailed her fingers along its length, moving as she did so along the platform to where the rock gave way to a sheer drop. There below her was a narrow chasm through which a turbulent river was pouring, dropping, falling, thundering into a deep pool far below.

For a long time she stood at the edge of the drop, her right hand on the dragon-scaled root to steady herself, watching the white water pouring, feeling the pull of it, the growing desire to fling herself over into it and be one with its awesome strength and speed. She was poised between the invisible, imperceptible power of the root, and the wild and visible violence of the water. In a state of tremendous agitation she at last forced herself to withdraw her gaze from the water. As she did so the white water became a still wall and the rock cliffs on either side of it flowed swiftly upwards.

It was the moment she was waiting for. The moment when the solid became fluid and the fluid solid.

She lifted both arms and the sunlight sparkled off the gems in her rings, the light from each of the stones dancing over the rock and across the chasm. Suddenly a rainbow blazed out above the pool. In that instant a fish leapt, its silver-dark form caught for an instant in the coloured spray.

'Now!' she screamed, knowing the magic of the moment must be taken swiftly at the zenith of the leap before the fall began.

Suddenly the invisible became visible and with her on the rock platform she saw a crowd of beings – bird forms and animal forms known usually only in myth and legend, human shadows and husks, strange supernatural formless gleamings and mists, winged beings flickering between light and dark as though they couldn't quite decide which way to be...

Triumphantly Urak turned to them.

'Friends,' she cried. 'I have found my heir. Soon she will be here among us. Soon we will begin her training. She will walk with you, talk with you, learn from you.'

The creatures writhed around her with delight. Soon they would have another physical vehicle to use, another voice to speak for them. They began to dance and sing, and Urak swayed to their rhythm on the very edge of the precipice – exhilarated by the danger and by the heady violence of their ecstasy.

Deva herself was not aware that any momentous change was about to take place in her life. The stare of the stranger puzzled and annoyed her and she took pains to turn away from him, dismissing his attention as being the usual male reaction to her beauty. And if he recognised her, that too could be explained by the fact that at the Temple she was well known as the daughter of the two great Lords of the Sun, Guardians of the Tall Stones. She told herself she had imagined the look of triumph.

Boggoron bided his time. The morning was almost gone before

he made the opportunity to talk to her. The people of the village, on hearing the story of the night, had persuaded her to rest with them while they sent a messenger to Hael to find out if Isar had returned there. It seemed the two villages were not a great distance apart, and linked by a well-worn track. The villagers were convinced Deva had been spell-led to wander in circles. They told her that none of them would venture off the path at nightfall. Several of them had tales to tell that made Deva shiver, and she was glad she did not have to pass another night in the forest. One man had heard the sounds of chopping wood on a windless, moonlit night, and when he went to investigate, puzzled that a woods-man should be working so late, a huge tree started to fall towards him. Terrified, he struggled to get out of its path. He remembered to this day the way the twigs and brambles tore his skin as he scrambled and tumbled through the undergrowth. He managed to get out of the line of fall, and, cowering under the shelter of another tree, he listened to the cracking of branches and the roaring as the giant fell, smashing and tearing everything in its path. He even felt the rush of the air it displaced. Afterwards, when the sounds died down, he ventured out to see if the woods-man who had felled the tree was injured. He found no trace of either man or fallen tree.

'What had happened to them?' Deva breathed, fascinated.

'I heard later that a woods-man had been killed by a tree he had felled on that very spot when my grandfather was a boy,' replied the man.

Others assured her that the trees themselves sometimes appeared to have a kind of malevolence towards people. One man had been deep in the forest in the late afternoon and had had an unnerving experience.

'It was a dark part of the forest,' he said. 'The trees were close together. Hardly any sunlight filtered through. I was gathering mushrooms. I was perfectly happy. I remember I was even whistling. My basket was filled to overflowing and my only worry was that I hadn't brought a bigger basket. I didn't realise how the time was passing and that the sun was already setting.'

Deva could see by the faces of those gathered around them that they had heard the story many times before, and that they both loved and hated to hear it. What was it about the darkness that both fascinated and terrified humankind? She had not heard one story about the dangerous animals that lived in the forest. The fears were all of the supernatural, the unknown. It was as though in daylight one easily forgot the mysterious vastness of the universe and all the things about it one did not begin to understand. But in darkness, without any other distractions, one remembered. The fiercest warrior was vulnerable and alone.

'Go on,' someone urged. 'Tell her what happened!'

'The sun set before I could get out of the forest,' he said. 'Suddenly. I've never known the night to come on so fast.' He paused again, for effect.

'Go on,' breathed his listeners.

'It was not so much what I saw,' he said. 'It was what I felt. I knew the trees were watching me. I could feel them moving nearer: crowding me, staring down at me, trying to crush me between them. I dropped my basket and ran, but it was as though the trees had made a wall round me and wouldn't let me through. I felt the trees would somehow absorb me into their bodies. They would suck me into themselves. I remembered that other people had disappeared in the forest and never been seen again. I began to think that I now knew what had happened to them. I beat at the trees with my fists. I screamed at them. It was terrible, terrible...' He was silent a moment, shuddering, remembering.

'What happened then? How did you get out?' Deva prompted.

He looked at her as though he had forgotten her existence. The audience was dead silent. And then he shook his head.

'I don't know,' he said. 'I never knew. I fainted. When I woke it was morning and I was all right. The trees were back in their places. I never went back there.'

Deva was disappointed. She wanted more.

'Did you have any dreams during that faint?'

'No.'

'Are you sure?'

'I remember nothing.'

'You remember nothing,' Deva said thoughtfully, 'but all kinds of things might have happened to you without your knowing it.'

'What kinds of things?' the man asked.

'Dreadful things,' Deva said darkly, warming to her own line of thought.

The audience drew closer, sensing a new twist to the story.

'Things that may have changed you – permanently.'

The man looked alarmed. His wife gasped.

'Nonsense,' he said sharply. 'I escaped unharmed.'

'How do we know you are the same person who went into that forest that day?'

'Of course I am!'

'But how do you know? You may have been sucked up into those trees as you thought and even now you are screaming to be let out.'

'But...'

She turned to the listeners and pointed her index finger at Berd, the storyteller.

'The man we see before us might well be a forest-ghoul given human shape.'

His friends and neighbours, even his family, drew back in horror.

'What are you saying!' cried the man. 'I am Berd. You all know me. I am the same.'

'Has anyone noticed anything different about him since he came out of the forest that day?' Deva demanded.

Berd looked from one to the other of his fellow villagers in growing panic. Not one denied what Deva was suggesting. He could see that the seed of suspicion she had planted was growing in each of their hearts. One by one they came up with incidents which, they said, indicated how they had noticed something strange and odd about him since that day. Not one of them had thought anything of it at the time.

'Stop it!' cried Berd. 'There's nothing different about me. The trees didn't touch me. I was just imagining it. I was afraid because of the dark. They didn't touch me! Nothing happened!'

'You hear how he denies it?' Deva said softly. 'You hear how angry he is that he is found out? You hear how he changes his story, the story he has told you scores of times?'

People were backing away from him, looking at him with disgust and horror. Several began to pick up stones and hold them ready, watching him warily.

'What are you doing to me?' Berd appealed to Deva. 'Do you realise what you are doing?'

'Why are you sweating? Why are you shaking?' she heartlessly persisted. She could feel the power of her words. She knew she could easily destroy this man. She knew she could sway the minds of all around him and destroy even the village if she wanted. The feeling was intoxicating. Her cheeks glowed. Her eyes were unnaturally bright.

Boggoron watched and listened – delighted. She was everything he had been told to expect. She would be a worthy heir for Urak, the owl-woman. He noticed how the people hung on her every word. He noticed how the children clung to their mothers' skirts. Even the big, tough men were pale with fear. But above all, he noticed how much she enjoyed the power she had over them.

And then – suddenly – Deva drew to a halt. She could destroy him – but she would not. Knowing that she could was enough for the moment. She would see if she could calm the crowd as easily as she had roused them. That too would demonstrate her power. She held up her hand as the first stone was raised.

'No,' she cried. 'I didn't say he was taken over by a forest-ghoul. I said he might have been.'

The man with the stone hesitated. The others waited, looking uncertainly at Deva.

'We can put him to the test. We can see if he has been invaded or not.'

'How? How can we test him?' the villagers demanded. Deva thought quickly. She did not want the responsibility of a death by stoning. She was already a little ashamed of what she had done. It had started as an idle game, a speculation, and taken on a deadly earnestness she had not originally intended.

'Leave it to me,' she said. 'I am daughter of the High Priest of the Temple of the Sun. I will be able to tell.'

The villagers murmured, knotted together in a tight band, leaving Berd and Deva standing separate from the rest.

She stood directly in front of him. She raised her hands so that the palms were close to his face – but not touching it.

'Breathe on my hands,' she commanded.

He breathed. His eyes were dilated with fear.

'Harder!' she snapped. 'Take a deep breath in and then let it out on to my hands.'

He did as she said. The sound of his breath was loud in the silence as everyone waited tensely and anxiously for the outcome. Deva had seen priests do this sometimes, but she had no idea what they did it for, or what they experienced when the breath touched their palms. She felt only the hot breath of a frightened man, and smelled onions and sorrel in the air. She noticed that he was trembling almost uncontrollably. She knew and he knew that his life hung on her next words. She herself began to sweat. Why had she done this? Why? It was in a different class from the tricks she had played on people all her life. With this trick she could take life. With this trick she could give life.

She looked at the faces of those around her and knew that if she did not play the game right through to the end, if the people suspected for an instant she had been tricking them, they could turn on her as easily and as ruthlessly as they had turned on their friend. 'How strange,' she thought, 'each one of these people is probably sensible and kind and harmless. But together they become a violent and unreasoning beast...' She was as afraid as Berd was now – trapped in her own trap.

With a voice that shook slightly, she pronounced that Berd was clear of any intruder. 'This is the man you have always known,' she said. 'Don't be afraid.'

Berd looked at her with desperate relief in his eyes. The villagers relaxed. She could feel the darkness that had welded them together lifting and each falling away now into his or her own individuality.

She turned and walked away, keeping her back as straight as she could, showing no sign of weakness. She heard some of his friends clapping him on the back, congratulating him on his narrow escape. She looked back only once – and wished she had not. She caught Berd's eye and in it she saw real hatred.

Boggoron moved up to walk beside her.

'What is it?' she demanded sharply. 'Why do you keep staring at me like that?' She had not been able to ignore his presence and it had not escaped her that he was the only one who had listened to her lies without believing them.

He bowed slightly, and she did not miss the knowing glint in his eyes.

'I know you, Deva, daughter of Kyra.'

'You've been to the Temple of the Sun?'

'No.'

'You've heard of me?'

He smiled, but did not answer.

'Where have you heard of me? What have you heard?'

'There is nothing I don't know about you,' he said with a sly and gloating grin.

For a moment she was discomfited and then she looked down at him coldly.

'You know nothing,' she said scornfully, and tried to move away from him.

'Urak does,' he said quickly, stepping forward and blocking her path.

She looked at him with distaste – but she was curious. 'Urak?' Suddenly the memory of the huge owl she had seen in the forest came to her. If anyone could know all there was to know about her, she would not be surprised if it were that owl. But this was madness! How could an owl...?

'Who is this Urak?' she demanded haughtily.

'Urak is prophet, seer, sorceress. She who knows all! She is the greatest who has ever lived. In three realms there is no one alive or dead to match her.'

Deva had never heard Khu-ren or Kyra mention her, yet surely they would know about such a being – 'if she exists,' she told herself hastily, trying to keep her growing feeling of awe under control.

'I doubt you,' she said. 'How is it that the mighty priests of the Temple of the Sun haven't even heard of her?'

'Oh, they've heard. They've heard of her!' Boggoron said darkly.

'I haven't heard her name mentioned.'

'Yet you know her name.'

Deva hesitated. It was true – she did know the name, but she could swear she had never heard it spoken.

'The man is simple,' she told herself defensively. 'He knows some petty witch-woman in his home village and has an exaggerated idea of her importance. He has no conception of the might of the Temple. If he had, his fine Urak would soon shrink to her proper size.'

Deva shrugged. 'I know a lot of names,' she said scornfully.

'She uses the form of a ghost-owl. She sees even in darkness,' Boggoron said quietly, watching her closely.

Deva shivered. He had her now. Her mouth felt dry and her skin cold. This could be no coincidence. Something was already in motion involving her and she had not been aware of it. She, who loved to control, was being controlled. She had been led to meet this man in this village, though she had thought every move she made since she left the Temple her own choice, her own decision.

She was very frightened, but also very angry.

'Tell your precious Urak,' she said fiercely, 'that I want nothing to do with her. I am Deva. No one knows everything there is to know about me. Not even my mother!'

'Urak knows,' Boggoron insisted. 'Urak has chosen you as her heir. She wants to train you to take her place.'

Deva looked at him, startled. Her heart skipped a beat. For a moment the temptation was enormous – but then caution reasserted itself.

'Tell your Urak I am my mother's heir. If she knows so much, she will know the stature of my mother Kyra... and what to be her daughter means. No sorceress, no matter how much her minions believe in her, could cast a shadow on her shadow.'

Boggoron smiled.

'She knows of Kyra – yet Urak still calls on you to be her heir.'

'Nonsense!' snapped Deva and turned away.

Knowing she was already halfway trapped no matter how she fought the net, Boggoron was preparing to pull the drawstring tighter when suddenly they were interrupted by the arrival of a group of villagers. Two figures had been spotted on the path from Hael – their messenger returning and, with him, someone who answered the description of Isar. In a very short while they would be at the last turn before the village.

Deva hardly waited for the end of their announcement before she was running along the track, her hair streaming, her cheeks flushed. As Isar and his companion swung round the turn, they were met by a flying figure, who threw herself into Isar's arms and almost knocked him off balance. Laughing, he swung her round and hugged her joyfully. The tight knot of anxiety that had tormented him since she disappeared, which had partially loosened when the messenger had come to Hael with the news that Deva was safe in this village, now unravelled completely. Whatever mood had bedevilled her when she ran off the day before had vanished and she was at her most loving and most cheerful.

'Where were you?' She was teasing, as though it had all been no more than a game of hide and seek. The shadows and fears of the night for both of them were no longer remembered, and – for a moment – nor was Lark.

Isar kissed the flushed and laughing face again and again, and the villagers, watching, drew their own conclusions. They escorted the couple back to the village and garlanded them with flowers.

That night, around the hearth fire of their host, Deva remembered Boggoron and looked around for him. He was nowhere in sight and when she enquired about him no one could remember seeing him since Isar had arrived. She told Isar about him, laughing, as though the whole encounter had been amusing rather than frightening. Isar listened and smiled, but took very little notice of what she was saying. It was only later, when events took the turn they did, that he recalled every word she had said and regretted that he had paid so little heed to them.

When it came time to retire for the night, their host insisted on Isar and Deva taking the bed of his wife and himself, while they joined their children. In vain Isar protested. Deva had led them all to believe that they were a newly wed couple and the way he kissed her in greeting had confirmed it. With dancing eyes Deva watched as Isar tried to back out of the situation without actually saying that she was a liar. She was amused and pleased to see he did not try as hard as she expected, and when the lamplight was doused and the chamber was lit only by the feebly glowing embers of the hearth fire, they were together in bed.

She allowed him time to lie stiffly on the edge as far away from her as he could get, and then, when his weariness got the better of him and he relaxed and rolled over, she was there, warm and close, twining around him, whispering in his ear, seeking out his mouth. But though there were shadowy filaments of memory from the long-distant past that drew them together – fleeting glimpses of the garden in Egypt they had left behind in that other life... the lily pond... the sound of bees and the rustle of palm leaves... the amaranthine lilies glowing in the shadows... an ibis gliding down... and then the dimness of the chamber into which they moved... the cool of shadow after heat... the touch of his hand on her breast – it was the dynamic of the present that really fired the blood in their veins.

In vain Isar told himself that he should not do what he was doing. It seemed at first that some part of himself was standing outside, admonishing him; another part was with Anhai, his great love, in that ancient time; while a third part was abandoning itself to deeper and deeper physical pleasure as Deva's warm and silken flesh pressed close and closer, her mouth explored and touched and kissed. There was a moment when he gave himself up completely to this third part and, from being the seduced, he became the seducer.

Deva emitted a sigh that was almost a moan as she felt the change in him, felt him rise to her as passionately as ever she had dreamed. 'At last,' she whispered. 'At last...' and then even she forgot the past, forgot everything but the rising surge of immediate and exquisite feeling that swept them up together in total abandonment.

When they both became aware again of the chamber in which they now lay, the fire had died down, and they were surrounded by complete blackness. Isar drew away from Deva and lay on his back staring, unseeing, at the reed ceiling. He listened as the pounding of his heart gradually calmed down and became a steady beat in an immense darkness. Deva did not move. She lay beside him, holding her breath, wondering what he was thinking, wondering if she dare touch him. Nothing had been resolved by their coming together. They both ached even more for what once was and what might have been.

In the morning Isar was withdrawn and distant, as though the night had never happened. He refused even to refer to it, as if not mentioning it automatically made it less real. Deva gave up trying to touch his hand; gave up trying to meet his eyes. She could see that he was ashamed of himself and had gone back to Lark in his heart.

When it came time to go, he told her he would not be going back to Hael and Farla's wedding with her. He had found someone who could guide him to the very part of the forest where he expected to find the oak burr he sought for Kyra's bowl. There were plenty of people who could guide her back to Hael, he said, and he hoped she would enjoy the wedding festivities. Even while he was talking to her he managed to avoid her eyes. He could have been politely addressing a stranger.

'So that is the end of it,' she thought bitterly – and in her anger and disappointment she conceived a plan that would change the course of many lives, though she meant only to teach Isar a lesson.

She pretended not to mind that he had chosen to ignore the night they'd had together. She made sure he and his guide were well provisioned for their expedition and bade them a cheerful goodbye, accepting with a grave nod the message of regret she was to deliver to Farla for his absence – and with a smile his remarks that she should hurry straight home as soon as the wedding was over.

When he reached the forest and turned to look back at her, she waved vigorously.

Did he hesitate to take the next step? Did he waver in his resolution to play the game the way he had chosen? He stood for a long while looking back at her, and for a moment she could feel his pain as deeply as her own. She stopped waving and they stood staring at each other. She felt an overwhelming urge to run after him – but before she could take the first step she felt a touch on her arm. It was Boggoron. She looked at him, startled that he should appear again just at this moment. Torn between her resolution and her love for Isar, she looked back to the forest path. It was empty. Isar had gone.

Chapter 5

The search for Guiron

When Isar returned home, he was weighed down with bags and pouches containing wood for carving, including the great oak burr he had set off to find. Lark ran to greet him as soon as word came that he had been spotted on the ridgeway, and at once tried to relieve him of some of the lighter burdens. He had been away longer than he intended and he looked exhausted. He kissed her and held her against him with his one free arm with a deep sense of relief. He was home, and it was where he wanted to be. He loved her and he felt safe with her. He tried to suppress the vivid flash of memory of his night with Deva. It had been disturbingly beautiful – a high point he would never forget – but it must never be repeated. Mixed in with the ecstasy they had shared, was something he could not put a name to. He had thought at first perhaps it might have been a sense of guilt – but he knew now it was not quite that. It was fear. Fear of losing his will for a separate and independent existence. Lark made him feel more wholly himself on every level: Deva reduced him to a point where he did not care if he was nothing in all the world but her lover. He could feel the pain of the separation from her even as he kissed Lark – but he was determined to ignore it.

Lark noticed that there was something wrong, something changed, in the way he held her – in the way he kissed her. She pulled back from him and looked enquiringly into his eyes, but he turned away at once and busied himself unpacking his precious pieces of wood to show her.

'Look at this piece,' he said, a shade too enthusiastically. 'It won't take more than a touch here and there to bring out the eagle in it.' He held it out to her and she stroked the wood thoughtfully. One form within another... nothing is what is seems...

Isar, looking down at her troubled face, hated himself for the feelings he had not been able to control. He put down the wood and took her in his arms again. 'It's all right,' he said gently. 'I've been away – but I've come back.'

She shut her eyes and abandoned herself to the warmth of the feelings that flowed through her as he kissed her. It would be all right – their love was as adaptable to life's irregularities as a river is to the boulders that lie on its bed. Whatever threatened them, they would face it together. She would tell him about the child – and what she feared. He was back.

When Deva did not return on the expected day, no one was particularly worried. Wedding festivities often trailed on well beyond expectation. But on the sixth day a visitor from Hael arrived with the news that the wedding had not taken place after all and that as far as he knew, Deva had gone with Isar into the forest.

Kyra called for Isar in some alarm.

As soon as she told him the news, she could see by his expression that he knew something that was relevant but which he would rather keep to himself.

She questioned him quietly and skilfully and soon found out, without his actually saying it, that they had spent the night together and had parted painfully but with a determination on Isar's part at least not to let it happen again.

She looked at the young man before her. She had always loved him – Fern's son, sensitive and gentle and yet with great inner strength. He was the kind of man who said very little, but when he spoke, people listened: the kind of man people turned to when they were confused or in trouble. Sometimes just being with him was enough to calm one down; sometimes it was some brief and poignant sentence that helped to put one's worries in perspective. She knew he loved Lark and would do nothing wilfully to hurt her. The pull towards Deva must be strong indeed to override all this.

So Deva had gone off to sulk? Kyra sighed. She remembered the time her wayward daughter had gone over to the enemy and become a worshipper of Groth because she thought the Temple was not doing enough to save Isar's life when he was a prisoner in Na-Groth's dark kingdom. She knew about their long history, and for a moment wondered if it would not have been better if they had married in this life after all. But then she thought of Lark and how Maal had chosen Lark to work through, and had placed Lark in Isar's way. Maal, the old priest who had been her friend and teacher when she, as a young girl, had had to face great danger. Maal, who had promised on his death to come back to her whenever she really needed him.

Much as she loved her daughter, she knew Deva was not right for Isar in this life. He had evolved far beyond her and she would hold him back – possibly even destroy him.

Kyra returned anxiously to her questioning, carefully sifting through what she was given and what she gleaned for herself.

Where would Deva have gone? Perhaps to her father? But Kyra knew Deva well enough to suspect that if she were hurting she would prefer to be alone. Besides, she would not know where to find her father – he was still on his travels and it looked as though it would be some time before he returned to the Temple. A dream message had told her that he was troubled by something he had found and he intended to get to the bottom of it before he turned for home. No doubt Deva would return in her own time. But Kyra couldn't relax. She had an uneasy feeling that there was more to this than one of Deva's moods.

'There must be something she said...' Kyra insisted.

Isar racked his brains. Hitherto he had been concentrating on the morning of their parting, but now he began to remember something she had told him. She had been joking about a stranger who claimed that she was the heir to someone called 'Urak'.

As soon as Isar mentioned the name 'Urak', Kyra stiffened and went white. The whole nature of the questioning changed. She was now truly alarmed and she insisted that Isar repeat every word Deva had said about the conversation with the stranger, whether he thought it important or not.

'Who is this Urak?' Isar asked, alarmed at Kyra's reaction to her name.

'I had thought she was long since dead!' Kyra murmured. 'Guiron spoke of her as an old woman when he was still a young man.'

Isar remembered Guiron. He was high priest of the Temple of the Sun when Kyra had first come to the area. He was another player in the ancient drama that he had thought was ended – until that night with Deva.

'What did he say about her?' he asked anxiously. It was not often Kyra looked so worried.

'She was a very formidable sorceress,' she said. 'People used to go to her when they wanted someone hurt or destroyed. Guiron warned me that if ever I heard her name I was to take care.'

'A witch-woman?' Isar said, puzzled. The only witch-women he had come across were relatively harmless creatures who cast minor spells for bringing 'good luck', or a lover, or fertility.

Some used their mild clairvoyance to help people. Some were even healers. It was true some misused their talents to curse people, but none of them would be a match for Kyra or any of the priesthood if it came to conflict. Why was Kyra so shaken?

'Her powers were immense,' Kyra continued. 'She had whole

communities living in terror of her.' She tried to remember everything Guiron had told her about the woman. She seemed to recall that Guiron had at last succeeded in banishing her to some mountains. Had she seen her in that flash from her crystal – that strange figure crouching in front of a cave entrance? 'I heard she could have been one of the Lords of the Sun,' Kyra mused, 'if she had only chosen to use her skills for good rather than for evil.' She frowned. Perhaps the trouble that was keeping Khu-ren away from home was connected with Urak, too. Kyra knew that nothing ever happened by accident or by chance – nor in isolation. If some shadow was on the move, it would be drawing with it the threads of many lives, and all who were being touched by it had a reason for being in its path. She shivered suddenly, remembering that she had heard the name another time – on the lips of Wardyke.

'She must be nearly a hundred years old if she is still alive. Are you sure that was the name Deva gave you?'

'Yes, it was. But there might well be another person called Urak.'

For a moment there was a flicker of hope in Kyra's eyes – but she knew in her heart that this was the Urak she had been warned against. It made sense of her feelings of foreboding, her impression of gathering darkness and of some great danger approaching.

'Leave me,' she said with sudden decisiveness. 'Tell no one what you have told me. Her name still has power to strike fear into any who have ever heard it.'

'What can I do?'

'Nothing. Go to Lark. Be with her.'

'I need to know what has happened to Deva. I need to help her if she is in danger.'

'I will call on you if you can help in any way. Now I must reach Khu-ren, and I cannot do that with you agitating beside me.'

'But...'

'Go!' she snapped with unusual impatience.

He went.

Kyra and Khu-ren were the only two Lords of the Sun in the Temple community, and to raise the energy necessary to bring the other Lords of the Sun from across the world in astral form, if she needed them, would be a major undertaking – involving not only all the priesthood at the Temple, but many of the local people as well. But it was not the time for that yet. First she must consult with the High Priest, her husband.

She returned to the Temple at sunset, the earth quietening down around her, long strings of birds winging home. The hearth fires in the villages that sprawled in the countryside around the great circle of standing stones were being stoked against the chill of the coming night. She stood against the tallest of the sacred three in the inner sanctum and began to compose herself yet again to reach Khu-ren. The sky was eggshell green shading to seashell pink in the west. It was pure and clear with not a single blemish of cloud. One star shone out, a focus and an inspiration.

Kyra seemed a small and insignificant figure against the huge and towering monolith, in its turn dwarfed by the immense arc of the sky above them. She leant her head back against the rock and tilted her chin so she was looking directly at the star. She stared at it, immobile, until the connection between them was so strong she could feel its light touching her forehead. Then she shut her eyes and the image and power of the star entered through the gate of her third eye and blazed out within her. At first she almost reeled back – but the stone held her upright. She could feel it growing hot with the energy that was passing through her, and her heart beat with excitement. No matter how many times she set off on her astral travels, it was never the same.

Perhaps this was one of the reasons this kind of activity was not encouraged among the uninitiated. It was possible for almost anyone in following a set pattern, a ritual, to take a few limited steps. But beyond this is deep and dangerous water where all ritual is transcended and the soul is obliged to make its own decisions, adjusting to every nuance of a changing and dynamic situation. In order not to be destroyed or lost in the frightening – because unfamiliar – realms beyond this one, the traveller must not only have a soul flexible enough to adapt and compromise at every moment, but also be well and thoroughly trained.

What a long way she had come since those early days in her small village stone circle when she blundered into the astral levels and faced the terrors of the Unknown. The Unknown was still there, and no matter how much she learned, she could never learn enough to master all of it. Each time she went into the Silence and stepped off comfortable and familiar ground, she was taking a risk – not only because she might not find what she was seeking, but because she might not find her way back again. She was very well aware that the only certainty of life is its uncertainty.

Kyra stepped out of the great hall of light within her head and took her course among the growing number of visible stars.

Khu-ren was waiting for her. He too was in the Silence – reaching out to her.

* * * *

Meanwhile, in Egypt, Userhet had left Guiron alone to puzzle out the hieroglyphics on a long strip of papyrus. The scribe had only half finished his work on this particular version of the spells for the Coming Forth by Day. These were being prepared for the tomb of the pharaoh Hatshepsut, the woman who had made herself ruler of Egypt when she should have been regent for her stepson, Thutmose. The papyrus would be buried with her, so that she would have the magic of the words to help her on her journey through the Duat, the Underworld, the long Night of the Dead, before she was given life again like the sun at dawn.

Guiron had been making good progress with his studies and found he could decipher most of the ancient text.

'You shall recite this writing when this spirit is pure,' he read. *'When it is made worthy and cleansed and when its mouth is opened with a wand of iron that has come from the stars... This text was found in a secret chest written in the god's own hand. What is written is a secret of the Underworld belonging to the Mysteries of the Underworld, a secret image in the realm of the dead.'*

Guiron's finger laboriously traced the glyphs, his lips murmuring the words. 'Ah to be pure...' he thought. 'To be made worthy and cleansed...' If these secret ancient texts could help him, he would learn them so well he would need no papyrus scroll in his grave to remind him of them as he progressed through the tests and trials of the Duat. But would mere words, however potent, however charged with magical significance, be enough to free him of the consequences of his deeds?

The Mogüd in that far northern country, among the darkness and the ice of that endless, harsh winter, had tried to teach him to transcend the limitations of the physical body while he was still alive and to 'fly' to the realm where the great spiritual beings most people thought of as 'the gods' dwelt – there, presumably, to ask face to face for release from the evil he had committed.

But he had his doubts that the regions he had visited were indeed the dwelling place of 'the gods'. He had felt he was seeing no more than images thrown up by his own imagination, enhanced by the Mogüd's cunning. Those regions constituted no more than the threshold of what was Beyond. To approach the highest realms, something more was required of him. What? Guiron buried his face in his hands. If he could not find it in these texts, he did not know where else he could search.

He was tired. He could read no more. He had been at the text for a

long while. He lay down on a couch and closed his eyes, bemused by all the instructions, by all the names to memorise, by all the promises.
'Whoever knows this text, he shall go out into the day, he shall walk on earth among the living and he shall never suffer destruction. This text is a million times true.'

'If only it were as easy as that,' he thought as he drifted into sleep...

As he slept he dreamed for the first time in years of the Temple of the Sun back in his birth-land. It seemed to him Kyra and Khu-ren were standing alone, hand in hand, in the centre of the inner sanctum, their faces anxious and sorrowful... Above them a huge bird hovered threateningly, its shadow falling on Kyra's golden hair. Guiron tried to see what kind of bird it was, and it seemed to him he was at once running across the fields trying to reach the Temple and flying high above it so he could see the great circle of Tall Stones, the ridge of earth surrounding it, the buildings and burial mounds that lay around it... He was both above the hovering bird and below it. For some reason, he did not seem to be thinking at all of the two human figures in the circle, but only of finding out what the bird was doing there and what kind it was. Just before he woke with a jerk he saw that it was a hunting-owl, its wingspan far greater than that of any bird he had ever seen, its eyes...

But he was awake, trembling, the name of Urak ringing in his ears...

Kyra sent a messenger to fetch both Isar and Gya to her side. When Khu-ren was back with her in the Temple they would find it easier to seek out Guiron and to know what was best to do for Deva. Meanwhile the agitation and anxiety she was feeling for her daughter would not let her rest. She had tried many times to reach Urak again as she had that time almost accidentally through the double crystal, but Urak had been warned by that incident and was not going to be caught unprepared again. She had ways of protecting and hiding herself if she didn't want to be found.

At her wit's end, Kyra decided she must at least set something in motion while she waited for Khu-ren's return. If anyone on the ordinary physical level could find Deva, it would be Isar and Gya – both loved her, and both were intelligent and resourceful in different but complementary ways. She would send them...

Maybe Urak would be so busy fighting the Temple and its priesthood that she would not even consider it worth her while to worry about the irritation of two such 'mayflies'.

* * * *

Lark had known that Isar was anxious about something ever since he returned from the expedition – but since his long talk with Kyra he had prowled up and down like an animal in a cage, hardly settling to anything. Even the knowledge that they were to have a child, though it pleased him, did not hold his attention for as long as she had expected. When he would not tell her what the matter was she tried to read his mind – but he deliberately blocked off his thoughts from her. Usually so sensitive to her moods and caring about everything that affected her, this time he did not even notice that she too was nursing a secret worry. She decided to keep her fears about Wardyke to herself until she felt she had more of his attention.

Gya, meanwhile, was making the most of Deva's absence. Never short of female admirers, he had no trouble in finding young women to share his bed. They were less exciting than his wife, but also less temperamental. He was rarely bothered by messages from the other realms and was totally unaware now that anything was wrong. As far as he was concerned, Deva was enjoying herself at the celebrations in Hael and he saw no reason why he should not also enjoy himself. He had wanted to go with her, but she had made it unflatteringly clear that she wanted to go alone. So be it. She might not want him – but others did.

When the message came from Kyra that he was to attend her at once, he was sleeping off a heavy night and was not at all pleased to be woken.

Still half asleep, his jerkin unlaced and his dark brown hair tousled, he appeared before the great lady. Isar was already there, looking pale and grave. The sun was barely up! What could they be thinking of to do a man out of his sleep like this?

Kyra greeted him quietly and politely. She did not smile. She knew very well things were not as good as they should be between her daughter and her husband, and, although she did not blame Gya for Deva's waywardness, she regretted that he responded to it in the way that he did.

Gya bowed as he should, but he left no doubt that he was disgruntled about being called out of bed so early. The protest was wasted on Kyra, who had been up and working for several hours.

'Gya,' she said, 'I think you should know that we are worried about Deva.'

'Deva? Why?'

'The wedding at Hael did not take place, after all, and yet Deva has not returned home.'

He was surprised, but not alarmed. Deva had wandered off before, visiting people without telling her family where she was.

'We believe she is in danger.'

Gya looked sharply at Kyra. He was fully awake now. He might lie with other women, but Deva was by far the most important to him. Kyra told him simply that Isar had seen Deva the day before the intended wedding, and she had spoken of a mysterious stranger who had invited her to visit someone called Urak, a witch-woman living in the western mountains.

Gya frowned. What was the girl up to now? There was enough magic and strange goings-on at the Temple. Why should she bother with a witch-woman?

'I'm afraid this woman is extraordinarily powerful and evil.' Kyra tried to keep her voice steady and calm, but both young men noticed the tremor in it. 'The sooner we fetch her back the better.'

Gya nodded at once. 'But surely it would be more effective if you used some of your Temple astral tricks to get her back?' he said.

Kyra shook her head. 'We will do what we can on the other planes, of course. But I will feel happier if you and Isar are there to escort her back, whatever happens.'

'Do you think any harm has come to her already?'

Kyra sighed and shrugged. 'No, not yet,' she said. 'But I think there is no time to lose.'

The general location of Urak's stronghold was known to be in a certain range of mountains in the west – but they would need some ingenuity to pinpoint it exactly. They were hoping for clues from the villagers and farmers nearby.

Gya was essentially a man of action and for some time had chafed at the quiet life he was forced to live among the Temple community. That he would be starting a journey soon and going into danger gave him a certain thrill.

Isar had no such eagerness for the adventure. He was anxious for Deva – but he hated leaving Lark so soon again, especially now she was pregnant and had had such trouble with her previous pregnancies.

There were very few horses in the community and most of those were kept by the Spear-lords. Gya went straight to Karne and requested the loan of two of his, telling him as much as he knew about the reason for the expedition.

'They'll not be much use in the high mountains,' Gya admitted. 'But they will get us most of the way, quickly.'

Karne agreed at once and advised the young man how long he could expect to ride per day without straining the steeds.

'Take care of them,' he said. 'The chestnut is old and will tire easily. The grey is young and skittish.'

Fern had joined them and was listening quietly to what was being said.

'Take the grey yourself,' she said to Gya. 'Isar is not as experienced as you and needs a quieter horse.'

Gya grinned and nodded. He was not sure why Kyra was insisting that Isar come at all. As far as he was concerned, he would have been much better off alone. But one did not argue with Kyra when she spoke with the full authority of her position in the priesthood. She had a reason – but she chose not to explain it.

Gya sprang lightly on to the grey and sensed the restless energy of the young stallion at once. Fern stepped aside hastily as the hooves trampled close to her; Gya had not yet taken proper control.

'Whoa! Whoa!' laughed Karne, and stroked the silvery mane and sensitive nose. 'You'd better ride him a while in the field until you both know what to expect of each other.'

Gya and the grey were off at once.

Karne put his arm round Fern's shoulders as they stood and watched the young man and the young horse galloping around the field, hair and mane flying, eyes bright with excitement. He looked down into his wife' face and saw that she was worried. He kissed the top of her head.

'They'll be all right,' he said. 'They'll find her and bring her back in no time at all.'

'I wish Isar didn't have to leave Lark at this time,' Fern said. She knew that although Lark had made it public that she was expecting a baby, she had not yet told either Isar or Kyra about her fears regarding Wardyke.

'She'll be all right,' Karne said soothingly. 'He won't be gone long. Kyra's probably making too much of this anyway. Deva's always going off on her own. If she were my daughter...' Karne left it at that, but Fern knew there were many times Karne had shown his disapproval of Deva's waywardness and Kyra's indulgence of her. 'You'd think a woman with such an extraordinary understanding of others would be able to see what was wrong with her own daughter!' he had said more than once.

Now, Fern wondered quietly to herself, if she had been Deva's mother – would she have let her get away with quite so much? She made the sign of the sacred circle on her forehead and thanked the Nameless One that Deva was not her daughter – nor indeed her son's wife.

Gya galloped the grey back to where they were waiting and reined in skilfully.

'They are two of a kind,' thought Fern, looking at the man and the horse. 'So young. So vigorous. So reckless and impulsive. Kyra knew what she was doing when she wanted Isar to go along. Gya needs him – though he doesn't know it.'

Chapter 6

The scarlet dress

Boggoron and Deva arrived at Urak's spectacular gorge at noon on a brilliantly sunny day. Every leaf blazed and not a shadow warned her of the true nature of the place she was entering. She looked around her with delight. There had been a heavy shower earlier and the limestone walls were still strung with the gleaming threads of waterfalls glinting in the sunlight. Their voices sang out from every crag and gully, and it seemed to her she was walking into an enchanted place where everything was light and bright and joyous.

Boggoron looked sideways at her and grinned to see her so pleased with what she saw. There had been a few times on the journey when he thought he would lose her. She had been so determined at the beginning, but as they travelled further and further from her home she began to have doubts. He used all the cunning Urak had taught him to stiffen her resolution. He described instance after instance of Urak's amazing powers – her ability to raise storms; her ability to manifest anything she wished; her ability to travel anywhere in the world, and beyond.

At first Deva counter-boasted by quoting the wonders her own parents could perform, but in every case Boggoron managed to top her story and leave her gasping. The adventure, which had started because she was angry with Isar and wanted to learn a spell to put him under her power completely and for ever, was turning into something very different and much more important. She was sure Kyra and the Temple had never heard of Urak, and she began to persuade herself that it was her duty to investigate and report back. When she realised how far she would have to travel and how long the 'investigation' might take, however, she decided she should send a message to her parents and Gya. She considered carefully what she would say. Her instinct told her that they would forbid her to continue if they knew exactly what she was doing, but she was sure that if she did not communicate at all they would send someone to look for her and, with their talent for far-seeing, she would certainly be found and forced to return. Having decided on what she would say in her message she then had the problem of finding someone to deliver it. Boggoron had been avoiding the villages and they had scarcely seen a soul anywhere along their route. For the first time she became aware of this, and a faint shadow seemed to pass over her heart. Was she, after all, doing the right thing?

But within a short while they came across two young herdboys out looking for strays – and Deva told herself that she had been mistaken about Boggoron deliberately avoiding people. She called out at once and started running towards them, not noticing that Boggoron had tried to seize her arm and lead her off towards a copse on the left where they would have avoided confrontation. Too late to stop her, he stood silently and watched. He could not hear what she was saying but he could see the boys listening intently and the elder of the two accepting something from her hand.

Deva persuaded the elder boy to set off for the Temple with a message for her father that she was safe and would return when she was ready.

'He is not to send anyone after me,' she stressed. 'There is no need. Tell him that. Tell him that I am with friends.'

She handed him one of her rings – a garnet clasped in gold. The boy's eyes opened wide as he gazed at it.

'This is payment for delivering the message safely. If you do not deliver the message this ring will bring about your death,' she promised darkly. The boy looked terrified – but could not bring himself to hand the ring back. He had no doubt that he would deliver the message safely.

Boggoron watched as the elder boy slipped away from the other, running eastwards. The younger one, rather disconsolately, continued along the path driving the strays they had already found before him.

Deva returned to his side. She offered no explanation and Boggoron asked for none. He gave no indication that he was disturbed by what she had done.

A short while later he suggested a rest, and wandered casually off while she refreshed herself at the stream. She should have been concerned that he was out of sight for so long, but she was feeling so good listening to the water bubbling over the rocks and the birds singing in the trees that she dozed off. She gave a shiver when she woke to find Boggoron standing beside her looking down at her. She did not like the expression on his face – but could not decipher it. She stood up hastily and suggested that they moved on.

She did not know that over the hill that lay between them and the road to the Temple, a young boy was lying bleeding to death with a dagger wound in his back, and that the garnet ring she had given her messenger, was now in Boggoron's carrying pouch, along with a disgusting jumble of raven's feet and wolves' paws, tufts of human hair tied with nettle stems, and a mildewed hunk of bread.

As they proceeded Deva became more and more excited at the prospect of meeting the sorceress. Kyra had not allowed her to train as a priest at the Temple, and on the whole Deva was glad of it. She was too familiar with the gruelling tests the novices had to face to envy them. But to have the powers of the priests without all that hard work! Her eyes shone at the prospect. She had no intention of taking Urak's place in the mountains and living in isolation for the rest of her life, but she would learn enough to control Isar, astonish her parents and give her an advantage over anyone she chose, at any time she wanted – and then she would go back. She swung gracefully along beside the awkward, shambling figure of Boggoron and dreamed of all the things she would be able to do if he was telling her the truth about Urak.

Once deep in the gorge, they left the valley floor and the swiftly flowing river that had been their constant companion, and began to scramble up and along rocky slopes, sometimes so steep that they had to cling to bushes and saplings to prevent themselves sliding back to the torrent below.

Urak watched Deva coming. So this was the apprentice with whom she would live out the rest of her life. She looked strong and healthy; a child of the sun, slim, firm, agile. She liked the way she did not hesitate to leap quite dangerous gaps on the mountainside when it was necessary, and never once wavered over a hand or foot hold. When Deva was nearer, Urak studied her features. Her black hair was twisted and pinned up at the nape of her neck to keep it out of the way. She wore leather tunic and trousers like a man – women often did for travelling – but Deva looked as though she were more comfortable in them than she would be in a skirt. Her nose was straight, her black eyes slightly slanted like a cat's, her chin determined. She was beautiful, yet unselfconscious about it. Urak nodded with satisfaction. She would do very well.

Suddenly the old woman stepped out from behind a huge old yew tree growing incongruously among the slender birch and hawthorn. Deva stopped in her tracks and gasped. She had been told that Urak was old, but she had not realised how old. The woman was almost a skeleton, with a layer of skin as thin and white as a frosted leaf. Her hair was snow-fire, her eyes as bright and blank as jet beads.

Deva swallowed hard. Suddenly she was not so sure she had done the right thing. She was aware that she was facing someone who would be able to see right through any of her tricks, and deep into her most hidden thoughts. Moreover, she would not be bound by any of the Temple laws regarding the safeguarding of an individual's privacy. She thought of turning round there and then and retracing her steps. But Boggoron was close behind to prevent her escape.

Urak held out her hands in greeting, and the flash of her rings momentarily dazzled the girl. On every finger a gem as big as a bird's egg sparkled and gleamed. As the light caught them, Deva seemed to be surrounded by a net of light beams of every conceivable colour. She stared with astonishment at stones she had never dreamed could exist – huge wine-red garnets, topaz like solidified sunlight, emeralds and sapphires, and one that had no colour in itself but threw out shafts of colour more vivid than the rest.

Seeing how she stared at them, Urak made a swift, almost imperceptible gesture with her right hand and Deva saw that she was holding something out to her – almost as though she were offering a titbit to a robin. She raised her eyebrows enquiringly and looked into Urak's eyes. The old woman smiled and nodded and moved closer. As nervous as a bird, Deva took one step forward and reached out. Another lightning gesture from Urak, and Deva found that on her own bare brown hands a ring now gleamed. She stared into the translucent depths of a piece of amber the size of one of her finger joints. Inside, a fly was caught, its wings spread out as though it was in mid flight. Her heart began to race and she felt almost as though she too were sinking deeper and deeper into some heavy substance out of which she would never be able to escape.

'Greetings, child,' Urak said softly. 'Don't be frightened. You are safe here.'

Deva was tugging at the ring on her finger, alarmed to discover that she could not get it off.

'You're very kind,' she said, trying to keep the tremor out of her voice. 'This is a beautiful ring – but I'd rather not...'

'Keep it,' said Urak graciously. 'It is yours.'

'I – I would rather –'

'There will be others... but those you must earn.'

'I – I think this is a mistake... I came here –'

'You came here to train to be a great sorceress.'

'Well, I –'

'Did my servant not tell you that you are to be my apprentice and my heir?'

'Yes, but –'

'Out of all the world, you have been chosen. It is a great honour.'

'I – I know that, my lady... but –'

'You are tired. Come – rest a while and eat. I will not hold you here against your will. Stay with me this one afternoon and night and in the morning – if you still wish to go – I will not hold you back.'

Deva frowned. She was afraid of this woman – this place – but she was tired and hungry, and to negotiate that hazardous route again without rest would be foolish. She would rather not spend the night with this extraordinary and terrifying witch-woman, but she saw no alternative. 'At least it will be interesting,' she thought, the curiosity that had led her into trouble more than once stirring again. 'I'll have some tales to tell when I return home!' She looked back at the ring on her finger, and she no longer saw it as a poor trapped creature but as a winged being living perpetually in light.

Urak, watching, smiled – well satisfied.

She led the girl to her cave, and from a great wooden chest she carefully drew out a shimmering red dress. As Urak suddenly shook it out, fold after fold of almost transparent scarlet fabric floated in the air. Deva gasped. She had only once seen a weave as fine, and that was in the piece of Egyptian cotton cloth her father had given her mother. But this surpassed it. Pleased by the effect she was creating, Urak held it out to Deva.

'Your clothes are dusty from the journey. I'm sure you would be more comfortable in this,' she said softly.

Deva nodded, speechless with delight. Urak gave a signal to Boggoron, who had been hovering behind Deva all the while, grinning and nodding at every move that Urak made, every word she spoke – but now he melted away and left the two women alone.

The girl peeled off her well-worn and dusty clothes and, trembling with excitement, lifted the filmy fabric to her body. The touch of it made her shiver and think of Isar and the pleasures of the night she had spent with him. If only he could see her now! He would not walk away so easily. Suddenly her fierce resolution returned. She would bargain with Urak for this dress, and when she left in the morning she would have it with her. Isar would see her in it – come what may.

Urak watched her arrange the soft folds around her body. How young she was! How fresh! How ready for everything she had to offer her.

The dress was very different from anything Deva had ever seen before in this life, but as she robed herself she knew exactly how to wind the fabric around herself... how to tie the knots at waist and shoulder that held it safe yet did not spoil the line. One breast was left uncovered, and this seemed all right to her – though no one she knew would ever have exposed herself in this way. She fingered the cloth, astonished at the numerous narrow pleats that sprang back into place no matter how she smoothed them out.

Urak stooped again, and once more lifted an object from the chest. This time it was a deep necklet of gold and precious stones. Smiling, she fastened it around the girl's neck, and it fitted as though it had been designed for it. Almost breathless at its beauty, Deva dropped her chin and peered at it lying just above her breasts. She recognised the flowers although she had never seen them in this life, except in the frequent dreams and visions she had had as a child of her past life in Egypt. Lotus lilies of turquoise on stems of gold were joined by leaves of lapis lazuli and tiny bubbles of water-coloured crystal... Gingerly she touched it and a thrill passed through her body. This too seemed familiar to her.

Then Urak reached into the chest again and lifted out a polished bronze mirror with a handle of ebony carved in the shape of a swan, its beak biting the edge of the mirror to hold it in place. She held it up to Deva, and the girl gasped at the image it reflected back to her. Her hair had loosened and flowed down over her shoulders like a black river. The light shafting through the cave entrance picked out the blue lights in it, and the gold of the necklace was reflected on the scarlet fabric. She had always taken it for granted that she was beautiful – but even she was astonished at the way she looked now.

Yet again Urak reached into the chest, this time lifting out a fillet of gold. She gathered up the long tresses of Deva's hair and slipped the golden circlet around them. Deva stared and stared at herself in the mirror while Urak watched. Above her forehead a turquoise lotus flower rose from the golden band, so life-like Deva was almost sure she could catch a whiff of its scent...

Chapter 7

Farla

When the day of Farla's marriage dawned, the bride was nowhere to be found. She had slipped away in the night, leaving a hurt and bewildered groom and a disappointed village. Only Farla's mother was not surprised. She had watched her daughter closely over the past weeks and knew, though she said nothing, that Farla's heart was not in the marriage. She was not sorry that her daughter had backed out of it, only that she had done it the way she had.

When Farla left her home she had no idea where she would go. She just knew that her life as an ordinary village wife would not work out, and the only other life she was familiar with – as a Temple priest – frightened her. Restlessly she searched her mind for an alternative, but could think of none. The one thing she was certain of was that she was a failure and a misfit. She utterly despised herself.

Perhaps if she lived with strangers for a while, she thought. Perhaps if she gave herself another name, another identity. Perhaps if she was someone else to others, she would become someone else to herself. But where should she go? Who should she be? As she hurried through the night shadows, many personae came to her and she toyed with each of them, but each lacked something she needed.

When she was tired of wandering, she came to a village she was satisfied was far enough away from both the Temple and her childhood home for her not to be recognised. She was pale and exhausted when she arrived. The clothes she was wearing and the pack on her shoulder were dirty and ragged. The villagers who greeted her regarded her with suspicion, and she knew that she wouldn't be allowed to stay if she did not give some kind of account of herself.

'My name is Urak,' she said without thinking. She had never heard the name before, but now it just popped into her head. It sounded a fair enough name to her and to most of the villagers – but an old man, bent almost double and leaning heavily on a stick, suddenly uttered an exclamation under his breath and stepped forward to peer at her closely.

'What is it? Do you know her?' the head-man of the community asked sharply, seeing the way his father looked at her.

'If she is Urak, there is enchantment at work here.'

'Why?'

'Urak is a witch-woman as old as that hill there...' he said, pointing.

'Are you Urak the witch-woman?' the head-man demanded, and Farla noticed how the whole community, apart from the man who had asked the question and the old man who had recognised the name, shuffled away from her, staring – fascinated, but terrified.

She hesitated and then repeated firmly that her name was Urak. By not denying that she was the witch she tacitly suggested that she was. 'Why am I bringing this on myself?' she thought. Perhaps because she had sought a new identity and here was one ready-made being given to her – or perhaps because she couldn't help herself. If Urak was a witch and her name had spoken itself through her, there was indeed enchantment at work. Farla trembled – but remained silent.

At that moment a figure emerged from one of the wooden houses, and Farla was astonished to see that it was Khu-ren – in the flesh this time – in his travelling clothes. He recognised her at once, but instead of greeting her warmly as she would have expected, he stared at her with deep suspicion and hostility.

Farla did not know what she wanted now: to acknowledge her true identity or hide behind another. Again she felt caught between two worlds. What, after all, was her true identity?

'Urak?' he asked coldly, his handsome face almost expressionless.

'You know my name, my lord,' she said in a low voice.

'Aye,' he said. 'I know your name.' But his voice did not soften.

She could feel the tension as the whole village hung on his decision as to what was to be done with her. He stared at her steadily. The silence was unbearable. She longed to explain, to plead, to justify – but her throat was so constricted she could not bring out a single sound.

At last he turned away from her and faced the villagers.

'Give this woman food and drink. When she has rested we will leave your village together.'

Farla breathed a sigh of relief. She did not understand why she had said what she had, and she did not understand why he had not exposed her lie – but at least the hostility of the villagers was lessened.

She was led to the house out of which he had emerged – the chief Elder's house. As she entered the darkness of the interior she fell forward in a faint. The chief Elder and his wife stared at the figure on the floor and couldn't bring themselves to touch her.

Khu-ren looked down on her for a moment and then lifted her in his arms and carried her to the bed. He stood beside her for a long time, looking troubled and thoughtful. Then he stooped and made the sign of the sacred circle, clockwise, with his right index finger on her forehead. Without regaining consciousness she slipped into a more natural sleep. He drew up a three-legged stool and sat beside her, his eyes never leaving her face.

Uneasily, the woman of the house prepared food and brought it to Khu-ren. He indicated, without looking away from the girl's face, that she should lay it beside the sleeping figure. She did this, and retreated at once to stand with her husband at the other end of the room.

At last Khu-ren rose and came towards them.

'She will sleep for a while,' he said quietly. 'Don't be afraid of her. She will not harm you.'

'Is she...?'

'No, she is not.'

It was clear the great priest did not want to be questioned further. He left them and went outside.

From time to time the woman of the house peered at Farla, but she slumbered on.

When at last she awoke the day was half gone and the food beside her cold. She was alone in the house. She had had strange dreams and was afraid. It seemed to her she was the agent of death in some way. Wherever she walked, people died – and when she looked down at them in growing horror she found that they were not people at all but voles or field mice or hares, their furry bodies ripped apart and their entrails spread out around them ritualistically.

She was shivering when she woke, and pulled the rug on the bed up around herself. Then, because the feel of the fur reminded her of the bloody fur in her dream, she pushed it aside, trembling. She wanted to get out of that dim room with its bad dreams, and tried to stand up. She found as her feet touched the floor her legs buckled under her as though she was very weak after a long illness. She cried out as she fell, grabbing the edge of the stool on which Khu-ren had been sitting. What was happening to her? She felt in some way that she was no longer in charge of herself.

At that moment Khu-ren came back into the room and saw her struggling, saw the bewilderment and fear in her eyes, and strode quickly towards her. He lifted her up and placed her back on the bed. Then he stood at the foot gazing down on her. His face – a moment ago full of sympathy – was now stern and angry.

He lifted his right hand and pointed with his index finger at the centre of her forehead.

'Leave her!' he commanded, his voice like a whiplash.

Farla had never seen Khu-ren angry and was filled with terror. The room seemed to grow dark and light again alternately, as though a lamp were flickering, though there was no lamp lit.

'Help me!' she cried, holding out her arms.

'You must help yourself,' he said firmly, but more gently now. 'Assert your Self. Remember that you are unique and special, the result of millennia of your own actions and reactions. You cannot be anyone else. You don't want to be anyone else. You are as you are – and as you are you will face life!'

She remembered how she had wanted to take on another persona and realised with horror that this might well have laid her open to another person taking her over.

'I can't,' she sobbed. 'I'm ashamed...'

'There is nothing you need be ashamed of.'

'You don't know what I have done... what thoughts I've had...'

'I know,' he said quietly.

She flushed. He knew her. He knew all her doubts, all her vacillations, her impatience, her dissatisfactions – maybe even her desire for Gya! Even now she longed to be someone else – someone strong, someone single-minded, someone...

'No!' he shouted, suddenly stern again. 'Farla! Look at me. Look into my eyes!'

But she wanted to hide. She wanted Farla to disappear. She put her hands to her face and hid her eyes from his gaze.

She felt his hands on hers, pulling them away. But she fought him. Whoever this Urak was, she would rather be her than Farla. Strong as he was he could not prise her hands away from her face. It was as though she had superhuman strength to cling to her adopted name. There was a roaring and a thundering in her ears... and through it she could hear Khu-ren's voice faintly calling a stranger's name: 'Farla... Farla... Farla...' A name she did not want to hear.

Suddenly he gave up trying to loosen her hands and took her by the shoulders and shook her violently.

'You think I, Khu-ren, have nothing in my thoughts to shame me?' he shouted. 'Look at me! Look into my thoughts. See what hides there. I live with it! So can you.'

She dropped her hands in astonishment. She looked at him. She looked into his thoughts and there... and there she saw the frustration of a man who had chosen one life and would rather have another. What other life? What other life could the most honoured and powerful person in the land, the High Priest of the Temple of the Sun, the mighty Lord of the Sun, the Guardian of the Tall Stones... what life would he rather have? She saw him as a child beside his father in a field of barley and felt his yearning for the simplicity of a peasant's life in his homeland, the smell of black earth and ripening grain. She saw that more than once he had wanted to give up the responsibilities of his position, wanted to weep and hide his head, and go back to his childhood land. She saw his waves of resentment that he had given up so much, yet still more was demanded of him. She saw his impatience with fools and his momentary lapses of self-discipline. She had thought him so strong, so perfect, so god-like.

She became calm. No longer did the light flicker, the storm rage in her heart. If he could live with imperfection, so could she.

'Farla?' he asked gently.

'Yes, Farla,' she replied, and smiled wanly.

Khu-ren insisted that he and Farla should at once start on their journey back to the Temple of the Sun. When they were alone on the road he cross-questioned her about the name she had tried to claim as her own. She told him she knew nothing about it: that it had just popped into her head and she had used it without thinking. But when she mentioned her dream he was very interested and insisted on her going over every detail several times.

He walked beside her for a long time after this in silence. She could see that he was thinking deeply, and she did not interrupt him.

It was twilight when they saw the smoke of a village in the distance, and she expected him to hurry to reach it before full dark. But suddenly he stopped and turned to face her, his expression grave.

'What is it?' she asked in some alarm.

'I would like to ask your help,' he said, 'but I'm afraid it may involve you in a very great danger – and I don't know whether I have the right.'

'What do you want me to do?' she asked. To be given a definite task with specific guidelines might well mean she could put off the vexatious task of finding her true Self and her true calling a little while longer.

'You will agree, I think, that the name "Urak" did not come to you by accident?'

Farla nodded, but waited for him to continue.

'It is possible her thoughts were ranging far and wide looking for someone she could use. You appeared to be the perfect vehicle. Your self-esteem was at its lowest. You were even contemplating changing your name and everything about yourself. I can see how you would be an excellent tool for her if she could get you. Your soul-energy is strong – or you would not have been chosen for the priesthood or lasted so long through your training. Yet you allow yourself to give up too easily. You gave up the priesthood. You gave up your marriage. You were even prepared to give up your name!' Farla knew that to an Egyptian that was almost unthinkable. 'In the gap left by the failure of your own self-confidence and will, it would be easy for another to step in.'

Farla hung her head. With every word he confirmed her worst criticisms of herself.

'Look at you!' Khu-ren said sharply. 'Even as I speak you are sinking into self-pity and self-condemnation!'

'What am I to do?' cried Farla in despair. 'That is how I am! I can't stop myself.'

'What do you want to do at this moment?'

'Kill myself!' she muttered, so low that he barely caught it.

He gave an exclamation of disgust and then he took out a knife from his belt and handed it to her, hilt first.

'Kill yourself now and you will have to face all this again – worse – because to kill yourself is the greatest failure of all. Live and win your own self-respect, and you will be free to use all that potential Kyra – and I – believe you have. What is it to be?' He held the blade steady, his gaze never wavering. 'Choose,' he said sternly.

'I choose to live,' she whispered, 'but I –'

'Good,' he said quickly, as though that minor detail being settled, they could now get on to the serious business in hand. He flipped the knife over in the air, catching it neatly by the hilt, then replaced it at his belt and looked at her. He could see the conflict still in her eyes between what she was and what she wanted to be. 'What I want you to do will not only take courage, but your will, your confidence, your strength of purpose. The lives of many people will hang on your success or failure.'

'How can you ask me to do this – knowing what you know about me?'

'I believe you can do it. You are not as you were yesterday, nor yesterday as you were the day before. It is a mistake to believe that you will fail now because you failed then. You have changed. You are not the same.'

She shook her head doubtfully.

'You can't see it. You may not even be able to feel it yet. But it is so. Look around you. Since we began to talk has anything at all stayed the same?'

She looked around her. The landscape was almost lost in darkness. The colours had changed, from subtle shades of green to dark purple and auburn, black and indigo. A cloudless sky was studded with stars. The village fires were glowing.

'What you can't see is that every leaf has grown a little; that stem is moving in the breeze now, when it was steady and still before; a bee has left that flower. You are older. My words are in your heart: my thoughts have become part of your experience. You will never be exactly as you were. To say you will behave exactly the same is nonsense.'

She straightened like a poppy about to open in the sunlight. She felt different. She was different. She had gone through the fire of his disapproval and her own, and she had come out the other side the stronger for it. He was looking at her with affection.

'You see?' he asked quizzically.

She managed a tentative, watery smile in response.

'I see,' she agreed. 'But what is it you want me to do?'

'I want you to accept Urak's invitation to follow her; make her trust you enough to find out where she is. Then you must communicate with us, but only then. She must not suspect you and the Temple are still connected. But you must promise that once you know her whereabouts, you will call on us. Go no further by yourself.'

Farla looked alarmed. 'What if she sees through me?'

'She won't see through you if you use the blocking techniques you learned at the Temple.'

'What if I am tempted really to follow her?'

'Temptation is one thing; succumbing to it is another.'

'But...' She was thinking how many times she had given in and given up.

'Remember – this time is different. You are different. If you hold out this time and see your commitment through –'

They were interrupted at this point by a voice calling out to them. It seemed that news of their approach had reached the village, and a party had been sent out to greet them.

Farla and Khu-ren were separated in the excitement. She followed, almost forgotten, as they escorted the High Priest to their village with drums and cymbals and noisy chattering. Such a visit was a great event for them and they intended to make the most of it. The venison was already roasting on the spit in preparation for the welcome feast, sparks from the crackling log fire spiralling up high into the air to join the stars. Farla began to think about what Khu-ren had proposed. She knew enough to realise the dangers of being taken over and used as a channel by a malignant force. That Khu-ren had suggested her risking this showed the measure of his anxiety about the woman. But it also indicated his great faith in her abilities and integrity – in spite of all that had happened. She was afraid, but she was very keen to be worthy of his trust. Also – more important, she now realised – if she could do this without wavering, she would regain her own self-respect. But where to begin?

She was offered meat and ale by smiling villagers. She drank, she ate – but all the time her mind was working. How could she bring herself again to the attention of this Urak? And how could she keep control of herself when she had done it, so that Urak would suspect nothing?

Chapter 8

Gya and Isar

Gya and Isar had been good friends since Groth's war, though two more different personalities it would be difficult to find. Isar, quiet, reserved, ever conscious of the complex and varied levels of existence; Gya, accepting only what his five senses could provide for him, quick to love and hate, quick to act without thinking. It was Gya who had turned a motley band of rebels into the efficient army which had been largely instrumental in defeating Na-Groth's formidable forces on the physical plane, while Isar, with the help of Lark and Maal, had destroyed their leader in a different and more subtle way, from within, by playing on his most secret fears.

There had been no animosity between them when Gya married Deva. Isar was delighted. He believed at the time that his love for Deva was more the love of a brother for a sister – in spite of all they had shared in that previous life – and he threw flowers over the bride and groom with as light a heart as anyone else. But now, as the two young men set off on their quest, there was an awkwardness between them. Gya, on the whole, was never bothered by feelings of guilt no matter what he did, justifying all his sexual adventuring by blaming Deva for her mischievous and sometimes deliberately cruel treatment of him – but he would still rather Isar, who was as close to her as a brother, did not find out about the other women he had taken to bed. Isar, for his part, could scarcely look Gya in the eye because of the night he had spent with Deva and the feelings that now raged within him and would not be brought under control.

The two young men rode silently side by side, wondering how they were going to keep their secrets.

It was not until they reached the foothills of the western mountains that they met anyone who had ever heard of Urak. Up to that time they had had no difficulty in finding food and shelter, but information was very sparse. In the more remote communities of the western hills, often cut off by snow and flooding rivers from their nearest neighbours, they found the people less friendly. But some had tales to tell about Urak. Isar noticed that when Urak's name was mentioned, the older people instantly made the sign of a circle over their hearts – the holy sign, the sign for protection. They were told of children, talented psychically, who were abducted and never heard of again. Only one was ever returned, and the old woman who told this story shuddered as she spoke.

'One morning, years later, the mother opened her door and found her son bound and hanging from a tree outside her house.'

'Dead?'

'No, not dead – but his wits had gone and he was never right in the head again and he could never tell them what had happened to him or where he had been all that time.'

The villagers moved closer together as though for protection. Many looked fearfully over their shoulders to the swirling mists and mysterious crags and chasms of the mountains.

'The hanging boy had strange markings on the soles of his feet,' an old man suddenly said.

'What kind of marks?' Gya questioned.

'Tattoo marks.'

Isar suddenly started as though he had remembered something.

'What did the designs look like?' he asked.

'What does it matter!' cried Gya impatiently. 'Is it not enough that we know what she is capable of and that Deva is in her clutches?'

But Isar insisted that he wanted to know what the tattoos looked like. There seemed some disagreement on this subject. Some had heard one thing and some had heard another. And then the old man who had first mentioned the tattoos stepped forward and, with a hand trembling with age, traced out the design in the dust with a long stick.

Gya saw that Isar recognised the pattern and was considerably shaken by it. When they were alone later he asked him to explain.

'When I was a child I once saw the soles of Wardyke's feet,' Isar said slowly, and then stopped.

'And?'

'They were covered with those very same tattoo designs. I asked him about them and he said he had earned them, but that it had cost him a lot. He looked as though he was remembering something he would rather forget.' Isar frowned. He was wondering if Wardyke was somehow connected with Urak and what had happened to Deva. At the thought, Isar's blood ran cold. Wardyke and Urak together? What a terrifying combination!

'Well, if even Wardyke found her a bad memory we are up against something really frightening.' Gya looked steadily into Isar's eyes. 'Are you ready for it – or shall I go on alone?'

'I'll not leave you,' Isar said, ashamed that Gya should even think of it.

'After all, she is my wife – and you have your own to think of.'

Isar stared into the darkness that was gathering over the land. 'Your wife and my wife,' he was thinking. 'How easily we take possession of people!' Had he imagined it or was there an edge to Gya's voice? Did he suspect that Isar and Deva had been lovers – not only in some far-off time, but here and now? Should he confess? Should he apologise? Once spoken in words, would the beauty of the memory of that one precious night survive the jealousy and the wrangling... the anger and the bitterness? He and Gya had been through so much together in Groth's war, and together they were facing a difficult and dangerous adventure again. Now was not the time to speak openly of such matters. What was known for sure could not be ignored; what was only suspected, could.

'Lark is in good hands,' he said at last, quietly – and he could tell by Gya's face that he was relieved. The young bowman was strong, agile and almost fearless, but he was used to handling enemies he could fight with physical weapons. He was not at all sure he could tackle an old witch-woman by himself.

They stocked up well with food and set off through the hill country, aiming at the mountainous terrain beyond.

Isar had been expecting some message or sign from Kyra. He knew the priests were searching for Deva in their own way and he had great faith in their methods. He was surprised that they were taking so long. He tried continually to be alert, watching for signs, ready for any suggestions Kyra wanted to implant in his mind.

Gya had his doubts that any help would come from the Temple. The place had always been a puzzle to him. He had been told that the priests, particularly Khu-ren and Kyra, could travel across the world without leaving the Temple, but he was not prepared to believe it. He had been present once when the Lords of the Sun from across the world were supposed to be there. It was during one of those rare occasions when the ordinary people were allowed into the Temple – but only as far as the outer circle. There they joined hands to form a vast ring and they were supposed to move in a certain rhythmic way, round and round, alternate male and female, the energy of their united bodies, the vibrations of their united voices raised in an ancient hymn... adding power to the circle of Tall Stones to draw in the astral-entities from thousands of leagues away.

He remembered he had been excited at joining the ring, thinking that at last he would see if what the Temple claimed was literally true or just a fantastic tale aimed at impressing the people to keep them docile and content. He had taken the hands of the two women on either side of him and started moving with the rest, following the drumbeat, watching as the huge, unwieldy line of people rippled and swayed around the perimeter of the Temple. At first there was faltering, some missing the beat, some bunched too close... but gradually the rhythm settled down and the spacing became more comfortable. The whole circle reminded him of a sinuous serpent, powerfully coiling around the stones to bite its own tail. He remembered thinking of the Temple teaching that the earth itself was alive with flowing currents of energy, which they represented as serpents in their iconography. The site for each circular temple of Tall Stones was carefully chosen where this energy was at its most powerful and most easily accessible. Isar had tried to explain it in terms of a whirlpool or vortex into which several streams or currents fed, becoming in the centre far more powerful than they were as separate streams.

'This is why we are not allowed into the Temple,' Isar told him. 'We would not be able to handle the energy.'

'How would it affect us?'

'I don't know exactly – but Kyra once said to me it heightened whatever energy you carried with you. If you came into the Temple, say, in happy mood, you would soon feel that you were floating in ecstasy. But if you came in feeling annoyed with someone, you would leave filled with hate and murderous intent. When you have been trained to handle and control your own energy, only then would you be able to control and channel the energy of the Temple the right way. Only the Lords of the Sun are capable of using the full potential of the inner circle.'

Gya had more questions than Isar could answer and eventually even Isar's patience was exhausted.

'Look, if you want to know so much,' he cried in exasperation, 'ask Kyra if you can join the priesthood and learn all their mysteries. I'm a wood-carver. Ask me about wood!'

Gya laughed. 'Can you see me as a priest?'

'No,' Isar grinned, relaxing. 'But just accept that these things are true. I can't prove them to you.'

Gya stopped questioning Isar, but not himself.

When he started moving with the serpent he had been sceptical and cynical. But afterwards? Afterwards he was confused. What had he witnessed? What had he experienced?

As the line of dancing people moved, and he with them, he had gradually forgotten his questioning mind and become one with the flow of energy. He could not remember when this happened or how it happened... but after a while he seemed to be flowing like a river... at first slowly, and then building up speed so that he felt he was a torrent roaring down a chasm, leaping over rock, cascading over cliffs...

Once, amidst the swirling and the whirling, he tried to pull his mind away and think as an individual again. For a moment he glimpsed the Stones of the inner circle where Khu-ren and Kyra were standing, their backs and the palms of their hands to the rock, their heads tilted back – eyes shut. Were there other figures? Had the mighty Lords of the Sun come to their call from across the world?

Desperate to see, Gya's head was filled with excruciating pain as he fought the pull of the energy that joined him to his fellow men and women. He couldn't see clearly enough through the sweat that poured from his forehead. He tried to release his hands from those of his neighbours so that he could rub his eyes clear, but his hands were locked tight and with all his strength he couldn't move them. He thought he saw figures through the blur of his vision – but he could not be sure. The moment was gone and he was back as the river...

He remembered the exhaustion he felt when at last they were released and returned to their homes. He remembered the headache. He and Deva fell down on the bed fully clothed and knew nothing more until the morning. When he woke his head was still pounding. He had fought. Deva was fresh as the dawn. She had accepted.

Today he was still doubting. He had more faith in his own efforts to find Urak than he had in the Temple's. In fact, he took it as a personal challenge and was very anxious that Isar and he should reach Deva before the Temple did.

'They will find a way,' Isar said confidently. To him there was no doubt that the Lords of the Sun had the power to do what they claimed.

When Deva woke after that first night's sleep, she found that she was alone. She sat up and stared around her. A shaft of sunlight penetrated to the furthest wall. There Deva noticed for the first time that the rock was fissured and she began to wonder how far the fissure ran into the mountain. She stood up and went to the entrance of the cave. She peered out along the open mountainside to see if she could see any sign of Boggoron or Urak, but all she could see was the cliff wall of the gorge opposite her, still in shadow, while close around her every leaf was ablaze with light.

She noticed that there was a double row of footprints in the dewy grass leading away from the cave and she was tempted to leave now before Urak and her companion returned. She didn't think she would be kept back against her will, but she knew Urak would try to persuade her to stay. She turned back into the cave and began to dress herself in the clothes she had been wearing when she arrived. How shabby and rough they seemed after the feather-light touch of the scarlet Egyptian dress, but she knew she had a long way to travel and she had to be practical. She laced up her boots over the worn leather trousers, belted her leather tunic and emptied her carrying pouch of everything that was not absolutely necessary to make way for the fine fabric and the jewellery. Then she paused. She was determined not to leave without her new clothes, but if she took them without permission, would Urak not pursue her? She had nothing of comparable value to leave in their place. While she was hesitating, her eye fell on the chest from which Urak had taken them, and curiosity got the better of her.

She ran to the entrance of the cave and looked out once again to make sure the others were not returning. The only change was that the sun had begun to dissolve the dew near the cave, though it still sparkled in the more sheltered places. She ran back to the chest and hauled it out of the shadows into the light. With trembling hand and many a glance back over her shoulder to the entrance she gingerly opened it. What she saw inside made her gasp. The dress she had worn was only one of many: the necklace and fillet that had so astonished her with their beauty were the least of those she now lifted out. She forgot everything else as she held up dress after dress and bedecked herself with string after string of glowing jewels, even rolling up her sleeves so that she could see how the golden bracelets looked upon her pale arms. She had necklaces of amber and jet and gold at home. She had fine clothes for fine occasions – but never and nowhere had she seen such luxurious goods as these except in those strange visions of Egypt she had had as a child. Deeper and deeper she reached into the chest. There seemed no end to its treasures. Suddenly she withdrew her hand with a cry. She had come upon a cobra, its head raised to strike, its yellow eyes staring malevolently into hers.

She heard a laugh behind her and spun round, the excitement of a moment before turning to guilty fear.

Urak had unexpectedly emerged from the fissure at the back of the cave and had been watching her for some time – amused. Now she stepped forward into the light and Deva was transfixed between the cobra's golden eyes behind her and the sorceress's black and mocking eyes before her.

'I wasn't stealing them...' she stammered. 'I was just... just looking...'

'And do you like what you see?' Urak asked smoothly, not taking her eyes off Deva's for an instant.

'Yes... oh yes, of course...'

'And would you like those beautiful things to be yours?'

Deva's heart was pounding. Still horribly aware of the cobra in the chest, she wanted to look round or move away – but she did not dare.

'Of course... of course...' she muttered.

Urak moved nearer.

'If you want these pretty things, my child,' the old woman said softly, 'all you have to do is reach down for them.'

Deva stared at her – shocked. Did she mean she had to put her hand in there and risk the deadly cobra? Was this Urak's way of punishing her for her thoughts of stealing the clothes and the jewels? 'I wouldn't really have taken them,' she told herself desperately. 'I was tempted – but I wouldn't have taken them. If she's so clever, surely she knows this.'

Urak was moving closer and closer.

'They are yours,' she purred. 'Just reach in and take them out.'

Deva tried to step aside, but suddenly the woman clamped her strong skeletal-thin fingers on to her arm and pushed her slightly towards the chest. Deva was caught between her terror of Urak and her terror of the cobra.

'I – I don't really... I really don't...' she stammered.

'They are yours,' hissed Urak. 'Take them!'

White and trembling, Deva put her hand into the chest and touched a necklace of gold and turquoise. Every muscle in her body was tensed to leap aside as soon as the cobra struck. Urak suddenly gave her another push and she almost fell into the chest. She screamed as she and the cobra came face to face – and then she realised it was as inanimate as the rest of the treasure. Its yellow eyes were made of topaz.

Shamefaced, Deva looked up and met Urak's eyes. The old woman threw back her head and laughed. The sound echoed and re-echoed through the cavern, and rumbled into the mountainside through all the corridors and fissures and caverns of the elaborate cave system that was the owl-woman's dark domain.

Chapter 9

The seeking spell

When Khu-ren arrived back at the Temple of the Sun he was alone. Among his colleagues, the enthusiasm of his welcome was muted by the knowledge that his daughter was in danger, but the ordinary people who lived in the valley of the Kennet river and on the hills that surrounded the great Temple at Haylken knew nothing of his anxiety. They came flocking along the ridgeway to greet him and surrounded him with singing and rejoicing, hundreds of them struggling to get close enough to touch him; others holding back, content just to catch a glimpse of him. He walked calmly through the throng, a tall, impressive man, giving strength by his very presence to the weak and wavering.

Kyra was waiting on the wooden causeway that led into the Temple. Behind her, at a discreet distance, the priests were gathered, waiting in absolute silence. Her hair, spun gold, was brushed out to surround her like a shining aura. Her soft and flowing robes, like her eyes, were the colour of the summer' sky. On her bare arms gleamed the bracelets he had given her and at her throat the necklace of faience beads that had been a sign of love between them long before they dared acknowledge it.

Khu-ren stood still when he saw her. The crowds fell back, leaving the two facing each other, poised on silence like a falling feather on an upward draught of air.

The two lovers looked at each other and longed to race into each other's arms... but the two priests kept a dignified distance, each bending the knee to the other in formal and ritualised greeting. Both made the sign of the sacred circle with the full hand, palms outward, in the air before them.

At last Khu-ren stepped forward and joined her. The watching crowd saw him by her side, she turning to lead him into the Temple, he taking her arm lightly as he walked beside her. Many sighed with pleasure, knowing the love between the two, glad they were reunited. Some had noticed that the Lady Kyra's expression had been sad and abstracted lately and they were sure it was because she was missing her handsome Egyptian. Now they were together, the crowd gradually dispersed, content that the Temple's full complement of priest-guardians was present and nothing evil could therefore befall them.

When Khu-ren had greeted his colleagues, they turned their attention to the most urgent matter in hand: the question of Deva and Urak.

Everyone in the Temple had been questioned about Urak before Khu-ren's arrival, and many of the older priests could tell tales that made Kyra shiver with fear for her daughter. The younger ones had not heard of her. It seemed she had either been inactive for years or had turned her attention to matters that did not come the way of the Temple. Most of those who'd heard of her had thought that she was dead. No one knew where she was to be found, or anything that would help them find her.

Kyra had suggested that as soon as Khu-ren was with them they should join together in a seeking-ritual. This they now prepared to do.

They joined hands in a circle within the inner circle, surrounding the central Sacred Three Stones, and, stepping rhythmically to the drums beaten by the novices, began to chant the ancient words of the calling spell.

They called on all beings to help them in their search: the trees that reached up to the sky yet were rooted in the earth; the rivers that flowed so swiftly from mountain to ocean; the birds that ranged the currents of the air. All natural beings they asked. And then they called on the beings that could not be seen – those entities that slip between the nearest and most familiar worlds, and the great shining beings from beyond the realms humankind can visualise and understand.

Gradually the heartbeats of all present matched the slow and rhythmic drumbeats of the ritual. The clutter of agitation and disorderly thought fell away, and each and every one in tune with each and every other reached out beyond themselves so that they experienced the steady vision of the tree; the continuously adapting vision of the river, the far, wide vision of the bird, and the timeless vision of the other realms.

Some chose to seek north; some south; some east; some west.

But in all the seeking they did not find Urak. For the owl-woman knew that they were hunting her and had hidden as only a high adept can hide.

* * * *

Deva watched as Urak drew an elaborate system of geometric figures on the flat platform of black stone that lay in front of the entrance to the cave.

One moment the old woman had been telling her enthusiastically about all the things she could teach her if she would stay, and the next she turned her head and seemed to be listening to a sound Deva couldn't hear. Suddenly she rushed to the entrance, calling as she did so to Boggoron, who was lurking outside somewhere, to come into the cave.

'At once!' she snapped, as he did not respond as quickly as she would have liked.

As though he knew what that tone of voice meant and was terrified of it, he shot into the cave like a startled cat and squatted down on his haunches at the entrance to the fissure at the back, facing Deva and fixing his slightly bulbous eyes unblinkingly on her.

Bewildered at the suddenness with which things had started happening, and curious as to what it was all about, Deva tried to forget his stare and looked back to where Urak was now marking the stone with a large piece of chalk. She went a little nearer the better to see, but Urak, without looking round, snarled at her to stay where she was.

As soon as she had covered the platform with what were, to Deva, incomprehensible signs, the sorceress sat cross-legged before them, shut her eyes and began to sway and hum. At first the motion of her body was almost imperceptible, the sound not unlike a bumblebee, but gradually the movement became more marked and the humming louder. Deva watched, fascinated, as the woman, apparently rooted to the ground, swayed in wider and wider circles until she was almost bent double and moving so fast it was incredible to think she, at her age, could do it. Deva was not sure that as a young woman she could have mastered half that speed and agility. All the while she was swaying, the hum was growing louder and louder. Her mouth opened and formed the strangest shapes, and from it flowed the eeriest sounds Deva had ever heard. Deeper and deeper the notes sounded, more and more resonant. They began to vibrate everything in the cave. The earthenware cup on the small wooden table began to jump about and before long it crashed to the floor.

Deva put her hands to her ears as the sound roared around her and the pain in her eardrums became unbearable – but still she heard it. Through the fissure, violent echoes were beginning to return from their journey through the hollow mountain and, magnified, join the fresh sounds Urak was still uttering. It began to seem as though a hundred different voices were raised in that un-human, monstrous, all-pervading chant.

From notes so low they seemed to come from the centre of the earth, Urak gradually worked her way up the scale until a lark flying as high as only a lark can, dropped from the sky as though hit by an invisible arrow.

Weeping, Deva was convinced she would die if the deadly sounds did not cease. And at last Urak graded the sounds down as skilfully as she had raised them until there was silence.

But the silence Deva had longed for seemed now as terrifying as the cacophony. The contrast was so great it left her like an empty shell, lying on the floor of the cave, all feeling and memory gone.

At the great Temple the circle broke up, defeated. Their search had failed. Their seeking spell had not found its mark. One by one the weary priests dispersed; the drummers removed their drums. But at a sign from Khu-ren Kyra stayed behind, and together they paced the perimeter of the Temple. They were tired but not as tired as their fellow priests. Apart from the extra training they had had as Lords of the Sun, their anxiety for their daughter would not let them rest.

They discussed the seeking-ritual and its failure, trying to discover why it had not worked. They were both hoping it was something lacking in the ritual itself, for if the failure was the work of Urak, they knew they were up against an enemy more formidable than any they had encountered before. To block such a calling spell, she must have known it was being cast – which meant that even now she might be observing them in their moment of discouragement and despair. Simultaneously the thought struck them and they paused, looking into each other's eyes in some alarm.

'We could build our own barrier,' Kyra suggested.

Khu-ren frowned. They could, but then they would be isolated – and no messages could be received or sent. They would be cut off from the rest of the world, from the people it was their responsibility to help.

Kyra tried again. 'If she is observing us, perhaps we could follow the beam of her attention back to its source.'

'*If* she is observing us,' Khu-ren muttered. And then he looked up as though he had thought of something. 'What did you notice when we were calling – just before we knew that we had failed?'

Kyra tried to think back. She was tired and worried, and none of her faculties seemed to be functioning properly.

'Your ears?' he prompted. 'Did you notice anything about your ears?'

'They tingled a bit and then... and then they hurt.'

'Precisely. She was using sound to block us.'

'Does that mean she is near?' Kyra asked, suddenly hopeful. The vibrations sound made did not travel as far or fast as the minute but powerful vibrations of thought. It was a relatively crude medium.

'Not necessarily. Someone like her would be able to project such powerful sound, so concentrated and condensed, in a way that its vibrations would reach much, much further than one would expect. We did not hear it. We felt it.'

'Could she have "heard" our chanting?'

'Maybe, if she was not too far away – but we were not concentrating on projecting sound, we were projecting thought. She might have picked up our attention. If that is so, we must have reached her even if only for an instant. Try and remember. There must be something that between us we can piece together.'

Kyra tried hard, but could remember nothing that seemed relevant.

'I'm tired, my love,' she said. 'Perhaps if I had a moment's sleep?' She had often found that a moment or two of sleep would clear her mind of all irrelevancies and throw up an unexpected gift of insight. She could feel that strange, sudden drowsiness coming on now as her body prepared to 'step aside' to give her inner consciousness its head. Khu-ren reached out his arms and, still upright, she lay against his breast, supported totally against his standing body. She sighed. 'If only the circumstances were different,' she thought, and then she went limp in his arms. Gently he rocked her; gently he kissed her golden hair. But even before the bird that had taken flight from one side of the Temple alighted on one of the Stones at the other side, she had woken, refreshed and bright-eyed. She had remembered a fleeting glimpse of two figures.

'In a cave...' she murmured, trying to bring the vision into focus with her waking mind and give a description of it to Khu-ren. 'A sort of cave... the one a skeleton... no – almost a skeleton... the other...' And here she cried out because it was Deva.

Khu-ren questioned her sharply, trying to draw out a description of the cave. How big was it? What shape? What colour and texture was the rock? These clues might give him some idea of the location. From her description it was clear that the rock was limestone. Was the sun shining directly into the cave?

He questioned on and on until Kyra had told him everything she could.

'You made the contact,' Khu-ren said, and she winced at the sharp edge to his voice. 'And you lost it because you let your emotions get in the way.'

It was true. This was not the first time such a link had been broken because she couldn't control her feelings. It was probably the passionate strength of her love in the first place that had enabled her to reach Deva, where Khu-ren's more controlled and sober affection had not. But if only she had not given way like that, if only she had kept control, held her attention steady – behaved like a great priest and initiate of the Mysteries rather than as an ordinary woman with a child... She shuddered at the memory of that skeletal figure and at the hints Guiron had given her so many years before about the power of this woman.

How had Urak escaped the attention of the Temple all this time? Khu-ren had told her of the village he had visited where an entire family had been destroyed by curse, and of the name that had come unbidden into Farla's mind. Had she been active all these years, but so cunning she had escaped detection even by the Guardians of the Stones? Or had she lain dormant – biding her time until she knew she could win? Was that why she had taken Deva – as a hostage? If this was so, she feared Khu-ren would say they had to put the good of the community above the survival of their daughter. Her lips tightened. What would she do then? What would she do! This time her prayer was addressed beyond the ancestor helpers and the spirit beings who roamed the shining realms, to the Being beyond all beings, the Nameless One beyond all names. 'Let it not come to that! Let me not be faced with that decision!' she cried.

But she could not tell if her prayer was heard, Khu-ren touched her arm.

'If we are to outwit this woman, we must have Guiron's help. He has had dealings with her in the past and got the better of her. He will know her weaknesses.'

She sighed. Guiron had been gone many years and in all that time had had no contact with them. He was old when he left. How could they assume that he was still alive, travelling as he did among strangers, sometimes in alien and barbarous lands?

Khu-ren knew it would be difficult. He called a young student and sent him off with messages for all those he needed for the task.

Guiron's contact with Urak had been when he was a young man, not long after he became High Priest of the Temple of the Sun at Haylken. She had almost defeated him – but not quite. High adept as he was, it had taken him some time to realise that the Temple was under threat from her. His predecessor had warned him about her, but as one year went by and then another, and he saw or heard nothing of her, he had put his wariness aside. Even when he first began to notice something was wrong, he did not immediately think of her.

One morning Guiron woke more weary than he had been when he went to bed. He thought nothing of it. But when day after day he found that he was so tired he could hardly carry out his duties he began to wonder what the matter was. 'Why is everyone so slow?' he thought irritably. For some reason everyone he encountered seemed to be working at half speed. Even young priests were dragging their feet as they walked, as though they were either very old or half asleep. Things that should have been done were not done, and he found himself spending his time cajoling and criticising. One by one the people seemed to be ailing. There were no specific illnesses – only lassitude, headaches and nausea. To make the great Temple operate even at the most mundane level became a difficult and exhausting matter.

Only when he tried to use the energy of the Stones to communicate with his fellow priests across the country did he realise finally that something was very wrong – and that he could not look for the explanation, as he had been doing, among the vagaries of the ordinary world... diet, overwork, the weather... The Stones themselves were 'tired' and the energy that was always there in such abundance for the priests to tap had disappeared.

They called on the Shining Spirits; they called on the Nameless One who spoke with the voice of the Sun; but more and more it became clear that someone or something was blocking the flow and draining the energy of both the people and the Temple itself. Once he was sure of this, he used all his skills to find out who or what it was. And then it was he came upon Urak.

She was living in one of the houses in the valley of the Kennet. To her neighbours she was no more than a rather eccentric elderly woman, keeping very much to herself: a stranger who had moved into the community that year, but who had rejected all friendly invitations to take part in community activities and festivals. Guiron's attention was drawn to her on the day he decided to involve everyone in the immediate vicinity of the Temple in a concerted and desperate attempt to call on the Lords of the Sun for help. Every man, woman and child was there, joining in the serpent dance... only the stranger who kept herself to herself was not present.

The drumming started. The movement started. It took longer, much longer than usual for the people to fall into the necessary rhythm – but they did so eventually and Guiron, alone among the three Tall Stones of the central sanctuary, concentrated all his strength and attention on reaching out to the Lords of the Sun. For a moment it looked as though he had succeeded. A shadowy figure appeared... but it was against one of the other Sacred Three and not against the ring of Stones that surrounded them. It was not where the Lords of the Sun were supposed to appear.

Sweat was running down Guiron's face with the effort to hold the energy level high enough for the Lords of the Sun to manifest. Who was this intruder? The figure was so dim he could not at first make it out. Why were none of the others appearing? The serpent dance was well under way now... but no one was appearing around the inner circle. For a moment the mist-like wraith beside him took on a clearer form and he found himself looking into the staring round eyes of an owl... a woman with an owl's head! He was so shocked he lost concentration and the vision was gone immediately. He felt all the energy drain out of him, his eyes rolled upwards and he pitched forward in a dead faint. At the same time the continuous line of the serpent dance broke. Some people fainted... others stood about, dazed and confused. The drummers lost impetus and gave up the attempt to keep the beat going.

It was not permitted that anyone not of the highest rank should enter the inner sanctum, so Guiron had to lie unaided until he recovered consciousness. When he did so he dismissed everyone and insisted on remaining in the Temple alone.

Night was coming on. The night of the hunting-owl. He had been challenged and he knew he would never leave the Temple alive unless he defeated his formidable adversary.

It was full moon and he had cancelled the full moon ceremonies.

When she came he wanted to be alone with her.

When she came he *was* alone with her.

He saw her first, her wings dark against the huge silver disc of the rising moon. He heard her haunting, eerie cry. He knew it was she who had found a way to drain the energy of the people and the Temple. He knew she wanted his position, his power – but she wanted it for her own glory and not for the good of the land itself.

Carefully he prepared himself for the duel. He cleared his mind. He took his stand. Quietly and meticulously he constructed a web of light, a net of glimmering ethereal gold.

She swooped. He flung it into the air and with a cry she swerved and avoided its clinging folds. It shimmered for a moment in the night sky and then fell to earth and dissolved instantly like snowflakes on hot embers.

She banked and wheeled. She swooped again.

This time his arms were above his head, his palms outwards, inscribing the sacred circle time and again so fast there was no way through the invisible barrier of swirling rings.

Once more she flew away unharmed, and soared to the high realms of the sky to bide her time for the next attack.

This third time would be the final test. They both knew it. He was exhausted. He knew he could not hold out much longer. What was there in his armoury that would save him now? He squatted on the ground, trying to rest, trying to gather his strength. He looked up fearfully at the sky. Usually it seemed to him to be an immense dome, blue by day and black by night. From somewhere up there the owl-woman was watching him. But now, suddenly, it didn't seem like a dome at all. He was looking into a vast hole that had no end. He was terrified. He buried his head in his arms, curled into a ball like a hedgehog. He never wanted to look at the sky again. How could he have lived all this time with that gaping void above his head!

This time when she swooped she saw him as a small and helpless creature. No vole or field mouse could have been more vulnerable. She screamed with triumph as she plunged.

But even as he felt the rush of air from her wings, his confidence in meaning and purpose returned... the secret spark of the spirit that never dies sprang into flame and he uncoiled like a spring. The sky no longer appeared to him as an endless negative – but as a rich and fertile region of infinite possibility. He leapt... he soared... he was a giant! He strode across the universe and in his hand he caught the tiny fluttering creature that had attacked the Temple and all it stood for. He held her by her wings and laughed into her eyes. He knew he could have killed her there and then – but he knew he had no right.

'I banish you,' he cried. 'I exile you to the mountains – to the rock prison of the high peaks – until you no longer seek to drain the life-blood of the world... until you help and not hinder the great design...'

And so it was that she had been confined to the mountains ever since, brooding on the wrong he had done her, denied the power that she claimed was rightfully hers.

Now, Guiron and Userhet, the two old men, retired from active life, stood on the bank of the great river Nile and watched the sun set over the island forested with palm trees that lay between the living and the dead; between the ephemeral city and the mountains of eternity; between the east and the west bank. There was a solemn hush in the city as everyone stopped what he or she was doing. Where they could, they made their way to the river bank; where they could not, they climbed to the roofs of their houses. Behind the walls of the temples the priests prepared for the evening rituals. Everyone was turned towards the west. Even the young children playing in the dirt of the streets were slapped by elders and made to face the west before they were taken off to bed. This was the moment of uncertainty; the moment of awed and breathless waiting; the moment when, they had been taught, Nut, the sky, swallowed the tired sun, Ra-Atum, and took him into her arched and starry body. There he would pass through the twelve portals of the night one by one, until the dawn, when he was born again with splendour and rejoicing.

Guiron heard Userhet murmuring and tried to catch the words.

'You who encompass all in your arms... beautiful beyond imagining. Lady of Stars – hold us against the night...'

This was the same sky that arched above his distant home; this was the same sun that set over the gently curving chalk hills that surrounded his own Temple.

'Before all things. I was. I am. The great He-She. Ra-Harakti at dawn; Khephri at noon; Atum in the evening. What name I am named is of no matter. I speak the word of the secretly named, whose name is not known.'

The evening rituals performed by Kyra and Khu-ren far, far over the great green ocean were not very different. How he longed to be part of them again! He might learn much from this alien land, but he would never feel at home in it.

Above them the birds were winging back to their nests. A flight of heron – their long necks stretched, their grey wings heavily beating the air – passed over, leaving the fish safe for one more night. Then came the strings of ibis, the birds sacred to Djeheuty, to Thoth. Guiron bowed to the ground at their passing, for Djeheuty, the ibis head, was close to his own heart: the protector of scribes and scholars, the wise, the peacemaker, the honourable judge... Behind them came the arcing and darting swallows that never settled on the earth but were the harbingers of Shu, the divine breath... dancing with delight high in the clear air. Guiron knew them from the summer evenings at home. Above them, close to Nut herself, the falcon soared, his brown wings blazing momentarily fire-red, caught by a ray from the dying sun. Horus, the one who soars above all others, the one who sees further than all others, the fierce and beautiful one, the strong, stern, powerful one, Son of Osiris who is the Lord of the Duat, the giver of resurrection, the renewer of life...

Then even the birds were still as the mighty golden disc sank lower. Guiron was tempted in a moment of despair to step out on to the brilliant path the great Being had laid on the water. What if he reached out, calling, drowning in the golden light? What if he began the journey through the underworld this very night? What if he followed Ra through the twelve portals of transformation? What if he was born again in the dawn with Ra-Harakti... a different and a better person?

Userhet touched his arm and held him firm. 'We do not choose the time,' he whispered. 'We do not know the secrets of the ever-living Ba.'

Guiron sighed. 'No, we do not know the secrets of the ever-living spirit,' he thought. 'We do not know the time of its coming forth, nor the time of its going in. But we know it is the quick of our being, the essence that is never lost no matter how many times we change our form – that which was with the "secretly named" at the beginning and will be at the end...'

The sun had gone but it had left the vast cloudless sky the colour of fire.

For a long, long time the two old men stood and watched the awesome sight. The beauty of it brought tears to their eyes and they thought how privileged they were to have taken form on this earth and to be able to witness such a scene.

'If this is the cipher of the god,' thought Guiron, 'what must the reality be like?' He knew he was not ready to face that reality yet, and Userhet knew that Guiron would no longer think of taking his own life.

The molten gold of the river and the scarlet after-glow of the sky slowly, slowly faded. In the breathless silence of the last moments of light, Guiron thought he heard his name called. He looked around quickly. The palm trees and tamarisk beside the water were still as stone. No breath of air stirred. The people who had watched the god depart had themselves departed. He and Userhet were alone beside the river.

'Did you hear my name called?' he asked his friend.

'No,' said Userhet.

Guiron shrugged. It was cooler now. They would go home to bed.

Chapter 10

Urak's treasure

Deva's confusion of memory after the extraordinary chanting suited Urak very well and she encouraged her in every way to wander in the no man's land between identities. She dressed her in Egyptian clothes and fed her food that would have been strange to the contemporary Deva, but familiar to the young woman who had lived long ago in the valley of the Nile. Boggoron chuckled as he served it, knowing that it was not what it seemed. He enjoyed having the company of the young woman: enjoyed watching Urak prepare to shape and mould her as she had shaped and moulded so many others. Every time a likely candidate for training came to the mountain, either of their own volition, like Wardyke, or drawn there by Urak's cunning and enchantments, Urak believed she had found a worthy heir and companion. But each time something had gone wrong. Either the acolyte proved disappointing as material to work upon and had to be discarded – and that usually meant destroyed, a victim of Urak's vindictive spells – or he or she grew so restive under Urak's domination that they tried to escape, and in doing so met the same fate as the others. Wardyke was one of the few whom Urak respected and sent out into the world with her blessing when she saw that she could no longer hold him. Boggoron had seen how she suffered to let him go – but he had promised that he would one day be back.

How would it be with Deva? Boggoron stared at the young girl incessantly – much to her annoyance. She was much more beautiful than any who had ever come their way before and she had a quality about her that awed even Boggoron. It was a quality of regality, of command. She would never pass unnoticed in a crowd; when she wanted something she would get it, and when she spoke she would be listened to. If Urak could win her loyalty she would have a powerful vehicle indeed to do her work for her in the world after she herself was dead.

One day Deva asked what lay beyond the fissure she could see at the back of the cave and out of which she sometimes saw Boggoron and Urak emerging. Urak commanded Boggoron at once to take her through it and to satisfy her curiosity.

Deva caught the eagerness with which Boggoron rushed to do the old woman's bidding. Hastily she said she would rather wait for a time when Urak herself could take her. But Urak insisted that Boggoron and she should go at once. She lifted up a cloak of black lamb's wool and carefully arranged it around the young woman's bare shoulders, fastening it at the throat with a huge silver brooch.

'You'll find it cold so deep in the earth,' she said. 'Take this – and take a lamp.' She thrust a small earthenware oil lamp into her hand, while Boggoron lit a flaming torch from the hearth fire.

'Won't you come with us?' pleaded Deva one more time. She dreaded being alone with Boggoron.

'Not this time, my dear.' She smiled as though she knew very well what was in the girl's mind. 'Boggoron will not touch you. You'll be quite safe.'

Boggoron looked up at his mistress sharply, as though annoyed that this taboo had been put upon him. She had not always been so protective of her female acolytes. But perhaps, he thought, it was because this one was not properly broken in yet. Perhaps it was because this one was special in some way. He knew the way Urak was looking at him meant that he would be in serious trouble if he laid a finger on the girl.

Only a little comforted, Deva folded her cloak closely around herself and followed Boggoron into the hollow mountain. For a long time they walked down a rough and sloping corridor, a continuation of the natural fissure that had its mouth in Urak's antechamber. The air became cold and clammy and smelled stale. Deva was more and more convinced she had made a mistake in showing an interest in the place and wished she was back in the comparative comfort of the outer cave.

'I'd like to go back,' Deva called, as the slope of the corridor became steeper and the gap between the rough side walls narrower.

'No. No!' he said, grinning and nodding ghoulishly – a small figure contained in a monstrous shadow. 'Soon. Soon. You'll see.' And he beckoned her eagerly on.

She stood for a moment, irresolute, wondering if she could bear to return alone with only the one very small lamp. She had seen several dark passages leading off the main fissure. Boggoron had ignored them and it seemed as though they had been going straight, but what if she could not find her way back? She did not feel like being left alone, even if the alternative was to be with Boggoron.

'Take me back at once!' she commanded sternly.

'Soon. Soon,' he chuckled, and scampered on ahead even faster than before.

'He'll pay for this!' she thought angrily – but she followed him, as he knew she would.

Not long after this they came to a sharp bend in the corridor. It looked to Deva as though the natural formation of rock had here been altered artificially. Perhaps the fissure had come to an end and the rock had been excavated further by pick and axe. She touched the walls and was astonished that such hard rock could have been worked in such cramped conditions. Boggoron told her to wait where she was and not move – and then he disappeared. She waited in the narrow corridor for what seemed a long time, angry and fearful.

And then she heard his call.

She worked her way round the sharp bend gingerly and was suddenly in open space. She gasped. A huge cavern stretched before her, hung with shimmering curtains of crystal. Columns of crystal rose from the floor; threads of crystal hung from the ceiling. Everywhere torches flared. Boggoron was standing on a huge flat table of crystal in the middle of a vast hall, waving his torch above his head. When he saw her astonishment he began to dance and crow with delight.

Although the cavern was a natural feature of the mountain, Urak had transformed it into a place of unbelievable luxury. Couches with silken cushions were arranged around side tables which were dressed with tall silver goblets filled with wine and baskets brimming with every kind of exotic food. Deva forgot her annoyance and rushed from table to table, crying out at what she saw. Boggoron led her away to the side alcoves around the main cavern, and there she saw gold and jewels, ornaments and clothes that made her head spin. She had never dreamed that there could be such things in the world: statues carved from every kind of stone... braziers holding lamps so intricately and exquisitely worked in different kinds of metal, yet as fine as lace, that the light shining from them threw up on the walls amazing shadows of dancing figures and flying birds, of strange beasts and flowers never seen in Britain...

She didn't know where to begin to explore all the riches and wonders, and Boggoron seemed more intent on dazzling her with the profusion than allowing her to examine any of the marvels too closely. As soon as she tried to pick up one object, he hurried her away to gaze at another.

'Where did this all come from?' she gasped.

Boggoron clapped his hands. 'All Urak's!' he cried. 'All Urak's!'

'But where from? I've not seen such things ever...'

'These are nothing. Baubles! Rubbish! If you stay with Urak you will have more than this. Much more. Much, much more! Better. Much better!'

'Have?' murmured Deva. Her eyes were glowing as she looked around her. The chest of treasures in Urak's outer cave was nothing to what she saw now. She reached out to take a necklace of rubies, but Boggoron snatched it away from her.

'Don't touch. Mustn't touch. We'll go back to Urak now.'

'But...' She tried to seize the necklace back from him but he flung it out of her reach.

'You'll have these things... more... more... don't worry. But not now. Not now. Urak will give – not Boggoron...'

She hated leaving such delights. He had to take her by the arm and physically drag her back to the corridor, while she pulled and struggled.

'Just a little more time. We don't have to go back yet,' she pleaded.

'Urak is waiting. Urak will be angry if we don't go now.'

'But we've only just arrived!'

'Urak said show – not touch. Come!' He tugged at her arm and his strength and determination prevailed. They were back in the narrow fissure and Boggoron was hurrying her along.

'Perhaps I'll stay with Urak a little longer,' Deva thought. 'It would be good to have some of these things to show when I go home. I'll have gifts for everyone that will make them fairly gasp.' She visualised herself in some of the clothes she had seen and she visualised her home with some of the couches, the statues, the lamps... Their lives would be transformed. They would have to have bigger houses, of course – more rooms, space to put them all in. But would Urak let her take them? She began to worry about the problem of how to gain possession of them and how to transport them home. 'Some of them' – and here she stopped in her tracks as a thought struck her – 'some of them are too big to bring down this corridor.' She could not understand how they could have gone down it in the first place to reach the cavern. 'There must be another entrance,' she thought, 'and if I find it I'll be able to use it and look at everything as much as I like without being dependent on Boggoron.'

'Hurry!' Boggoron urged. 'Hurry. Urak angry.'

Urak angry. Boggoron was obviously terrified of Urak. Why should she be angry? It was on her insistence that Boggoron had shown her the cavern. Deva frowned. What did Urak want with her? Why had she wanted her to see the cavern full of wonders? 'Just showing off her possessions I suppose,' Deva thought. 'Trying to impress. Well, she has succeeded.' Deva thought hard about what she had seen and knew that she would never be happy again unless she herself possessed everything in that cavern. 'She's old,' she mused. 'She's very old. She won't live much longer and if I stay – as her heir – everything will be mine.'

Her thoughts broke off suddenly as she caught Urak's amused and watchful eye on her. She had been so preoccupied with her plans she had not noticed that they were already back in the antechamber and that Urak was waiting for them.

'You like my baubles?' the old woman said slyly.

Deva flushed, wondering if she knew what she had been thinking. She wished now she had been priest-trained so that she could block her thoughts off at will from people like Urak. There had been times when she pleaded for the chance to be a priest, seeing what skills they had, what power... but her mother always fobbed her off, saying that she was not ready for it yet... that this or that had to happen first before they could even put her name forward to the High Council as a prospective student. Kyra never said outright that Deva could not train or that she was not suitable, even when Deva wept and pleaded and demanded, reminding her that as the daughter of the two great Lords of the Sun she must surely be a natural for the training. Kyra always stalled for time, knowing that the whim would pass and that a while later the last thing on earth her daughter would want to be would be a priest.

The girl nodded eagerly. Yes, she liked Urak's 'baubles'.

'Come, my dear,' the old woman said. 'Eat. I have prepared a meal.'

'Perhaps she didn't see what I was thinking,' Deva thought with relief. There was no sign of the anger with which Boggoron had threatened her. 'In fact,' Deva decided, 'I don't know why Boggoron is so frightened of her. She's a very nice old lady.'

She allowed herself to be led to a table laden with the most delicious and varied food she had ever seen. The sight of it made her realise just how hungry she was and she was soon wolfing it down. She never once wondered how strange it was that Urak could get such things so high in these remote and rocky mountains.

Chapter 11

The island

Farla was thirsty and she had walked a long way. The village she was approaching looked deserted; the inhabitants, no doubt, were out in the fields at this time of day. She saw that a little stream ran below the group of houses with a well-worn path leading to it. She followed this and knelt down on a flat rock by the water's edge, cupping her hands to drink. Suddenly she felt that she was being observed and she looked up. On the other side of the stream a strange figure was standing: an old woman with fine white hair spread around her like a cloak and a hat in the shape of an owl's head. Farla called out at once, greeting her and asking her where the rest of the villagers had gone. The woman didn't reply, but just stood staring at her. Farla stooped to drink from the stream. When she looked up, the woman had gone. She was not sorry. The woman made her uneasy.

At that moment Farla heard a child call out from one of the houses and a mother reply. She went at once to the place and made her presence known. Soon she was being given food and drink and being made to feel welcome. Over the meal, when the rest of the villagers had returned, she mentioned the old lady, wondering to which family she belonged. No one claimed her – indeed no one seemed to know her at all. Intrigued, Farla described her in detail. Still no one seemed to know who she was.

Was the old woman Urak?

Farla shivered.

That night Farla encountered Urak – or the 'fetch' of Urak – in what she thought was a dream. Curled up in a sleeping rug beside the smouldering hearth fire in one of the village houses, she found herself drifting through darkness, her limbs as weightless as smoke. After a time she began to make out dim shapes, and gradually they took on form. She found she was floating through a forest of giant trees, their trunks so tall they appeared to disappear into the sky. She saw no leaves, no branches, no ferns or lichen growing. This was a dead forest, stark and bare... She began to feel very alone and very afraid. She found she had no control over her body in the normal way – if body she had. She wished the forest was more like a living forest with leaves and twigs and ferns and birds, and as the wish crossed her mind the whole place became as vibrant as a living forest.

And then – just when she had accepted that everything she could see was produced by her own thoughts, and was less afraid – she heard a sound that she knew she had not conjured: the sound of an owl uttering its low, melancholy call... that eerie, haunting sound that filled the hearts of so many warm-blooded creatures with terror.

Farla jerked awake in the close and smoky darkness of the village house. The forest was gone, but the sound of the hooting was still there. She crept to the doorway and stepped out to get some fresh air – relieved to see that there were stars and a moon shining down on the village and on the cluster of thatched wooden houses. But her skin was prickling with premonition and she was sure something evil was surely about to happen.

Suddenly from above she heard the sound of beating wings and, looking up, she saw that the light from the moon and the stars was blotted out by the wingspread of a gigantic hunting-owl. She put her arms over her head, convinced for the moment that she was as small as a mouse and about to be torn to pieces.

But nothing happened.

The shadow of the wings passed over her. She was unharmed. She looked up. The moon and the stars shone down once again. The bird was gone. The night was silent.

After a while, cautiously, she moved. She no longer felt as if she were being watched. But damage had been done, though she was not yet aware of it. Her old doubts, her old fears and uncertainties were back – and worse than before.

'I'd never be capable of being a priest,' she told herself. 'I lose control far too easily. Besides, who wants to be a priest! It's far too bound about with rules. We are trained for power and never allowed to use it except on the authority of the High Priest.' She found she was beginning to resent the role of Khu-ren and Kyra in her life and could not understand why she had thought to go back and take up her training again. 'I'd be much happier if they left me alone,' she thought. 'Let Khu-ren find his daughter himself! Why should I risk my life?'

She turned to go back into the house – and then she changed her mind. She decided to leave now before she needed to give any explanation for her decision. 'I am nothing to these people,' she thought. 'They gave me hospitality because that is the expected thing – but they'll not be sorry to see that the stranger has gone. I'll not contact Khu-ren – neither will I seek Urak and Deva. I'll go my own way. It's about time I did what *I* want to do for a change!' She set off to the west along the road that led out of the village, having no idea that the independence she thought she was so fiercely asserting was in fact nothing of the kind.

Farla walked through the rain as though she did not notice it. She had come a long way since her decision not to return to her family or friends, nor to undertake the task set for her by Khu-ren. The tops of the highest hills were under mist, blending with the sky, the trunks of the trees wet and black, the leaves weighted down with drops. Her clothes were in fact soaked through. The only concession she had made to the rain was to take her shoes off and to walk barefoot through the long grass, mud squelching up through her toes. She felt remarkably free.

She had no idea where she was going or what she intended to do with her life. She knew only that she was not going back.

It was in this mood she came upon a lake; a slate-grey sheet of water, pockmarked with rain drops, the shoreline indistinct with reeds. She was contemplating which way to go around it, when she noticed a coracle of hide and reed tethered to an old log half in and half out of the water. She found herself stepping into the muddy water without thinking, and climbing into the boat. She cast off and half in a dream began to paddle. Once on the water the lake seemed much larger than it had before and what had appeared to be the opposite shore turned out to be only an island.

The rain eased off at last and the water became as still as a mirror. Farla leant over the side and peered at her reflection. Her hair hung in long damp strings, her face was pale and tired. This she expected. But what she did not expect was that there were other faces reflected beside hers... a crowd of them, young and old, male and female, eagerly pressing in around her to peer over her shoulder. Startled, she looked around her – but she could see no one. Quickly she looked back at the surface of the water, but the rain had started again and the surface was disturbed. There were now no reflections. Uneasily she paddled on until her craft struck the pebbled shore of the island.

Still in this strange mood of allowing things to happen rather than making choices, she stepped ashore. There were the burnt out remains of a few wooden houses not far from the beach, and prominent at the top of a small rise that could scarcely be called a hill were a few standing Stones. Farla looked at them more closely. She could see even from where she was that the temple circle was not complete, and when she drew nearer she saw that it had been a circle of twelve fairly small Stones, now with only seven still standing. Brambles had grown over the sacred space and everywhere there was the impression of neglect and desertion. A flock of screeching birds flew up, scolding, as though warning her off their territory.

'This could have been a casualty of the Na-Groth war,' she mused. But she thought all the circles had been restored since then. It had been an enormous task but one which the great Temple at Haylken had been most careful to carry out. Without the network of small local circles and the priests who served them, communities across the vast forested land would be seriously cut off. The great Temple of the Sun was the heart of a powerful and caring system. To be isolated in spirit from its strength and its wisdom was to be alone and helpless in a dark and dangerous world.

Farla wondered about the faces she had seen reflected in the lake. Were they the souls of those who had met some ghastly death upon this island, unprotected because their temple circle had not been restored after the war – or had some disaster struck in spite of the circle and its priest? She knew that, powerful as the priests were as Guardians of the Tall Stones and their people, there were other powers and other forces at work in the world, continually threatening and challenging.

She touched the tallest Stone and felt nothing – no answering tingle. The Stones were dead, the circuit broken. A chill wind had started up and her wet clothes were heavy and uncomfortable. She began to shiver uncontrollably. There was something unclean about this island – and she turned in panic from the Stones and ran down the slope to where she had left the boat. The grey water of the lake was breaking on the shore like the ocean. The coracle was gone! She could see it far out on the water, lurching awkwardly, pushed hither and thither by the choppy waves... every moment sinking lower and lower until at last it vanished beneath the surface. She was trapped!

She retreated from the beach, where the wind was at its fiercest, and tried to find some shelter. She was cold and hungry and frightened and ended up curled like a babe in the womb against a rock that broke the main force of the blast. She wept. She had no idea how to swim and, even if she had, it would have been a strong swimmer indeed who could have made headway on those wild waters. She was convinced that some malevolent force was at work and that if she fell asleep some evil would befall her.

The clouds became heavier and lower. A driving rain came

beating in on the wind. The reeds and trees on the far mainland shore disappeared and then the mist came rolling in across the lake, cutting her off completely from the outside world. Was this how it had started – with the isolation of the people on the island? She buried her head in her arms and felt like screaming. The mist was now so thick around her she could see nothing, but at least the wind had dropped.

When she first heard the whispering she thought it was the sound of the rain among the leaves, but then she began to make out words and she knew she was surrounded by figures. She peered at them but could hardly distinguish any individuals through the thick mist... yet the whispering seemed near, some of it close against her ear. At first she was terrified; then she decided to try and find out what was being said and by whom. She lifted her head and listened. There were as many voices as there had been faces reflected beside hers in the lake. All were talking at once and it was difficult to distinguish anything that was being said. The overall impression was of great urgency. They were clamouring to explain something to her and they were pleading for her help.

'Stop! Stop!' she cried, putting her hands over her ears – though that did nothing to make the voices less persistent. 'I can't understand if you all talk at once. I want to listen. I want to understand. One of you speak. One of you tell me what you are all trying to say.'

As suddenly as the voices had started, they all ceased. Then there was a tense and frightened silence as though they had heard something she had not and were staying absolutely quiet hoping not to be noticed. There was no sound that she could hear – only the lapping of the water at the grey lake edge.

She stood up. 'Speak!' she called again. 'I'll listen. What is it you are trying to tell me?' The mist was much less dense now and she had the impression of shadowy figures crowded just beyond her range of vision. But as she took a step forward and reached out her arms to them, she heard another sound – the flapping of wings. A huge owl blundered out of a nearby tree and lurched across the island, winging its way low across the water. She shivered – remembering her dream. When she looked round again, the figures were gone. Had they seen or heard the presence of the owl before she had? Was that what they feared?

She began to think of the mission Khu-ren had given her. She had turned her back on it, but had it turned its back on her? The ghost-owl was not going to let her go after all. Had she been led to this place deliberately? Was she trapped here until she agreed to cooperate? Farla had set off to find her independence – but there didn't seem to be such a thing. In whatever direction she turned she seemed to end up facing the same way.

The work of the great Temple had to continue as usual. Kyra and Khu-ren knew that too much depended on them to concentrate only on their daughter. Every priest of every far-flung circle had been alerted that a dark force, bearing the name Urak, was active again and asked if they knew anything that might help them find her. Meanwhile the teaching and training went on day by day, the purification ceremonies, the ceremonies of sunrise and sunset, moonrise and moonset, the discussions between the High Council and the representatives of the Spear-lords and the Elders of individual communities about their particular problems, the ceremonies to initiate new priests, the testing and the judging, the greeting of new students and the sending off of those who had completed their training successfully.

The Temple knew that the training of people first to know themselves and then the nature of the realms in which they lived was a slow and often a painful process. No stage of it could be hurried... no step omitted. The students committed themselves to years of training and they expected equal commitment from their mentors. The whole depended on the strength and integrity of the parts – so each student was given close attention while at the Temple and no one left with the final mark on his or her forehead, the sign that the deepest and most awesome Mysteries had been experienced, unless capable and worthy of using that experience responsibly.

It was during the time when Kyra and Khu-ren would rather have been seeking Deva and Urak that the day arrived for one of the most important ceremonies of the Temple year: the placing of the mark of the true priest on their foreheads – the mark invisible to the ordinary man, but apparent to all those who themselves had earned one – and the sending off of the initiates to take up their positions in their designated temples.

As Kyra began to robe for the great day she thought about Wardyke. He had come to their village in the far north when she was a child, and, apparently invested with the power of a priest, had all but destroyed their quiet and harmonious community. It was only when it came to their attention that Guiron, the High Priest, had refused him this final mark upon his forehead that they knew just who they were dealing with. His dark shadow was near now – she could feel it. She would not be surprised if he had something to do with Deva's abduction. But she must not think too much about Deva today. There must be no mistakes in this ceremony.

First she robed in white, then in blue. Over this, covering her completely except for her eyes, she drew the black robes. Against her skin, as always, she had the simple blue faience necklace that Khu-ren had given her as his first token of love. Over the white robe she wore a wide necklet of beaten gold, engraved with spirals of moving energy and circles of still containment. Over the blue lay a necklace of silver with rock-crystal beads interspersed with amethyst. The black had no adornment. On her arms were torcs of gold. At her shoulder, holding the folds of her robes in place, pins of gold. But on the outer garment they were so cleverly placed that no gleam showed through the cloth.

Khu-ren would have yellow against his skin – yellow for the sun – and a breastplate of gold studded with gems carefully chosen for their associations. Clear rock-crystal for clarity of purpose and thought. Amethyst for spiritual enlightenment. Emerald for nature-wisdom. Garnet for blood-wisdom: the wisdom of deep emotional commitment without possessiveness. Topaz for joy. Rainbow-tourmaline for health and harmony. Banded-agate for Time and sapphire for eternity. Over this would be a veil of white, and then a heavy robe of purple studded around the shoulders with gold pins; and over the whole, like her, a robe of sombre black. Other priests would be in red and green – but in each case overlaid with black.

The procession outward from the sanctuary, down the long, sinuous avenue of Tall Stones that led to the heart of the great Temple of the Sun, was a solemn and somewhat frightening one. Only drums sounded and they with a slow and sombre beat. The three candidates, clad in simple white shifts, walked behind, heads bowed, and, if they were anything like Kyra had been when her time came, terrified and filled with self-doubt. Once this final mark was in place there was no turning back. They were committed to the selfless service of their community and they were tied by vow to the mysterious God whose fearsome eye blazed down on them, the only part of the great Un-Named and Un-Known physically revealed, the disc of light too bright to look upon, the mighty source of energy that had given shape and meaning to their temples.

The crowd watched without a sound. This part of the ceremony represented the Void: that which would Be if there were no life force... no consciousness of any kind... The return procession, if all went well, would be very different. There would be no sign of black: all would be colourful and joyful... the music from pipe and drum fast and celebrational. The new priests would be cheered and congratulated at every step. The Void had ceased to be, and the priests were masters of Becoming.

As Kyra took her place in the inner circle beside her husband, she began to feel very strange – as though her spirit was drifting off somewhere, without her permission. She tried to pull herself together. This was not part of the ceremony. This was not as it should be. She thought she might be at last picking up the presence of Deva, but in fact it was Farla she saw: Farla struggling to climb a hill towards some standing Stones and being held back by a crowd of screaming people. On wings of shimmering invisible gold she flew to see what she could do to help.

Khu-ren looked hard at the figure of Kyra. There was something wrong. The ceremony at the Temple of the Sun was about to commence. From all over the world the Lords of the Sun would be coming to lend their blessing. The call had gone out, the materialisations were already starting. He felt momentarily at a loss. But if Kyra's soul-self was somewhere else, he knew there must be a good reason for it. The real work of the Temple, after all, was not only to give people positive help in making the difficult spiral journey upward through the realms – but to protect them, to heal them and to rescue them from immediate danger in *this* realm...

Farla stretched up her arms and howled as a wolf might howl.

'I'm tired,' her heart was crying. 'I want a simple life. No decisions. No difficult tasks on which the lives of others hang!'

From stretching as high as she could, Farla sank down and curled up on the ground in the foetal position. 'If only I could start again,' she muttered. 'If only...' Who were these people who crowded round her? What were they expecting of her? Who was this fearsome ghost-owl? 'Why me? Why? Why *me*?' Surely the mighty priests of the Sun could deal with one witch-woman however skilled. Why did they need her – failed and inadequate, hopelessly confused, imperfect in every way...? Tears came from behind her closed lids and streamed down her cheeks and, like rain after drought, they brought a kind of relief. She fell asleep sucking her thumb like a very small infant.

Kyra's soul-self found her, muddy, dishevelled, lying on the ground, clinging to sleep as a small child clings to a favourite blanket or toy. Around her a crowd of shadowy figures was gathered, swaying and keening, watching her for any sign of waking. The image of Kyra stood before them in a cloak of golden feathers, shining hair floating in the air... When they saw her they turned instantly towards her, their voices clamouring for her attention as they had for Farla's. Kyra listened.

Since before anyone could remember the island had been considered a holy place. It was almost a perfect circle – set at the centre of a circular lake. A hermit had lived on the island and pilgrims had rowed across the lake to lay their troubles at his feet. He was gentle and strong and wise. Miracles happened in his presence. People were healed. People who came in despair left in hope.

Kyra glanced across at Farla, whose tears were still wet on her cheeks, and back to the anxious, tormented faces of the ghost-crowd surrounding her.

'What went wrong?'

It seemed the old hermit had died and another came in his place who had neither the wisdom nor the compassion of the old one. It became the custom to bring offerings because the new hermit would not listen to them if they did not bring something of value. Families worked hard to raise what he demanded. It became the custom to ask for success and power and vengeance instead of for understanding, for healing and for wisdom.

More and more people came flocking to the island, noisy, demanding, greedy... The ancient place was no longer peaceful and beautiful. The constant tramp of feet around the circle loosened the foundations of the Stones and some of them fell down. Others were dragged down and thrown into the lake to make room for more and more people to crowd in on the so-called 'holy man' who could grant almost everybody's wishes.

One day the man left.

The people came and found the island deserted.

They could not believe it. They had grown so accustomed to turning to him for everything – for every problem, for every desire – that they had forgotten how to work things out for themselves. The 'holy man' would tell them what to do. The 'holy man' would provide for them. They loved him. They worshipped him.

He would come back, they believed, and they waited and waited. So terrified were they that they would miss his arrival back, many of them would not even leave the island for an instant to get food. The winter came. Storms lashed the lake into a fury. Those who were left, huddled together and died. And still they waited, clinging to the place. Waiting to be told what to do. Waiting to be given everything they wanted.

No one came to the island any more. It was said to be an evil place... haunted by lost souls.

Farla had come and they, the waiting ones, had crowded round her eagerly, wanting to know if she had news of their lost provider: wanting to know if she had come to take his place. She had not understood.

Kyra stooped over Farla and covered her tenderly with her golden feathered cloak. She whispered into her dream what she, in soul-form, had learned.

'I want to leave,' Farla's dream-shadow whimpered, 'but I have no boat.'

'Build one,' whispered Kyra. 'Don't wait like these people for it to be provided. Build one. But before you leave this island you must cleanse it... you must free its people... you must show them how to help themselves.'

She touched Farla's forehead as Khu-ren at that moment was touching hers. Farla stirred in her sleep and straightened out. She no longer lay like an infant in the mother's womb, but like a young woman resting on a grassy bank.

When Farla opened her eyes at last, it was a clear night. She was cold, but no longer weary or afraid.

Kyra's soul-self returned to the Temple of the Sun before the last of the Lords of the Sun had materialised. Her body suddenly stiffened, her head lifted, the flow of vital energy restored. Khu-ren smiled at her in relief.

Each Stone of the sacred inner circle was now occupied by a figure. The candidates and the two local Lords of the Sun were there in the flesh; the others were in astral form, visitors from across the world, from China, from Egypt, from the high Himalayas and the low-lying rainforests of the tropics... Quilla was there from Crete, the Island of the Bulls. She was no longer as young as she had been when Kyra first encountered her – the fearless acrobat who danced with bulls – but her body was still lithe and firm and her carriage proud. She might teach more than she performed these days but the crowds still roared with admiration at her appearance among the athletes in the great bull-yard, and she had lost nothing of her physical, mental and spiritual agility. Kyra and Khu-ren allowed themselves a quiet moment of pleasure in their greeting before they returned to the severe concentration of the task in hand.

All the visitors were in black, too. The first chant was delivered as a solemn invocation. As it neared its end the robes were shed and all were found to be clad in shades of blue and purple. Even the light surrounding them seemed tinged with blue. The mood of the chant lifted. It started rich and deep, but soon the words began to soar. At last, high and fine, one thin note vibrated in the crystal-clear air. All other sounds ceased. Only this one persisted. Now all were in white or gold. The new young priests blinked as a blinding light dazzled their eyes. The pain was at first almost too much to bear – but when their eyes adjusted enough to see what was before them they gasped and fell down on their knees.

From the forehead of each Lord of the Sun a narrow beam of brilliant light projected, and where they met in the centre of the circle was a vision so magnificent none of them would ever be able to forget it, nor would they ever be able to describe it. It was as though they saw in one marvellous moment the beauty and the harmony of the whole of existence represented in a kind of living, vibrant tree of spheres that was growing at once upward and downward, rooted in the realms so high no one had ever penetrated their mysteries, its trunk bearing branches shimmering with life, reaching down till they brushed the earth... While simultaneously it was rooted in the earth and reaching up through all the green and growing spheres to the high realms of the Shining Spirits and beyond. There was a continual flow through trunk and branch and leaf and root. No part was left without change and movement and meaning – from the gigantic stars on their majestic and ordered courses to the minutest component of the tiniest and most primitive cell. Each had its place and purpose. Each contributed and was essential to the whole.

They felt faint with awe. This was theirs. All this was theirs! They as human beings had the gift of consciousness beyond all others in the earth-realm to glimpse such reality. They could no longer justify any action they might take that did not take this vision into account.

They bowed their heads, and as they did so they felt the High Priest's finger upon their forehead and knew that the vision had been sealed in; it was now their responsibility to guide and protect and teach those who had not experienced it.

Farla started to build a raft. There was no axe on the island, but there were plenty of branches she found she could prise loose from the trees, or logs that had broken off in storms or fallen off with age. To bind them she used a combination of narrow strips torn from her leather jerkin and wands of reed.

'This might not keep afloat,' she thought. 'If only I could swim.'

Well, swimming could be learned. She had seen people swim and she would see if she could do the same. As the days went by she practised in the shallow waters at the eastern edge of the island.

The rain had died down and the fog had lifted. The days were clear and warm now; the nights still cold – but at least her clothes were dry.

She began to feel almost happy and wondered if she really wanted to leave. She did not forget the clamouring voices and the anxious faces: neither did she forget the ghost-owl – but she was so busy she forgot to worry about them.

She had not realised that she could be so resourceful. She was finding things to eat, although she had thought she would certainly starve to death. She built herself a reed lean-to against a flat-faced rock and began to feel quite comfortable at night. She even thought of resuscitating the small temple on the hill. But how could she lift the Stones?

And then she remembered what Kyra had once told her. The Stones were not the temple. They were there to help concentrate the energy, but the energy they concentrated came from the minds of the people who worked there, the earth, the sky, the wind, the water under the ground... everything below and above and around... It might be difficult to resuscitate a temple when one could not complete the circle of Stones – but it should not be impossible. If she were in tune with all the natural forces and with the invisible realms as well, she herself should be a strong channel for the kind of energy she needed to clear the island of malevolent influences and bring it to life again.

She began to use the chants she had learned at the Temple of the Sun. Chants that were designed to clear away evil influences – doors of sound through which she could pass to the deeper levels of consciousness.

Then she changed the rhythm and walked round and round the circle, weaving in and out of the Stones that were still standing – and in and out around the places where the others had once stood. She visualised the missing Stones in their original places clearly. It was not difficult, because she soon found that some part of the energy the Stones had once transmitted lingered on. The pattern of the sacred circle was still complete – it just needed a little more skill and effort to make use of it.

She began to weave an invisible web around the Stones... linking the ones standing and the energy impressions of the ones missing. As the web grew tighter and stronger she began to feel she had a working circle once more and, as she finally stood inside it, she knew what she had to do.

She called the people she had seen – the anxious, crowding faces, her lost and frightened people. The sky was cloudless. The air still. Her voice rang out across the mirror-waters, skimmed the surface like a kingfisher, bright and fast and clear.

She knew she could not leave this island as she had found it – a broken, sad and haunted place. Urak might have led her here to keep her from finding her – but the weave of the great design was complex and one person's motive sometimes served another's purpose. She had lost not only her way but her Self. Now she thought she saw how she could regain both. She thought she understood why the people on the island clung there so forlornly.

Was it a dream, or had Kyra really visited her and explained it all?

She called them to her and they came flocking... pale wraiths not unlike the white moon seen in the blue sky on a sunny day. Almost invisible...

She could understand what they were saying now and she could answer them.

She drew them to the edges of the circle. She did not let them enter – for no one not trained for it could withstand the power of such a circle when the energies were charged up to their peak. She had never felt so confident. It was as though everything in her life had come together for this moment. Her training at the Temple... the restlessness that had driven her away... her coming to this place... everything had been intended. She knew she was in the right place at the right time and good would come of it.

She lifted her arms, and the words that came from her at that moment were more persuasive, more lucid and more powerful than any she had ever spoken. She drew the lost people to her and sent them away prepared to rejoin the journey through the realms they had abandoned.

Some tried to ask her which way to go and what to do, but she refused to tell them. 'Each journey is different... unique to the person who makes it. I'm prepared to start you off by showing you some of the ways to consult the wisdom of your own eternal spirit – but I cannot tell you what only It can tell you, and the ways I show you may not be the right ones for you. Those too you will ultimately have to find for yourselves.'

She taught them as Kyra had taught her, to go into the Silence.

Suddenly, one morning, Farla woke and knew that she was free of any feelings of guilt or regret for the past. She knew who she was and what she wanted to do, and those old doubts about herself were no longer standing in her way. She was not as noble as some people, and she was not as ignoble as others. She was herself, and as such she would live her life. She knew also that the ghost-people had left at last – ready to seek their own way through the realms, confident that they too had a contribution to make.

She had decided she wanted to return to the Temple and finish her training, but she still felt slightly uneasy that she had not carried out Khu-ren's suggestion for finding Urak. She knew the transformation she herself had undergone in transforming the island had made her ineligible as bait for Urak. The sorceress needed a weak, disgruntled and vacillating person – not Farla as she now was, at the height of her confidence. But should she help in finding Deva in some other way? She could not decide.

Part of the Temple training had been to learn how to follow the clues in what they called 'the secret trail'. In finding one's way across a landscape one followed the obvious indications laid down by other travellers... the paths, the notched trees, the stepping stones across streams, the sighting lines from one marking stone to another, from one hill cairn to another... The 'secret trail' they spoke about at the Temple was more subtle. It was not part of the physical landscape. The clues to follow came from the depths of the subconscious or the heights of the super-conscious – where one was in touch with far more than seemed to exist in normal waking life.

Farla had always particularly loved butterflies. She saw one now, a rich and vibrant red, sunning its wings on a yellow dandelion. On its wings were two blue circles with white centres. She read this cipher without any hesitation. The dandelion flower was the sun. The winged being was her soul. The two circles, the circle of the Temple and the circle of herself. Red is for death. The butterfly is the symbol of resurrection and transformation.

Blue is for Spirit. The butterfly is the symbol of resurrection and transformation. White is for the pure light from the Nameless One. The butterfly folded its wings briefly, so that the two circles were placed over each other. She was one with the Temple: its task was her task.

The butterfly lifted from the flower and flew off towards the west. To the west she was to go, to find Deva: not to the Temple, which lay to the east. Her decision was made. She was glad – for in the depths of her heart she knew that this was what she had to do.

Chapter 12

Deva

Deva sat at the feet of Urak and learned everything she was prepared to teach. The woman was tireless, working late into the night, determined that by the time she died Deva would know enough and be loyal enough to her to disrupt, if not utterly destroy, the hated Temple of the Sun for ever.

Deva was fascinated by what Urak was teaching her. This was better than the Temple training. Leaps and strides were made in no time at all. None of those wearisome preparatory exercises, that tedious training in self-discipline and those long, long years of steady, step by step advance. Here there was no talk of 'essential groundwork' or 'responsibility'. Each day she could try something new whether she had grasped the previous day's lesson or not. Why did the Temple make such an issue of being 'ready' for knowledge? She was ready for anything Urak cared to tell her.

Yet sometimes she had a twinge of regret that she no longer saw her family and friends, and once or twice she thought she glimpsed her mother out of the corner of her eye – but the image disappeared as soon as she turned her head.

Urak missed nothing, and whenever she saw the slightest hesitation on Deva's part – the merest shadow of nostalgia for her home – she took her 'travelling' to whet her appetite and to show her what could be hers if she followed this new path single mindedly.

She dressed Deva carefully in pleated white muslin, draping the cloth so that every curve and promontory of the girl's beautiful body showed. She hung a broad jewelled necklet around her of lotus blossom in turquoise and lapiz lazuli, seashell and gold. She plaited her thick black hair with threads of gold until it framed her face like an Egyptian wig. Then she bound a golden snake upon her upper arm and placed a gold signet ring on her finger. At first Deva was disappointed that the ring had no jewel – but then she noticed that it was engraved all over with signs and figures, so small that she could scarcely make them out.

'What do they mean?' she asked, curiously holding up her hand to the light.

Urak smiled. 'Look at them carefully,' she said softly. 'It is important you decipher them.'

Deva frowned and squinted at the minute grooves and lines.

'Look closely,' Urak urged. 'Of what does this first figure remind you?'

'An animal,' Deva replied after a moment's puzzlement.

'What kind of an animal?'

'No, it is a woman – but with a lion's head.'

'Sekhmet,' sighed Urak with satisfaction.

Deva did not consciously hear her, but the name was now in her head. The girl stared at signs and slowly, gradually, began to figure out one after the other. She found herself murmuring as though she were reading what was written on the ring aloud.

'Sekhmet... lion lady... lady of blood and storm... In one hand you hold the riches of life... in the other...' Deva peered closer and closer into the glimmering gold seeking out the tiny hieroglyphs, but she could not make out the last one. She looked up, thinking to ask Urak for help. But Urak was nowhere in sight. The cave, the mountainside, the tree-clad valley of her homeland were all gone.

She was standing in a chamber very different from any she had experienced in her present life, though memories of the distant past made it seem familiar. The whitewashed walls were covered with painting in vibrant and varied colours – trees so lifelike she could imagine she heard birds rustling in their branches, flowers twining and blooming in every possible space between them – but all very different from the verdant green woods of Britain. She looked around the chamber itself. A shaft of burning white light came in through the window and shone on a chair so richly embossed in gold it fairly dazzled her. Beyond this was a chest finely worked in gold and glowing enamels, with scenes of wild fowl – nesting in the reeds on one of the panels, and taking to the sky in another, their wings creating a marvellous pattern that gave the impression of freedom and yet order...

Deva began to move about the room, delighted with everything she saw. Across a bed of ebony and gold rich fabrics were draped. She saw an ivory headrest carved like a sleeping gazelle, a table of cedarwood inlaid with precious stones, small, exquisitely carved boxes, and files and bottles of alabaster and chalcedony containing aromatic unguents and oils. A mirror lay on the table beside an ostrich feather fan. Deva peered at her own reflection in its polished copper surface and could not help smiling. She could not remember

Urak touching her face, but the face that looked back at her with such satisfaction was carefully painted with black lines of kohl to emphasise the graceful slant to her eyes, green shadow on her lids, red on her lips... She had never looked so beautiful. She found boxes of jewels and ran them through her fingers: golden chains of lotus flowers, earrings of bees, huge pectorals of linked gems carved to represent the Egyptian gods and their symbols, golden cobra coronets.

The door was slightly ajar and she was tempted to explore further and yet unwilling to leave the treasure of this chamber. She stood at the entrance, hesitating a moment – and then stepped forward. The second chamber was very different, reminiscent of an underwater scene painted in cool turquoise and blue and aquamarine. Fishes and water-lilies decorated the walls, and in the centre was a sunken rectangular area – a pool with steps leading down to it and jars of perfume ranged along the sides.

Deva looked anxiously around to see if she were still alone, and when she found that she was, she tiptoed to the pool and knelt down beside it. She stirred the water with her hand and the light shafting through slits near the ceiling cast a flickering, dancing net of golden light over the surface. How she would love to plunge in! How she would love to live in such surroundings!

Suddenly she felt herself slipping forward, and as her face touched the surface, the water seemed to break up into a million brilliant droplets of light. When her vision cleared she found herself back on Urak's rocky and inhospitable mountainside.

'No!' she screamed. 'No. No. No! I don't want to come back. I don't want this life! I want that one! Let me go back. Let me go back!'

She found herself kneeling in front of Urak and pulling at her clothes – the cloth so coarse and ugly compared to what she had just seen.

Urak looked at her sternly.

'Be still, child. Be still. You shall have all that – but not yet. Not yet, I say!'

But Deva would not be comforted. She lay on the ground and beat her fists like an angry child. 'I want it. I want it now!'

Urak gave a sign to Boggoron and he, always waiting and watching, slid forward and seized Deva by her shoulders. Grinning, he shook her violently backwards and forwards and sideways, until she almost choked on her sobs. At last she gave in and was silent. On another sign from Urak, Boggoron let her fall to the ground. There she lay whimpering for some time, thinking about what she had seen and comparing it with the simple things that had contented her until now.

Urak and Boggoron withdrew and left her to her thoughts.

Gradually, exhausted, she fell asleep.

One day Deva pleaded with Urak to teach her manifestation-magic. She had never known anyone at the Temple perform this. Indeed, she could not recall ever having heard of it before. She knew Kyra and the rest could summon up illusion when necessary. But manifesting was not illusion. Illusion worked by releasing or implanting thoughts and images in the minds of others. Urak could actually materialise something before Deva's eyes and Deva could touch it and use it.

'It is not making something out of nothing,' Urak explained. 'It is changing the whole inner structure of something by the power of the vibrations emanating from the mind. A healer sometimes uses these vibrations when he disperses a tumour or unblocks an artery. I use them when I want something that is not available to me on this mountain.' She picked up an ordinary pebble and within moments held a jewelled ring in its place. She smiled at Deva's delighted response, and handed it over to her to examine.

'But I have seen you do it out of the air – starting off with *nothing*.'

'You said "out of the air", child. That is not nothing.'

'I can't understand why the Temple priests don't do it. They could provide all sorts of comforts for themselves and for their people.'

'Perhaps they don't want their people too comfortable.'

'Why not?'

Urak shrugged. 'Who knows what devious reasons they might have,' she said scornfully.

'Can I learn how to do it?'

'Certainly.'

'Now?' Deva thought how she would return to the Temple and bring this skill with her. Perhaps the priests did not know how to do manifestation-magic. Perhaps this was a skill only Urak had. How impressed they would be if she could teach them something they did not know... if she could make their lives easier and more comfortable. She thought of the presents she could give Isar. Gya's eyes would open wide at what she could do! She began to see herself as a great power in the Temple community. No, she would not teach them how to do it themselves – not until she was very old, like Urak. She would keep the secret so that they always had to come to her when they wanted something. She would provide – and as provider she would control.

Urak smiled. How eager the child was! What a pleasure to teach.

'Not quite yet,' she said fondly. 'In a little while. There are a few things you need to know first.'

In everything Urak did she took the short-cut. There was no concern for the future, no protective caution about the long-term effect on others. Why should she care? She was only interested in herself. Even her desire for an heir was a combination of not wanting to be forgotten and of vengeance. Guiron had removed her from the mainstream of the world's affairs, banished her to these uninhabited mountains – well, her physical form was held in this isolated spot by his spells, but over the years she had learned how to slip out of the body and, in the form of her totem, the hunting ghost-owl, she had ranged far and wide, making her mark where she could, showing that she was not entirely crippled by his edict. Even with his restraining bonds, she still had power to punish and wound and avenge if she wished.

Wardyke suggesting Deva as her heir and Boggoron managing to capture her were the greatest strokes of good fortune she had ever had. What a wonderful vengeance both for Wardyke and for herself: to turn the daughter of the High Priest into the very thing Guiron would most hate!

The Temple had put no restraints on Deva. She could go about as she pleased. In fact, she would be welcomed with great joy when she returned to the Temple community. What mischief she could do before they even realised what she was capable of – and how Khuren and Kyra would suffer when they did! So Urak would avenge herself on Guiron – for she was sure he would hear of it; and Wardyke would avenge himself on both Guiron and Kyra, for limiting the use of his psychic powers.

Urak had learned much of what she knew from renegade priests who had studied at the Temple but left without the sacred mark. But her own ingenuity had carried her far beyond any of them and, if she had not been banished by Guiron, she was sure she would have become famous in the land as a powerful alternative – and eventually replaced the Temple altogether. She was particularly interested in manifestation-magic, for this was something the Temple was particularly against. One of her acolytes reported what Guiron had said when he requested instruction in it.

'Life doesn't consist of what you have,' he had said angrily, 'but of what you are. The danger of believing that possessing things is a measure of life is incalculable. We're on a long and difficult journey through the realms of being, and if we are held back by the weight of our possessions and the business of accumulating them, caring for them, protecting them and so on – we'll be that much slower in reaching our goal, maybe even that much more unlikely ever to reach it.'

She knew, by the eagerness with which her students asked her for the instruction in this branch of magic, that this would be the way she could most easily undermine the authority of the Temple. It had taken her many, many long years of trial and error to reach the degree of mastery in the forbidden skill she now had, and she guarded it jealously. In training her apprentices she always held this back to the last, and, because none had stayed the full course with her, none had so far mastered it. This time, with Deva, she would make sure that her student learned from her all there was to learn. She sensed it was her last chance to destroy the hated Temple.

More and more Urak encouraged Deva to 'travel' – and when she did she almost always chose her ancient homeland, Kemet, the Black Land, Egypt. There was something comforting in the way Egypt had changed so little since her day. The peasants still tilled the fields after the inundation had subsided in the same way; still drew water from the river or the canals with counter-weight and goat-skin bucket hinged on a palm-trunk cross-beam; still built their homes with sun-dried mud-brick. The desert still ran beside the river like a hungry hound. Only the temples and the palaces were even grander than she remembered – and it was to these that she invariably gravitated.

One day she found herself standing in the cool shadow among a gigantic colonnade. Where the shadow did not fall the sunlight blazed down with an extraordinary ferocity. Through the dry, clear air she heard chanting – but whether it was from far away or from nearby she could not tell. At first she thought the words were in some outlandish foreign language, but then she began to understand them. She started to walk along the colonnade, keeping as much to the shadow as she could. The walls, out of reach of the searing sunlight, glowed with rich-coloured paintings of boats and birds, of trees and flowers, of stately gods and goddesses. In the corners vultures with every feather picked out in scarlet, blue and gold, spread their wings wide, their claws clutching the ring of eternity. Horus, the falcon head, with penetrating eye glared down at her. Hathor, the Lady of the Sycamores, the mother of us all, passed by.

Deva could see that the building was not completed. A group of workmen were gathered around the foreman or architect, listening to his instructions. He was a thickset man with a vigorous and energetic way of waving his arms as he talked, and a dark and dynamic eye.

He knew what he wanted – and he wanted it passionately. He would not allow his dream to be spoiled by shoddy workmanship.

Deva noticed two old men sitting in the shade of an avenue of trees beside a pool. The garden was laid out but did not give the impression that it was fully established yet. One tree was still in a pot and lying on its side, wilting in the heat. Deva was amazed that such verdant green, so many flowers and bees and so much plashing water, were here in this baking desert place. The inner chambers of the building seemed to have been cut into the bedrock of an enormous yellowish-red cliff face, the columns arranged by the architect to echo the cracks and fissures of the natural stone. Men were trundling huge statues on rollers up stone ramps to terraces higher than the one on which she found herself. The building and its garden lay between the yellow desert, bone dry and parched, and the silent, towering cliffs.

Deva left the shadows and walked across the hot sand to where the green of the garden began. The frankincense trees rustled with birds, fishes leapt and played in the pools, some wax-white flower was giving off a heady scent.

As she approached the two old men, one looked up and saw her. The shock on his face was unmistakable. He scrambled to his feet and stared at her as though he had seen a ghost. The other was deep in thought, staring at the ground, and was unaware of her presence. She wondered at the recognition in the old man's eyes and it crossed her mind that he seemed familiar to her too... but – as suddenly as it had come – the whole scene vanished and she was back with Urak in the fastness of the British mountains.

Userhet came out of his reverie to find Guiron standing beside the bench in the garden of Hatshepsut's half-finished mortuary temple, shaking uncontrollably.

'What is it, my friend? What is the matter?' he asked anxiously, taking his companion gently by the arm and trying to bring him back on to the bench.

'Did you see her?'

'Who?'

'The young woman.'

'Where?'

'There!' Guiron pointed frantically. The figure had appeared out of nowhere, walking under the trees, shimmering as the ghost-lady of the lake had shimmered, beautiful as she had been – his friend's wife, Anhai... the woman who had killed herself rather than be disloyal to her husband. 'The same!' his heart cried. 'The same... the same... the same...' Would he never be free of her? Surely now in his old age he would not still be haunted by her?

'I saw no one,' Userhet said, shaking his head. And then he looked into Guiron's troubled face more closely. 'Tell me, friend,' he said solicitously. 'What is it?'

'Nothing,' muttered Guiron. 'Nothing at all. An old memory. An old dream.'

Userhet pressed him no further. He too had old memories, old dreams, he would rather keep private.

Chapter 13

Lark challenges Wardyke

One early dawn, after a night of tossing and turning, Lark made a decision. She climbed the slope of the hill that led to the great burial mound overlooking the valley where her village lay. The grass that covered it was wet and the lower part of her skirt was soaked through by the time she stood upon its brow. The entrance to the mound was sealed by a gigantic slab of stone. There was a small courtyard where the mortuary priest performed his ceremonies, but this was now deserted. The ritual of the ancestors usually took place at night, when the living felt themselves much closer to the dead.

Wardyke's urn of ashes was here, and although Lark hoped that his fell soul was long gone from this place, she knew that the remains of a person, or something that had been very close to him for a long time in life, might sometimes be used for recall.

Desperation had driven her to such measures. She knew she should enlist the help of the mortuary priest and do the thing properly at the appropriate time of the night... but from what she had heard of Wardyke she would not want to encounter him at night. No, the dawn was the best time – when all light and growing things, hope and love and joy were at their strongest. Let his shade come now when it could do the least harm. She had to find out about her child – one way or another.

Isar had kept Wardyke's dagger. It was well wrapped up and hidden, but for some reason Isar did not want to part with it. She had respected his wishes, knowing that Wardyke was his natural father in this lifetime, and, for a brief period when he was a child, he had been close to him. She knew also that whatever later grief had come their way, in the ancient days they had been close friends. She hated having it in the house, especially now, when she feared that Wardyke was beginning to overshadow them again. It seemed to her that it might well be acting like a lodestone to draw him back.

This day she had it with her. She trembled at the risk she was taking, and she had told no one of her intentions. Not even Fern. She felt she had to do this thing alone.

Lark stepped into the small forecourt before the entrance slab and composed herself for her task. She had no clear idea of how she was going to achieve what she wanted to achieve – or even if it was possible. She stood facing the centre of the long corridor she knew was behind the sealing stone. She pictured the small chambers that led off on either side, the dark little cells containing the bones and relics of the ancient chieftains and their families, and, more recently, the Spear-lords and those whom they wished to honour.

She tried to picture Wardyke – not as ash, but as he was in life, as she had heard him described. He had been a huge man, tall and powerful, his eyes fierce and dark, his nose aquiline. She shuddered as she carefully unwrapped his dagger and the cold bronze touched her hand. It had a wooden haft, held by hundreds of tiny gold pins driven well in, their heads flush with the wood and outlining a series of neat geometric patterns. She turned it round with trembling hands and held the wood. Was it her imagination, or did the gold pinheads burn her hands? It was as if the dagger was humming with an energy of its own, impatient to be used.

Lark laid it hastily down on the paved ground directly in front of the centre of the sealing slab – the point towards the darkness within the mound. She knew that any object used for many years by a single person would soak up a great deal of that person's energy... and something that had belonged to such a man as Wardyke – priest turned sorcerer, evil genius and ruthless dominator of his fellow men – was best left alone. But she had already gone too far. She found she could not take her eyes off the dagger; she could not lift her hand from it. She was crouching beside it, stroking it as though it were a living thing. The tingling in her fingers that had seemed so frightening when she had first touched it now seemed pleasant. The years away from the light had done nothing to dim the shine on its polished surface or blunt the sharpness of the blade. Wardyke's energy was still in it... she could feel it and she was fascinated by it. Would it be such a terrible thing if her child had Wardyke's power and strength? She loved Isar, but sometimes, just sometimes she wished he would be more assertive, more determined. He never saw through Deva's wiles: never refused a plea for help no matter how difficult it was for him to honour. For the first time in her life she began to admire the callous, the selfish, the cruel.

Then suddenly she realised what was happening – Wardyke was there, his thoughts insinuating these things into her mind. She jerked her hand away from the dagger and retreated, leaning her back against the outer wall of the forecourt. It seemed to her the dagger was glowing with a faint but sickly light. She was horrified at what she had done. What could she have been thinking of to play such a dangerous game? How naive her original plan now seemed. She had thought she would call upon his shade to manifest, and then she would ask him face to face if he was intending to incarnate through her. Was she crazy? Would such a man give her a straight answer? And what if he were to say 'yes'?

She could feel the forecourt filled with the presence of evil. She could see nothing but the glowing dagger – but she knew she was not alone.

The cry Lark gave barely reached the peasants who had begun to work the fields beside the hill. One looked up, thinking that he heard something, but decided it was the cry of the crow that was flying over at that moment.

She could not let this ghastly force use the body of her child for its fell schemes! She rushed forward and seized the dagger by the haft, raised it and, with a sudden rush of desperate energy, aimed it at her own breast.

'Wardyke – I know I cannot destroy you... but I can seal this one door against you!'

With all her strength she plunged the dagger towards her flesh.

The sun had risen while she was in the forecourt and at this precise moment the first rays penetrated a crack in the eastern wall. A thin shaft of light caught the polished bronze and gold of the dagger and for a moment distracted and dazzled her. The infinitesimal hesitation caused her aim to deflect, and though she fell to the ground in agony as the metal pierced her, it missed her heart and she did not die – but this she did not yet realise.

It seemed to her she was falling into darkness and could hear screaming all round her. At first she thought she was surrounded by shrieking demons, but gradually she grasped that the voices were one voice and that it was her own, echoing against the walls of darkness all around her. Her own voice, and yet she had no voice! She was inside the burial mound – of that she was sure. 'I am dead,' she thought. 'Wardyke cannot use me now.' But Wardyke was before her, looming large in his cloak of ashes, his eyes boring into hers.

'Woman, why are you here? Why do you meddle in matters that are beyond you?'

She tried to conquer her fear of him – to regain the courage she had set off with in the morning and meet his eyes.

'You will never enter my body now. You will never use me to be reborn!'

It seemed to her Wardyke didn't seem to understand what she was saying at first, and when he did – he started to laugh. The whole dark place shook with his laughter, hollow and mocking, cold and cruel.

'Woman, what I want I will have – and nothing you can do will stop me.'

'I have stopped you,' she said boldly. 'I am dead. I cannot bear a child.'

He looked at her with scornful amusement.

'Dead, are you?' he sneered – and then his image faded and the darkness surrounding her seemed to grow less.

'No!' she whispered, beginning to realise at last that she had failed.

She opened her eyes and looked into the eyes of Kyra.

How could this be?

She was lying on a couch in Kyra's chamber and healing leaves were bound upon her breast.

Kyra leaned forward and kissed her gently on the forehead, and smoothed her hair with gentle hands.

'Don't move, my child... the wound is deep... lie still.'

Kyra held her by the shoulders to keep her still while the young woman gradually came to terms with what was happening. Lark remembered the flash of light. Had that been help from the Shining Beings – or one more cruel trick played by Wardyke? She was alive, yet she still did not know the answer to the question that most troubled her. She looked into Kyra's eyes and put her hand on her womb.

Kyra thought she understood, and smiled. 'Your child is safe.' And then, seeing the mixture of relief and disappointment on Lark's face, she sat down beside her and took her hands in her own.

'Listen to me, my child,' she said softly. 'When you are well we will talk about your child. I blame myself for what has happened to you. I have been too busy with my own problems to help you with yours. You did a foolish and a dangerous thing... but you are safe now.'

Lark turned her face to the wall and Kyra could see the tears welling out from beneath her lids. She stroked her hair.

'Sleep now. Rest. When your wound has healed we will talk.'

Lark did not want to sleep. She wanted to hear what Kyra had to say about her child... about Wardyke... about Isar... but the great priest's hands were firm and gentle as they massaged her head, and within moments Lark was fast asleep and the process of healing and renewal had started.

Much later, when she had rested and was calmer, she heard what had happened. It seemed that the mortuary priest had felt an urge to go to the burial mound that morning, although he would normally not have done so at that time. There he had found Lark lying on the paving stones of the forecourt, a dagger stuck between her ribs, slowly bleeding to death. He had pulled the knife out and bound the wound as best he could to stop the bleeding, before carrying her back to the Temple. Kyra had been called.

'The dagger?' Lark asked Kyra anxiously in sign language. Kyra shook her head. There had been no dagger with the girl when she had been brought in.

Lark kept repeating the sign for the dagger more and more anxiously. Puzzled by her insistence, Kyra sent for the mortuary priest. When he finally arrived and was asked about the dagger he looked embarrassed. He said he did not know what had happened to it. He remembered pulling it out and putting it down beside her... but when he had returned to wash the blood away and purify the place for the next ritual, the dagger was nowhere to be seen. He swore on oath that there had been no sign of the dagger.

Lark looked so terrified at this news that Kyra immediately dismissed the man and sat down beside the girl.

'What is it?' she asked. 'What is so special about the dagger?'

Lark tried to explain, but at first her hands were moving too fast and too wildly for Kyra to follow what she was trying to communicate. Then she caught the meaning, 'Wardyke', and she was extra alert at once. As Lark made the signs over and over again for her, Kyra realised that was what they were talking about – Wardyke's dagger, kept all these years secretly by Isar.

If she had only known that dagger was in Isar's possession! If she could not have persuaded him to part with it, she could have at least exorcised it. And now, who knew whose hands it had fallen into! She thought about the mortuary priest – but she trusted him. His story had rung true. There would have been plenty of time for someone to visit the forecourt and take the dagger while he was carrying Lark to the Temple. Some of the peasants working in the fields nearby had certainly become aware of what was happening and had even helped the priest carry his burden. One of them might have taken it. But Kyra knew that the ordinary person's fear of the burial mound was so strong it would be very unlikely for any of them to have actually ventured near enough to see the dagger – let alone steal it from the forecourt of a burial chamber. That Wardyke's dagger was somehow loose in the world again was a terrifying thought. Whoever had it might well be influenced by it, as Lark had been. Now that she knew more about the circumstances, it was not so puzzling to her that Lark, who had always struck her as such a deeply calm and well-centred person, should have tried to commit the stupid and wasteful act of suicide.

Kyra spent a lot of time with Lark as she healed, and learned everything about Lark's fears for her child, her despair, her horrific encounter with Wardyke in the burial chamber... and Isar's strange desire to keep the dagger in spite of Lark's ill-ease about it.

To comfort her about the child, Kyra told her her own anxieties about the birth of Deva. She described what she had witnessed on the Holy Mound just before Deva was born and how she had been convinced she was being used for a birth that would kill her. When she had not died, in spite of giving birth in a burning house in the middle of a war, she learned not to trust premonitions so easily. Khuren had teased her quite a bit about it over the years – whenever she too hastily interpreted some sign or omen.

'Besides,' she said at last, 'even if the worst comes to the worst and it is Wardyke who comes to birth through you, the child will not be Wardyke. He or she will be in a new setting. New influences will be at work. With you and Isar as parents, I expect very little of the bad side of the old Wardyke will be able to develop.'

Lark was partially comforted – but not wholly. If only Isar were here. It was his love she needed. How could she ever have doubted his strength? She longed for his arms around her – for his words of comfort and wisdom.

Isar, resting in a small shepherd's shieling on the lower slopes of the mountains, felt a wave of longing to be in the comfort of his own home with Lark. Gya seemed to be enjoying the adventure and took each day as it came, as though sometimes he had forgotten what they were travelling for. He was the busier, because, as an experienced hunter and bowman, he was in charge of providing the meat. Isar never quite got used to eating what he had seen flying or running a short while before and exerted himself to find the roots and leaves and berries Fern had told him were good to eat.

The shieling was deserted; it was probably only used by the shepherd in midsummer when the sheep were high on the slopes. The two young men intended only to shelter one night, but the morning dawned almost imperceptibly, the dark giving way to driving rain so heavy that the mountains completely disappeared, and even Isar, who was impatient to finish what they had started and return home, had to admit that they could not make their way through that deluge. After a while the wind dropped, but the clouds continued to sit heavily on the slopes. There seemed no reason they would ever lift. The rain poured down steadily, hushing on the thatch of the little hut, gurgling and muttering in a hundred little rivulets as they rushed over the rocks down to the valley.

Isar lay on the pile of dry straw in the hut and listened to it hour after hour. Gya slept soundly. He had woken once or twice, established that it was still raining and fallen back to sleep with a grunt of disgust. Isar could not sleep. He was haunted by memories: Lark, whom he loved, and Deva, whom he could not get out of his mind.

Yesterday at dawn when they were still in the valley, clambering over boulders in a stream, he had had a strong feeling that Lark needed him. As usual he was trailing behind the agile Gya. He called out several times for Gya to stop, but his companion never looked back. At last Isar refused to go any further. After a long time Gya noticed that Isar was not with him. He called out impatiently a few times and then started to retrace his steps, thinking that perhaps Isar had met with some misadventure. He found Isar at last, sitting on a boulder in mid-stream, his chin sunk on his knees, deep in morose thought.

'What's the matter with you?' snapped Gya. 'I thought you'd drowned or something.'

'I think I am drowning,' Isar muttered.

'What?' shouted Gya irritably.

'No. I haven't drowned,' said Isar.

'Well, what on earth are you sitting there for? We've a long way to go.'

'I know.'

Gya looked at him. Isar seemed to have lost his sense of purpose. His face was drawn and tired – but not with physical weariness.

He leapt a few rocks over the white and turbulent stream and came to rest beside his friend.

'What's wrong?'

Isar shook his head.

Gya did not press for an answer. He squatted on the rock beside Isar for a while longer to give him a chance to confide in him, but when Isar did not seem to want to, Gya moved to a rock nearby and lay flat on his stomach, gazing into the water of a relatively still pool to the side of the main flow of the stream. Both young men were fishing: the one for a decision, the other for a meal. They were so still birds came down to the water to drink beside them, unafraid. Suddenly Gya pounced and brought up a struggling silver fish in his brown hand.

'Ha!' he shouted excitedly and held it aloft proudly.

His shout broke Isar's reverie. He shook himself and grinned. Gya had the right idea – live for the moment. If only he could!

'What if you go on alone to find Deva?' he asked when they were grilling Gya's fish and the scent of the woodsmoke was drifting through the branches of the forest canopy.

Gya looked at him sharply. 'So that's it. You want to give up.'

'I had a strong feeling Lark was in danger.'

'How can she be in danger?' Gya said. 'She's at home with all her friends around her. She is near the Temple – the safest place on earth! Nothing can touch her there.'

Isar looked unconvinced.

'We're probably in danger right now,' Gya continued, 'and Deva certainly is!'

'If I thought we'd find Deva...'

'Of course we'll find Deva!'

'I don't know... no one really knows where Urak is – except that she is in these mountains. But this mountain range is huge. She could be anywhere.'

'I thought Kyra was supposed to send messages.'

'Then where are they? The only strong message I've received is that Lark needs me.'

'Well, go to her then!' Gya said. 'I can manage.'

Isar looked uncertain and unhappy.

'I don't know what to do.'

'Go to your wife.'

'But if Deva...'

'I'll find Deva,' Gya said firmly. 'Don't worry about her.'

Isar knew that if any messages were going to be sent by Kyra, Gya would have very little chance of picking them up. Gya did not have the faintest idea how to make himself available for such thought messages. Isar knew that if he turned back now he might jeopardise their chances of finding Deva.

He stared into the coiling woodsmoke for a while, trying to come to terms with his anxiety. What Gya said about Lark was sensible. She was among friends, under the protection of the great Temple. Deva was the one in danger and he would never forgive himself if harm came to her...

Chapter 14

The Hall of Records

One night Urak woke from a troubled dream to see a crowd gathered round her bed. She sat up angrily, thinking that Deva's family and friends had finally located her and were come to take her back. But as she became more fully awake she noticed that there was a strange, eerie light in the cave, and the figures pressing so close to her were as insubstantial as smoke. She looked more closely and recognised one or two. There was the man whose whole family she had destroyed because he refused to allow his daughter to come to her on the mountain. There was one of her former students who had died in horrible circumstances because one of her spells went badly wrong. There was... As Urak looked round she recognised more and more people, and each one was someone who had been wronged by her. She would have expected them to be angry and vengeful, but what disturbed her most was the expression of expectation, of gloating triumph, on each and every one of their faces.

'What do you want?' she hissed. Behind them she could see Deva and Boggoron still asleep and she did not want to wake them. It seemed to her a ripple of amusement passed through the crowd, but no one replied.

She reached out to seize the figure nearest to her, but her bony hand passed right through his arm.

'Speak or be gone!' she snarled. She tried to think of ways of exorcising them which would teach them not to come bothering her in the night, but for some reason her mind would not function properly. She could remember nothing of all her knowledge, nothing of spell or incantation or ritual... She was blank and helpless, an old woman threatened by danger and incapable of defending herself. Anger turned to fear. She stared around her suddenly in stark terror. She experienced the terror each of her visitors had experienced at her hands in the past, and, as she lived through their particular pain, they disappeared from her sight. She was left at last a gibbering bundle of bones clinging to the fur rug on her bed. When she looked down at her hands they were the hands of a skeleton with no flesh on them at all. She tried now to cry out to Deva and Boggoron for help and comfort, but no sound came from her throat.

How long she lay like that she could not tell – but she must have fallen back to sleep, for the next thing she knew was that Deva and Boggoron were leaning over her solicitously and Deva was holding a polished silver mirror to her face. 'We thought you were dead,' Deva said, startled, as Urak opened her eyes. She took a step or two back from the bedside, trying to hide the mirror behind her.

The old woman lifted her left hand and looked at it. There was flesh on it.

'What are you staring at!' she snapped, sitting up. 'I'm not dead yet. Far from it!' But she knew in her heart that she had been given a premonition of her end and it would not be long now.

Boggoron cackled triumphantly as he hobbled away.

'I told you,' he said gleefully to Deva. 'She'll never die. She's not mortal like you.'

Urak was standing up now, her thin, spare figure alarmingly tall and imposing – powerfully alive once more. Deva drew back and let her pass. She paused at the door to take down the long cloak of black goat's wool and owl feathers that she wore when she was preparing for a particularly difficult piece of work, and strode out into the light without a backward glance. Boggoron and Deva looked at each other nervously. Something significant was afoot and they were not part of it.

Up to this time Deva had told herself that she was free to go at any time: that she stayed only because it suited her to stay. But at the moment when she thought Urak was dead, she knew she wanted to learn what Urak could teach her more than anything in the world. She could not bear it if Urak died before she passed on her knowledge – and she knew now she could not leave while there was a chance of learning any of it. There had been a time when she would have been delighted with a cave full of baubles to take home. But now that was not enough. She wanted the power to create anything she desired. It was true that what Urak did was not creation in the true sense. What she manifested was there already – but in different form. There was no end to the possibilities in following this path and Deva wanted to master all of them.

When she was a child she had thought she loved her parents but now she realised she carried a deep resentment against them because they had secrets they would not share with her. Well, she would soon have secrets she would not share with them. And her secrets would be more astounding and impressive than any they could have. She did not want to harm them – she did love them in a sense – but she wanted to prove herself superior to them, for they had implied in so many ways that she was not capable of following in their footsteps. They did not trust her to take the training for priesthood when she had shown them time and again her psychic capabilities were more than adequate. She still smarted from the words Kyra had spoken one day when she had been particularly persistent about starting the training. 'There is a great difference between the spiritual and the psychic,' she had said. 'Although it is true we choose novices from those who show particular psychic ability, and there is no doubt that if that were the only criterion you would be chosen – but there is more to the selection than that. We look at the past of the soul in question... how it has developed and evolved... how far it has progressed... how much it has already learned...' Deva had stormed out of the room in tears. What gave them the right to judge her unworthy! She was as 'evolved' as they were... as wise... as capable...

Where was Urak? What was she doing? A wave of impatience to be getting on with her studies drove Deva to the mouth of the cave. There was no sign of the woman. This was the time of day, refreshed by sleep, when Deva most enjoyed her training. She had grown to expect constant attention from Urak, and Urak had ignored her as she strode past her.

'Where has she gone?' she demanded of Boggoron. He shrugged his shoulders. Even he had been surprised at the way Urak behaved. He knew how important Deva was to Urak's plans, and it was the first time since Deva's arrival that she had left him without specific instructions regarding the girl. 'I suppose she thinks I don't need any reminders,' Boggoron thought smugly. 'No one will get away from me!' He squatted at the entrance to the cave with his eyes fixed on Deva. 'We'll wait for her here,' he said.

'I'm going after her. I want to know what's going on.'

'No. We'll wait here.'

Deva looked at the creature, his eyes bulging gloatingly as he stared at her. She knew it was only fear of Urak that kept him off her. She was not prepared to stay alone with him.

'You stay here. I'm going to look for her.' She strode purposefully forward, her head held high and haughty as she passed him.

He crouched like a malevolent brown goblin and then sprang at her. She tried to shake herself free but his gnarled hands were very strong. His weight brought her to the ground and he was all over her. She could feel the rasp of his tongue as he licked her face and neck like a dog. She could feel his knee forcing her legs apart. Silently she fought to free herself. There was no point in screaming for help because there was no one to hear her. At last she managed to twist her head away from him, and as she gasped for breath had the presence of mind to look over his shoulder and call out Urak's name, as though she had just seen the woman herself approaching.

Boggoron sprang off her as if he had been burnt by fire, and went scuttling off down the slope in terror, losing his foothold and slithering out of control for most of the way, coming to rest at last in some thorny bramble bushes. Bruised and shaken, Deva did not wait for him to discover that he had been tricked. She rushed off along the path Urak usually took when she was going to her a special place. Whether she was there now, Deva did not know, but she knew however angry Boggoron was, or however incensed with lust, he would never dare set foot on Urak's special territory. She was not sure she herself would dare – but at least she could be near enough to seek sanctuary there if Boggoron still would not leave her alone.

Urak's special place was a kind of natural amphitheatre of rock, the walls a dark intrusion into the silver-grey limestone. It was from here Urak had obtained the smooth black slab in front of her cave on which she performed her spells. The rock was fine grained, oozed out from the depths of the earth and cooled quickly many millions of years before. This was the place she came to when she wanted to call on the help of the dark spirits beyond this realm. Guiron had had the energy of his Temple to use when he wanted to call on the help of the spirits of Light; she had her temple, too – this remote and lofty place.

She had come here first not long after she arrived on the mountain – though it looked very different then – and called on whoever was 'out there' to come to her aid. She made no stipulation as to whether the force she called on should be positive or negative, dark or light, good or bad. She just wanted someone – anyone – to teach her how to be the mightiest sorceress that ever lived. She remembered thinking of the things she wanted to do with her power, and not one of them would have had the approval of the Temple. Will is the key that opens the door – but the door it opens is determined by motive. The door that opened for her that day was a door into darkness. The mountain shook and the skies grew black. Shrieking, she buried her head in her arms, and when she looked up again, the whole shape of this part of the mountain had changed. The limestone had been peeled away and thrown into the valley below, revealing this black and alien core of rock. She was physically unharmed, but before her stood the being she had invited, and his eyes were holes blacker than a starless sky, and his voice was like the ghost of thunder.

She had feared him... but she had learned what she wanted to learn from him.

She stood now at the centre of the rock platform – behind her the soaring rock wall, before her a gap in the mountains so placed that the view beyond was vast and uninterrupted... the low hills... the rivers and lakes... the villages and farmsteads.

This was the place from which Urak spied on the world outside her eyrie. This was where she flew from when she took on the shape of the hunting ghost-owl. Today her coarse black cloak floated around her, the broad collar of owl feathers ruffled at her neck. On her head she placed a circlet – a thin twisted coil of different metals joined over her forehead with one huge gem. The gem had no colour in itself, but mirrored all colours. It had no shape itself, but could take on any shape. This time she knew whom she would call: she knew who would be of most help to her.

She formed his name with her mouth – though no sound came from it. Deep in her throat the vibrations started, but they were not meant to be heard by earth ears and no earth ears would ever hear them.

'Wardyke,' she thought... she breathed... she called.

And Wardyke came.

The earth trembled as he stepped upon it. Loose rocks fell down and rattled into the chasm below her, but the mountain stood firm this time. Was it a cloud that obscured the sun, or did the light of the great celestial orb suddenly dim? Urak felt the chill and shivered. She repeated the inaudible sounds that, matched to their counterparts in the astral realm, would materialise the shadow of a shadow.

As before, first there was the darkness... then the feeling of foreboding... leading to that strange impression of being detached gradually from her body. Urak remembered it well. Her tongue became as heavy as lead in her mouth, her limbs as inflexible as stone. She was no longer in control of herself.

The impression of darkness increased steadily, though in fact the sunlight was strangely undiminished. It seemed to be gathering from every side. She could no longer move her eyes, but she had the impression that shadows were flitting past her and joining a greater shadow already on the platform.

Suddenly Wardyke stood before her.

He needed no words to tell him why she had called him. He knew about the visitation.

'Your death will be soon,' he confirmed.

'I am not ready!' she cried in despair. 'Can it not be delayed?' It seemed to her that all her sorcery was worth nothing if it could not win her one moment of extra time on earth.

'Your time has come,' he said. 'There is nothing you or I can do.'

'Deva is not ready. I will die, and our wrongs will be unavenged. When I'm dead I will only be able to work through her if she calls on me. And she may not call. Her parents are powerful priests and could easily persuade her to turn against me once she is back under their influence. I need more time! I need your help.'

It seemed to her the strange darkness that surrounded them increased its intensity. For a moment she had second thoughts. Death would release her from the dangers of this realm – but what of the retribution waiting for her in those other realms...

Perhaps she should do one good deed at least before she died. But Wardyke had been called and he was here – ready to help her. If she did not take this opportunity she would lose everything she had worked for for so long – the downfall of the Temple that had denied them both so much freedom and power.

'There are ways of speeding up the training so that you could complete it before your death,' Wardyke said.

'Tell me,' she pleaded. 'I'll do anything.'

'The girl could die – or go insane. I myself, were I in an earth body, would hesitate before I used these methods.'

'What choice have I? I am dying!' she cried.

'What choice indeed,' he said dryly, and for a moment she thought she caught a look of mockery in his eyes.

Deva, searching for the rock amphitheatre, had felt the earth tremble and was afraid. A falling rock had narrowly missed her head. She thought of taking this opportunity to leave the mountain. For the first time since she had arrived, neither Boggoron nor Urak was in sight. Beneath her the cliffs fell away to the valley far below, where a river flowed. She could hear the sound of water hurrying over the boulders, racing to the sea. If she were to reach the river and follow it, she would surely find her way out of these rough and precipitous gorges. Where the land was flatter, she would find people.

But... did she want to leave yet? Once again she decided to stay. 'I can leave at any time if I want to,' she repeated to herself. 'But this is not the time.'

The path she was following branched and branched again. She thought she would find Urak's special place easily, for she had gone that way many times when Urak was training her. But for some reason, this time, she could not find it. She could only think she had inadvertently taken the wrong fork and she retraced her steps. But however many times she did that, and however convinced she was that she had at last found the right way, she never had.

It was Urak who found her when she was on her way back to the cave.

The drums were brought from their secret hiding place in the mountain. There were two large ones and three small ones carefully wrapped in hide. Boggoron was sent off to take them one by one to the basalt amphitheatre. He staggered under the weight of the largest, but Urak would not allow Deva to help him. As she stepped forward and reached out to steady his burden, Urak's angry voice cracked like a whip, and she withdrew her hand at once.

'Don't touch them. Don't ever touch them!' Urak snarled.

'I was only trying to help,' Deva muttered defensively.

'The drums must only be touched by the drummer,' she was told. 'The power of their speech is broken if they are mishandled.'

Deva had forgotten that at the Temple too the drums were always kept separate and when one drummer left the community, his drum was handed over in a special ceremony to the new man – as though it was a living being transferred to the care of a new guardian. Drums had voices. Drums could speak. Drums could rouse passions; manipulate emotions; affect thoughts, dreams and decisions. At the Temple they were used to induce the mood that would make the mundane sensitive to the sacred; the mortal to the immortal; the natural to the supernatural

For what was Urak going to use them? Deva could sense the nervous excitement in the air. Urak was planning something that even she found alarming. Boggoron knew that something special was afoot, but knew no more. He staggered off along the path with his burden, his face alight with anticipation.

Deva had to content herself with watching and wondering. Urak was robing carefully as though for a great ceremony, fetching special ritual objects from their hidden places and preparing them for use.

When it seemed at last that she was ready and Boggoron had completed his transportation task, Urak turned her attention to Deva. She was given a dress of fine white Egyptian linen to wear, but this time, instead of jewels, she had the skin of a lynx-cat hung over her shoulder. Her hair was combed out fully with an ivory comb, scraped back and fastened with gold pins so that no strands strayed across her face. Then Urak fetched out a small box of pigments and unguents and started to paint the girl's face with a strange and elaborate design so that, at the end, when she saw herself in a mirror, she was unrecognisable. It was as though she wore a mask. Her skin was taut and uncomfortable where the paint had dried.

Then Urak painted her own face and Deva watched in growing alarm as the formidable old woman took on all the characteristics of a fearsome hunting-owl. She painted out her eyebrows and rounded out her eyes in such a way that even when she blinked it seemed as though her eyes were still staring. Then she fitted on her cap of owl feathers and announced that they were ready to go.

'Go where?' Deva asked.

'The question is meaningless,' Urak said enigmatically, and led the way along the path to her special place.

Deva followed silently, filled with trepidation. She could sense that this was not going to be an ordinary lesson. Urak was preparing something really special... something that even she might never have tried before.

When they reached the place, the sun had gone behind billowing clouds and soon the whole sky was a mass of swirling white, grey and black, as though it too was preparing for the drama about to be acted out in the mountains.

The drums had been set up in their places by Boggoron and he was already squatting beside the group of three smaller drums.

Deva stood where Urak had placed her and watched as the owl-woman paced the area of the platform, weaving in and out around each drum, creating a kind of pattern as she did so. The air became very silent. Deva could hear no bird call, no insect rasp. The clouds above continued steadily piling up as though they were gathering in a theatre to watch a performance. In and out Urak wove, while Boggoron sat as still as stone and Deva stood watching, fascinated.

The bodies of each of Urak's five drums were hollowed from the wood of a single tree. The surface of the wood had been rubbed smooth and kept pliant with regular oiling. Deva had seen Boggoron working on them time and again. She had always been surprised how different he appeared when he was working on the drums. His expression became almost gentle, almost beautiful; his hands deft and sensitive. Now she could see something in his face, as he squatted beside them, that made her wonder if there was not an alternative Boggoron hiding in that uncouth, warped body, that sly and cringing mind. What he felt for Urak was fear and gratitude; for her, lust; but for the drums he felt love.

Over the wood hide had been stretched taut, fastened with wooden pegs and tied with thongs. The slightest touch would make them sound.

At last Urak stopped in front of the second largest and Deva could feel from Boggoron's sudden alertness that the work was about to begin. But what was she to do? She had been given no instructions. Since they had arrived at this place she had been virtually ignored.

The thought of moving towards the biggest drum crossed her mind. She was affected by the atmosphere of tense excitement and longed to be part of it. Besides, if she was not to be involved in what was about to happen – why had she been brought along?

Suddenly Urak looked across at her, and, as though she had spoken aloud, Deva knew that she would be in trouble if she made the slightest movement. It was only a glance, and almost immediately Urak's full attention was back on the drum, but Deva knew she was fastened to that place as surely as if she had been bound to it.

Another long moment of intense silence, and then both Boggoron and Urak began touching the hide with their drumsticks. Deva saw no signal pass between them but they moved in unison. At first it was a mere tremble of wood on hide, so faint it was almost inaudible. But Deva knew the silence had ended and that they were now committed to something mysterious and terrifying.

The faint sound grew stronger. She listened, almost holding her breath, as it swelled. It reminded her of raindrops falling singly at the beginning of a storm, and then by their millions, pattering on leaves and thatch. The hands of Urak and Boggoron moved faster and faster until they no longer could be seen as separate hands. The drumming was swift and powerful. She could feel the skin on her scalp prickle as the sound became a mighty wind roaring through a forest. It swayed and swelled and grew and faded. The wind had passed, but the rain continued. Behind the sound of it she thought she heard the murmur of distant thunder.

Deva trembled and shut her eyes. She felt herself caught in the midst of a huge storm, the sound of the thunder reverberating throughout her body. She swayed and keened with terror, convinced that lightning was striking nearer and nearer to her. The noise of the storm that was not a storm grew louder and louder, fiercer and fiercer. At last it reached such a pitch Deva could bear it no longer and struggled to open her eyes. She was determined to find somewhere to hide from its fury, even if it meant making Urak angry. What she saw when she opened her eyes filled her with even more terror than before. The sky was pitch black and, surrounding them on the platform and on every flat protruding rock above them on the mountain, were other drums and other drummers. Urak and Boggoron were now only part of a huge orchestra of drummers. Urak's largest drum was being beaten by a huge being, so fearsome in aspect that Deva nearly fainted with alarm. Dark mists were swirling on the mountain, and through the murk it seemed to Deva some of the drummers were floating in the air... some appeared to be in the clouds themselves.

Urak, enclosed within a ghastly glow, was moving so fast it was almost as though the sticks were playing her, rather than she playing the sticks. She and Boggoron seemed unaware of their companions, unaware of anything but the tremendous energy they were raising.

Deva could sense the swirl of energy around her growing stronger, until she felt as though she were being sucked into a vortex. She tried to cling to a nearby rock with all her strength but she was tugged and pulled by a force greater than she had ever known before. The sound of an immense and violent wind was howling around her, but no leaf was stirring. Thunder cracked and roared, but no lightning flashed. She tried to scream – but as she opened her mouth it was as though the dark, motionless wind poured into her throat and she was taken over by it. Outside and inside she was possessed by it. Her fingers bled as they were ripped from the rock and she was whirled away. She became the wind... a dark and bodiless force that left the mountain and the drummers far behind and rushed through the darkness, cleaving her way through the clouds... seeking... seeking... What? A nameless need drove her on... a fierce desire... a desperate and violent passion... an overwhelming greed...

She found herself at last in an immense circular chamber. Its ceiling consisted of overlapping slabs of rock placed so skilfully that they formed a huge vaulted dome. A narrow and powerful shaft of light shone down from a small round hole at the apex, causing a brilliant disc of light to fall at the very centre of the floor, where it illuminated a radiating series of paving stones, each circle of which was of a different type and colour.

As her eyes became more and more accustomed to the contrast between the brilliance of the light-shaft and the dim regions of the hall beyond, she noticed that there were rings of alcoves or niches at every level around the walls. In each alcove stood either a stone jar of the type used for storing the ashes of the dead – or a shallow stone basin on which there was a collection of dusty skulls. She shuddered. Was she to be sealed up – living – in a tomb?

She started, icy with fear, as she heard a sound and sensed a movement from the other side of the column of almost solid light. Clenching her fists and biting her lip to stop it trembling, she prepared to face whatever lurked in this weird place. Was that a figure she could dimly see – almost human, but larger than life-size? With a great effort she controlled her terror enough to call out in a loud voice that wavered only slightly.

'Is there anyone there?'

The walls picked up the echo and suddenly a hundred voices

seemed to be crying: 'Is there anyone there? Is there anyone... anyone... there... there... there...?'

Was she being mocked?

Suddenly a figure emerged clearly and came to stand before her – a tall man, taller than any she had ever seen. Was it her imagination, or could she see through his body, as though through a black veil, the walls of the opposite side of the vast chamber? He looked into her eyes and it seemed to her she had never seen eyes so dark, so cold, so cruel.

'What is this place?' She struggled to hold her head up – to meet his eyes boldly. 'What do you want with me?'

He smiled, and his smile chilled her blood more than his formidable and sinister gaze.

'I hear you are ambitious, Deva, daughter of Kyra,' he said, and she noticed that for some reason his voice did not set up an echo, nor did his body cast a shadow. The sound of her name pronounced by such a one drove more terror into her heart. She looked frantically around, but the chamber had no doors – no possible way of escape.

'Don't be afraid,' he continued smoothly. 'You have come here to learn and I am here to teach you. This is the Hall of Records. Here is stored the memory of all that has been, all that is and all that will be. Are you not curious? Are you not anxious to know what I can show you?'

She was curious. She was anxious. Her intuition was warning her to beware, to refuse what he was offering... but something in her overrode the warning. Here was an opportunity not to be missed – no matter what the cost.

'Come with me,' he said silkily. 'Come, let us start the lesson.'

He reached out his hand to take hers, but she shrank from him. She was thankful he did not insist. She followed a few paces behind him as he strode across the paving stones. They came to a halt before one of the more accessible alcoves. He reached down and lifted up a skull and, before she fully realised what he was doing, he had placed the skull in her hands. Horrified, she stared into its sightless eye sockets, and for a moment thought that she was going to retch. And then...

And then it seemed to her she was experiencing a battle. She was galloping across a plain with thousands of horses beside her. She and her fellow warriors were emitting a strange, ululating howl as they bore down on the enemy, a fearsome war-cry. She felt tremendous excitement and a fierce impatience to kill and kill again. Hate flowed in her veins as hot as blood itself. Hooves drummed and thundered... arrows whined... men screamed... She had never felt so glorious, so powerful, so certain that what she was doing was right.

She suffered excruciating pain in her head as the events she was experiencing speeded up. The battle was over and she was witnessing the victory celebrations... the drinking... the singing... the taking of women. How strange, she thought, to feel what it was to be a man taking a woman...

Then her guide placed the skull she was holding back in its place and handed her another. She was instantly part of a different experience as vivid as the first had been. This time she was a rich merchant inspecting with satisfaction his vast estates and his cowering slaves. She fingered bales of exotic cloth. She ran her fingers through gold coins and pearls beyond price. She ordered her slaves to whip the beggars that clamoured at her door.

Another skull gave her the experiences of someone else in another time and another place. This went on many times until she had as rich a store of experiences and memories as the merchant had had chests of treasure.

Then her guide placed in her hands one of the sealed jars and indicated that she should open it. She almost reeled back and dropped it as a stream of unfamiliar consciousness in the form of thick and acrid smoke came billowing out of it. She could not help but breathe it in though it nearly choked her. Everything that Urak had learned in her long years of trial and error, of cunning and of unscrupulous experimentation – Deva now learned. The secrets of manifestation-magic were hers at last!

But the strain of holding all this new knowledge together was tremendous and it seemed to her that if she took in one more detail she would split apart, disintegrating into a million fragments, and each fragment an agony.

She turned to her guide to plead for a respite – but he was no longer beside her. She looked around and found that he was standing now some way from her, facing a new figure: that of an old man clad in a shabby blue cloak. She could not understand why her powerful companion should apparently fear this slight old man, and yet it seemed that he did.

The two men locked eyes, and Deva could almost see the beam of thought-energy that thrust and parried between them. Not for a moment did the old man waver.

'So, Wardyke, we meet again?' he said in a quiet, steady voice.

'Maal!' Wardyke spat – and the black fire of his gaze flared up, but stopped just short of the old man as though he were invisibly protected in some way. Deva realised that she was witnessing a duel of wills.

Suddenly the light shaft at the centre seemed to expand and flash out in every direction. It illuminated with stark brilliance the whole cavernous hall – and then shrank again to the centre. There was now no sign of the dark being who had been her guide. Beside her stood only the gentle old man. She looked at him in astonishment.

'Deva,' he said gently. 'You have been misled.'

'On the contrary,' she said, 'I have experienced all things – and seen the truth.'

'Have you?' he said quietly. 'Look again.' He directed her attention to the first skull her previous guide had shown her. It seemed to her that perhaps the place was lighter than it had been before, and she could see more clearly.

She was back in the same battle, but this time she was a young boy on the ground, retching with fear. All around her men's limbs were lying severed, blood was turning the soil to sticky, stinking mud. She looked up in time to see an axe coming down towards her head and knew that she was going to die. She screamed with agony and with regret for all the things she would have liked to do with her life, had she been given a chance. She felt no hate... only despair at the waste of it all and disgust at the degrading role men chose to play when they could have been so great.

Everything the first guide had shown her, the second showed her also. But in every case, although the same events occurred, she saw them differently.

When she reached the life of Urak, instead of being filled with pride as she had before, she shuddered at what Urak had had to do to acquire her knowledge, and was shocked at how she had used it.

'Go home, Deva,' the old man said. 'Your mother is waiting for you.'

'But, tell me – which is the true picture I have seen?'

Maal – Kyra's old friend and teacher – smiled sadly.

'If you don't even recognise truth when you see it,' he said, 'what makes you think you can play at being a god?'

Kyra sat quietly in her chamber with her eyes closed and one of her crystals pressed against her forehead. Each of her crystals was as clear as mountain water, without blemish. Each one was faceted at both ends. There were other crystals, beautiful, but not so perfect, in use in the Temple – but Kyra's double-ended quartz crystals were famous for their perfection. They had come from all over the world. Many had been brought by travellers in fragile ships from distant lands – magical crystals, once used by priests and shaman in the forests of Africa. Others from the deep, dry canyons of America, where for generations they had been used in the spirit-talking ceremonies. Some had come from the far north, where Guiron had encountered the Mogüd. Kyra used them mostly for healing, but this day she had chosen a soul-seeker that had come to her from Africa. A merchant had brought it, and told a tale of how he had been drawn to find it through distance and danger by the power of visions and dreams. When he had it he had wanted to keep it – but again dreams had played a part and led him to Kyra. It was almost as though her name were secretly engraved on it.

She had known as soon as she first touched it that it was charged with a very powerful energy – so powerful indeed that she had not dared to use it before this day. Today she needed all the power and energy it could give her.

First she spoke with her guardian spirits and asked for their protection, as she did before any hazardous undertaking. Then she dedicated its use for the purposes of light. Finally she raised it to her forehead. She felt at first the discomfort of the cold surface against her warm skin – but soon it grew hot and she could feel its energy coursing through her body.

Although she knew what she was doing was dangerous and the crystal energy could, if she were not careful, burn out her mind, she kept control of herself and, in a calm and steady voice, she asked the soul-seeker to find her the priest of her childhood, Maal, her friend and teacher, long since dead. He had promised to return whenever she truly and seriously needed him.

And so it was that Maal had come and Maal had found Deva and, once again, foiled Wardyke.

Suddenly Deva found herself lying on the mountain at Urak's feet, utterly exhausted. The drumming had stopped. Boggoron was resting with his head on his knees, his clothes soaked through with sweat. Urak was standing over her, waiting to see how she had come out of the experience... waiting to see if she had learned what Wardyke had promised to teach her...

Chapter 15

The fire-mare

Whether Isar and Gya would ever have found the entrance to the great gorge in which Urak had her lair, had Urak herself not been too preoccupied to guard her domain, it would be impossible to say.

When the two young men made camp one evening, they were unaware how close they were to the end of all their searching. In fact, even Gya was beginning to lose hope; he tethered the horses and helped Isar collect the wood for the fire silently and morosely.

What if they did not find her? What if she was already dead – or 'taken over', as Kyra seemed to fear? So many memories came crowding into his mind: Deva riding beside him with her hair flying out behind her... Deva biting her lip as she concentrated on drawing the bow when he was teaching her to shoot... Deva bathing naked in the lake... Deva making love...

He strode away from the campsite into the gathering shadows of the night, not wanting Isar to see how disturbed he was. Sometimes he hated Deva... but the hate was bittersweet and very close to desire. Now, in this remote place, abandoning for the first time the sense of adventure that had born him up through the journey, and thinking only of what it would mean if they did not find her, Gya felt that without her his life would be bleak and featureless.

Isar watched him walk away and sensed his despair. It matched his own.

Everything gradually became very quiet, the last birds winging home, the stars coming out. Isar wrapped himself in his cloak and sat watching the sparks rising from the fire. He heard Gya returning, but he did not look up. The bowman put another log on the fire and found a place to settle for the night on the other side from his companion. Neither felt like talking. Neither felt like sleeping. The crackle of the flames was the only sound.

How long they sat thus neither afterwards could tell, but suddenly they were shocked out of their sombre mood by a terrifying and extraordinary event. Urak's vigilance may have been less than it should have been, but the weird bodiless beings, the macabre and grotesque flotsam that haunted the interface of the realms, choosing neither one plane nor the other, clinging to earth-beings like Urak, who provided them with an open door into this realm, were vigilant. They were ready to guard her territory and drive unwanted visitors away.

Suddenly the last log Gya had put on the fire exploded and huge flames roared up. Both young men leapt up – alert to the danger to neighbouring trees – but they could not get near enough because of the searing heat to assess exactly what was happening. They drew back and then both saw, though neither could believe what he saw, within the soaring flames... a gigantic white mare rearing and plunging, trampling the red-hot embers with her glowing hooves.

The two horses, safely back at the edge of the woods, neighed and reared in answer to her call, and, breaking tether, came galloping wildly towards her. Demented by a combination of their lust for the extraordinary mare and their fear of the fire, the horses circled frantically around, nearly trampling Gya and Isar to death as they did so. Gya leapt about, trying to seize the bridles, while Isar, never very confident with horses, retreated, terrified, behind a large boulder.

The white mare seemed to be dancing in the fire, unharmed by the heat, her mane flying free, unsinged, her magnificent flanks as smooth as silk. The two horses, driven wild with the frustration of not being able to reach her, began to fight each other. Gya was flung aside and was in serious danger of being killed. Isar rushed out to try to save him – but was too far away. Gya looked up at the huge creature leaning over him... saw the deadly hooves coming towards him... and shut his eyes. The fall had winded him and he could not move. He was finished. He was sure of it.

Suddenly the figure of a woman appeared from nowhere and seized him under the armpits. She heaved and tugged and got him away from death by a hair's breadth. Then Isar arrived and the two of them dragged him to safety. Gya struggled to regain his breath – the earth was shaking with the thunder of hooves, the air hideous with the screams of the beasts as snapping teeth tore at neck and flank, drawing blood.

Farla looked at the huge mare, the shining red eyes, the silver mane. It had a fearsome and a cruel beauty... but it was illusion. Yet she feared it had taken on a life of its own – as illusion sometimes does if someone needs strongly enough to believe in it. The two stallions would not let it go, though Farla stood on top of the boulder and used all her powers to dismantle it. Bewildered, the two men watched and listened as the woman chanted, as the woman glowed within an aura of vibrant and pulsing light. Sweat poured down her face. Her voice grew hoarse. The images she tried to hold in her mind – the images vital to freeing the two stallions from their lust and their obsession – kept wavering and fading. Whoever had produced this mare was powerful indeed, but Farla knew that now it was the horses themselves who were holding it. She was fighting their need to believe in what they saw, and until she could change the image in their minds she could not destroy the image of the mare in the fire.

If the mare galloped away or even simply disappeared, the horses would still fight for her... still seek for her. They must lose interest in her somehow. Fiercely she struggled to bring the mare down – to make her less attractive. Fire was the energy that was being used, fire was keeping her going. Farla thought of water; imaged water; dreamed of water. She raised her arms to the sky and visualised the rain pouring down on their heads and on the flames... But the fire burned brighter – the water merely spitting and spattering as it touched the heat, turning at once into great billowing clouds of steam – and still the image of the mare grew stronger.

Did she hear laughter? She dared not look away from the fire, but she knew that on every branch of every tree surrounding her and lurking in the shadows under the trees were figures – Urak's friends, Urak's demonic and disembodied cronies. Isar could see them too and shuddered. Gya could not – but even he sensed that someone was watching from the shadows.

'Come out, you bastards, and take your damn mare away!' he shouted – rushing at the trees with his dagger drawn. 'Show yourselves! Fight, you sons of filth!' He lunged at every shadow desperately, but nothing but the bramble thorns fought him back.

Still, his apparently futile action served a purpose. The old chestnut stallion had been badly hurt and forced to retreat. The victorious grey, now free to mount the mare, was distracted by Gya's shouting and the flashing of his dagger in the firelight. In that moment, Farla – holding her attention steady – acted. When he looked back to his beautiful mare she was stumbling, she was drooping, she was withering. When, snorting, he came to her side, she was lying dead in the grey ash of the dying fire. He sniffed her, but the powerful scent of her femaleness was gone. He turned away from her before even she crumbled into white ash and was no more.

Then Farla turned her attention to the watchers in the trees and directed her angry thoughts to them. Astonished at her power, they went scurrying off, melting back into the darkness from which they had come.

The chestnut was almost dead. The fight had been no illusion, though the cause of it had been. Gya had to finish him off with an arrow through the head to stop him suffering – Isar kneeling beside him stroking his flank.

Farla gently called the grey to her and soothed him with soft words and gentle touches. He was ringing wet with froth and sweat, trembling in every limb. She told Isar sharply to build up the fire again so that she could see what she was doing, and, from her carrying pouch, she brought out certain herbal salves that she rubbed into his wounds. He snorted and trampled restlessly, but allowed her to attend to him.

When all was done the three sat down around the fire, shaken and exhausted.

'You saved my life,' Gya said gratefully to Farla. 'But where did you spring from?'

She smiled. 'I've been following your trail,' she said. 'I want to help find Deva.' She noticed how her heart beat faster as he looked into her eyes. 'If only...' she thought. 'If only...'

Isar wanted to know if she had come from the Temple and what was happening there.

'We've received no guidance,' he said, somewhat aggrieved. 'We've no idea where to look for her.'

'We must be getting very close,' Farla said, 'or why would those... those creatures... play that trick on us?'

'I noticed a gorge up ahead when I went for a walk earlier,' Gya said, 'that would be a good hiding place for someone who didn't want to be found.'

'That's it, then,' said Farla. 'In the morning we'll...'

Her voice trailed off. She was weary beyond belief after the experience she had been through, and she began to slump forward. Gya, nearest to her, took her in his arms and held her close. 'Steady,' he said sympathetically. 'You need some rest after all that excitement.' He wrapped his own cloak around her and lowered her to the ground. He arranged her pouch as a pillow under her head and stroked her hair. 'You'll feel better in the morning,' he said. 'We'll find her. Don't you worry.' Farla looked up at him, the firelight bringing out a warm glow on his suntanned skin, his eyes in shadow... She knew she loved him – and she no longer felt ashamed.

Chapter 16

The silver vortex

Deva was confused. Since her encounter with Maal in the Hall of Records she had begun to doubt that anyone had the right to the secrets Urak was offering her. She was also in doubt that the secret knowledge Urak was purveying was worth having. She had been considerably disillusioned by the way the akashic records, which she had thought would give her the real and ultimate truth about everything, gave her no more than differing and subjective versions of the same events. Either these were not the real akashic records – in which case Urak was trying to deceive her, or they were – in which case she would have to revise her understanding of what the akashic records were. She kept contrasting the eyes of the two Beings she had met there: the first guide – provided by Urak – with eyes that chilled her to the marrow; the second, with eyes that were kind and wise.

Her first instinct after the experience was to leave Urak at once. But Urak must have known something had gone very wrong with the first lesson, because she took great care that Deva was not out of her sight for an instant. She was promised that at the next lesson she would at last be allowed to work the magic herself. No more watching open-mouthed as Urak materialised objects before her. She would be able to do it herself. The temptation of this was too much for her embryo doubts and misgivings.

'I'll just learn this one more thing and *then* I'll leave,' she thought. 'What could be the harm, as long as I keep control of myself and don't let myself go too far. After all, I would only use it for manifesting good things.'

Urak led her into the depths of the mountain, down the narrow fissure she and Boggoron had already traversed several times, through the great cavern of treasures and into another fissure even narrower than the first. The deeper they went the colder it became. She was shivering almost uncontrollably, partly with cold and partly with fear. Where were they going? Would the woman never stop!

Urak strode on relentlessly, negotiating almost impassable hazards. In trying to keep up with her, Deva grazed her skin several times and bumped and banged her shoulders and her head. Boggoron slithered behind them, whimpering and muttering to himself.

Then she began to notice a noise somewhere way ahead and below them... a kind of rumbling. She feared for a moment that it was the beginnings of an earth tremor that would surely bring the whole mountain down upon their heads – but Urak seemed unconcerned and strode on.

At last they came to the end of the long tunnel they had been following and stood on an open ledge looking down at a pool far below them, the water milky white where several waterfalls fed into it and swirled it around. As Urak held up her lamp and Boggoron his torch, she could see that it was a fearsome whirlpool... a great swallow-hole... a place of terror. There seemed to be no river running away from it. All led in – none out.

The path Urak and Deva and Boggoron were on had come to a dead end. There was nothing before them but the sheer walls of an almost circular funnel stretching far above them into the darkness and far below them into the angry, whirling water.

'This is the place,' said Urak calmly.

Deva's heart missed a beat. What did she mean? How could she perform any magic on this narrow and slippery ledge? She began to be overcome by a feeling of vertigo and took a step back from the edge. Her foot slipped, and if Boggoron had not seized her at once with his immensely strong and bony hands, she would have fallen.

Her heart was pounding with terror.

'Urak,' she whispered hoarsely, 'let's go back... I don't... I can't...'

'Stand still, girl,' Urak commanded. 'This is the place. This is the door.'

For a brief, wild moment Deva was comforted. There was a door in the rock! She looked round at the dark walls frantically, feeling with her fingers to see if she could find any trace of it. The sooner they were away from this dangerous and fearful place the better. She did not like the way Urak and Boggoron were looking at her. They were crowding her, one on either side, and were showing no interest in finding the door in the rock.

'What is it? Why do you look at me like that?' were the last words Deva said before Urak and Boggoron together pushed her over the lip and into the cauldron of boiling, icy water hundreds of feet below.

'This is my death,' thought Deva as she fell, and a strange calm came over her. There was the moment of terror – the scream that ricocheted against the dark rock, that pierced every nook and cranny, that battered itself against the walls like a bird caught in a chamber. But then everything went silent. She could not even hear the roar and the rumble of the water that was rushing up to meet her. The water was rushing, but she was still. She seemed to float, motionless, poised for a long, long time above a terrible beauty. The liquid had become light... silver and diamond drops whirled in a spiral dance... filaments of gold spun and twirled... aquamarine, emerald, sapphire – all the jewels she had dreamed of – were spinning in this mighty silver vortex and she was going to become part of it. The walls of rock had completely disappeared now. She was in a world of white and silver spray. As though it was her own choice – like a salmon choosing the moment and the angle of his leap – she aimed at the centre of the whirlpool and was caught instantly in the powerful downward tug, the violent thirsty swallow of an ancient force...

As her head hit the solid muscle of the water she lost consciousness.

From above, Urak and Boggoron saw her whirling like a fragile black twig for a few moments and then disappear.

They stood in silence, lamp and torch held high, straining to see if she would reappear. When they were sure that she would not they turned and hurried back down the tunnel – in such haste that even the agile Urak knocked herself against the walls.

Kyra woke with a shriek. It seemed to her the walls of her chamber were swirling around her. There was roaring and thundering and everywhere she looked everything was in motion... tables and chairs... clothes... everything... She shut her eyes and covered her head with her arms. Even in the darkness she could feel herself turning.

Suddenly Khu-ren was there. He took her in his arms – he anchored her. She clung to him and sobbed against his chest.

'You are safe, my love,' he was whispering. 'Safe, with me. Open your eyes and look around you – we are together.'

Timidly she opened one eye and then the other. The walls and the objects of the room were no longer moving. Khu-ren held her close. She could feel his lips against her cheek... her neck... her breast...

'If this is death,' thought Deva, 'it is not how I expected it.'

It seemed to her she had no body and yet was conscious. The order she had come to expect on earth was nowhere in evidence. There was no 'up' and 'down', no 'left' and 'right'. It was like an immense darkness in which minute specks of light pulsed for a moment and then disappeared. They appeared at random and disappeared at random. 'No order,' Deva thought, and realised that this was the most frightening thing she had ever experienced. Was she one of those specks? At any moment would she be snuffed out and never reappear?

'It's unfair,' she thought. 'I was taught to expect more than this after death. Where are the Spirit-Realms Kyra taught me about? Where the orderly gradation of Being... the gradual passing through stage after stage until one has reached a plane high enough to understand all things...'

She despaired.

'I'd rather not have been born at all if this is all there is,' she thought. 'How stupid. How pointless.' To be shown so much beauty, so much complexity! To have had a mind capable of such great things – such leaps, such flights, such splendid understandings – and all there is at the end after all one's effort was this, this chaos, this void, this nothing!

Suddenly the guide from the Hall of Records with the cold eyes, Wardyke, appeared.

'Am I dead?' she asked.

'No,' he said. 'You have come here to learn about the nature of matter – and the nature of will and thought. You are in the vortex of energy out of which a million worlds have been created. There is nothing here but pulses of energy – you may shape them into whatever you wish.'

Deva had seen a priest stand naked in snow and experience no cold and sustain no frostbite. She had seen a priest stand on burning embers and experience no pain and sustain no burns. She had never doubted that mind was more powerful than matter, but she had never thought that she could use it in this way.

She was tremendously excited. It was as though the universe was hers and she could mould it any way she wished. Images of how she would like things to be if she had the power came to her mind – and with them came the urge to sing. She found herself uttering high, strange sounds, unlike any she had ever made before. Astonished, she noticed that the pulses of energy in the vast darkness were coming together and forming into objects. Her ideas were beginning to take shape. It was as though she were singing and thinking a universe into being. She remembered how Urak had recently shown her a piece of hide stretched tight between pegs and covered with a layer of fine dry sand. Boggoron and the old woman had been sitting on either side, chanting something – something that grew louder and louder until Deva had had to put her hands over her ears. She had noticed how the skin began to vibrate and that, as it did so, the sand shook on its surface and somehow formed into a geometric pattern.

Was this it? Was this the key to manifestation-magic – sound causing vibrations which altered the pattern of the vibrations inherent in an object? She thought back to the times she had witnessed Urak manifesting something. She had supposed it was the concentration of thought that was bringing about the change – but now she remembered that each time Urak's throat had moved as though she were making a sound and Deva's ears had tingled as though she were hearing one – though more often than not the sound Urak emitted was beyond human hearing. Delighted with her new understanding, Deva gave herself over completely to thinking up images and producing sounds to go with them.

But suddenly she was afraid. Things were happening too fast. She could no longer control her thoughts or the sounds that she was making. Terrible, fearful ideas were coming to her and terrible, fearful things were coming into being. The more frightened she became, the more her thoughts raced about and the faster the world became peopled with monstrous and misshapen forms. The song she was singing had become ugly and discordant – each note worse than the last – and she could not think how to stop it and start again.

Wardyke smiled and held up his hand. Instantly everything froze. She was appalled at what she saw. Was this what she would do if she had the power to create a universe?

Her thoughts swung to Kyra, her mother. She longed for the time when she was a child and life had seemed so safe and simple. 'What a terrifying thing it is to be responsible for how things are,' she thought. She was no longer sure she wanted this power. Why had she not listened to Kyra's teaching? Why had she always turned away from her?

At that moment she noticed that Wardyke, who had been watching her with gloating satisfaction, fell back a step with an angry and startled exclamation. He seemed to dissolve before her eyes and then re-form into the figure of Maal. Beside him, and hand in hand with him, was the image of her mother. They both lifted their free hands to her head, and it seemed to her a beam of light was coming down from above, passing through their hands and into her head. In that light she saw clearly the dangers of what she and Urak were playing with. Create one thing, change one thing, and, however minutely, everything else had to change to accommodate it. The Unknown One who had created the universe could take into account the repercussions to the millionth, billionth degree – but their own limited minds could never encompass such a vast, complex and subtle design.

And then, suddenly, it seemed as though Time that had stopped, had started again where it had left off.

Deva heard a roaring in her ears and felt herself buffeted in the tremendous force of the whirlpool. She fought to stay afloat, catching a glimpse for a moment of the faces of Urak and Boggoron looking down at her. Then they were gone and the water closed over her. Her lungs ached as she tried to hold her breath. Her eardrums nearly burst. But suddenly she was clear. Torn and battered, she was swept through a narrow opening in the rock and then borne along at a great pace on the surface of an underground river speeding to the ocean. There was just enough space above it for her to take in great gulps of air. She wanted to live. She wanted to go back to Kyra. Oh, what a fool she had been! If only... if only...

She was almost blinded as the river burst out into the sunlight on the mountainside. There was a fall – and she dropped to the turbulent pool at the base of it, more than half drowned, but clinging to life with all her willpower.

'Hurry! Hurry!' screamed Urak, pushing Boggoron aside as he stumbled into her way. They had burst out of the mountain and were rushing along a precipitous path to see if they could find Deva as she was washed out into the open.

Urak was gasping for breath and it seemed to her that a huge hand had hold of her heart and was squeezing it tighter and tighter... but she had to find Deva. She had to know if she had learned what she wanted her to learn; she had to know if she was ready to be sent back to the Temple – Urak's creature, Urak's slave – prepared to undermine all that the Temple stood for and capable of wreaking vengeance on behalf of both herself and Wardyke.

'Ai...' she screamed. 'Ai... Ai...' How her body pained her and held her back! How that loping fool Boggoron irritated her! 'Carry me,' she shrieked at him. 'You dreg, can't you see I need...'

Terrified, Boggoron cringed back. He had never in all the years he had been with her dared or been allowed to touch her.

She lashed out at him with her bony hand and ripped the flesh on his cheek with her sharp nails. She had to lean against a rock, doubled up with pain.

He stood, indecisive, shocked, trembling... but the look in her eye decided him at last to obey. Shuddering with fear, he lifted her. She weighed almost nothing.

'Run!' she hissed. 'Run... you... you...'

He ran. Sure-footed now as a mountain goat, he negotiated the hazards of the uneven track – knowing that not only would he be dead if he stumbled and fell but he would probably be cursed for ever and ever as well.

But even so, Urak knew they would never get there in time to catch Deva as she came swirling out of the mountain. Fragments of images were flashing before her eyes and she knew someone else was near... someone from the Temple seeking Kyra's daughter. Urak was too distraught to be sure who it was and how near they were, but she dreaded that the Temple might once again snatch victory from her. She must get to Deva. She must be sure of her. If there were any chance Deva would not do what Urak wanted her to do when she returned to the Temple, the owl-woman wanted her dead. That in itself would be a revenge. She might not destroy the Temple, but she would hurt those who were most powerful in it.

But she needed help. That fool Boggoron was too slow.

She tried to compose herself enough to send out a call. The soundless sound went out – broken, almost incoherent... but nevertheless understood by those it was meant for.

At the bottom of Urak's narrow valley three figures picked their way carefully through the boulder-strewn stream. Occasionally they could clamber along the banks, but mostly the rocky sides were too steep or the forest growth too thick. The grey horse had had to be left behind on a long tether, with water and lush grass well within reach.

Isar and Farla were tense and nervous, fearing the confrontation that they sensed was near. Gya was leading the way, full of excited anticipation that at last things were going to come to a head. His weapons were ready, his senses alert.

They had gone some way thus when Farla noticed that the birds had stopped singing. Even the sound of the stream had changed – the gentle bubbling murmur that had accompanied them the whole way up the gorge was now more of a threatening grumble, and it sounded as though ahead of them there were rapids or a waterfall.

Farla wanted to call out to Gya to be careful, but he was too far ahead and the water was making too much noise.

Isar turned and looked back at her, his face worried. She hurried to catch up with him and stayed close as they rounded a bend and were suddenly faced with a forest clearing. Their stream was feeding into what looked like a very deep pool, and a waterfall thundered into it from a hole in the side of the steep cliff face to the west. Gya was already there, standing on a rock that jutted out into the water, looking around in some surprise. The gorge had opened out so suddenly. None of them had expected it.

Farla was looking up at the waterfall when she gave a cry and raised her hand to point. She had seen an object come bubbling out of the dark hole in the mountain and go tumbling down to the pool with the white water – and the object looked remarkably like a human figure.

The two young men looked round at once, but before they could establish what exactly they had seen they heard a terrible sound above their heads and looked up. Hovering over them was a swarm of the strangest and nastiest beings they had ever seen – and even Gya saw them this time. Some resembled vultures, but with remarkably human faces. Others had no bird form at all but were shadowy shapes twisting and writhing and constantly changing – the only thing constant about them was that they shut out the light of the sun and cast a deathly chill on the three horrified humans. Gya drew his bow at once and let fly at one that seemed more solid than the rest, but his arrow went straight through it and out the other side, falling harmlessly into the water. The creatures were screeching and swooping with eyeballs red as fire, and talons that shone like polished metal. There was a rush of icy air as they brushed past.

Isar had drawn his knife and was slashing above his head with one arm while he tried to protect his face with the other. Gya was frantically shooting arrow after arrow, though none had any effect on their attackers.

Farla looked back to the water, suspecting that they would not be suffering this attack if they were not very near to finding Deva. A figure was floating in the water, limp and apparently unconscious, the swirl half dragging it under. Farla could see that it was Deva, and she was being swept along to where the river poured out of the pool on the other side, to drop down over another ledge of rock and another waterfall.

Farla screamed as a ghastly talon fastened on her shoulder and she could feel the hot and stinking breath of the monstrous creature that was attacking her... but she managed to shake herself free somehow and plunge into the water. She had taught herself to swim to escape from the island, and now this skill served her well. Isar and Gya managed to keep the creatures fully occupied as she swam out to Deva at the centre of the pool. After a struggle with the fierce tug of the water she managed to get a grip on her and started to drag her back.

Isar rushed to help her. Together they got Deva on to the bank and did their best to pump the water out of her lungs and staunch the bleeding of the numerous cuts and scratches she had sustained on her journey through the mountain. Gya fought on. Although he was causing no casualties, the bombardment of the constantly flying arrows was apparently discomfiting and confusing their attackers.

Seeing that Isar was attending to Deva, Farla turned her attention back to the creatures. If physical weapons could not disperse them, perhaps other methods could. If they were not of this earth-realm – and it was obvious they were not – someone's will must have brought them in and be holding them here... It would be Urak, of course.

At that moment Farla heard a sound from the cliff face above her and looked up. An old woman and what looked like a misshapen dwarf were standing beside the cave out of which the waterfall was pouring, looking down at the scene below.

Urak!

Farla tried to compose herself in spite of the noise and danger. For Kyra's sake, for all that she had done for her, she wanted more than anything else in the world to bring her daughter safely home to her – but, tugging at some buried part of her heart, was the painful thought that Deva was also Gya's wife, and if she succeeded she would never have Gya herself. 'No,' she said fiercely, crushing the thought. This form of distraction had been her undoing once before. She still felt the sick child's death on her conscience. She must think of Kyra. Only of Kyra. Kyra and Khu-ren. The Temple. She must call on the strength of the Temple and through it on the strength of the great Shining Beings from the higher realms... the 'birds' that sang in the mighty Tree of Life.

Powerfully she imaged the great Lords of the Sun, and around them the circle of energy that was the Temple.

'Urak!' She framed the name in her mind though no words came from her lips. She dared not take her eyes off the woman, but she had the impression that the noisy and violent swarm had gone back where they had come from, frightened off by the strength of the light that was channelling through her. The old woman high on the cliff staggered and fell back.

'It's done!' thought Farla exultantly. 'It's done!' And – a moment too soon – she swung round to see if Deva was all right.

But Urak was not finished yet.

She had felt the power of Farla's gaze... she had seen the image of the ring of Standing Stones... she had caught the message and the warning from the Beings of Light. She was too weak now to match image for image, power for power. She could scarcely stand. But she was determined that Deva would carry her vengeance to the Temple or she would not return at all.

Urak was frantic. She could see that Deva was alive, but she could tell nothing more. She tried to call Wardyke to help her... but she could not muster the psychic strength. Farla and her hateful priests had closed the entrance between the realms and isolated Urak from her familiars.

But there was one last thing she could try.

Suddenly a huge hunting-owl swooped down on Deva's soaked and battered body. It began to tear at her in rage with its talons and beak. Horrified, they tried to beat it off – but soon retreated, astonished at its size and ferocity.

Gya set his last arrow and took careful aim. The shaft flew true. Blood spattered Deva as the huge bird shrieked and flapped its wings, losing its grip on her flesh. It lurched off – for a moment looking as though it was going to be able to limp away. But the arrow was still in its breast and its life's-blood was rapidly seeping into the soil.

Farla caught the look on Isar's face as he lifted Deva into his arms. She was sobbing and clinging to him, her blood – where the owl talons had torn her flesh – staining his tunic. In that moment there seemed to be no one else in the world but the two of them clinging together through Time, lovers forever... Farla looked quickly at Gya, wondering if he had seen what she had seen.

He was standing where the owl had fallen and he was staring at something on the ground, bewildered.

'What is it?' Farla went to him.

At his feet was an old, old woman with an arrow in her chest, thin as a skeleton, white hair as long as a cloak.

Urak was dead.

From the cliff above them they heard an unearthly howl and when they looked up they saw a strange, wild man beating his head with his fists, sobbing inconsolably. Boggoron had lost the only family he knew.

That night Isar and Gya built a ring of fire around their camp, isolating themselves from Urak's hastily dug grave. They had given her something of a funeral at sunset. Farla praying over her fragile and discarded body that she might be taken into the care of the Shining Ones... that her soul might realise where it had gone wrong in this life and be prepared to change for the better in the next.

Gya strode away from the little group and stood staring into the pool where they had found Deva, listening to the roar of the river as it poured out of the mysterious regions within the limestone mountains, turned round and round in the pool below, and finally made its way down the valley towards the great ocean. He was not sure that he believed everything the Temple taught... He was not sure that our body on this earth is no more than a cloak we, as eternal beings, put on and take off, and continue to do so many times until we have, as Kyra once put it, 'grown out of the need for it and are ready to go on to the higher realms'.

'What are these higher realms?' he had asked her once. But not even Kyra could describe them.

'Can an infant just born describe to you the delights of lovemaking between a man and a woman?' she asked when he pressed her. 'Ask me again when I am further on in the Great Journey.'

'But how do you know they are there at all?' he persisted. 'How do you know there is anything at all after the worms have eaten us?'

'There have been glimpses,' she replied. 'Moments of insight given. Not only to me but to anyone who is prepared to look and listen...'

'Are you saying that the infant catches a glimpse of a man and woman making love, but doesn't understand yet what they are doing?'

She laughed. 'Something like that. He or she will look back one day and be amused how little they understood then and how much they understand now.'

'I can't wait for that day!' was Gya's laughing reply. And that was how he was prepared to leave it. One day he would understand – but meanwhile there were other things that interested him more.

He had collected the wood for the fires while the others finished off the strange little ceremony Farla had insisted on having for Urak.

Unnoticed by any of them, Boggoron had been hidden behind some bushes watching the whole thing, tears pouring down his dusty cheeks.

The next day, when the four young people had departed, leaving only the minimum rocks necessary to keep her grave safe from scavenging animals, Boggoron crept out and, sobbing openly, built a huge cairn of rounded river-worn pebbles above her grave.

Kyra knew that Deva was coming home. It was as though a fog had lifted and she could see clearly at last. She was not sure what had happened, but she knew that she was no longer being blocked by

Urak's tricks. She called Lark to her side and told her that Isar would soon be back with her. Lark bowed her head thankfully. She did not think she could bear the separation much longer. She needed his support, his understanding, his strength. That night when she went to bed she was not aware of the join between waking and sleeping... all was one piece of cloth. She had no bad dreams. Isar was coming home to her at last!

Chapter 17

Deva's return

Deva walked the muddy streets of her home village and yearned for the grandeur and the space of the mountains, the magnificence of the palaces and colonnades of Egypt. She was impatient with the smallness of the houses, the contentment of the people. 'Why are they satisfied with so little,' she asked herself impatiently, 'when there is so much more they could have?' She spent more and more time telling them what they were missing, describing her Egyptian journeys, the chairs inlaid with ivory and gold, the cloth so fine you could see through it, the exotic foods, the fans of ostrich feather, vases of alabaster... Most listened fascinated to her tales and looked around their little houses of wood and thatch, with their few practical vessels of earthenware and wood, and began to feel deprived.

'I don't know how you can live like this,' she said to her father. 'You, who've known such luxuries in Egypt.'

'It's the water I drink, not the cup. There is no purer water than that which springs from these hills.'

'But your people can write words down on papyrus or on stone, We have nothing like that here. Don't you miss anything from your home?'

For a moment Khu-ren hesitated. He did miss many things about Egypt. His present home was beautiful – the gentle feminine curves of the chalk hills, the soft and waving grass, so green that emeralds would pale beside it, the wheat fields richer than any gold, the forested valleys, flame-red in autumn, delicate mist-green in spring. He loved the Temple with its stark attention to essentials... the Tall Stones marking the circle – the cipher for the sun – which in its turn was cipher for that which is limitless and nameless: the One in which All is contained. He loved the rituals closely bound to the seasons, the rhythms of the earth, the sun, the moon and the stars. He had grown impatient with the complexities of the religious rituals of his own people, the priests often paying so much attention to the physical representations of the gods that they forgot what the images in stone, in gold, in lapis lazuli, actually stood for.

Ah, but his daughter had touched a nerve. He did miss Egypt. He missed the sunsets over the desert – the fire-red after-glow, the ever-deepening crimson and purple. He missed the great river and the sails lifting to the breeze. He missed the dawn – the stillness of waiting, the moment of transformation. There were sunsets and sunrises here, but never so stark, so clear, so basic. He missed the mountains on the west bank, holding their silence and their secrets. He missed the rust and ochre colours of the desert, the great space.

He missed so much!

He looked at Deva sharply. 'This is my home now,' he said. 'These are my people. We need no words chiselled in stone to tell us what we need to know.'

Gya was suddenly alert. A shadow had moved in the chamber. He was sure of it. Deva was fast asleep beside him, her bare shoulder catching the faint glow of moonlight from the window. He had dozed off momentarily after their lovemaking, but had drifted awake not long afterwards. He had lain still, thinking of the woman beside him. One moment she was passionate towards him and he could scarcely keep up with her demands. But then there were times when he felt he meant nothing to her, and her attention was far away. He had seen the way she and Isar had looked at each other, but he had no fear that they would ever do more than look. Isar had a deep and abiding love for Lark and he would never, being the kind of man he was, do anything to hurt her.

There had been a kind of desperation in the way Deva made love this night. Both of them were bruised. Both of them were exhausted. But he could not sleep. Something was bothering him. He lay questioning his love for her. He felt no tenderness for her as Isar felt for Lark, only a kind of frenzy – almost a pain. But a pain he feared he could not do without. What if she left him? Since her return from Urak he had felt his hold on her becoming more and more tenuous. She refused to speak about Urak, as though it were a part of her life that was shut off for ever – but she was restless... abstracted... impatient.

When he noticed the movement in the shadows he was thankful he was indeed awake. Slowly and carefully he slid his arm out of the rugs and reached for his clothes beside the bed. There was a dagger in his belt. Deva felt the movement of his body and stirred with a sigh, but he had made no sound and she did not wake. His eyes never left the place where he had detected the intruder.

Suddenly there was a swish and a creak as a body leapt on top of him. He had not yet grasped his dagger, but he was alert enough at once to raise his arms and seize his attacker. The shout he gave woke Deva and she sat up, startled.

'I have him!' yelled Gya. 'Light the lamp! Light the lamp! We'll see who comes creeping into our room at night!'

Bewildered, Deva fumbled with the fire-stones, shivering with fright as the bodies of her husband and his attacker rolled and lurched, falling at last off the bed and on to the hard floor. She could hear Gya's cursing and another voice she thought she recognised.

At last the lamp was lit and they could both see that it was a vicious, spitting Boggoron whom Gya held helpless in his muscular grip.

'Gya, let him go!' she cried. 'It's only Boggoron.'

'Only Boggoron!' shouted Gya. 'Tell him to drop his knife if he is a friend of yours!'

'He's no friend. Boggoron!' she snapped authoritatively, holding the lamp high. 'Drop the knife. My husband will kill you. Drop it at once!' Gya was a much bigger man than Boggoron and, although Urak's slave still held the knife, he now had no chance of reaching Gya with it. Whimpering and snarling, he dropped it – his hand almost blue from Gya's grip.

Gya shook him as a cat shakes a mouse and flung him away from him on to the floor. But before he could crawl away, Gya seized his own dagger and stood threateningly over him.

'Who is this weasel?' he asked Deva with contempt.

'Don't kill him. He's Urak's slave.'

'Urak's companion. Urak's helper. Urak's avenger!' almost sobbed Boggoron. 'No slave... no... no slave...'

'Let him be,' Deva said calmly. 'Without Urak he is nothing.' She felt sorry for him. She knew he had no life apart from Urak and for all she had hated him on the mountain, he was at least some tangible evidence that she had not dreamed the whole incredible incident. 'Who knows,' she thought, 'he might be of use to me.' He might have some of Urak's lore stored in that low, beetling forehead. She felt strangely elated at the sight of him.

'He tried to kill me,' Gya growled.

'I know,' said Deva soothingly. 'But he was upset because you killed the only friend he had. Look at him. He's no threat to you.'

Certainly the wizened figure lying on the floor with his arm above his head to ward off blows did not seem a worthy adversary for the famous bowman and warrior.

'Boggoron,' she said firmly. 'We're going to save your life if you swear never to attack my lord Gya again.'

'What is my life worth to me with Urak dead,' muttered Boggoron. Gya raised his knife.

'Boggoron,' she snapped. 'Your life is mine now. Urak named me her heir. You heard her. You know it. You are mine.'

Boggoron looked at her from under his arm. He was silent.

'Acknowledge it!' she said sternly. She had pulled a garment loosely around her and was standing in the lamplight with her hair, as blue-black as ravens' wings, flowing over her creamy bare shoulders. Her eyes, as powerful as Urak's, were glaring into his. He began to tremble. It was as though Urak was a young woman again and he was the infant she had found in the bracken.

'I acknowledge it,' he whispered.

'Let him go,' she said to Gya. 'You'll have no more trouble from him.'

Gya lowered his dagger arm and looked from one to the other in astonishment. All Boggoron's fierce anger was gone and he was cringing at Deva's feet like a beaten cur. Gya felt extremely uneasy about the whole situation but he too seemed to be, temporarily at least, under the spell of Deva. He could not have disobeyed her if he had wanted to.

'You may sleep outside our door this night,' Deva told Boggoron haughtily. 'Tomorrow I'll find a proper place for you.'

Gya stared with open mouth as Boggoron crawled to the door and curled up outside it like a dog.

'Deva...' he began to protest.

'That is enough,' she said coldly. 'It is over. It is the middle of the night and I'm tired.'

She dropped the garment from her and, as white as alabaster, climbed into the bed. Meekly Gya climbed in beside her and lay flat out on his back – not daring to touch her.

Within moments she and Boggoron were asleep, while Gya lay awake.

Boggoron soon became a familiar sight. He followed Deva everywhere and she only had to snap her fingers for him to do her bidding. Kyra tried to explain to her that she had no right to keep another human being in such subservience to her, but Deva parried by saying that Boggoron knew no other way of life. He would go to pieces if she took her yoke from his shoulders.

'I doubt it,' Kyra said. 'He might be temporarily confused, but he'd soon learn to live his own life like the rest of us. You are damaging yourself more than him by this attitude.'

Deva tossed her head impatiently and walked away. Kyra did not understand. Kyra had not seen Boggoron's relationship with Urak. The creature wanted to be a slave. 'Besides,' and here Deva had a moment of honesty, 'I need him.' She needed him so that she could recapture something of the belief in the power and privilege that would one day be hers if she followed Urak's path. She needed him to remind her of Urak... to remind her of some of the aspects of Urak's teaching that were already slipping from her. They would sit for hours and talk about 'old times', Boggoron at her feet, she on a tall oak chair.

She began to gather a little group of friends around her, people who hung on her every word; people flattered to be the intimates of the daughter of the High Priest; people who chose to do nothing with their lives and then complained that they were bored. They listened fascinated to her tales of the riches she had seen and the luxuries of other countries, and grew even more dissatisfied with their own lives.

'You must help me,' Deva said one day to Boggoron, tired of talking and describing. 'I want to do something to astonish these people.'

His eyes gleamed. He had not been party to Urak's deepest secrets, but he had observed enough over the years to be of some use to his new mistress.

Deva had chosen what was called 'the field of the grey gods' for her experiment. It was in a valley some little way from the Temple and out of sight of the villagers, strewn with huge slabs of grey rock. In very ancient times Deva and Isar, in their former incarnation together, had had a palace there and some remnants of it were still visible. One in particular: a roughly shaped throne. It was to this Deva always gravitated. She had sat on this throne before things started to go so very wrong in her ancient life. Here she felt the strength she had had as Radedef's beloved. She knew it was unlikely that Boggoron and she would be disturbed – for the local people feared the field and claimed that it was haunted. Occasionally students were brought to it to learn to sense the vibrations and the emanations of stone before they went on to the delicate task of choosing the right stone to be used in the building of sacred circles. But she had taken the precaution of finding out when the next group of students would be brought to the field, and it would not be for several days yet.

She settled herself on the stone throne and commanded Boggoron to squat at her feet as usual. He opened his mouth to say something, but shut it again when she raised her hand warningly. The stone was cold when she first sat down, and uncomfortable – but almost immediately she began to have a very strange sensation. It was almost as if it were humming. It was warming very rapidly to her body heat, and she was finding that she was beginning to feel very comfortable in it as though it were thickly cushioned. She gazed across the field with its scattering of grey slabs, to the hawthorn trees in full blossom growing at the edges. A rook landed on a nearby boulder and stared at her boldly with a round, yellow eye. She stared back at it for a moment, wondering how it saw her, wondering what thoughts were going on in its head without words, wondering if it was indeed a rook... or some shaman or sorcerer, a master in shape-shifting.

When she looked away from the bird again, she found that a thick mist was now obscuring the limits of the field. The hawthorn trees were already fading from sight and the white cloud was rapidly rolling in, consuming the huge blocks of stone on the way.

She could not suppress a shiver of fear. She wanted the magic to start, the field to be charged with an energy she could use, but she was alone now, no powerful Urak at her side to orchestrate it. She leant forward and touched Boggoron on the shoulder. 'Move closer,' she whispered. 'Don't leave me.' With alacrity he shifted until he was right up against the edge of the stone chair. He glanced apprehensively at the strange mist moving in and wriggled closer until he was against her leg. Surprised that she did not withdraw at once, he looked up at her. She seemed transfixed. She was sitting bolt upright in the chair, her hands gripping the sides, her feet close together on the ground. She was staring straight ahead. What was she seeing? He peered back at the mist, straining to see what she was seeing... but he could make nothing out.

Deva was wandering in the ancient palace that had once stood on this site. The huge blocks of stone were fitted together once again to form great high walls. Warriors were standing guard at the gate. Her women, chattering, were following her down the long corridor to the throne room. There sat her lord, Radedef – her beloved. He looked up when she entered and her heart almost melted at his smile. Around her were the courtiers, gold at their throats and on their arms, gold on their fingers and in their ears...

'My lord.' She heard her own voice distinctly. He reached out his hands to her and she moved towards him, totally content in his love.

But before she reached him she caught her sandal on an uneven paving stone and stumbled. When she looked up again he and all the court had disappeared. The hall had gone, with its fine trappings, and the corridor and walls... She was in an empty field, Boggoron crouched at her feet and a mist rolling away into the distance.

She gave an exclamation of disgust, tears filling her eyes.

'If only,' she murmured, 'if only... if only I could go back to those days!'

'Mistress.' Boggoron was tugging anxiously at her skirt. 'What is it? What is it, mistress?'

'Nothing,' she said sharply, wiping her eyes on the back of her hand. 'Old memories. Foolishness. We can't have the past back, Boggoron. I've learnt that. The golden age for you and me is irretrievable – but there are still things we can have! We'll not let Urak's skills die with her. Come, Boggoron – let's see if I learned anything from the great owl-lady!'

She had experienced illumination in the vortex with the help of Kyra and Maal, but her own nature and the poison of Urak that still flowed in her veins fought against it. Was it Urak's voice whispering in her ear, or her own, that persuaded her that a few manifested luxuries would not alter the world too drastically and would certainly make her life easier and pleasanter?

She stooped down and picked up a small piece of stone. She told Boggoron to stand in front of her and she put it in his hand. 'Hold it out straight – like that,' she said. 'Don't move. Don't dare move. Don't even tremble! I am going to make a golden cup out of that valueless little stone, Boggoron, just as Urak would have done. You are going to hold it steady and concentrate on it being a cup, a golden cup. Understand?' He nodded. 'It is important you don't let your mind wander. Understand?' He nodded again more vigorously. He was filled with a sense of importance. Urak had never let him actually take part in this way.

Deva described the cup in detail to him – the cup she wanted him to visualise. It would be of fine beaten gold, ridged and ringed, but the lip would be as thin as a leaf. There would be a handle at the side. He would be holding it by the handle when it changed. She did not know if it was necessary for him to take part in the visualisation process, but she thought it could not hurt, and it might well help. She was not sure she had enough power by herself.

When she was satisfied he had got the idea and was standing very still, staring unblinkingly at the stone in his hand, she began to make sounds. She began to sing. This time she did not let her mind wander to old hurts or seek images in the mist. As clear as if she were seeing it in physical reality, she visualised a golden cup at the centre of the silver vortex she had entered when she was pushed into the underground whirlpool by Urak. She thought she understood now the meaning of the ring-spirals that had been carved in the ancient days at the entrances to tombs, on the inner walls of initiation chambers and on the wooden columns at the entrance to their own Temple of the Sun. They represented the vortex – the powerful inrush of energy that one experienced outside Time as one passed from one realm to another...

At first there were moments when her image wavered and her voice seemed to break – but her desire to make the magic work was so strong, her concentration soon returned.

It seemed to her she was burning up as though with a fever. Her head ached, sweat poured down her cheeks. But she held on... held on. Boggoron had become like a stone himself. He never moved. He was locked into the beam of energy that poured from her as surely as the stone that he held.

Suddenly he gave a groan and dropped to the ground.

The thread of her concentration broke. She stared at him for a moment, bewildered, wondering who he was, and where she was, and what was happening. Then she remembered what she had been trying to do. Without a thought as to whether he was all right or not she rushed to his side and reached for the object he had been holding. In his hand when she prised it open was nothing but dust. The rock had disintegrated but had not changed its nature.

Furiously, she turned on him.

'We were nearly there!' she screamed. 'Why did you move?' She began to beat him on his unconscious head, feeling the bone of his skull against her fists with satisfaction.

'Dust!' she screamed. 'If only you hadn't moved!'

After a while she came to her senses, and looked at him more calmly. Was he dead? Had she killed him with the energy she had felt pouring from her? She was more curious than sorrowful as she turned him over.

When he groaned she was relieved. How would she have explained his death?

Chapter 18

Wardyke's 'friend'

Fern was very worried about the behaviour of her younger son, Jan. He had always been an eagerly adventurous boy, often into mischief of one kind or another – but never anything secretive or harmful. He was the sort of child who climbed trees too high for him and got stuck; who fell into the river when he was supposed to be watching that the baby did not; who did not turn up at mealtimes. He was his father's close friend, liking nothing better than riding off with Karne, sitting high above the world on the Spear-lord's horse, his arms firmly wound around Karne's waist.

But lately he had changed. He had become morose and silent. He refused the opportunity to ride with Karne in favour of going off by himself into the woods. When people came upon him suddenly he started as though he had guilty thoughts.

Karne thought it might well be the onset of puberty and suggested they should start thinking about the initiation rites all boys underwent on the threshold of manhood. But Fern sensed something in him that had not been there before and she believed it was not due to the natural changes in his body.

Jan had a secret and he had never kept a secret from his parents before – not a serious one. Every autumn he hid his special store of hazelnuts from his siblings, but it never took them long to discover the cache. This time he knew his secret must be kept. If he told anyone, he knew the object of his fascination would be taken instantly away from him – and that he could not bear. Not yet, anyway.

He had been playing in the fields near the great burial mound that day when Lark had gone to confront Wardyke. He had seen her toiling up the hill and disappearing behind the great stone slab at the entrance. The question of what she was doing there occupied his mind for a moment or two... but then he had thrown some grain for a group of sparrows and was busy watching how the fluffy young birds vibrated their wings and still called to be fed by their parents, even though they were quite capable of picking up the grain for themselves – and indeed capable of flying in search of their own food. It was only when he turned to go home that he noticed the commotion and saw the priest and another man carrying Lark down the hill as though she were dead.

He was shocked. He liked Lark. She came often to the house and although she could not speak, she often played hide and seek with them. Sometimes in the evening when it was difficult to go to sleep she sat with them and plucked that little harp of hers, making it sing beautiful melodies until they drifted off.

He looked at the tomb, wondering what had happened. It lay as it always had, a long green mound on a hilltop, close against the blue sky. But today he thought he saw a kind of black smoke drifting over it. He could not be sure. It was so faint and so fleeting, gone almost before he registered it.

Curiosity had always been Jan's undoing. He decided to investigate – and ran up the hill.

No one was around.

He could see nothing unless he ventured behind the great entrance slab into the forecourt. Should he? He paused, terrified but fascinated, at the little flight of steps that would take him up and over the side wall of the forecourt.

'Perhaps I'll just climb to the top and look down. I won't go down,' he vowed.

When he saw the blood – and the dagger – he nearly turned and ran at once... but the dagger gleamed and glinted, its gold pins catching the sunlight. With beating heart he clambered down the steps on to the paving stones and seized the dagger. Without a pause he was up and out of the forecourt again and pounding down the hill to hide in the woods by the river, the dagger clutched in his sweating little hand.

Trembling, he washed it in the river and stared as the metal shone under the moving water, deforming under the ripples and eddies so that for a moment it looked more like a face with a long pointed beard than a dagger. In his panic at this apparent transformation, he dropped it – and it spiralled down to settle on the riverbed among the smooth, rounded pebbles. He plunged in his arm and tried to retrieve it. He lost his balance and slipped into the water, nearly drowning as his arms became entangled in the waterweeds that grew at the side. The centre of the river was so clear that its depth was deceptive. The dagger was further than he had thought, and no matter how he struggled he seemed to get no nearer it. But something must have dislodged it from its resting place for suddenly it floated free, uncannily swept by the current towards his outstretched hand. With bursting lungs he slashed the tendrils that held him down and rose, gasping, to the surface, carrying the dagger triumphantly with him.

It was his! He had risked his life for it – and it had saved his life for him. No one would ever make him give it up!

Hastily he searched the woods around him for a suitable hiding place. He knew he would have to be cunning because the whole area was familiar ground to the village children.

At last he found a place he was sure no one would find and laid the deadly blade down.

'Wait there for me,' he whispered. 'I'll be back.'

As he turned to run home he thought he saw a shadowy figure move among the trees and turned, alarmed to think someone might have seen him bury it. But there was no one there. He called and searched – but he found no one.

That was the beginning. He kept the dagger secret and it became for him more precious than a holy talisman, more beautiful than the jewels his mother wore – even more precious than his father's grey horse. It was his in a way that nothing else was his. The possession of it gave him a secret and a terrible strength. He would never use it, he told himself. It was just the having of it.

One day he had taken Wardyke's dagger out of its hiding place and was crouched down on the ground turning it over and over in his hands, admiring the design on the hilt, when suddenly he sensed he was being watched. Hastily he put it behind his back and scuffed a few fallen leaves over it. Then he looked guiltily up and saw, a few paces from him, the figure of a stranger leaning against a tree. He could see his clumsy attempts to hide the dagger were pointless. The man's expression was one of ironical amusement. He had seen everything. Jan did not know what to do. He estimated from the distance between them that he would not get far if he started to run. He looked at the man more closely. There was something odd about him. He was dressed in a long shadowy black cloak though it was a warm day. His face was cruel and hard, and yet he appeared to be smiling. His eyes, even from that distance, seemed to bore right into Jan's mind. The boy felt he could see into his most secret thoughts. 'That's not fair,' Jan thought resentfully. 'He's doing it without permission.' The priests at the Temple had the art, but would never invade a person's privacy without first requesting permission – unless, of course, it was a matter of real danger if they did not. This man was spying on him from outside and from in, and Jan did not like it.

He picked up the dagger again and stood up. He lifted his chin and stared boldly into the stranger's eyes. His heart was beating very fast and he was extremely frightened, but somehow, holding the dagger gave him bravado. He would not give it up no matter what. 'Even if I die for it!' he thought fiercely.

The man laughed – but there was no mirth in his voice.

Sweat was trickling down Jan's forehead and involuntarily he used the back of his left hand to wipe it away. In the moment his vision was obscured the man disappeared. Jan gasped and looked round uneasily. He had completely vanished. The boy ran to the tree against which the stranger had been leaning and looked behind it and all around it. Jan felt extremely uncomfortable. Somewhere the man was hiding, watching – and laughing. He clutched the dagger more tightly. Wherever he hid it now, he could not be sure the man would not see him and, when he was gone, take it. Jan could not contemplate losing the dagger.

He slipped it under his tunic and into his leather belt. It would be difficult keeping it hidden on his person, but he was no longer prepared to risk its being found by someone else. If it were found on him, at least he would have a chance to argue – or fight – for his right to keep it. But if that cold, harsh man took it, he would never see it again, nor know where it had gone. The man was not a local – of that he was sure – and by the bitter cast to his features he doubted if he had come to train as a priest at the Temple. They had many strangers in this valley, passing through on the way to the Temple, for it drew students from all over the world. But they had the look of people eager to learn... of people with a good and satisfying purpose in life. This man looked as though he was an enemy of life.

Jan took to hiding the mysterious dagger under his rugs at night and on his person during the day, knowing that he should give it over to his parents or to the priests at the Temple, but deciding, as each day went by, that he would keep it one more day, and give it over the next. He found, however, as more time went by, that it became increasingly difficult to admit he had it.

At the beginning there had been quite a hue and cry about it – his father questioning everyone who could possibly have been near the entrance to the ancient passage grave at the time Lark tried to take her own life. Jan had lied then – and he had had to continue lying, until now he was lost in such a labyrinth of lies there seemed no way out. All the fun and joy seemed to have gone out of his life. He became morose and bored. He would not play with the other children, yet at times he longed to do so. He was obsessed with the fear that they would find the dagger on him. He had restless nights and bad dreams, and Fern worried as she saw him getting thinner and paler by the day. Whenever she questioned him, he insisted that there was nothing wrong and withdrew even further into his shell. He longed to tell her and to free himself of the secret that had now become a burden to him. But somehow he could not.

One night he was lying sleepless, when suddenly there was someone at the foot of the bed. He thought at first it was his father, who often came in at night to see if the children were warmly tucked up, but the shadowy outline of the man seemed too large for that. He stared at him in alarm, too frightened even to call out. The stranger beckoned to him and without a murmur of protest he crept out of bed and followed him, it was a very dark, moonless night. Low cloud obscured the stars and only a very few of the many hearth fires in the valley still had embers that glowed. Jan was terrified. He could see nothing – but he could feel the presence of the stranger beside him.

'You have my dagger?' the man asked in a low voice. Jan shivered as he noticed how hollow and distant it sounded, though the man himself was close by him.

'I – I didn't know...' Jan stammered, 'You – you can have it back! I – I – didn't know...' He turned to rush back into the house to fetch the dagger, now desperately eager to get rid of it. But the doorway, though apparently empty, had a kind of curtain of ice-cold air over it, through which Jan could not bring himself to pass. Terrified, he looked back over his shoulder. It seemed to him he could make out the figure of the stranger – a form of darkness blacker than the night itself.

'I don't want it back,' the being said softly. 'I want you to keep it. It is yours.'

Jan gasped. Keep it? His heart skipped a beat. Something in him was wanting to insist that Wardyke took it back – for now he was sure that the stranger was Wardyke himself – but something else was making him long to keep it.

'I – I would rather...'

'Keep it,' whispered Wardyke out of the darkness. 'It is yours.'

'Mine?' murmured Jan. Wardyke's dagger, given him by Wardyke himself!

He felt he had left his family and friends a long way behind. He felt he had become a man without the complicated rituals and tests other boys had to endure.

'There is just one thing...' Wardyke's sly voice interrupted the flow of his thought.

'Anything,' answered Jan without thinking, filled with excitement at the thought of keeping the dagger... at the thought of meeting the mysterious and almost legendary Wardyke himself...

'I am lonely – I need a friend.'

'I'll be your friend,' Jan offered at once.

Wardyke smiled and the darkness of his shadow seemed to intensify.

'Our friendship must be a secret.'

'Of course!' Jan said, feeling bolder now, filled with importance, not even noticing that far from getting rid of the one secret that had been bothering him, he now had taken on another.

'I will help you in any way you want,' Wardyke said smoothly. 'Friends always help one another.'

'Certainly,' Jan replied, almost cheerfully.

'Go back to sleep now,' Wardyke whispered. 'Keep the dagger safe. It will be the sign between us of our friendship.'

Jan was so bemused by the possibilities open to him with a friend as powerful as Wardyke that he actually waved as he turned to go. It was only when he was back in bed, with the rugs pulled up to his chin and the sound of his siblings breathing softly beside him, that he suddenly had misgivings.

After that Wardyke appeared to him quite often. Whenever he beckoned, no matter what he was doing, Jan followed him. Usually the boy could not remember what had occurred between the two of them when he returned, but he found that his attitudes were changing. He had less and less respect for his father and began to despise him for being content with the small community he controlled. He had dreams of how, when he was Spear-lord, he would expand his territory. 'I'd keep a proper army of trained warriors so that everyone would fear me and do what I wanted.'

Under Wardyke's influence he began to dislike everything about his home and the Temple community. He began to brood on the way he would takeover and change things if only he were in power. But when he had not seen Wardyke for a while his old feelings reasserted themselves and he knew that these thoughts and this way of thinking were not his own. Sometimes he dreaded meeting Wardyke and longed to be free of him. But at other times he looked forward to the contact.

One morning, as the mist swirled around the villages of the Haylken valley, Wardyke demanded that Jan steal a certain crystal from Kyra's private and very precious collection. He was told exactly where he would find them and which one he should take. Jan remembered seeing the crystals once. They were exquisitely beautiful and he had longed to hold them in his hands. But... to steal one! This he did not want to do.

'Why don't you get it yourself?' he asked sulkily.

Wardyke smiled grimly. 'I have my reasons,' he said.

'What reasons?' Jan pondered. If he could appear anywhere he wanted at any time, why did he not just appear in Kyra's chamber and take the crystal? Then it struck him that if the man was as insubstantial as he appeared he probably could not actually pick up material objects and carry them around. He needed a human agent for that. He needed Jan. Jan wondered if he dared refuse to steal the crystal. He looked at Wardyke's cold and wary face and decided he did not dare refuse.

He had already done things for Wardyke that he regretted. On one occasion he had stolen Kyra's faience necklace – the one possession Kyra valued more than any other. Normally she wore it all the time, but on this day the thread had broken and the beads were lying in a small birchwood box in her chamber. Kyra had been heartbroken at the loss and had searched high and low for it. To her it was much more than a necklace – it was her youth, it was her love for Khu-ren and his love for her, it was protection against the dark forces, the link between her husband's land and her own, and it was her one personal and private thing that had nothing to do with the Temple and its rituals. It expressed her individuality as Kyra, the woman, as opposed to Kyra, the priest. When Jan stole it he had been relieved that it was not more valuable. 'She'll never miss a few broken beads,' he had thought. But when he saw how distraught she was at the loss – he was sorry.

'Why?' he had asked Wardyke. 'Why did you want that necklace? It's not very valuable. Let me put it back in her room and I'll get you her golden torcs and collars, her rings and her bracelets...'

Wardyke smiled. 'Gold is of no interest to me, boy,' he said.

'But why that particular necklace?' Jan persisted. But Wardyke did not answer.

He was already thinking about her crystals. To drain her strength, to reduce her confidence... to increase the possibility that she would make hasty and ill-advised decisions...

'If I get the crystal for you...' Jan began nervously, 'will you promise not to ask me to steal anything again?'

'You will get me the crystal – and then we shall see,' Wardyke said coldly.

Jan bit his lip. He had not the courage to stand his ground this time, but his urge to break free from Wardyke was growing stronger every day.

* * * *

Farla settled back to serious work at the Temple as best she could. Most of the time she managed well, knowing now that this was what she wanted to do. But some nights she found it difficult to sleep and took to walking about until she felt she was ready to relax. It was on such a night that she had an experience she found difficult to explain afterwards.

The student and priest houses were built to the west of the Temple among a grove of trees. An almost full moon caused deep shadows to alternate with strips of light. It was the deepest part of the night – the hearth fires had long since died down. Farla, heading quietly along the moon-silvered walkways between the buildings, could almost feel the touch of other people's dreams and see the shadowy night-riders pass.

Just as she reached the avenue of river-sculpted stones that led to the High Priest's house she thought she saw a small dark figure emerge from the door and run off, brushing past without seeing her. Briefly she caught a glimpse of his face and was astonished to recognise Jan, Fern's son.

'Jan!' she called out – but he did not stop and was already gone, melting into the shadows.

She thought of running after him, but was not sure which of the many paths he had taken. She looked back at the High Priest's house, puzzled. What on earth was the child doing out at this time of night – and so obviously being furtive. Had she imagined it? No – she was sure he had come out of the house. There was no light showing – which indicated that Kyra and Khu-ren were either asleep or absent from their home. Farla began to have suspicions that she did not wish to have, for, like everyone else who knew him, she had always liked Jan. But lately there had been quite a few robberies in the village, and no one could imagine who was responsible. Surely not Fern's son?

She moved nearer and was standing somewhat irresolutely in front of the door wondering whether to rouse Kyra and Khu-ren when suddenly she felt that someone was standing behind her. She swung round and saw a dark shadow move back and merge with the shadow of the house.

'Who is there?' she asked sharply, her heart missing a beat.

There was no reply and there was now no sign of anyone.

She was frightened, but she was determined to get to the bottom of what was going on. She moved closer to the shadow and challenged it again – louder this time – half hoping the sound of her voice would awaken the sleepers in the house.

Suddenly it felt as though a cold hand touched her forehead, and she jumped back, startled. It was a light touch, almost instantly gone. Nothing else happened. Nothing moved. Puzzled, she found herself standing in front of Kyra's house in the middle of the night in her shift with only a light cloak over her shoulders – and she could not remember what she was doing there, how she had got there, or anything at all about the figure she had seen running from the scene. She stood still for a long while, trying to remember; but nothing came to her. Slowly she began to wander back to the student house where she belonged, a little dazed, her step wavering and uncertain as though she were drunk or drugged. She found her bed and curled up in it. She was instantly asleep.

Jan had had every intention of stealing one of Kyra's crystals. He was not sure if Wardyke's arguments had finally persuaded him that she had so many she would not miss one – or that his fear of Wardyke had conquered his scruples. He had crept into her house when he thought that all the village was sound asleep and had stood in the chamber where she kept her collection, now housed in Isar's beautiful oak bowl. A thin needle of moonlight came through a hole in the shutters and fell directly into the bowl. This in itself was unnerving. It was as though the bowl glowed and the crystals in it were giving off light. He stared, awed by their beauty. He wondered if he should not take two – the one Wardyke wanted and one for himself.

He drew nearer and hovered over them... They were silver-white, translucent, numinous... He reached out his hand. He hesitated. Did he hear a sound in the next room? Khu-ren turning in his sleep? Kyra sensing that her crystals were in danger? What if he were caught? Silence again. He hardly dared breathe. Never had he seen anything so exquisite in all the world. He lowered his hand and delicately touched one, careful that he did not cause the others to tumble as he dislodged it from the pile. He had it in his hand. He could feel the cool surface of it; his fingers traced the smooth and shining planes and facets... Another one. Just one more! One for himself. He touched another and jumped back. It seemed to him a sharp tingling pain shot through his finger and up into his arm.

'Nonsense,' he told himself and reached out again. The moonlight seemed to fill the bowl and he had the impression now that the crystals were floating in clear water. He leaned over the bowl to get a closer look and was startled to see his own face reflected in it... his own face multiplied many times as each facet of the many different crystals gave back an image of him. Each image had a different expression – some happy, some sad, some frightened. Fascinated, he stared and stared. It seemed to him some of the faces were not as he was now, Jan, son of Karne, but were of different people – and yet in some way he knew that they were all himself. Some seemed near and some seemed far away. All these people were him. He had the strength, the knowledge, of all these people. He was not just one small boy terrified of disobeying Wardyke... He was the equal of Wardyke. His being had roots every bit as long and strong as Wardyke's. He had free choice and if he, Jan, did not have the courage to reject Wardyke, these others that were also him – the many facets of his being, his journeying soul, his eternal spirit – they would give him the courage to reject him.

He put back the crystal he had picked up and ran out of the room and out of the house as quickly as he could. He did not notice Farla standing in the pathway. He did not notice Wardyke lurking in the shadows, his face angry and disappointed.

The next day Jan sought out his brother Isar. He found him in the roofed but unwalled shed he used to store and season his timber. He had just begun a new carving and invited Jan at once to stay with him and watch what he was doing. He was glad of a chance to talk to the boy alone. He, like his parents, was worried about the way Jan had been behaving lately.

Jan sat on the woodpile and shifted his position several times, trying to get comfortable – and also trying to formulate what he wanted to say. Now that he had decided to confess about the dagger, he was glad Karne was away from home for a few days. His father had been known to lose his temper. But Isar – never.

Suddenly, behind Isar, he saw a shadow move and he knew that they were not alone. Isar, looking up, saw the terror on his brother's face as he looked at someone or something over Isar's shoulder. He spun round but he could see nothing. Jan scrambled off the woodpile and the logs began to roll and tumble everywhere. Before Isar could stop him he had run out of the shed. In leaping aside to escape the avalanche of wood, Isar lost time. And when the confusion had died down, there was no sign of Jan. He set off at once in search of him, but the boy must have run fast. Isar went straight to his mother's house – but Jan had not returned there.

Jan did not know where he was going. As far as he knew there was nowhere he could go that Wardyke would not follow him. But, summoning all his courage and strength, he was determined that at least he would not be used to destroy his family and his friends. He had matured a great deal since he had had the dagger in his possession. Under Wardyke's influence he had become devious and dishonest – but the very deviousness of his thinking had led him to realise what Wardyke was up to. He would go as far away from the Haylken community as he could while he still had enough independence of thought to do so. He would become an exile and a wanderer over the face of the earth and never see his loved ones again, if necessary – but he would not stay and be used in this way.

He ran and ran, his heart burning in his chest with physical effort and fear. But for the first time since he had touched the fatal dagger he felt he was making his own decision... and this, in itself, gave him strength. He remembered what his mother had once said: 'We are never alone. We are always under the influence of those around us – whether we can see them or not. But remember, influence is one thing – succumbing to it is another.' She had stressed that no one could make us do something we refused to do. They could kill our bodies, but they could not make us obey unless we chose to obey. Jan did not want to die, but he decided that if that was the only way to free himself, that was what he would have to do. He thought of Lark. Was that why she had tried to kill herself?

Had she been under the spell of the dagger too?

'Perhaps that is what he wants me to do,' he then thought. It would be a good revenge on Kyra and Karne and Fern if the people they loved committed suicide one by one. 'I must get rid of the dagger,' he thought. 'That's the only way.' He had tried to do this several times before – but had never been able to. This time he would go to a deep lake he had been to with Karne, where they had had a good time bathing. Karne had warned him not to swim too far from the shore. 'No one knows how deep it is,' he had said, 'but a child was drowned here not long ago.' Surely it would be deep enough so that no one would ever find the dagger again and come under its malevolent influence.

He realised with extraordinary clarity that he had not been able to dispose of the dagger before only partly because he did not know where he could put it so that it would not be found by someone else. More important, he had not been able to dispose of it because he had not wanted to. Now he did. He seriously did. Perhaps now it would be possible to get rid of it – and with it the ghoul that haunted it. If the lake accepted it, he would be free and he would be able to return to his home. If not – he would never go home.

Isar made enquiries for anyone who might have seen Jan leaving his workshed or in the vicinity of the village that morning. At last he tracked down a woodcutter who had spotted the boy running through the woods.

'He usually stops to talk to me,' the man said, 'but this morning he didn't even greet me.'

'Where was he headed?'

The man could give him the direction, and from there he worked his way west, following clues. Was the boy trying to reach his father? Isar could not forget the terror on his brother's face and was really worried about him.

In speaking to Fern that morning, Isar realised that he was not alone in the feeling he had that there was a mysterious shadow hovering over the Temple and its people. Fern was convinced of it.

'It is not only Jan,' she said, and she told him about the increased instances of theft and violence among Karne's people, and the way so many seemed to be waiting for something to happen instead of getting on with their lives in the normal way.

Lark too was a worry. She seemed so pale and listless, and no matter how he and Fern and Kyra tried to persuade her that they had put every protection around her and that, even if Wardyke's fell soul was incarnating through her, the changed circumstances of his new family and environment, and the concentration of love and care and prayer, would effectively guard against the worst parts of his old nature recurring. 'After all,' Kyra stressed, 'we all have to work out our difficulties through life after life – and to be born into your family, here and now, might well be just what the soul of Wardyke needs to turn him around from the dark to the light.'

Lark listened – but there was still no joy in her eyes when she felt the infant stirring in her womb.

Isar was horrified when he heard what had occurred with his father's dagger and blamed himself angrily for not burying it with its owner. The fact that it had not been found worried him a great deal. He was sure that somehow the increase in violence Fern spoke about had something to do with it. What an irresponsible fool he had been to keep the weapon of a renegade priest and master sorcerer! He could only excuse himself by the fact that he had been an ignorant child at the time – and that his feelings towards Wardyke had not been as easy to understand as they were now. A child could be excused – but he was no longer a child and, for all he said to comfort Lark, he dreaded the possibility of Wardyke's return as much as she.

He had made his own enquiries about the whereabouts of the dagger after his return with Deva – indeed, this had occupied nearly all of his time – but he had had no success. Now, as he followed Jan's trail, he began for the first time to wonder if the change in Jan's behaviour were due in some way to the presence of the dagger.

And so it was that he was not at all surprised when he found Jan at last, standing on the shore of a lake, holding the weapon in both hands out in front of him, his face contorted with the strain of an inner conflict.

Isar felt it was important that Jan himself threw the dagger into the lake – but he had moments of terrible fear that if he left the boy alone, some force might take him over that would drive him beyond his reach for ever. The water of the lake was mirror-still, the sky above it dark grey. It was as though a storm was brewing but the rain was being held back like an infant in a long and difficult dry labour.

The boy's hands were trembling with the strain of holding the dagger out ahead of him and suddenly Isar leapt forward as he realised the point of it was gradually rising towards Jan's chest like a divining rod. He remembered Lark – and dashed towards his brother.

Jan!' he shouted. 'Jan – no! Drop it! Drop it!'

Suddenly a dark and fearsome wind sprang up. The water of the lake became choppy and wild and the trees on the shore bent almost double. Jan was straining against the wind, leaning into the dagger.

Isar jumped towards him and knocked the deadly metal out of his hand. He heard it chink against a stone and saw a brilliant spark fly upwards from the strike, illuminating the boy's face for a moment to reveal an expression of incredible hatred.

Isar seized his shoulders and shook him violently.

'Jan, it's your brother. Look at me. It's Isar. Your brother!'

The clouds were thunderously black now and the waters of the lake slate-dark. Isar could feel the difference in Jan as he fought against him. His thin child-arms were unbelievably strong. Isar, the man, was thrown backwards.

Jan!' he shouted desperately. 'Remember who you are. Remember Fern. Remember your mother!'

At the mention of Fern's name the wind gave a howl that was so human, so tortured, that it made Isar's blood run cold. Wardyke remembered Fern! Wardyke remembered the begetting of Isar.

Jan shuddered violently and fell to the ground in a faint. The dagger lay beside him, apparently inert. Isar did not know what to do. His instinct told him that Jan would only be truly free if he himself chose to throw it away; on the other hand, he had been the one to keep it back from the grave. Perhaps it was up to him to get rid of it finally.

He made a decision and picked the dagger up.

'Wardyke!' he yelled. 'I know you are here. Listen to me. Listen.'

His words were blown backwards. He had to brace himself against the gale. If he threw the dagger now into the lake there was a chance that it might be blown back to the shore – back to himself and to Jan.

It was even possible, with Wardyke's power behind it, that it might lodge in the heart of one of them.

He raised it above his head and held it steady with all his strength.

'It is over. Leave us alone! You harm no one but yourself by clinging to your old ways and your old resentments. I call on the Nameless One and all the Beings of Light to help us. Against these you cannot ultimately win, Wardyke. You know it and I know it.'

A livid lightning flash rent the black clouds and a clap of thunder almost deafened him. A tree not far from them disintegrated in a cloud of yellow smoke.

Jan had regained consciousness and crawled towards him, and was crouching against his legs. Both brothers were terrified.

There was another flash, which seemed even nearer. The water at their feet sizzled and boiled. Another – and the dagger in Isar's hand scorched his flesh. Grimly he held on to it in spite of the pain.

'Throw it,' whispered Jan hoarsely. 'Throw it!' He now knew as well as Isar that the dagger was the door through which Wardyke's malevolent energy was pouring.

Isar gathered all his strength and, before the next lightning flash, flung it with all his force as high and as far as he could.

Astonished, the two watched it rise beyond the range of Isar's strength to throw, turn at the zenith, the gold pins of the hilt momentarily throwing out shafts of light, and then slowly spiral down to the surface of the water at the centre of the lake. As it touched, the rains came. A deluge of heavy drops pockmarked the grey water. They clung together, knowing that this danger, at least, was over.

Chapter 19

Sekhmet and Ra

Under Deva's restless guidance many people began to dabble in the Mysteries which the Temple had always been so careful to guard, knowing how dangerous they could be if only partially understood. The 'field of the grey gods', and sometimes the home of one or other of Deva's acolytes, became venues for secret rites. Deva passed on as much of Urak's teaching as she thought fit, in order to develop a strong group who could join their effort and energy to hers in order to try to manifest objects. She became obsessed. She had seen it done. She had received instruction. She was determined the secret would not die with Urak. What power would be hers if she could master it!

What power was already hers, she thought, as she looked round the rapt faces of those who had gathered round her.

At first Boggoron had been an integral part of the enclave that met in secret, but more and more he tended to present an excuse for not being there. Deva did not care. She had vowed him to secrecy and had no fear that he would break the vow, for it had been sealed with a fearsome curse. The first time he did not appear, she wondered where he was and questioned him. But his excuse was good – Kyra had asked him to do something for her, and he could not refuse without rousing suspicion.

The meetings always started with a ritual learned from Urak, to hide what they were doing from the deep-seeing eyes of the priesthood. So far Kyra did not suspect how seriously her daughter was seeking forbidden knowledge. When she saw her she appeared to be living a normal life, and Kyra was relieved that so little of Urak's poison seemed to have attached itself to her.

Deva, in her turn, did not notice that Boggoron was changing. His back was straightening up. He seemed taller. His eyes were beginning to look into her eyes when she spoke to him instead of at the ground at her feet.

Kyra had noticed one day the way Boggoron was watching the drummers at their training: noticed the way his body was responding to the beat. Quickly she offered him the chance to play one of the drums discarded from the sacred 'herd'. She marked the gleam of excitement in his eyes as he took the sticks from her hand, and she was astonished at the power and skill of his playing. Gradually she encouraged him to play, and gradually she manoeuvred a place for him in the group that was responsible for the drumming in the Temple. Khu-ren suggested she might be moving too fast and that she must not forget that Boggoron had been Urak's closest companion and was bound to be still under her influence – but Kyra would not listen. She felt that Boggoron was ready to change; that all he needed was to be respected for himself and what he could do. She gave him every chance and she was rewarded by seeing him winning the respect of the other drummers, and respond to this in turn by the gradual opening up, almost the flowering, of his own self-respect.

Deva did not miss him. She had more acolytes than she could handle and her experiments were going well. During the latest attempt they had managed to change an object from one thing into another, for a brief, uncertain moment. In its new form it had hovered fleetingly, and then reverted to the original. But the fact that anything had happened at all, after all their work, gave them tremendous encouragement to persist.

Deva decided they needed help – and she knew where she could get it. She would 'travel' as Urak had taught her. She would go 'home' to Egypt. She would call to Sekhmet and Ptah. She knew in which temple to find them. Sekhmet the 'Mighty One', the Lioness, the woman of strife and war, the Destroyer. She, with her husband Ptah, the Creator, surely carried the secret that lay at the fulcrum of being and non-being. She would promise anything, give anything, if only the Great Lady would let her glimpse something of this secret.

In the darkened room of her home at Haylken in Britain, she began the incantations that would take her into the presence of the Egyptian goddess with the seductive body of a woman, the head of a lioness, crowned by the burning and relentless disc of the sun and the fearful hood of the cobra. She had feared this deity in her former life, and, as a child, had crept past all images of her with her heart in her mouth. But now she seemed drawn inexorably towards her. She remembered Urak's respect for her. Her statues, carved out of fine-grained black stone from the heart of a volcano, stood silently beside the still, dark water of a sacred lake. As the moon hovered over the desert mountains behind her, the eyes of the goddess seemed to be looking out of the lake, instead of being reflected in it. Deva shivered. She had achieved what she wanted to achieve and was in the presence of the powerful being she had set out to find. Now she must not falter in speaking the words that would enable her to communicate with Sekhmet... no matter how many realms apart they might be.

'Goddess of the Fire, Mighty One who melts whole worlds with the breath of your mouth – if you would lend me but a tiny part of your knowledge, your strength, your power, I would make your Name ring out among the people of the earth... No part of it would be without your Name.'

Did the eyes in the water move? Deva could not raise her own eyes to the Being herself, for the reflection of her stone image in the dark water of the lake was more terrifying than she would have dreamed possible.

She waited breathlessly, her heart pounding, whispering under her breath the words of power Urak had taught her, trying not to obey her instinct to flee. Where was her comfortable home now, the houses of wood and thatch, the sacred Stones of the familiar Temple? Khuren himself would have trembled in this presence. Was she insane to seek out such a one? But she was desperate: so near to achieving what she desired more than anything in the world, yet – without help – so far from it that she might as well never have started on this dangerous path.

'No going back now,' a voice inside her was telling her. 'Go back now – it is not too late,' another whispered.

She bowed her head to the ground and could feel the grainy sand of the desert pressing into her flesh. Over and over again she spoke the incantation, asked the questions, made the promises...

Suddenly the moon went behind the mountain and she was in total darkness. At this point she decided to abandon the attempt and flee back to her body, left in her chamber at Haylken. But she found that she could not do so. She seemed to be turning to stone herself.

Horrified, she realised that she was getting her wish – the Mighty One was changing and transforming matter in answer to her prayer, but the matter she was changing was Deva herself! She - would be stone for ever! She could feel her thoughts like fluttering birds leaving her and a terrible coldness and emptiness and loneliness taking their place.

What would have happened to Deva, had Guiron not been wandering by the lake at that time, she would never know. He had heard a strange sound and come to investigate. He stood now with the flame of his torch lifted above his head, staring cautiously at the giant statues of Sekhmet that sat so silently beside the water.

Surely they had not given that cry of despair? He moved closer to them and lowered his torch slightly. Then he saw another figure at the lakeside – smaller, human-sized – a woman. He gasped. It was the woman who haunted him, who had always haunted him... Even here he was not safe from his desire for her!

He stood and gazed at Deva, noticing with aching heart how beautiful she was. And then he noticed her eyes.

He started. What suffering! What fear! He suddenly realised with horror that she was a living woman in the process of turning into a stone statue. His thoughts were in turmoil. How could this be? How and why had he come to this place at this time, to witness this fearful thing? One thread of thought led him into the dark regions: he thought it would be no bad thing for him to have a statue of his beloved, so that he might see her whenever he wanted without the fear of succumbing to his former sin. But another thread, and this one was mercifully the stronger, led him towards the light. Fervently he prayed for her release, invoking all the Spirits of Light he had ever heard of, and the Nameless One beyond all these...

As though she were mist dissolving in the sun, Deva's 'body' became more and more insubstantial until there was no trace of it beside the dark lake in Egypt.

Guiron stood alone – and wept.

Deva was exhausted and shaken after the experience with Sekhmet, and lay for a long time in her chamber curled up in bed with rugs drawn up around her ears. Should she give up?

She began to wonder at the power of the energy she was playing with and fear its unpredictability. She remembered Kyra's warning that to try to use a force you did not understand was not only to risk failure but to court death. But she still badly wanted the power that mastering Urak's knowledge could give her, though she was near to despair at ever obtaining it.

It was several days before she could summon up the courage to try again. Perhaps she had invoked the wrong force. It was Sekhmet who, at one time, had almost destroyed the human race. Perhaps she had not made it clear it was the point of balance between Sekhmet, the Destroyer, and Ptah, the Creator, that she was looking for – the fulcrum on which 'being' and 'non-being' turned. Perhaps she should go to Ra himself – a source higher than either Sekhmet or Ptah. Ra, whose cipher was the sun, the Great Spirit worshipped in so many different lands under so many different names. She could choose to use the prayers of Kyra's Temple to invoke his help – or she could choose to use the prayers of Egypt.

She decided she would go to the 'haunted mound', the place she had turned to so many times as a child – the place she had haunted for so many centuries when she was waiting for her beloved to return. From its height at noon she would reach towards the sun. No one saw her climb its grassy slope. No one saw her stand upon its summit.

She was alone. She was frightened. Then – for a moment – she thought she saw two shadows at her feet – and one of them was Urak's.

She spun round – but there was no one there. The second shadow was gone. She must have been mistaken.

But strangely now she did not feel so afraid.

She prepared herself for the moment when the sun would be at its zenith. Prayers from her former life in Egypt came to her which she had never consciously known before in this life.

'Hail to you, Ra, in the full strength of your glory, sailing in your golden boat among the invisible stars. More divine than the gods – self-created, self-perpetuating...'

She bowed her forehead to the ground as the great Lord stood above her.

'I have worshipped you since the beginning of Time and I will till the ending of it. Beyond all things you are the One. Take me as your daughter; teach me the secrets in your heart; let me serve you and love you, and be your hand upon the earth...'

She looked up, suddenly confident that she was being heard.

The full light of the sun blazed into her eyes and for an instant she felt that she was melting with the pebble she held in her hand. The light was so strong she experienced it as excruciating pain. Involuntarily she raised her arm and hid her face in the crook of it. There were sounds roaring in her ears, at first unrecognisable and then taking on the form of music – strange, throbbing, weird.

Cautiously she eased her forearm away from her eyes, terrified to face the full light of the sun again, but too curious not to. The scene had changed. She was no longer on the haunted mound of Haylken. She was standing at the centre of an open courtyard in an Egyptian temple: a colonnade of tall columns that seemed to reach to the sky surrounded it. Her flimsy sandals scarcely kept the heat of the sand, baking in the sun, from scorching her feet. In front of her was an altar carved with all the images of the sun-god: RaHarakti the Falcon of dawn; Khephra the Scarab of noon; and Atum of evening; the beginning, the ending and the beginning... Her eyes were drawn to a giant scarab of green nephrite bearing the golden disc of the sun before it, just as the dung-beetle from whom Khephra had taken his image bears the ball of dung containing its future.

She was trembling.

'Khephra,' she whispered, 'Lord of transformations, help me.'

That she was before the very form of the god most associated with transformation filled her with hope. Could it really be – at last?

She was aware that someone had entered the great open court behind her from the shadows of the colonnade, but she did not look round. She was anxious not to take her attention off Khephra, lest he refused to grant her request. She was still clutching the flint pebble from Haylken in her hand, though everything else about her had changed. Her clothes were of fine transparent linen, her arms were bare apart from golden bracelets, and she could feel the weight of a circlet upon her head. She could even smell the scent of the lotus blossom that drooped over her forehead.

'Khephra,' she whispered again. 'I do not ask you to transform this stone into gold for me. I ask you to teach me how to do it myself. I need the sounds... I need the song that transforms one thing into another. Help me. I'll do anything for you. Anything! Just give me the sounds.'

It seemed to her she heard a voice, and the voice was neither unfriendly nor friendly – a voice passionless, strong and quiet.

'A Word begins all things and a Word ends all things... the Word that is the secret name of the Nameless One.'

'But there must be other words, lesser words,' she pleaded. 'I do not seek to end all things but to change only one or two small objects. Surely there would be no harm in that? I vow to do no more.'

'A word is sound and thought. A word has material vibration and immaterial meaning. The key to what you ask lies in the combination of the right sound with the right thought. This is the safeguard. Neither one nor the other is sufficient alone, and the chances of anyone finding that combination and having the strength of Consciousness to hold it in balance are very slight.'

'I ask no more than Urak already had. I will be careful. I'll change no more than one or two small objects.'

'Even one change could start a chain that could destroy a universe.'

Deva felt like screaming. She felt like seizing the statue of Khephra and dashing it on the ground. Why was she thwarted at every turn. Why? Why? Why?

Guiron, who had entered the sun's sanctuary with his friend Userhet, stood as though transfixed. Before the altar, where no one apart from the High Priest, the first Prophet, was supposed to stand, was a young woman – *the* young woman! He took Userhet's arm and held him back. The old man looked at Guiron in surprise and then his eyes followed his friend's to the altar. There he could see nothing but the noonday sun blazing down on the golden disc at the head of Khephra.

'What is it, my friend?' he whispered, though it was sacrilege to speak in the sanctuary unless addressing the god. 'What troubles you?' For Guiron's face was full of despair.

'It is she,' he murmured. But Userhet did not know what he meant, for Guiron had not yet told him anything about the guilt that still haunted him.

Deva would not let the matter drop. If the gods would not help her, she still had her own skill and ingenuity and Urak's teaching behind her. She had found the right combination once in the vortex, and she would find it again.

After a while things started happening. It became easier and easier to disintegrate objects into fine powder. Even this astonished and impressed her group of friends. But it was not enough for Deva. She chanted late into the night sometimes, and concentrated so hard her head ached and her cheeks grew pale. She had jars full of dull grey powder – and no jewels.

But one day, just when she was beginning to lose heart, she found a small blue crystal in the palm of her hand. She was not sure how she had managed it, but somehow she had hit the right note at the right moment. After that there was no looking back. She had found the key at least to what Urak knew.

If she had been asked to explain how she had done it, she would not have been able to. As far as she could tell, it just 'happened' when her mind was in a particular state. To get into that state there were certain steps she had to take, and if she skimped or omitted one single part of the preparation nothing would happen. On the other hand, even if she meticulously did everything correctly, it was still possible for her to fail to reach the state. It was as though there were something extra needed which was a mystery to her, but which sometimes she inadvertently stumbled upon.

No one else could do what she did and she did not attempt to teach them, for it was the exclusivity of her skill that gave her status and power. She swore all her followers to silence and the meetings were held in secret, but somehow the numbers were growing.

'Urak would be proud of me,' she thought, and she told Boggoron of her successes. But he showed little interest. Watching manifestation-magic had been commonplace to him in his life with

Urak. He was far more interested in the life he had now as one of the leading Temple drummers. In Urak's service he had always been lonely, isolated, lost. But now, basking in the warmth of Kyra's appreciation, he felt a tremendous surge of 'belonging', as though he was part of the earth itself in some way – not standing on the surface of it, separate from it, apart from it... but feeling the throb of its heart as the throb of his own heart. He believed now that any harm that would come to any part of the earth would come to him; any joy that would come to any part of the earth would be his.

Gya began to notice that their home appurtenances were gradually becoming more and more sumptuous and that Deva often disappeared for hours at a time with people he did not like. But he thought very little about it and assumed she was obtaining the luxuries from the merchants who always came to Haylken in the summer – and this year in greater numbers than ever before. He did not really care. He and Farla had become lovers.

Neither of them had intended this to happen – but happen it had. Since their time together during the rescue of Deva they had been good friends, and it was to Farla – as a friend – that Gya had turned when Deva had teased him beyond endurance. He was tired of her playing hot and cold, and felt he would go mad if he did not complain to someone about it. He met up with Farla the day after she had seen Jan running away from Kyra's house. She still did not remember the incident, but she was haunted by the feeling that there was something important about the night she ought to remember. She was in an uneasy, vulnerable mood, beginning to wonder once again if she were indeed suitable material for the priesthood.

They had met unexpectedly, walking by the Kennet river in a secluded part of the forest, both seeking solitude, yet finding solitude no answer to their problems. They sat beside the river for a long time, talking – pouring out all their thoughts and feelings and worries – both finding comfort in someone else understanding exactly what they meant with very little explanation. It was when they rose to go and Gya took her hands to pull her up that, for the first time, they came close together and in that closeness found more than comfort. Gya, sensing the tremor that went through Farla's body when it touched his, looked down into her eyes in surprise. There he saw what she felt for him. The moment was right. He needed what she could give. And she – she had hoped for such a moment for a long time.

He drew her closer and stooped to kiss her. Even then he meant no more than friendship. His painful passion for Deva was not dead and he liked Farla too much now to use her in the game he sometimes played... But the kiss lasted longer than he intended and the warmth of Farla's response felt good. Neither could bring themselves to draw apart, though both knew they should. Wonderingly, as though seeing her for the first time, he kissed her lightly freckled nose, the rust-brown of her hair at the nape of her neck. He pushed back the shoulder of her dress and explored the skin beneath. And then he kissed her breast... For both of them the rest of the world had ceased to exist, and as they lay on the soft grass beside the stream, they felt neither twig nor pebble beneath them – only the mounting pleasure of their union.

At last, sighing, they drew apart and Gya raised himself on his elbow and looked down into her face. She was flushed and starry-eyed, the loose curls of her hair mingling with the moss and ferns of the earth. He had never thought her beautiful before, but she was beautiful now – and he was more content than he could remember being for a long, long time. They said nothing to each other, but smiled into each other's eyes. After a while he lowered his head to her breast and went to sleep. She stayed awake – running her fingers through his thick dark brown hair and over the firm skin of his cheek and neck and shoulder. She looked up at the leafy canopy of the forest above them and watched the sun move through the leaves, touching one after the other into emerald splendour.

When he woke they still did not speak – though they had spoken so much before. They stood up and stretched and dusted off the twigs and grass, and walked quietly home.

They smiled at parting, but said nothing. Neither knew whether this would ever happen again. Both wished that it would.

Chapter 20

The seven doors

Guiron told Userhet something of the long history of his relationship to Deva, how he had murdered her husband in a former life long ages before, raped her and been the cause of her suicide.

'But worse,' he said regretfully, 'I had so scarred her that she refused to move on; refused to incarnate again. She clung to the same place, a ghost, waiting, shut off from the riches of all the other realms – making one small memory a prison...'

'That was her choice,' Userhet said quietly. 'Your guilt was in the murder and the rape; hers was in the refusal to continue the journey of the soul.'

Guiron, the old man, lowered his voice so that his companion had to lean closer to catch what he was saying. He told how his guilt did not only belong to that ancient lifetime, but to the present one as well. He had once again forced himself on her.

'The ghost?' asked Userhet, unable to keep the note of astonishment out of his voice.

He was told about Panora, the mischievous, half-human, half-ghost offspring of that strange union, who had finally chosen to die and enter the human process of soul-evolution. But only after she had almost destroyed the Temple.

'And this young woman you keep seeing?'

'She is Anhai at last reborn. She is known now as Deva, daughter of Kyra.'

'You should be glad she has chosen at last to move on.'

'I am. But I find, even at my age, the old fire has not died down. I left my country and all that I wanted to be near so that I would not be tempted again. Is there to be no escape – ever?' Userhet could hear the despair in his voice. He put his hand on his friend's arm.

'Something is left to do,' he said. 'She is being sent to you for a reason. Find out what it is. Then you and she will both be free.'

'Help me, my friend. I cannot face this alone!'

Userhet looked at him long and compassionately.

'It has to be alone,' he said at last. 'I feel it.'

Guiron buried his face in his hands. Even now he could see her in his mind's eye. Would he ever be able to shut her image out? It was then he decided to go into the mountains – alone, as Userhet said – and try to discover what it was that was still left to do.

Guiron crossed the great river Nile to the west bank as he had done scores of times, the light boat sailing the clear blue waters, the mast pointing straight to the clear blue skies. He and Userhet had spent a great deal of time on the west bank, watching the workmen building the pharaoh's magnificent mortuary temple against the cliff of the western mountains. Userhet knew the architect, Senmut, well and they had passed many a pleasant hour with him, caught up in his enthusiasm, admiring the scope and splendour of his designs and the determination with which he saw that every detail was carried out to his exact specification.

Guiron had not missed the expression on his face when Hatshepsut came to view the work. Hatshepsut, daughter of the great Thutmose I, who, not content with being regent while her young stepson was too young to reign, had declared herself the rightful pharaoh and taken over the power of government. It was natural that a ripple of excitement should go through the whole community of workers at her approach, but Guiron caught something more in Senmut's eyes, and something that should not have been there in the eyes of the pharaoh when she looked at him. He did not dare ask Userhet outright if they were lovers, but he would not have been surprised if they were. There was a feeling in the air around them, a kind of tense excitement. The pharaoh walked calmly and regally around the site, commenting on this and that, enquiring and praising. Senmut, at her side, answered gravely. No one could have faulted them in their behaviour, but Guiron could feel it: the passion, the desire – held in check, but only just. They were two of a kind – restless, brilliant, impatient with fools. They matched each other in every way.

Guiron wondered about Senmut and Hatshepsut now as he set off across the plain towards the silent western mountains. Did the guilt of their illicit love affair torment them as much as his desire for Deva? Would it too end in centuries of retribution? It was sad that fate had not given them to each other under different circumstances. Yet perhaps the very tension of their forbidden love was the spark that lit the brilliance of what they were achieving together.

Guiron had never seen a building more beautiful, more

harmonious to the landscape in which it was set, so evocative, so holy. He and Userhet went there so often because there they could sense the thinness of the veils between the realms: because there, more than in any other place, they knew they were in the presence of the great spirits some called the gods. This was no ordinary temple. And it needed extraordinary circumstances and extraordinary people to bring it about. Guiron remembered the two of them standing on the rough stones of the upper terrace, the architect and the pharaoh, the man and the woman. He had caught the look that passed between them and he had trembled to think what the energy generated between them might achieve. If they had been man and wife there was no doubt they would have loved each other – but that violent, secret, creative energy would have lost much of its impetus and power.

He wondered about his own relationship with Anhai – now Deva. What had been the point of it? They had produced nothing between them but sorrow and suffering. His had been a totally destructive love. Why? Why? Why? If he did not find the answer to what troubled him in these mountains, he would die. He was determined not to return to the world of living people until he was free of his obsession.

He reached the foot of the mountains about noon. Behind him was the green flood plain of the Nile, the villages, the fields of grain, the rich and fertile land, the black land of inundation silt. Before him was the red land of the desert, guarded by a rocky wall of mountains. There he would strip away everything and face himself.

He had supplies of food in a pouch at his side – but when it was finished he would eat lizards and snakes or starve to death.

The sun was burning the land with a terrible intensity and the rock underfoot was unbearably hot. The heat haze reduced everything to shimmering unreality. He became faint and nearly lost his footing on the edge of a precipitous cliff. Suddenly he felt cooler, and when he looked up to see what was giving him shade, he saw that it was the shadow of a huge falcon, turning in narrow circles above him. Userhet's god, Horus.

The mountains stretched ahead of him, yellow-bronze in the blinding light of the sun. He climbed and climbed, leaving the green strip of verdant land on either side of the Nile far behind. There was now no sign of man or his works. Here he would find no companion – no one to give him comfort and tell him what to do. He was alone among the raw peaks of rock, dust closing in behind him – and dust lying before him. Painfully he clambered over the hot boulders, reaching towards the dark, dark blue of the sky where the solitary falcon wheeled and soared.

He rounded a cliff and came face to face with the mighty pyramid-shaped peak that dominated the desolate valley where Hatshepsut's father and grandfather had chosen to be entombed.

The silence was total.

He looked towards the peak that housed Mertseger, 'she who loves silence', the guardian goddess of the valley of the tombs. His heart was pounding uncomfortably. The climb had been steep, but he was afraid as well. Would she let him pass, the fearsome cobra goddess?

But nothing stirred and it was under Mertseger's mighty pyramid-shaped peak that he found a small cave in which to shelter from the heat of the sun at midday and to lay his head when he wanted to sleep. To the west, although he could not see it because of the giant battlements of rock, the desert lay – the Unknown, stretching apparently to infinity. To the north was the great scar of the valley of the tombs where the pharaohs waited out eternity.

The food he had brought with him into the mountains soon gave out and he grew gaunt and thin living on a sparse diet of lizards and an occasional bird hit by slingshot. He tended to sleep in his cave through the hottest part of the day and creep out as the great sun lowered to the horizon. In the cool of the evening and in the early morning he hunted. In the night he stayed awake watching as the stars wheeled slowly and majestically above him. It was at night he wrestled with his thoughts and tried to see the way out of the trap he was in. But it was at night also that he kept seeing Deva – not in clear vision as he had seen her in the avenue of frankincense trees at Hatshepsut's temple... nor before the fearful statues of Sekhmet... nor even before Khephra at the sun altar... but as a memory that would not die and an image conjured by longing.

He had thought when he came to Egypt that he would find truth written down in the ancient texts, and by learning to read them he would learn what he needed to know. At first he had been excited by the new form of scholarship and his eyes had ached with the long hours he had spent with the rolls of papyrus. But as he became more and more skilled at deciphering them he began to notice inconsistencies, inaccuracies. In copying the same text one scribe wrote one thing and the second another. Some texts made beautiful sense – but others were nonsense, copied so often that the mistakes of one generation of scribes had been carried over and further exaggerated by the next generation, each moving further and further from the original. He had learned that he could not trust the written word any more than he could trust the Mogüd's smoke. From both he had learned something – but not enough, and not what he had set out to learn.

One morning, when he was out hunting, the earth gave a shudder and he was almost killed by an avalanche of falling rock. He came back to the cave, much shaken, having found no food that day.

He lay down, weak and exhausted, in his customary place and tried to compose himself for sleep. Hunger pangs prevented him, and he opened his eyes at last and lay staring idly at the rock ceiling above him. Eventually his eyes wandered and he discovered that there had been a rockfall in his cave as well. The whole back wall seemed to have collapsed, and there was a gaping hole behind a mound of rubble that indicated that his cave continued into the mountain.

He struggled to his feet, his curiosity kindled and his hunger forgotten. With difficulty he lit one of the few pitch torches he had brought with him and began to scramble up onto the pile of debris that had accumulated beneath the hole. He knocked his shins and grazed his hands and his elbows, but at last he was in a position to look into the darkness beyond the cave he knew. The flickering flame illuminated a long corridor. The walls seemed curiously smooth, as though man had had a hand in their shaping. Feeble as he was, he had to explore it!

Another great effort, and he was on the lip of the rubble and over into the corridor, flakes of rock skittering away from him down both sides of the pile. Once firmly on the floor, he raised his torch above his head and strained to see as far as he could. The corridor was long and narrow, becoming lower as it went deeper into the mountain, the end of it lost in the darkness. He knew he was foolish to explore it by himself and in the condition he was in. If he were to die now with his problem unresolved, he would suffer for it in the next life. This time he wanted to be clear of the past when he entered the future. But his curiosity was too great.

'I'll take care,' he told himself. 'I won't go far. Just a little further to see where the corridor leads. I'll come back another day when I feel stronger.'

He did take care – inching his way along step by cautious step – but he did not stop when he could see the end of the corridor, for at the end he could see that it opened out into a chamber.

He could not think of stopping until he was standing in the chamber itself, with his torch held high, illuminating every corner of it. He was in a half-finished tomb. Of that there was no doubt. There was no coffin or sarcophagus, but the walls were half-decorated with the sort of paintings and hieroglyphics that were always put in tombs to guide the deceased through the complicated tests and trials of the Duat, the realm after death, and to bring them safely and triumphantly through to new life. Userhet had told him that though these paintings were always associated in the minds of most people with the death of the pharaoh, to the adepts they also formed a guide-plan for the living to achieve transformation into enlightenment – a state in which there were no barriers between the realms – and an individual might enjoy and understand the higher realms while still in a physical body. Each figure in the elaborate scheme had to be read as a multi-layered symbol – the deceased would read it one way, the living another.

Guiron stared, fascinated, following the line of the narrative from wall to wall, sometimes seeing it clearly, where the artist had filled in the vignettes with pigment; at other times only faintly, where the lines had been sketched in lightly.

He found himself particularly intrigued by a painting of seven doors and stood in front of it for a long time, staring at it, trying to 'read' it in the way Userhet had taught him, on many levels.

Whether it was the oppressive stuffiness of the place, the smell of the burning pitch, his lack of food or what... but Guiron began to feel very strange, as though he were floating off from his body.

He was alarmed. These were not his gods, these strange beings painted on the walls with stylised human bodies and animal heads. He had come to know a great deal about them from Userhet – but he still felt they were alien. No matter how Userhet explained the symbolism to him and assured him no one in his right mind actually believed the god Thoth had a human body and the head of a sacred ibis, they still made him uneasy. Guiron's people made no representations of the Shining Spirits or of the Nameless One beyond them. The nearest they ever got to thinking of a visible image of the invisible force they worshipped was the sun itself, the moon representing another aspect of it. The stone circles were constructed, not as representations, but as practical and effective catchment areas for the potent, life-giving energy that powered the universe. The long passage graves of his people sometimes had reminders of the vortex, through which one passes in order to reach the other realms, carved into the rock, but there were no figures represented, no writing to tell how life begins again after death. This message was conveyed by the beam of sunlight that came through a small aperture in the deepest part of winter. When the earth was at its coldest and darkest and one might very well despair, sunrise brought this ray, this beam, this messenger of hope and renewal into the tomb.

Guiron felt himself to be alone in the desert – walking.

'Careful,' he told himself. 'Careful of the illusions weariness can bring. Careful of the power of images charged with ritual magic.'

One part of him abandoned itself to the experience; but another kept watch: kept control. He stepped forward, saying a silent and fervent prayer: 'Great God beyond all gods, Creator of all the universes and all the realms... who sends servants of light throughout all Time and Space to help and guide those who are struggling, guide me now. Protect me and lead me without fear and without weakness, that I may come forth from the darkness into thy light.' It seemed to him that this was the first time in a long while he had directed his prayer to the right source.

Before him he suddenly found a huge door, locked against him. He could see that the door was standing clear of any building and that if he wished he could walk round it rather than try to go through it. But he knew that if he did so, he would miss something very important. It was of very heavy wood, set between two huge slabs of stone. A third slab served as a lintel above it, carved with many strange devices.

Before the door stood three figures: the Keeper, the Guard and the Recorder. He looked at the figures and they looked at him. No words were spoken but he knew that he had to name each of them before he would be allowed to pass through. He knew also that the names were not names in the ordinary sense, but complex, secret ciphers that would give a meaning to the door and a meaning to his passing through it. He knew also that if he made one single error the door would not open for him.

He who takes on many shapes that he may learn.
He who listens to the secret teachings.
He who remembers what he has learned.

The door opened and he passed through. Beyond it in the desert he saw another door.

He who discards all that is not needed.
He who is prepared to change.
He who burns with the will to change.

The second door opened and he passed through it. Beyond it in the desert stood another door.

He who examines again what he has thrown away.
He who is vigilant.
He who protects what he has received.

The third door opened and he passed through it. Beyond it in the desert was another door.

He who records and keeps what he has understood.
He who is ever watchful that he is not misled.
He who defends what others try to take from him.

The fourth door opened and he passed through it. Beyond it was yet another door.

He who has earth-knowledge: serpent knowledge.
He who is a flame.
He who has power.

The fifth door opened and he faced another.

He who nourishes the soul.
He who is alert.
He who is sharp of eye.

He passed the sixth door safely. The seventh stood before him.

He who is strong in what he knows to be right.
He who speaks out against the wrong.
He who is the powerful defender of the secret wisdom.

Strangely, though each name he called out was so clumsy, as the door opened for him and he passed through, layer upon layer of esoteric knowledge was revealed to him. Much of it he already knew from his own training as Lord of the Sun, but there were nuances that he had missed even in those things he thought he knew.

Suddenly he had a revelation, a direct experience of the Eternal. He saw in a blinding flash that the secret wisdom to be sought and held was *Love* – not the physical, possessive love he had for Deva, but love as he felt it now – for the mysterious, wonderful, dynamic *Whole* of which he was joyfully a part.

He had travelled all this way and endured all that he had endured only to find a truth that was with him all the time. Perhaps he had only known it before with his mind – but now it rang in his heart like a true note in a beautiful and harmonious melody.

At this point his physical weakness overcame him at last and he slumped on the floor in a faint. How long he lay there he did not know, but when he regained consciousness, his torch was almost burnt out on the dusty floor and he had to hurry to reach the entrance of the corridor before he was in complete and absolute darkness. He groaned as he crawled back to his cave, stiff and sore, but beyond hunger. Determination kept him going though his body protested at every movement. He did not want to die yet. Userhet had been right – there was one more thing to be done.

Bruised and exhausted, he fell at last into the dust of his cave and lay there resting for a long time. In the end he fell asleep – and in his sleep he suffered a terrible dream. He saw Deva again... not as the beautiful and desirable woman who had haunted him for so long, but as a child straying among the most fearsome dangers. She had two mouths: with one she was calling for help and with the other she was warning any and everyone to keep away from her. 'I'm all right,' she was saying. 'Help me!' she was saying. His heart was filled with a new emotion towards her – a caring, unselfish kind of love, no longer desire. He knew he had to help her, for he had been partially responsible for the danger she was in.

When the dawn came he awoke and struggled to his feet. After the dream of Deva, he had had other dreams. He had seen violence in the Temple... he had seen destruction...

Chapter 21

The Festival of the Moving Stars

With Deva safely home, Kyra and Khu-ren felt it all right to leave Haylken for a while and journey to the north, where there was to be a huge festive gathering of clans and tribes and priests, of dancers and singers and musicians, of farmers and traders and miners. Karne and Fern were to go as well, accompanied by a good many of the priests of the Temple, the local Spear-lords and the most prosperous of the farmers.

At this time of year every year it seemed as though the stars grew restless and jostled for different positions in the sky. The night sky was brilliant with meteors and meteorites, and the custom had grown up over the centuries to hold annual ceremonies in each individual community, and then, every third year, a major celebration hosted by a different community in a different part of the country. Feelings towards this time of celestial restlessness were ambivalent. Some feared that harm would come to them when the ancient order of the stars was disturbed; others welcomed the breaking of old patterns, and the changes it might bring. Each year at the time of the meteor showers there was a great deal of Temple activity and many tales of events happening in this realm that better belonged in the next, but the third year was always thought to be special – not because there were more meteors, but just because it was the tradition. The people moved about the land seeking new experiences and new relationships and connections just as the stars moved about the sky.

Before Kyra and Khu-ren left, protective spells were pronounced, and then those who were staying behind watched the cavalcade of those who were going and waved them on their way. It would be a long journey and no one knew exactly when the pilgrims would return. When it had been Haylken's turn to hold the Festival of the Moving Stars some of the guests had stayed for three moons. One or two had never left.

The pack horses were heavily laden, the dogs yapping excitedly. Isar put his arm round Lark's shoulders and held her close. He could see by her face that she was not happy that Kyra and Fern were both leaving. They had assured her that they would be back long before her baby was due – but she was frightened. Fern had tried to get out of going, but the occasion was an important one for making contacts with people across the country and Karne, as Spear-lord, really needed to be there. Fern had missed the others because her children had been too young to take, but this time Karne insisted he wanted her with him. Friends were looking after the baby, and Jan and Inde were being left with Isar. Fern looked back and saw them standing by the roadside, Isar with one arm around Lark, Jan close by his side, waving. She had been so relieved to have the mystery of Jan's behaviour solved, and to know that the dagger was no longer in his possession. She was particularly glad that Isar had been the one to throw the deadly thing away, for she knew he would not have kept it in the first place if his father had not still had some kind of hold on him.

Kyra too had had her misgivings about going – but Khu-ren insisted that, after the strain of all that had happened, she was looking pale and a journey and a festival would be good for her. 'The timing is perfect,' he told her. 'Urak is dead. Deva is safe. Wardyke's dagger has been disposed of. Lark's baby is not due for another two moons. We can spend some time together away from the worries and the duties of the Temple.' She was tired. It had been a difficult year. She and Khu-ren had hardly been together in a peaceful and relaxed way since early spring. On the journey they would stay close – she would ride on his horse with him, held close in his arms – and at night they would be curled up in a small hide tent together after the singing and the story-telling round the cooking fires had stopped. She loved the old stories. She loved the songs, the flute players and the harpers. She would enjoy the camaraderie of the group, and being with her brother Karne and her friend Fern again. Since they had come those many years before to the Temple of the Sun that she might train as priest, they had not had much time together. They had all been too preoccupied – she with her training and her responsibilities, Fern with her children, and Karne with his duties as a leader in the community. She would walk with Fern again and talk as they used to talk, long ago in their home village. A tear of nostalgia came to Kyra's eye at the thought of those far-off days and that far-off place. It would mean a great deal to her to be on a long, slow journey with the people she loved.

She tried to persuade Deva to come with them, sensing that they were growing too far apart. But the girl said she had been away from Gya too long earlier in the year and she did not want to leave him again. He had been asked by Karne to guard the community in his absence. Kyra was pleased with the reason her daughter gave, and never questioned it. Deva seemed cheerful and content with her life now and Kyra was delighted. She was tired of worrying about Deva. 'Gya will look after her,' she thought. 'And Isar and Lark are staying.' She thought of the priests they were leaving behind. 'Everything will be taken care of while we're away,' she added to herself contentedly.

She told Khu-ren she would come and he smiled to see the eager light in her eyes. There had been too many shadows lately.

Deva too was watching the travellers leaving, and she could not believe her good luck. Just when she was making a breakthrough with the manifestation-magic and was in grave danger of being discovered by her parents, her parents were going away. She found herself grinning openly at the thought. Kyra was out of sight now, and, after watching the others idly for a moment, her eyes wandered to those left behind who were still standing at the roadside, gathered in groups, talking.

She spotted Isar, and her heart gave the familiar leap. But her smile soon faded. He had his arm around Lark and was looking down into her uptilted face. As Deva watched, he stooped and kissed her on the lips. Deva flushed angrily. There was such tenderness in the way they were standing together and in the way he kissed her. Deva tossed her head. 'I've had him and I'll have him again,' she muttered to herself – but first there was a great deal she had to do.

With the people who were most likely to stop her away, Deva's ambitions grew apace. Merchants far and wide got wind of the extraordinary luxuries appearing at Haylken and flocked there. People were puzzled by the affluence that seemed suddenly to have come to some of their neighbours, but thought it had something to do with the traders. They still did not suspect what Deva and her small group of confidants were up to. Homes were extended to house the new furniture that was being acquired and many an angry quarrel started between neighbours because the expansion of one property caused encroachment on another.

The way things were going came to Isar's attention first when he witnessed a fight between two men he had always thought of as good friends. He stepped in and separated them and by so doing got caught up as arbiter in their argument. He asked to see their two houses, unable to understand why either of them should so heatedly seek more land. When he stood inside the first one he could not believe his eyes. The chambers, which before had been perfectly adequate to house everything the family could possibly need, were now piled high with exotic and outlandish furniture and goods that he, for the life of him, could not see the reason for owning. The place was oppressive with possessions; the light from the windows was cut down by curtains of such rich colour and texture that they would have looked more at home in a palace than a village house in Haylken. The woman of the house was standing in the middle of it all, arms akimbo, and an expression on her face Isar found hard to describe to Lark later. It was a wariness: 'These are my things and don't you dare touch them!' – combined with pride: 'These are my things and I am better than you because I possess them!'

Isar was sickened.

He was then shown the other house, and found that there was not much to choose between them. The only difference was that in the second house the children were fighting viciously over a toy.

'Where have all these things come from?' he asked in amazement.

'Never you mind,' said the mother of the fighting children sharply. 'You can see we need a bigger house.'

'Or to get rid of some of these things,' Isar remarked mildly.

The woman turned to her husband. 'What's he doing here? Why did you bring him here to criticise us?' She could see by Isar's expression that he did not approve of what he saw. His disapproval made her particularly angry because she knew that he was right. Somehow, although she loved all the wonderful things that were coming their way, something was wrong. They did not seem as happy as they were before. There were worries that they had never had before – and one of them was that they would be robbed. There had been several instances of this recently. And the children – the children never seemed content. The more she gave them, the more they wanted. They were soon bored with the artefacts she brought home from her sessions with Deva, although when they first saw them they were wild with excitement, even fighting over them, as they were now.

By dint of skilful questioning Isar finally learned that Deva was somehow the spring from which the stream was being fed.

When Isar came to Deva's house he found her dressed as an Egyptian, in scarlet cloth, so fine it afforded only the flimsiest veil over the curves of her body; one breast was exposed entirely. Around her neck she wore a collar of lapis lazuli scarabs with turquoise wings set in gold. From her ears swung turquoise and gold lotus flowers, on her arms coiled golden snakes, and on her forehead was a translucent gem of aquamarine, the size of a pigeon's egg, swinging from a fine gold chain that was anchored somehow in the midst of her elaborately dressed hair. He caught his breath. Never had he seen or imagined anyone so beautiful. He had approached the house angrily, determined to get to the bottom of the mischief for which she was no doubt responsible. He had rehearsed what he was going to say a hundred times, knowing that it was not going to be easy to confront her. He had thought that the struggle between his feelings for her and his love for Lark was over. The moment when they found her in the mountain pool had been one of the sweetest of his life and he would never forget what he felt as he held her once again in his arms and knew that she was alive. She had been so childlike on the journey home from Urak's mountains: so vulnerable and tearful, so in need of love and protection. He had ached to carry her the whole way, to keep her close against him, to murmur words of comfort which he knew would soon lead to protestations of undying love. But mercifully Gya had been there and he had managed to control himself. But when they were back in Haylken he had heard about Wardyke's dagger and how Lark had attempted to take her own life with it. All his attention had at once focused on her, and he hardly saw Deva from one end of the summer to the other. He had almost convinced himself that his old feelings for Deva were quite dead, and he was sure he could handle the present situation sensibly in Kyra and Khu-ren's absence.

He could not understand what was happening. The whole nature of the community that he had known all his life seemed to be changing. There was a kind of feverish greed, a bad-tempered possessiveness, a locking-of-doors against neighbours that had never been there before – or, if it had, only among a very few individuals. And it had all happened so suddenly. Natural change was inevitable, but it was usually slow and almost imperceptible. He could not help thinking this must be unnatural, and, in thinking that, his next thought was of Urak. Had they been too late after all to rescue Deva?

Deva now stood before him and all the words he had prepared to say froze on his lips. He had forgotten how stunningly beautiful she could be... and her dark eyes looking into his told him that she had forgotten nothing of that night when he made love to her.

He swallowed hard.

'Is Gya here?' he asked lamely. She smiled and stepped back for him to pass her. She had not answered and he knew in his heart that Gya was not there. But he stepped forward nevertheless.

He could have been in the chamber of an Egyptian palace.

Shadowy memories from the distant life they had shared in Egypt before they came to Britain teased his mind. There was a couch of ebony wood, with lion paws for feet – the wood inlaid with pearl and silver. The room was curtained and dim though it was broad daylight outside. One small lamp burned, casting a flickering light on rich fabrics, on vases of alabaster, on golden goblets and ostrich feather fans. He took a step backwards, determined to leave.

But she took his arm and drew him forward. He did not resist.

'Don't you remember...' she breathed, the heady scent of lotus blossom almost making him swoon. She kissed the lobe of his ear and he trembled. But he still tried to draw back.

She called him by his ancient name and his heart cried out for those days.

'I remember,' he whispered hoarsely.

She took him in her arms and her lips were on his lips. Memories of making love to her, and not all of them from that former life, came crowding and almost broke his resolution. But under the softness of her flesh he could sense something else, something alien, something hard... some shadow that Urak had left behind.

With a great effort of will he pulled apart from her and held her at arm's length.

She used his name again – but this time he resisted.

'Radedef is long since dead, Deva, daughter of Kyra. And so is Anhai, his beloved.'

'No!' she said passionately. 'Anhai lives! Radedef lives!'

He shook his head. His hands dropped from her arms and he stood looking at her – but no longer under her spell.

'Deva...' he started gently.

'No!' she screamed. 'Anhai!'

'Anhai is dead, Deva. Long, long dead. You have another life to live. Live it. Don't throw it away on shadows and dreams.'

She was angry now and she turned slightly away from him. When she spoke again her voice had a bitter edge to it.

'You came for a reason. Why are you here, Isar, son of Wardyke?' She almost spat the last words out. He was shocked to hear the appellation. Although he knew he was the natural son of Wardyke, no one ever called him that. He had always been Isar, son of Karne.

He looked at her flushed and angry face. He desired her, but he did not love her. There was a restless bitterness in her, a need to harm and hurt, an unscrupulous will to power. All this he knew about her. She was a dangerous and destructive woman, very different from the little girl he had protected and loved before Na-Groth's war. Very different from Anhai, his lovely and loyal wife in those long-dead times. Maybe even very different from the woman he had made love to in the spring.

He took a deep breath.

'I came because I'm worried about what is happening in this community.

'Should you not speak to Karne – he is Spear-lord of this community – or my father, who is High Priest of this community?' She repeated the word 'community' with sarcastic emphasis. She was denying her influence on those around her, and she was mocking him for his earnestness.

He flushed and bit his lip.

'Deva,' he pleaded. 'You know what I mean. Something bad is going on – and somehow you are at the back of it.'

She raised her fine black eyebrows and looked at him scornfully.

'Why do you assume that I should be responsible for it if it is bad?'

'I don't assume,' he said. 'I know.'

Her eyes snapped dangerously.

'Who has been lying about me?'

'No one.'

'If I am accused I have to know who accuses me.'

'No one accuses you.'

'You speak in riddles. We are not children now to play games.'

'No, we are not children,' he thought, 'and we are not playing games.' He knew that if he told Deva who had used her name, that person would be punished. 'How could I love this woman?' he thought. But he knew his body still yearned for hers and he knew also that somehow he was partially responsible for her bitterness. If he had not married Lark – or, even if he had, if he had not been so vacillating and shown Deva that he still desired her. If he had not made love to her that night. If... if... if...

'No one accused you,' he repeated firmly. 'I used my wits and found out that you were behind the flow of all these changes.'

'What changes?'

He indicated the room around him with a sweep of his hand.

'No traders brought these goods.'

'How else did they come here then?' she challenged.

'You tell me.' He had regained his composure and was looking into her eyes steadily. She met them as steadily for a few moments. She was wondering whether the time was right for her to reveal her power to him: whether she would be able to turn his knowing to her advantage.

'Come,' she said at last. 'Sit, Isar. I have something to show you.'

He remained standing. She shrugged her shoulders slightly when she saw that he was refusing to relax.

'Stand if you will. But watch my hand carefully,' she said. She held out her right hand, palm upwards. Her arm was bare apart from the slender golden snake that coiled around it. An eye of topaz stared at Isar unblinkingly from just above her wrist. He remembered later that he had made a precise note that there were no rings on the fingers of that hand. He stared now, fascinated. She seemed to be humming a strange little tune. Suddenly a small object materialised on the bare palm of her hand from nowhere. Had he blinked and missed something? She was watching him very carefully. She did not even glance at what was on her hand – but she held it out to him.

'For Lark,' she said quietly.

He looked at it. It was an exquisite ring, gold with a device of flowers in precious stones. Lark would love it.

He looked up at her, astonished.

She was smiling.

'What trick is this?' he gasped.

'No trick. Magic,' she said.

He was silent and took the ring she was holding out to him gingerly in his hand. He turned it over and over carefully as though it were alive and might bite him. It was solid gold and precious crystal. His heart began to beat very fast. Was this Deva before him? Or was it Urak?

He tried to hand the ring back.

'No. It is for Lark.'

'Lark doesn't want it,' he said quickly.

'Ask her.'

'I don't want her to have it.'

'Ah, I see,' she said knowingly. And then, looking at him mockingly, she suggested that it was perhaps because it was too fancy for plain little Lark. Instantly she produced, apparently out of nowhere, a bone needle and a woollen thread.

'Deva,' he whispered, and he had gone very pale. 'What is this?'

'Manifestation-magic, my love,' she said sweetly, pleased with the effect she was having. 'There is nothing I can't manifest if I choose.'

'Deva,' he muttered again, and even in her triumph she was disturbed by the sorrow in his voice.

'Why are you sad? It is a wonderful gift!'

'It is a deadly gift!'

'How can you say that? The people were miserable and poor. They are now rich and happy.'

'Rich, maybe – but not happy. Where will it end? We could have everything – and nothing.'

She looked at him impatiently.

'I intend to have everything,' she said, 'and you will have nothing if you reject it.'

'I have everything I need and want, without your magic.'

'Everything?' she asked pointedly.

'Everything!' he insisted.

Suddenly her expression changed and softened.

'Ah, Isar, I could have everything – but I would throw it all away if I could have you.'

'You know that is not possible. Neither is it true.'

'I would,' she insisted. 'I'd swear never to use this power again.'

He looked at her – caught in a terrible situation. But no, he must not listen to her. This was not the Deva he had known. Urak's cunning was in her.

'You could take me to Kyra. She could put a binding spell on me so that I could never break the vow.'

'Vow anyway – without conditions. Deva, you don't know what you are playing with. The Temple has good reasons for forbidding the practice of manifestation-magic.'

'The Temple is past its useful life,' Deva said harshly. 'Things have to change and now, during the time of the Festival of the Moving Stars, is as good a time as any to change them. The people are tired of the Temple's ways. They want the things I can give them. They are grateful to me.'

'They will not be grateful when they find out where all this will lead them. They will not be grateful when they find out you have grown bored with the first stages of this new power and want to carry it further...'

'I'll give it up,' she interrupted sharply. 'But only if I have you. It is in your hands.'

'No!' he shouted. 'It is in yours.'

'I'll give up nothing... unless I have you,' she repeated coldly, and, looking into her stone-black eyes, her hard but beautiful face, he knew that she meant it.

'Then you, and all of us, are doomed,' he muttered, and turned and left her house.

Isar took Gya aside and told him what Deva was doing, although he did not tell him on what terms she had offered to give it up. Gya listened lightly and did not seem at all perturbed by what he heard.

'I knew she was up to something,' he said cheerfully, and Isar could see that, far from being dismayed, he was quite proud of her.

'Don't you see the harm it can do?' Isar asked.

'Oh, nonsense!' Gya laughed. 'It keeps her out of mischief.' He was delighted that she had been so occupied lately, for it gave him more time to be with Farla. He could not see why Isar should be so worried.

Isar looked at him, surprised. 'You haven't noticed anything wrong lately?'

Gya shook his head. 'What kind of thing?' He had noticed very little lately but Farla's nut-brown eyes and well-rounded body.

'Never mind,' said Isar and left him. He found it difficult to explain what was wrong. He just had the feeling this was a wrong turn somehow and that if they pursued this way, gaining more and more possessions with less and less effort, they would soon lose touch with all the wisdom of the inner realms that had kept them sustained for so long, and begin to be trapped in the material world like a bird that is locked in a box when it should be flying freely in the sky.

The child in Lark's womb had moved its position and all the women she knew were telling her that it would not be long before it was born. She dreaded giving birth, but most of all because Kyra and Fern were still away. For a short time after Jan and Isar had rid themselves of Wardyke's dagger she had been almost happy. Isar had pointed out that Wardyke would be unlikely to be the child in her womb if he was still roaming about the world encouraging Jan to bring about harm to the community; and now the dagger was gone he was sure Wardyke had gone too. But as her time grew nearer so did her fears return. Something was very wrong. She could sense it. When Isar told her about Deva she was not surprised. She retired to her room as she often did these days, in tears, and Isar wished he had not mentioned it.

He felt helplessly caught between these two women. Lark he loved, but as she retreated more and more into her fears she became less easy to be with, less approachable. Nowadays she often cringed away from him when he tried to touch her. If only she could talk, she might have made him understand that it was not because she did not love him that she withdrew – but because she felt somehow that her body was not her own any more. But she could not talk, and the sign language they used was not subtle enough to convey such things. There used to be a strong link between their minds – but that seemed very much weaker now.

Isar began to wonder if it would be such a terrible thing if he succumbed to Deva's plea. After all, it might save the community from a great deal of grief. But here he stopped himself. He knew that if he made love to her it would be because he desired her and not for the good of the community. He knew also that it would bring no benefit, but only loss, to those he truly loved.

He began to look as tormented as his wife. He avoided Deva and shut himself up in his workshed, working morosely on his carving and finding that not one piece came out as well as he had hoped. 'Why bother,' he thought irritably one day. 'Why do I take all this trouble when I could get Deva to manifest in an instant something better than I could carve in a week!' All the satisfaction had gone out of the creative act, all the joy.

Gya told Farla about Deva's activities more as a bit of amusing gossip than anything, and was startled when she took it as seriously as Isar had done. This news made sense of a lot of things that had been worrying her for some time. It seemed to her that the ceremonies in the Temple had been performed very cursorily since Kyra and Khuren had been away. At first she thought it was just because the incentive to keep up the high standards was now missing; but after a while it seemed that the falling off was even more than this. Quite often priests did not turn up at all, and when they did their minds seemed on other things. Farla noticed that some of the priests seemed to possess all sorts of riches that they had not had before, and that some of them now seemed more interested in their appearance than the words they were saying. Deva had kept her activities well hidden from Farla, for she knew that if she were going to have trouble from anyone it would be from her. She was not wrong.

At first Farla blamed herself for having been so preoccupied with Gya she had not realised what was going on – and then she set about assessing how much damage had already been done. She found a great deal. Having once possessed great luxury it was not easy to give it up – and no one intended to do so. Somehow everyone's thoughts were on the acquiring of more and more things, on outstripping their neighbours, and on protecting their belongings from thieves... They soon had more to worry about than local thieves, however. Raiders and robbers from far and wide got news of the unexpected wealth that was appearing at Haylken and they soon began to close in on the area.

Farla decided that she could not tackle the problem alone and sent urgent messages to Kyra and the others to return.

* * * *

Kyra enjoyed the Festival of the Moving Stars this year more than ever before. The relief of having Deva safely home after the danger she had been in contributed a great deal to her happiness – but not all. She had always loved this festival. People came from many different communities – some even from the islands off the coasts, from Ireland and from Brittany. There was always the chance of meeting old friends. There was feasting and story-telling, music and dancing. There were demonstrations of physical skills and demonstrations of psychic abilities – all in good humour, none in pride or envy. It was a time of exchange, a time of learning. There were racers and jugglers, speechmakers, bards and traders. There were also a fair complement of charlatans and tricksters... but they were in the minority and did not manage to spoil the event.

At night Kyra liked to climb to the top of the festival hill and look down on the hundreds of cooking fires encircling it and up to the stars above them. There would be many people watching the stars – for that was the main entertainment of the occasion, and when a star streaked across the sky, a cheer went up from thousands of throats.

Now, she was sad that it was once more over and she remembered with a little shiver of delight the sound of that cheer, the rising cadence of it, the joyful, triumphant ring to it. She remembered also the sadness and the beauty of the final ceremony.

After all the nights of the moving stars, the display of lights was over and the sky was still again. All who were there gathered round the hill, hand in hand – and there were so many the small hill was ringed several times – and, gazing up into the sky, sang a hymn so beautiful, it brought tears to Kyra's eyes every time. They sang to freedom and to change, they sang to choice and movement and new beginnings – but the end of their song was always the same: gratitude to the Nameless One that there was harmony and order behind all the changes, that, in spite of the individual having freedom to choose, there was still an overall pattern to existence into which each one fitted and which might be enriched or impoverished in the matter of detail, but would never be destroyed as a whole.

Boggoron had come with the drummers and this was his first experience of such a hymn. He did not catch all the words because he was beating his drum, and a thousand voices together tended to make an abstract musical note of a word – but he caught the excitement of it, the awe in it, the tremendous feeling of relief. The stars had moved... but the star pattern was the same. Everything had adjusted so that the heart of the universe still beat with the same beat, and Boggoron beating his drum was expressing it – was part of it!

When the time to disperse came there was many a tear at parting and many a promise to meet up at the next festival. The holding of the festival itself was part of the rhythm, part of the pattern. It gave comfort and stability – it gave shape and regularity. Within it, every time they came together, there were changes – but the overall pattern was the same.

Farla sent out the call for Khu-ren and the others just in time. That night one of the worst raids the Temple or its people had ever known threatened to destroy them.

The community was just settling down for the night when a man came to Gya's door, shouting and banging. Gya opened to him – and just caught him as he fell. The stranger was covered in sweat and dust, his eyes wide and staring.

'What is it, man?' Gya said. 'What is it?' He hauled him in and put him on one of Deva's elegant couches, dust and dirt and all. Deva herself was standing sipping wine out of a tall crystal goblet. She looked with disgust and annoyance at the intruder. Gya grabbed the goblet from her hand and held it to the lips of the man. 'Drink,' he commanded. 'It'll give you strength to speak.'

The man gulped it back and then pushed Gya's hand aside.

'Enough!' he muttered. 'I'll drown in the stuff.'

Deva was even more incensed at this insult to her particularly fine and rare wine. She felt like punishing him with one of Urak's hurting-spells – a great many of which she remembered – but the urgency and desperation on his face made her curious.

'Raiders!' the man got out at last. 'Hundreds of them... from over the sea...'

'How soon?' Gya was already thinking of defence strategies.

'By midnight. I came as fast as I could.'

There was blood matting the cloth on his shoulder. Gya took it in at once, as he took in every other detail. His mind always worked best in a crisis. He was almost glad Karne was away and he was the one to make the decisions. He told Deva to bathe the man's arm and give him food and rest – and then he left in a hurry. To rouse the Temple and all its surrounding villages at such short notice was not easy, but it was done with a particular blast on the horn – a warning signal that had not been used for many a long year.

When the raiders came they did not take the community by surprise, but even so the battle that ensued was hopelessly uneven. The strangers were heavily armed with spears, axes, swords and bows. They had no other interest in life but what they were doing. They knew no other trade. Their loved ones – if they had any – were far away and out of danger. The villagers were at every possible disadvantage. They did not enjoy killing and their families were near them, constituting at once an incentive to fight for their protection, but also an anxiety that sometimes slowed down their responses and reactions.

Gya seemed to be everywhere. He was a brilliant bowman and leader and was now in his element – but the Haylken community was almost impossible to defend. It straggled along the valley and over the hills and was used to peace. Gya tried to marshal the people into the Temple, for its surrounding ditch and ridge embankment would make an excellent defence. In the confusion of the night some managed to get into the Temple, and they were the safest... but others could not reach it in time and were slaughtered. By dawn the raiders had retreated, taking everything of value they could lay their hands on and leaving scores of villagers wounded or dead. Farla and the other priests worked on, though they were almost too exhausted to stand, helping people find their loved ones, tending the wounded, encouraging and comforting as best they could.

Deva's house had been stripped bare and then burned to the ground. She herself had managed to reach the Temple and its relative safety. Farla came upon her about noon and asked how she was. She looked quite calm, as though untouched by what had happened.

'I'll soon replace what was stolen,' she said confidently.

Farla looked at her and felt the blood rushing to her face. She was so angry she could scarcely bring the words out – and when she did they were far less coherent than she would have liked.

'And are you going to replace so easily the people who have died?' She almost choked on the words.

Deva for a moment looked as though she had some regrets, some doubts. 'You speak as though I'm responsible for what happened.'

'And are you not?' screamed Farla.

'I don't see...'

'If there hadn't been all that wealth here the raiders wouldn't have come. Is it not enough for you that we have had sufficient to eat, warmth and shelter, love and family and friendship all these years? What do we need with all this gold... all this – this clutter... all this rubbish!'

Deva looked at her in astonishment.

'What is the matter with you, Farla?' she said smoothly. 'Is Gya tiring of you?'

Farla was thankful she did not have a dagger in her hand at that moment, for she would have been sorely tempted to plunge it into Deva's heart. She stood helplessly, staring at her, her mouth open, stunned.

Deva turned neatly on her heel and walked jauntily away.

Gya found Farla in paroxysms of tears and took a long time to calm her down.

'We haven't time for this,' he said when Farla was more herself. 'We're needed. Come – be strong. This is not like you.'

She pulled herself together. It was a day or two at least before those who had gone to the festival could possibly be back, but Gya believed the robbers would make another raid. Quite a lot of the newly acquired treasure had been carried into the Temple for safekeeping, and the robbers knew it. They had been repulsed after a hard struggle by Gya's men. But knowing there was more – they would be back.

Farla suggested that all the treasure should be taken out of the Temple and dumped on the hills beyond the villages.

'Let them have it,' Farla said rousingly. 'Rather than our lives!' But the owners of the treasure would not give it up. They would rather die, they said, than have it taken away from them.

Someone, thinking he was helping Farla persuade them to the sacrifice, pointed out that Deva could manifest more for them if they parted with the things they already had – and for a moment it looked as though the owners might agree. But then Isar unwittingly spoilt everything by saying that if Deva did this, the same thing would happen again and again. 'We'll never be free of these murdering raiders as long as we have something they want,' he said. The owners decided to keep what they had in case nothing more was forthcoming.

'Can't you raise the Lords of the Sun to help us?' someone asked Farla.

'I'm not ready for that yet,' she said regretfully. 'Khu-ren and Kyra will be back soon. If only we can hold on till then.'

But meanwhile there was a night to get through.

As expected, the second night the raiders came again. This time all who were left alive in the community were sheltering in the Temple. The embankment was manned by bowmen and spearmen, and the wooden bridges that normally spanned the deep ditches around the circumference were removed. The Temple had become a fort.

All had grown up to believe that the Temple was sacred ground, and no one but a priest should enter it. The only times the ordinary people were allowed in were those when their energy was needed to supplement the earth currents that flowed around the Tall Stones. There was something terrible to Farla about the Temple being desecrated in this way, but she could see no alternative. Messengers were bringing news of more and more raiders on the way. She had the feeling that Urak and Wardyke were both near – watching with satisfaction the fulfilment of their vengeance. Gya's motley crowd of half-trained bowmen and spear-throwers could not hope to hold off the hordes they were expecting. And, even if they did, what invisible damage had been done to the Temple? What subtle and delicate energies dispersed and lost? The place and the structure had been used in a particular way for millennia... and its energy had been built up painstakingly, meticulously, strength by strength, over countless ages. It had been used for the worship of the beautiful and harmonious force that created the universe – and for drawing on that force for healing, for communication, for understanding, for life itself. That the place and the structure were now being turned into a place of fear and slaughter might mean that new energies would take over, breeding hate and blood-lust and vengeance... and spoiling the place for ever.

Lark took her place with the others in the Temple. During the previous night she had escaped the raiders, but the strain of the experience had brought about the onset of labour. Although she had been feeling the pains for several hours, they were still fairly mild and far apart. Isar brought her to Farla, and Farla took the decision to place her apart from the rest, and in the inner sanctuary, the holiest place in the whole Temple – somewhere no one ever went except the very highest of the priesthood. Both Isar and Lark looked uneasy about the arrangement.

'Don't be afraid,' Farla said. 'These are desperate measures for desperate times. I'm sure Kyra would understand. You'll be safe here – and your baby will be safe.' She looked at Lark compassionately. She had heard of her fear that it was Wardyke who was waiting to enter through the door of her body.

'If it is as you fear,' she said gently to Lark, 'the holy place will keep him contained until Kyra can come to him and put a binding-spell on him. Maybe it will even influence him at the moment of birth to be a better person. There are strong energies here – and there is not one being born who cannot change.'

Lark allowed herself to be led into the inner circle and propped up against one of the outer Stones. They did not go near the three sacred ones at the very centre.

Isar stayed with Lark as the raid started. First came the ordinary arrows and then the fire-arrows. He remembered the night Deva was born. Kyra was in Fern's house in the middle of Wardyke's war and gave birth in a house on fire. Guiron was there then. He wondered where he was now and if he sensed at all the trouble they were in. Lark groaned and he put his arms around her and held her close.

His face was buried in her hair and he forgot Deva and all that she had ever meant to him. 'O Nameless One... O hosts of Shining Spirits... please, please help us now. Protect and guide us and aid us in every way.' He could feel Lark's grip tightening around his fingers and knew that her time was near.

Chapter 22

The last raid

When the desperate call came from Farla, Kyra and Fern were sitting peacefully side by side on a large boulder in the middle of a stream. Both had their shoes off and were dangling their feet in the water. Karne, who was gathering kindling and firewood a short, distance away, heard them talking and laughing together, their happy voices blending musically with the bubbling and gurgling of the silver water hurrying over the rocks to the sea. The tall trees of the forest arched over their heads, an occasional shaft of sunlight breaking through to create a dazzle on the water and make diamonds of the flying drops. Boulders covered thickly in rich green moss lined the banks, and underfoot the centuries of fallen leaves gave the earth a soft springiness.

Both women had unbound their hair and they looked like two young girls from this distance, Kyra's still golden, Fern's fire-red. If he were nearer he knew he would find a strand or two of grey, but the flickering sunlight that played on them now found only the purest of colours.

He collected his wood and set his fire, the site carefully chosen and lined with stone to protect the forest. The smell of wood smoke soon added to the exquisite and gentle pleasure of the day.

The fire was crackling well, and one of the others had arrived to do the cooking, so Karne decided to join his sister and his wife. In the few moments his back was turned to the sylvan scene, everything had changed. He found now that Kyra had her head in her hands and was swaying to and fro as though in great distress. Fern had her arms around her like a mother with a sick child. A cloud must have crossed the sun, for the forest was no longer a place of shimmering light, but a dark and gloomy place.

He began to run towards them.

'What is it?' he called. 'What's happened?'

Fern looked up and over her shoulder, relieved to see him.

'I don't know,' she said. 'She suddenly cried out, but I didn't catch what she said.'

Karne was crouching beside them now and had his arm around Kyra too.

'What is it? What is it, little sister?'

'It's... it's... Fetch Khu-ren. Where is Khu-ren?' Kyra's expression was quite wild as she looked around for her husband.

'I'll get him,' Karne said hastily. 'But what's wrong?'

'We must go. We must go home at once.'

Fern pushed Karne's arm. 'Go – fetch Khu-ren,' she whispered urgently. 'Now!' she added sharply as he hesitated.

He went.

The fear and desperation of the people of Haylken had reached Kyra. Weeping and almost incoherent, she told Khu-ren of the thought-forms that had come to her – and within moments he and Karne were arranging that a group of them should set off at once, the women with children and older people to follow at their own pace. Kyra was the first to be ready, impatient to set off. By dint of going without food and rest altogether, those who were on horseback came within sight of the great Temple during the second night of violence. Horrified, they stared at the flames in the distance and urged their poor exhausted steeds to one last effort. Fern had stayed behind to lead the group that had to move more slowly, but Kyra was with her husband and her brother right at the front.

When they were nearer they could see that the Temple was completely surrounded, the fires of the burning houses giving good light for spear-throwers and bowmen. Kyra and Karne wanted to gallop straight down from the ridgeway at once, but Khu-ren tried to restrain them, pointing out that this would achieve nothing but their own deaths.

'There are too many of them for us to attack them physically,' he said. 'We must think. We must use other methods.'

Normally Kyra would have been the first to agree with him, but now she could think of nothing but that her daughter Deva was in danger down there. Karne was thinking of his children.

'There's not time for your magicking now!' Karne cried impatiently. 'You can see what is happening. Your tricks might have helped when the attack was just about to start, but there is too much confusion there now. No one will see your fancy illusions!' And without waiting another moment he set off down the hill, with Kyra, abandoning all her wisdom and long training, following him, her love for Deva blotting out all other considerations.

Khu-ren uttered an angry exclamation and nearly rushed after her – but he knew they would all surely be lost if he did so, and he held back.

He sat his horse, gazing down into the inferno below, his face like stone. With all his strength he gathered up the power he had as High Priest and Lord of the Sun and sent out a call for help to the Shining Spirits of the upper realms, presenting his body as a channel for their use. Seeing him sitting so rigid and still, those who were left with him grew impatient and followed Karne and Kyra in their suicidal dash to the Temple. They had friends and family there too, and it was more than they could endure to sit idly by and watch them slaughtered.

Desperately Khu-ren held on to his concentration. It was never easy to summon these great beings – but alone, exhausted, and with emotions in turmoil, it was almost impossible. Yet the very emotions that made it so difficult for him to concentrate on the time-honoured ritual words of calling, and his burning trust that if he asked for help he would receive it, lent a charge of energy to the wordless message of the heart.

Lightning suddenly rent the cloudless sky and more than one of the raiders below looked up in astonishment. From horizon to horizon the huge dome above was filled with moving shapes. No one afterwards could describe what they saw – they only knew that they felt a presence that drove terror into their hearts, and many dropped their weapons and fled. Their leaders, less vulnerable to such fears and with more at stake, tried to hold them back, but the fact remained that just as the ditch between the Temple itself and the outer ridge was being stormed, a terrible confusion overtook the invaders, those in front on the makeshift bridge turning back and knocking into the ones behind. Farla and the other priests quickly took advantage of this and added further confusion with their own forms of illusion – which, up to then, hampered by their fear, they had been unable to sustain. Gya and his men, seeing Karne riding in, yelling and waving his sword, with other horsemen behind him, took heart and fought as they had never fought before.

In the night of fire and terror Lark gave birth. Determinedly she pushed her child into the world, Isar beside her, both oblivious of what was going on around them. In this inner sanctum they felt invulnerable. It was as though they were in a sort of cocoon of silence out of which they could see, if they wished to look, the rest of the world behaving in a violent and insane way.

Gently he encouraged her, firmly he held her in his arms, allowing her to push back against his chest, dig her nails into his hands. She was too busy now and in too much pain to think of Wardyke. She thought only of finishing what she had started.

At last, with one great effort, the girl-child broke free of her body and lay in Isar's hands, gulping in air, accepting life. Swiftly and neatly he cut the cord that had held her to her mother and put the little creature to the breast. Already she was sucking – already Lark's arms were around her and her lips were on her matted hair. Isar looked down on them, and there were tears in his eyes.

Then he looked up, thinking to thank the Nameless One and the great Shining Spirits for bringing his child safely to birth. He gasped at what he saw. The sky was filled with huge and mysterious forms constantly changing shape, the stars shining through them. He touched his forehead to the ground and his heart was so full of love and joy and gratitude that he thought it would burst. When he looked up again they had gone.

When Khu-ren came down from the ridge at last, the raid was over and the stunned community was trying to see who was left alive and who needed help.

'Where is Kyra?' he asked quietly.

Farla shook her head. She had not seen her.

There was no sign of her.

Khu-ren walked through the scenes of suffering and confusion as though he did not notice them. Of everyone he asked the same question – and got the same answer.

Kyra was not found until the morning, when the sun's light illumined the desolate scene of smouldering houses and mourning people. A young boy found her lying beside the track from the ridgeway, still some way from the Temple, and called Khu-ren. She was unconscious and there was blood matting her golden hair from a deep wound on her head.

With his heart breaking Khu-ren carried her to the Temple. Their home was gone, their community decimated. He laid her in the inner sanctum beside Lark and her infant and began the healing prayers. From the pouch at her side he drew the stone sea urchin she always carried as talisman. Isar brought water and healing herbs. They bathed her wound and bound it with leaves and linen. Then they placed the small and exquisite stone upon her head above the wound. She had found it many years ago when she was lost deep in the earth in a cave. It was a sea creature that had been transformed into stone. Kyra had always looked on it as a special gift from the Shining Spirits and a healing-power object – focus for rays of invisible energy. With Lark and Isar beside her and Khu-ren on one knee, his lean brown hands growing hot on her head with the healing energies that were flowing through him, Kyra fought for her life.

Outside the sanctum, the process of restoring some kind of order to the community continued. Temporary shelters were erected for those who had lost their homes, and people gathered together those of their families who were left alive – and tried to come to terms with what had happened.

Karne and Gya and Farla worked tirelessly. Karne organised the restoration of order; Farla healed and comforted. None of them was then aware of Kyra's plight.

But Deva heard of it and came running to the sanctum. She paused at the ring of outer Stones, almost as though she felt there was some invisible barrier there. She stared at the scene before her and her face was pale. Farla's words of accusation rang in her ears. Had her actions wrought all this?

'Kyra,' she whispered, for though she had gone against her mother time and time again, the love had always been very strong and deep – and it was now welling to the surface. She longed to rush forward, to take her in her arms, to sob out how much she loved her, to rail against and plead with the Shining Spirits Kyra believed in...

She saw Isar with his arm round Lark and their child between them, and she knew that all the gold she could bring into the world would never buy him back. She had lost him for ever and she was alone.

She lifted her arms to the sky and she howled with despair. Her father, Isar and Lark looked up briefly and saw her there – but Kyra groaned, the first sound she had made, and instantly their attention returned to her and Deva was forgotten.

Knowing that she was forgotten, Deva walked away. Her body returned to the charred remains of her home and sorted through the embers for something left of her former wealth, but her soul-self remained in the Temple, hovering beside the sanctum, yearning for forgiveness and a chance to undo what she had done.

Boggoron heard about Kyra and came to the outer Stones of the inner sanctum too. He brought his drum and squatted on the grass, his eyes never leaving the woman who had given him self-respect, his fingers working the drum. Its beat accompanied the feeble and fluttering beat of her heart; he was trying, by gradually steadying and strengthening the drumbeat, to steady and strengthen her heart.

At last she opened her eyes, the blue of the ocean in sunlight. She was very confused... she was in pain... but they could see that she was looking for something. Her gaze touched Khu-ren and he could feel her love... It moved to Isar and to Lark, and to each she gave her love... but she was still seeking. Her search stopped at the place where they had seen Deva standing, and it seemed to them that Kyra saw her standing there still. She smiled and with a very small and fluttering gesture she tried to raise her hand and hold it out to the Deva she could see standing between the Tall Stones... but the effort was too much for her and she fell back into unconsciousness.

'Fetch Deva,' Khu-ren commanded Isar. 'Bring her back.'

Isar looked at Lark. Lark nodded. She held her baby closer and looked down into her face. She knew now without any doubt that there was no shadow on this child. She was a child of light. She felt it on every level of her being.

Isar ran.

He found Deva sitting in the ruins of her house, making no attempt to clear it up and start again. Her shoulders were drooping and he had never seen her in such despair. Her hair was hanging in lank strands and there were streaks across her face where tears had run through the smoke stains.

He stood for a moment, looking down at her before he called her name. In the night his heart had been full of hate for her because he was convinced it was her encouragement of greed that had called down the raiders on their heads. But she looked now so like a small lost child that he could not bring himself to hate her.

'Deva,' he said softly – and then again, louder, when she did not respond.

Dully she looked up and saw him standing there. Had she been wrong? Was he hers after all? But this last flicker of hope was soon extinguished. There was no love in his eyes. Pity, maybe – but no love.

'What do you want?' she asked bitterly. 'Have you come to gloat and say you told me so?'

'No,' he said. 'I've come to take you to Kyra.'

Now there was a different expression in her eyes – a question.

'She wants you.'

'She's alive!' Deva sprang to her feet, her face lighting up.

'Yes, she's alive, and she wants you to come to her.'

Deva ran. She did not look to the left or to the right. She did not know if Isar was following, or whether she cared if he did or not. Kyra was alive. Sitting in the ruins of her house she had remembered what Khu-ren once told her – that Kyra had been afraid of her daughter's birth, that she had had a premonition that Deva would bring about her death. Kyra had survived the birth of Deva, though convinced she would die in labour. Now, believing that her mother was dying, and knowing in her heart that she had played a major part in bringing about the raids and corrupting and weakening the priesthood so that they were no longer capable of defending the

Temple, she realised that the premonition might have been right all along, only Kyra had misjudged the timing.

'If Kyra lives,' Deva said to herself fiercely, 'I will give up all that Urak taught me. I'll be everything that Kyra wants me to be! If only... oh, if only...'

She reached the inner sanctum as though she had wings on her feet. This time there was no invisible resistance and she fell down on her knees beside Kyra, tears streaming down her cheeks. She took her mother's hands in her own and prayed desperately, as she had never prayed before, that she would live.

There was a flicker of the eyelids and Kyra opened her eyes. She saw Deva's face close to hers and all that was in her heart written on it. Behind her she saw the strength of Khu-ren. Their child – so troubled, so difficult to understand...

Kyra knew that she was dying and knew the thoughts that were in Deva's mind. She made a tremendous effort to speak.

'No bargains with the Nameless One,' she murmured. 'For your own sake give up Urak's way.'

Deva sobbed.

'But if you die...''

'I *will* die, my love – it is my time – but you must live. Think, think what you have learned beyond Urak's teaching, beyond even my own. Think what you have *learned*...' Kyra's eyes closed again and for a moment they thought she had slipped away. But there was one more thing she needed to do. She turned her head painfully towards Lark, and as her eyes opened again Lark held her child close for Kyra to see. Again a faint smile played across her lips.

'It is not Wardyke,' she whispered. 'I'm glad. She will be the future of the Temple... she will be its High Priest. Look after her well – she is a messenger of light.'

This time her eyes did not close and the smile that crossed her lips was radiant – but frozen.

She had left them.

Deva took no part in the struggles of the community to recover during the next day or two. She had left Kyra's side and walked away. No one saw where she went and no one tried to follow her. She herself had no clear idea of where she was going. She only knew that her mother was dead and she had been responsible for it. She walked unseeing past the mourning people. She herself was holding the sorrowing at bay. She wanted to be alone – she wanted to think. But until she was alone she refused to think.

Some people saw her and greeted her, but she did not hear them. She walked past the woods where the men were already chopping the trees for the new houses and the funeral pyres. She did not go towards either 'the field of the grey gods' or 'the haunted mount', which had both played such a big part in her past. She followed the serpent-shaped processional avenue along its whole length and came at last to the sanctuary at the top of the hill, where those who were to enter the priesthood waited out the night before their initiation. She looked down over the valley – so bleak and scarred now, so full of suffering and loss.

The thoughts she had refused to think came crowding in on her. She faced herself honestly for the first time – and she did not like what she saw. Much that had hurt and saddened Kyra, and been against her teaching, she had done because of her obsession with Isar. She had been holding on to the shadow of a past that was gone forever, and spoiling the present and the future by her refusal to let it go. For centuries she had refused to undertake the great upward journey through the realms and had stayed clinging to a point in time and space that had already served its purpose and was no longer a growing point for the soul. She had been allowed to incarnate again at last in that same place with the same protagonists. She had been given a chance to unravel the knot, unblock the channel. And she had not taken it.

Now she allowed herself to feel the grief for Kyra's death that she had so carefully held back. Now she wept and ranted against herself for the time she had wasted in not appreciating her mother, in not being close to her, in not giving her joy. How much she had missed! She thought of Urak, who, in a sense, had tried to take her mother's place: and the two women stood side by side in her memory – the one so bitterly driven by feelings of hatred and vengeance, motivated by the desire for power for power's sake; the other, distrusting power and using it sparingly and only to help her fellows, motivated by love. The one had used her; the other had truly loved her.

'Take me!' she cried in despair to the dark shadows she could feel pressing around her. 'Take me – I am one of you! I am a dark spirit. There is no hope for me! I've rejected everything that is good and accepted everything that is evil.'

It was early autumn, and some of the leaves were on the turn and some were already drifting to the ground. A light breeze stirred them and in the dry and rustling sound she thought she heard Kyra's whisper... 'Think what you have *learned*...' She had not caught the significance of that stress the first time she heard the words. Kyra was telling her to ignore all the 'teaching' she had had, all the things she had been told and had accepted with her mind – and look only at those things she had understood in the depths of her being.

The smoke of the raiders' fires and the pyres that were now being lit covered the landscape at her feet like a ceiling, below which the people toiled, lived, loved and died, above which the sun shone and the larks sang.

'I had forgotten,' she whispered. 'I had thought the smoke ceiling, the cloud ceiling, was the sky, and all that we have to deal with is what we can see.'

Suddenly the view before her expanded to include realm after realm – some peopled with the spirits of those who had lived on earth and had not yet returned... others with beings who had lived on earth and were progressing beyond it to the next realm... others with beings who had never had bodily form... others with beings who had no form at all but only a consciousness that was close to the shining heart of the Nameless One who is beyond All, even beyond the sun who sails in his barque of millions of years.

In that context her obsession with amassing petty possessions and her desire for power over ephemera seemed absurd.

She sat down on the ground and buried her head on her knees. The burden of the vision and her shame at how she had betrayed it throughout her life was almost too much to bear. If only she could go back and start again! She thought and thought, working out ways to make up for what she had done. But at every turn, with every clever manoeuvre she worked out, she was brought up sharp against the fact that whatever she did she would still know how to manifest objects. It was a knowledge that could lead to terrible abuse and it was knowledge she did not trust herself to have. Deva wrestled with herself as she had never wrestled before. She had been through a great deal to acquire that knowledge and she wanted to keep it – but she knew, as surely as the sun was in the sky, that if she kept it, one day she would be tempted to use it; and all that had happened to her family and friends would happen again.

Time and again Kyra had warned her against the use of psychic gifts without pure spiritual intention. A knife could kill as surely as it could cut bread. Psychic power, she realised, was no more than a tool – and it could be used to reach a greater understanding of the invisible realms in which we operated as humans, and, by so doing, allow us to heal, to save, to encourage, to progress. Or it could be used to dominate, to manipulate and to destroy.

She knew that neither she nor those she had led halfway into her secret were spiritually advanced enough not to use Urak's knowledge for their own short-sighted gain – which might, in the long term, be disaster for the community. She despaired. She was trapped. She could almost feel Urak's satisfaction. She would give anything, do anything, to wipe out what she had learned from Urak. But how?

'Oh, Kyra,' she thought. 'I would listen to you now, if only you were here,'

She looked around, her heart aching, half hoping that Kyra would materialise before her. For one terrible moment the thought crossed her mind that if she could materialise inanimate objects perhaps she could materialise people.

As the thought struck her she recognised its enormity and knew that this was where Urak's road led and why Farla and Isar had been so agitated – and why her parents and the Temple had been so desperate to rescue her from Urak before it was too late. The world, peopled with constructs from the minds of anyone who took the trouble to learn the technique... however diseased however perverse...

'O God!' she screamed. 'God beyond all the gods, help me! Help me! Kyra, don't desert me – help me, please... please...'

At this moment she had a mental picture of two old men – one, Maal, Kyra's mentor who had helped her before, and one a stranger – no, not a stranger, someone she had known long ago and hated – in this lifetime known as Guiron, once High Priest at Haylken.

She could understand that her cry would reach Maal, who was always so close to Kyra and was no doubt close now because of her death. But Guiron?

But perhaps this was not so unexpected, after all. He had been responsible for much that had gone wrong. She found to her surprise that she no longer hated him. For the first time she understood how easy it was to take the wrong path and how difficult it was to get off it again. His obsessive desire for her was no different from hers for Isar. He had raped her... She, being physically weaker, could not rape Isar, but she had seduced him by cunning.

'Ah, Guiron, we are two of a kind,' she thought sadly.

Was there nothing about herself that she could now respect? She was almost ashamed to have Maal look at her with those compassionate eyes.

'Guiron,' she told herself, 'Guiron will help me. He will understand.'

She reached towards the image of Guiron she could see and she knew that the long, long thread that held them together was about to be broken.

* * * *

Guiron stood at the edge of the cliff overlooking Hatshepsut's temple. He could see the flat flood plain, greening towards the sinuous muscular thread of the Nile and fading back to the ochre colour of the desert before it reached the faint pink smudge of the distant eastern mountains. Exhaustion and hunger had gone beyond agony and he seemed to be poised above the landscape, contained in a kind of timeless fiery ball of heat.

He must have stood there for a long time only partly conscious, for the sun that had been near its zenith when he arrived was sliding down the sky, its rays lengthening across the barley fields and beginning to touch the river water with a faint glow of gold, when he became fully aware of where he was again. He knew he could go no further and that he had reached the end of his life on earth... but he knew also that Userhet had been right – there was still something left to do.

It seemed to him he heard his name called, faintly, hauntingly, despairingly. He turned his head slightly to the northwest, for the sound seemed to come from that direction. The mountains and the desert lay in ribbed and ridged desolation for unimaginable distances... No one was there.

The call came again, and this time Guiron shivered with recognition. He hardly dared accept it, but he knew who called him.

'She needs me,' he whispered. 'She needs me!'

He hoped he would be strong enough to answer her call, and tell her he was here for her, all passion spent, full only of love and caring and regret for what he had done to her.

And then he began to hear her thoughts... to feel her reaching out to him – and tears came to his eyes when he realised that there was no longer any hate or resentment there.

Beside her, in his mind's eye, he saw two figures. On one side was Kyra and on the other Maal. The girl herself appeared unaware of them – but they were there.

How could he help her... how? He could feel his strength fading. In some ways the visionary image he had of the three figures on the hilltop in the Haylken valley was clearer than the Egyptian landscape that lay at his feet. With a tremendous effort of will he held on to the consciousness of several levels at once.

'Let it be now before I die that I expiate my guilt,' he pleaded with his god. 'Let it be now.'

Across the deserts and the oceans he looked into the eyes of Maal and of Kyra and he saw there what he must do. Neither he nor Deva could see clearly enough what had to be done, but Maal and Kyra could – and they were ready.

Guiron strove to clear his failing eyesight and looked to the tall needles of stone that stood in the temples of the distant city on the other side of the Nile – the obelisks tipped with gold. Like the Tall Stones of his homeland, they reached towards the numinous regions of the heavens, carrying the heart upwards beyond the dust and flies to the shining realms.

The huge orb of the sun was sinking behind the mountains of the west, but before it went, its long rays touched the golden tips of the obelisks and rods of blinding light sprang out from them.

Through the power of Guiron's mind these beams shot out across the world, swifter than thought itself, to where Deva stood. With hands raised – palms outwards – Maal and Kyra reflected these rays into the heart of Deva. She screamed in agony as she tried to fight her way out of an extraordinary cat's-cradle made up of burning rods of light. A fire-arrow through the head would have hurt less. Inexorably the cage closed on her and wherever the light touched, it scorched her. She was beside herself with pain and terror. The fire seemed to be inside her as well as out.

Soberly and compassionately Kyra and Maal watched as she struggled to escape – but they did not for a moment cease to direct the rays. Guiron, more than a thousand miles away, could feel her agony and almost wavered in his task. He knew that if he blinked for a moment or took his eyes off the fiery obelisks she would be released from her suffering. But she had asked for help to forget Urak's teaching, and this was the only way. It was being burned out of her memory once and for all. After this there would be no lingering seed to grow again another time. The knowledge would be lost to her forever.

At last the strain was too much for Guiron and he fell to the ground unconscious. With the shutting of his eyes the great beams of light ceased to broadcast instantly, the sun sank below the mountains, and the distant obelisks were no more than faint marks in a darkening city.

He had done what was left to do – he had helped Deva with a love in his heart that was not lust.

At the shutting off of the rays Deva herself lost consciousness. When she regained it there was nothing to show what she had been through. Wonderingly she looked at her skin. There was no sign of burning. She felt no pain.

She looked round for Kyra and Maal, but they were nowhere in sight. In their place were two other figures – Wardyke and Urak.

'No!' Deva cried. '*No!*'

Both were as insubstantial as smoke, and both were reaching out their arms to her as though pleading with her to give them substance... to give them strength...

'We can help you,' whispered Urak, her voice as hollow as an owl's. 'You *need* us!'

'Trust us,' Wardyke mouthed, the sound of his voice as sibilant as a snake's. 'Your mother never understood you and she has now taken away from you the one thing that can give you status... that can give you power... We can help you.'

'No!' shouted Deva angrily. 'No! Never again!'

She turned and ran down the hill towards the Temple. She would never listen to Urak or Wardyke again – and to make sure of that she knew what she must do.

As the smoke figures faded off the hilltop she thought she heard a long desolate sigh, but she did not turn round.

Kyra's body was to be interred without burning. She was placed curled up in the earth as though she were in her mother's womb.

The stone sea urchin she had used so often in healing was placed in her right hand, the fingers locked around it.

Looking at her lying there before the stone slab that would cover her was lowered, Karne and Fern thought she appeared more like the young girl who had come with them from the far north than a great and powerful priestess. There was hardly a wrinkle on her face, or a grey hair in the gold. She was still a young woman; a woman who had much to do. But perhaps – Fern thought – it was to be done in other realms than their own. They must not hold her back, no matter how much their hearts ached to share her company again.

Fern, who was thinking these thoughts standing beside Karne and holding his hand, looked up through her tears to see Deva beside Khu-ren at the other side of the grave. The tall Egyptian's face was like stone, but Fern knew his heart was breaking. What was Deva thinking, Fern asked herself, as she stood so still beside her father. She could not read her eyes because Deva's head was bowed. From the way she was standing it seemed she too was sorrowing. 'Too late,' thought Fern, a little bitterly. 'If only she had shown that affection more tangibly when her mother was alive.' And then chided herself for the uncharitable thought, for she knew Kyra had loved her daughter and indeed would not be lying here now had she not rushed unthinkingly into the fiercest fighting to look for her. Kyra had believed in Deva, cared about her, tried everything she knew to protect her.

Fern had always had reservations about Deva, and was secretly glad when Isar had married the gentle Lark, handicapped as she was, rather than the High Priest's headstrong daughter. She had tried to love her for Kyra's sake – but had never managed it wholeheartedly. But there was something in the way the girl was standing now, something in the way she reached out and took her father's hand and moved closer against his shoulder, that softened Fern's heart. Perhaps Kyra had not died in vain. Perhaps – even – it was meant to end this way all along. She remembered the premonition Kyra had had at Deva's birth. But why? Why? It was hard to think of Kyra's death as anything but a tragic waste. Surely Deva, even if she now became what her mother had always dreamed of, would never be as valuable to the community as Kyra had been.

Karne was pressing his lips together, trying not to show emotion. He was seeing Kyra running across the heather-clad hills with him; he was seeing them that day lying on the grass on their bellies spying on the priest Maal at his secret rituals in the stone circle of their home village. If he had not insisted that she use her psychic abilities to find out what was going on... if he had not driven her and driven her until at last she came to Haylken to train as priest... would she be lying here so young? But he could not see Kyra as an ordinary matron in an ordinary village, baking bread and weaving cloth, growing old and forgetful and ugly. He saw her even now standing with her hair spread around her like a golden aura, lifting her arms to the rising sun while the birds flew out in long and chattering strings to greet the day.

Karne, who never saw visions, and only half believed what Fern and Kyra believed, suddenly turned his head. He could have sworn he caught a glimpse of her walking away beside an old man.

He looked back at her body – and knew that she was not there.

'She's with Maal,' he thought comfortably. 'What has happened, has happened. I'll not think of "if" and "but" and "maybe". I'll not let her down...'

After the drummers, Boggoron among them, had played their last... the mourners had sung their final farewell... After all who had come to watch her go had departed and the earth lay warmly over her grave... Deva asked Khu-ren if she might go to Egypt.

'Not in vision-quest or in astral-form,' she said, 'but in a boat, the way you came to Haylken, the way I came a thousand years ago.'

'And what will you do in Egypt?' he asked quietly. There had been no bitterness, no recriminations. He could feel that she had changed and he knew that Kyra would not wish him to dwell upon the past.

'It seems to me I've been spending all my time trying to change one thing into another – when I should have been trying to change myself,' she said quietly. 'I want... I think I am ready now to start preparing myself for the great journey through the realms Kyra tried to tell me about.'

'You could do that here,' he said.

'No,' she replied. 'This is not my way. Kyra once said there are many ways to the same end and each individual must travel the way that feels most comfortable and true. I have never felt at home here. Let me go home. Let me follow the way that feels most comfortable and familiar to me.'

Khu-ren looked at her silently a long time. There were times when he could not sleep for longing to be in Egypt. Should he go with her? Now that Kyra was not here... was he free to go to that burning, beautiful land of his youth again? But what would become of Haylken if both its Lords of the Sun left it? Kyra had said Isar's and Lark's daughter would be High Priest one day. Had he to wait for that?

'My lord?' Deva asked anxiously, puzzled at his long and heavy silence.

He brought his thoughts back to her. He could not leave Kyra's people yet.

'You may go,' he said. 'If you are sure.'

'I am sure.'

He said no more, but nodded and walked away.

About Moyra Caldecott

Moyra Caldecott was born in Pretoria, South Africa in 1927, and moved to London in 1951. She married Oliver Caldecott and raised three children. She has degrees in English and Philosophy and an M.A. in English Literature.

Moyra Caldecott has earned a reputation as a novelist who writes as vividly about the adventures and experiences to be encountered in the inner realms of the human consciousness as she does about those in the outer physical world. To Moyra, reality is multidimensional.

Books by Moyra Caldecott

Titles marked with an asterisk are available or forthcoming from Mushroom eBooks. Please visit www.moyracaldecott.co.uk for more information.

FICTION
Guardians of the Tall Stones:
The Tall Stones*
The Temple of the Sun*
Shadow on the Stones*
The Silver Vortex*

Weapons of the Wolfhound*
The Eye of Callanish*
The Lily and the Bull*
The Tower and the Emerald*
Etheldreda*
Child of the Dark Star*
Hatshepsut: Daughter of Amun*
Akhenaten: Son of the Sun*
Tutankhamun and the Daughter of Ra*
The Ghost of Akhenaten*
The Winged Man*
The Waters of Sul*
The Green Lady and the King of Shadows*

NON-FICTION/MYTHS AND LEGENDS
Crystal Legends*
Three Celtic Tales*
Women in Celtic Myth
Myths of the Sacred Tree
Mythical Journeys: Legendary Quests

CHILDREN'S STORIES
Adventures by Leaflight

Lightning Source UK Ltd.
Milton Keynes UK
UKHW041450160320
360414UK00004B/1413